Praise for *Nicholas Eternal*

"Libraries and readers ... will welcome the intrigue, relationship developments, and bigger-picture questions *Nicholas Eternal* evolves. It crafts satisfying twists and turns, possibilities readers might not see coming, and confrontations that test the boundaries of good and evil intentions. The result is a story that is fresh, original, and thoroughly compelling in the process of transcending definitions of paranormal romance, urban fantasy, or anything in-between."

—D. Donovan, Senior Editor, *Midwest Book Review*

"A sacred tattoo ... a painful existence and the nodes of fate ... *Nicholas Eternal* is a mesmerizing, stay-up-all-night story of sacrifice, survival, and just how beautiful a broken heart can be. A must-read urban fantasy from author Kim Conrey!"

— McKinley Aspen, award-winning author of *Praesidium* (Shadows in the Wind Book One)

"This roller coaster ride of a story is beyond captivating. It's the most heartfelt tale I have ever read and absolutely brilliant."

—KJ Fieler, author of *Shadow Runner*

"A well written novel with characters that come to life with internal struggle, ancient powers, and a touch of noir."

—Ben Meeks, author of *The Keeper Chronicles*

Also by Kim Conrey

Stealing Ares (Black Rose Writing 2022)
Losing Ares (Black Rose Writing 2023)

Emily,
I hope Nick & Noory's
journey inspires you!

NICHOLAS ETERNAL

THE WAYWARD SAVIORS
BOOK ONE

Kim Conrey

KIM CONREY

For George Weinstein, a wonderworker

Acknowledgements

Gratitude is everything.

As always, I am thankful to the Atlanta Writers Club for the years of knowledge, learning, and camaraderie. Not only has it brought me to this place in my journey, but it's allowed me to meet some of my closest friends. I simply cannot imagine writing without this fine organization. The Roswell critique group has been a great help in nearly everything I've written. The Wild Women Who Write Take Flight Podcast has been the supportive bunch of writing women I wish everyone had. Thank you, Kathy Nichols, Gaby Anderson, Lizbeth Jones, and Kat Fieler. To Ben Meeks, thank you for the encouragement, guidance along the journey, and for sharing opportunities. You are a beacon for other authors to follow. Thank you, Terra Weiss, for making sure I don't get hosed.

Thank you to Marta Dec for this beautiful cover design that captures the soul of Nicholas so completely.

In the interest of saving the best for almost last, thank you to my husband, George Weinstein, who works tirelessly to help other writers, especially this writer. I am forever grateful.

Without a doubt, I also wish to thank my readers. I know how much a good story means. I hope somewhere among these pages you find a respite from your troubles. If not, then at least a character to commiserate with, in whose heart you see a glimpse of home.

CHAPTER 1

The sun was beginning to set, backlighting the Atlanta skyline as if a finger of red-orange fire had been painted over the top of each skyscraper. The sounds of traffic blended with the distant barking of dogs, a couple arguing in the apartment complex to Nicholas' left, ten floors up. Someone screamed profanities in the distance. The cacophony of noise rose higher and higher, assaulting his senses until he looked at the crumpled newspaper in the alley before him. It slid slowly across the ground and made a faint scraping. He preferred it. He preferred all of it to the tracking he'd been doing throughout the day as he followed the teenage girl's signal from one building to another, slipping in and out of dimensions until the signal had suddenly stopped, which was a relief but also terrifying in equal measure.

He watched the paper make its way across the concrete. He took out his flask, tipped it up, and the ouzo made a pleasant and familiar burn down his throat. That's when the tingle—also familiar but, unlike the ouzo, not pleasant, began at the base of his skull, slid down his brain stem and crawled over his chest. *Ignore it.*

He tried. It squeezed his bones in its millennia-old grip. Much like himself, never changing with age. He sighed, put the flask back in his pocket, looked at the brick wall in front of him, thought about where he wanted to be, and disappeared through it. The ache in his chest, the electricity on his brain, took shape and form. It was the child in danger, the female, but that wasn't always the case. It was just what most people assumed. Boys were abducted, too.

Darkness closed in.

When he slipped out of the portal, a man, startled at first, started yelling at him. In Nick's haste to get back into the mortal realm where he could listen on a clear frequency, he'd materialized in the man's apartment.

"Did you come down my damn chimney?"

Nick noticed he was, indeed, standing right in front of his fireplace. He held out a hand to signal the man to stop talking. "Be quiet. I can't hear her," Nick said. He was getting closer. He could feel it.

"What the hell are you talking about?" The man was enormous and lunged for him.

Nick quickly and efficiently placed him in a sleeper hold and lowered him to the floor. The signal was clearest here. He couldn't afford to move without getting a lock on her location. As soon as he did, he disappeared again and traveled through three different buildings. The signal grew a little fainter by the time he arrived. It shouldn't have. Then the tingle vanished entirely.

It happened again. He didn't make it in time to save someone who needed him. He looked at the lifeless teenage girl lying in the alley as guilt sought the chinks in his armor but found no entrance. He knelt, gathered her in his arms, and drew the sign of the cross on her forehead as a light mist began to fall—offering the tears Nick was unable to shed. The streetlights illuminated the water that coalesced on her pale face; in every drop were rainbows suspended for a short breadth of time before sliding away, baptizing the wastelands of her youth and streaking her makeup, way too thick for a girl of fourteen. With a trembling hand, he gently ran his fingers across the purple marks forming on her neck. A sense of unease enveloped him at the idea that he could feel so little at such blatant brutality, but time had slowly entombed his heart, layer after layer, century after century, until a sepulcher stood where a man should be.

He had dreamed of her the night before and tracked her all day and evening as she moved from place to place. The grief of other lost children interfered with her signal, confusing his ability to locate her: a common problem in a crowded city.

Now she was gone from this life, but the embrace of eternity would wash over her as surely as the rising sun kissed the meadows longing for the dawn. He knew that, but it didn't change the fact that her future, all the beauty, all the blessed ups and downs of a mortal life, were lost to her.

After a moment, practicality took over. He knew what had to be done: he needed to call on John. He laid her gently on the ground and dialed the number with shaking hands.

Within fifteen minutes, Lieutenant John Abramson arrived. Nicholas looked at the man with the dark hair and olive-toned face and found his usual look of sympathy—Nick had grown weary of seeing it. "I don't require your pity. Save it for her."

"The dead no longer need it," John said, studying his face, which was no older than thirty but held the weight of the ages if one gazed too closely into his haunted brown eyes.

Here it comes. Nick braced himself for a familiar conversation.

John took a deep breath and spoke carefully. "There's an AA meeting at Sacred Heart this Thursday night. You know I'll go with you, Nicholas."

Nick's voice was flat as he spoke. "I've already told you. I'm a different kind of drunk. Those people can't begin to understand what it's like for me. Seventeen centuries of this." He gestured to the body lying on the ground.

"No, no different. You aren't special. You all drink for the same reason: afraid you aren't enough."

"It's been a long night, John. I don't need this right now."

"Right now, is exactly when you need it. Right now, is when you need to be clearheaded enough to do your job, but the liquor coming off you is about to knock me over, and there isn't even any wind."

"What are you suggesting? That she wouldn't be dead?" Nick said, goading John, pushing him to say it.

"You'd like that, wouldn't you? Another excuse to have a drink. You know I won't crawl into that hole with you." Nick heard John take a deep breath and try again. He always tried again. "You've saved thousands more than you've lost, Nick."

They're harder to remember. Nick looked at the horizon. The sky had begun to clear but few stars could be seen past the light pollution.

"Go home, Nicholas. Get some sleep."

Nick turned to go. John touched the back of his head before he walked away. He felt a temporary healing radiate from John's hand, the only other person alive who could understand the terrible burden of time, but he refused to turn around. He forced his feet to move, even as his body begged him to stay within the respite of John's healing touch.

The sidewalk blurred before him as he left.

Noory blew a wisp of platinum-blonde hair from her face as the man left the crime scene. She watched him and thought about following, then wondered why she would do that. It was borderline "stalkery." Instead, she sat just out of sight on the rooftop, picking at her chipped blue nail polish through the next hour. It was definitely the man who had left the donation at the shelter earlier. She'd watched from her office while he dropped off the boxes with the volunteer. He had the same thick, dark hair, muscular but lean build, and the same I'd-be-gorgeous-if-I-wasn't-so-damn-tortured-inside look on his face. There was something about him. Something different, like John, like her . . .

When all the other investigators had gone home, she watched as John crossed himself and stood silent for a moment. She wasn't one for prayer and contemplation, but her adoptive father was, and she respected him. After a few more moments of silence, Noory leaped from the four-story building and landed right behind John with the stealth of a cat.

"Scion," he said quietly, without turning around.

"You know I hate it when you call me that."

"Sorry, Noory. So, what business does the sci . . . what business do *you* have with Nicholas?"

"He left a donation at the shelter last night and bolted before anyone could thank him. The kids needed those shoes and jackets. It will turn cold soon. But I was actually looking for one of the girls from the shelter who's gone missing."

Noory watched John give a sad smile, but he wouldn't comment further on the stranger. "You heading back to Tech this fall?"

"Again, John, really?"

"You're brilliant, Noory. Females are sadly underrepresented in engineering. You're a 'rambling wreck' if there ever was one," he said, quoting the Georgia Tech fight song. "You could invent some amazing gadget to dazzle us all and make enough money to build a brand-new shelter for those kids you care about."

"I'm less worried about the shortage of female engineers and more worried about the shortage of people giving a damn. When you find out the name of the murdered girl, can you let me know?"

"It will only haunt you," he said softly.

"Not knowing haunts me more. She might have been Calista, the girl from the shelter. I didn't get a good look at her."

"Yeah, I'll stop by."

"Thanks, John."

Noory could see the exhaustion settle on John as he ran his hands through his wavy black hair. "Go back to school, Noory," he called out, but she had already sprinted away.

Chapter 2

Nick walked into his penthouse overlooking the Atlanta skyline. Exhaustion clung to him, but he knew he would only lie awake in bed thinking of his failure. He went to the liquor cabinet and reached, with shaking hands, for the ouzo. He poured it into a crystal cut glass and sat on the couch, watching the lamplight filter through the tumbler as he exhaled. The thick notes of licorice in the alcohol made him think of Greece, standing on the cliffs and seeing the sunrise over the ocean on the island of Santorini. It had been years. John had taken him there, back home where it all began, hoping to get him away from the drink.

John would not approve. He took another drink and laughed into the empty room as his vision began to blur. He was soon asleep.

Around ten the next morning, he woke with one thing in mind: getting to the shelter to donate some money. That helped almost as much as the ouzo. He showered, dressed, and then stood in front of the refrigerator, knowing he should try to eat something. His stomach clenched at the thought of it.

"I'd like to speak to the director, please," the dark-haired stranger said, adjusting a sleeve of his blazer.

"You're looking at her," Noory said, standing behind her desk.

She saw the same look on his face that she had seen so many times before: she wasn't what this man was expecting. She had long, platinum-blonde hair with dark roots, a nose ring, a worn army jacket over a black tank, jeans, and boots, with enough buckles running up the side to set off any metal detector within a mile.

"May I help you?" Noory's heart pounded as recognition washed over her. It was him. She tried not to let on that she had seen this man the night before mourning over a young girl in a dark alley. "Are you looking for someone?" she asked.

"No, I just wanted to leave a donation." He slid the check across the counter. Noory held back a gasp as she read the amount.

"Look, no one expects you to clean out your bank account," she said, worrying that he might have been grieving and unaware of what he was doing. She didn't know how he had known the girl from the night before, only that it wasn't him who killed her—if it were, John would have never let him go.

"Oh, I'm not. I won't miss it," Nick said.

"Okay, then." This amount of money didn't just help the kids, it helped her, too. It meant more sleep and less lying in bed awake trying to think of more businesses she could approach and grants she could apply for to keep the shelter going for the next year. "I'll go get a receipt for your taxes."

"Thanks."

She read the name on the check: Nicholas Theodoulos. Her curiosity made her hesitant to just let him walk away. Something in his eyes tugged at her gut and made her eyes well up just thinking about it. "Damn," she said to herself. The guy was loaded, but he was also haunted. Her overly suspicious tendencies didn't kick in at the moment, though she knew they should have. She was always wary of strangers bearing gifts. It wouldn't have been the first time: politicians had walked in with a check, hoping for a photo op. She usually accepted. Money to help the shelter trumped her desire to tell them to screw themselves and stop using these kids' shitty situations for a boost in the polls. This felt different.

"Here's your receipt. We truly appreciate it. Would you like a tour before you go?"

"No!" Nick said and then looked away in what she could only interpret as panic.

Noory was taken aback at how fast he refused. Though the center was always grateful for donations, it angered her that some would rather throw money at a problem than recognize that these were real people. The anxiety on his face morphed into something like grief before he regained the look of practiced control once more. Clarity washed over her as she remembered him cradling the young teen—clearly a street-walker—from the night before. She realized he was afraid to see their faces.

"All right. I understand," Noory said softly. They locked eyes for the briefest moment before he closed his blazer as if he were exposed, then shoved the receipt in his pocket and exited quickly.

Noory watched him leave. "Ava," she called to her assistant, "I'm heading home for the evening." She grabbed her keys and cell phone and left before Ava could respond.

She caught up with Nick but remained far enough back that she blended with the others on the busy downtown street. He walked from one block to the next, where he would stop as if listening to something. Once he even sniffed the air before dropping in behind a man in a business suit. Nick continued following as he took a left and crossed a set of railroad tracks as the skyscrapers and sleek apartment buildings gave way to warehouses and loading docks in the more industrial part of Atlanta.

Noory cringed, knowing the building they were approaching was a place where men brought prostitutes. She'd been there before, due to tearful calls from strung-out girls who had been in and out of her shelter for most of their teen years after leaving their foster homes and making their case workers insane with worry. The man Nick was following took out his cell phone as he opened the door. He was so preoccupied with a call that he didn't seem to notice Nick slip in or hear his footsteps over the creaking of the huge metal door and the crunch of the debris strewn across the old, abandoned warehouse floor. The door shut behind them while Noory climbed a fire escape on the side of the building.

By the time she reached the top of the stairs and found a broken window to peer through, the stranger's cell phone already lay crushed on the floor beneath Nick's foot.

"I'm here on behalf of Calista," Nick said.

The blood drained from Noory's face and roared in her ears as she fought to stay conscious. She knew exactly who Calista was. She put the pieces together and realized it was her body that Nick had been mourning in the alley the night before. Calista had come into the shelter with a black eye a week ago, and Noory had stayed up late into the night talking with her. Noory had not been able to see her face well enough as she'd looked down from the rooftop and saw Nick cradling her—or maybe she just didn't want to. John had been right when he'd said knowing who it was would only haunt her. Before Nick revealed her identity, Noory could've pretended that Calista was somewhere safe, cared for, maybe even loved. Now . . . .

"Who?" the man replied.

"You took her life and never even knew her name?"

The man's face went pale.

Nick casually removed his jacket as he spoke. "Now I, on the other hand, insist on knowing the names of those who are about to die." He pointed at the man. "Brad."

Noory watched Brad's Adam's apple quiver as he swallowed hard. "I have no idea what you're talking about."

"Don't lie to me."

Noory wondered if she had blinked because the man was suddenly flying backward through the air. Nick's extended arm was the only thing giving her a clue that he had even struck the man.

Brad lay on the floor gasping like a landed fish as Nick leaned over and spoke so softly that Noory was barely able to hear. She heard enough, and it made her heart skip a beat and her hands turn cold.

"As she lay dying in my arms and the last electrical impulses bounced around her brain, would you like to know what I saw there, other than terror?"

Brad inhaled a clearly painful breath.

"I saw *you*." Nick said with disgust as he jumped back to his feet.

It became clear that Brad knew trying to remain innocent was no longer an option. He shook off the punch and stood up. "You won't get out of here alive."

Nick laughed. "You've got no idea."

"So, you're here to get your ass kicked over one little whore?" Brad asked.

Nick became completely still for a moment, and Noory watched as raw fury settled over him like a cloak. "You know, there was some small part of me, way, way back in a corner of my mind that could see myself just beating the hell out of you and letting the courts deal with you. Now that part of me is gone."

A soft crackle filled the air. Brad looked around, as if trying figure out what was going on. "So, you think you're some superhero? Batman, Spider-Man, some shit like that?"

"You're missing a few," Nick said. "I'm a fan of the lesser knowns: Judah Maccabee, Kali, Saint Michael . . ."

The man picked up a lead pipe from the ground and came at Nick, who ran a couple of steps and then jumped so fast Noory could barely follow it. He shoved a foot into the man's chest, using him as a ramp, pushing off him, allowing himself to fall and grab Brad's collar on the way down and yank him to the ground. He continued where he left off, ". . . St. Joan, St. John . . ." Nick crouched, and no sooner did his arms extend from his sides then daggers appeared in each fist. The blades flashed with an eerie blue glow, ". . . and Saint Nicholas," he roared as he slammed a knife into each of Brad's shoulders and yanked him backwards as tendons ripped.

The man screamed in agony, and from what Noory could only surmise, a certain recognition that he was about to die.

Brad looked up at him with wild eyes as Nick yanked out the daggers before walking around to crouch beside him.

"Mercy," Brad croaked out.

"That's exactly what she said to you. Well, she mouthed it, right? Because your hands were crushing her windpipe at the time."

"Please."

"If I let you go, you'll be back on the street in no time—doing the same shit over and over." Nick shrugged as he continued to speak. "There were no witnesses. And here you are, a respected businessman."

He wiped his blades off on the lapels of the Brad's suit jacket. "And she was just one more girl, lost in the system, no one looking out for her. No one will mark her absence."

Noory thought she heard Nick's voice crack a little as he spoke. As brutal as the scene was, she knew he was right. She knew it firsthand.

"They are known only to me!" Nick thundered, as the rafters of the old warehouse shook, and Noory had to brace herself on the rickety old fire escape. He shoved one of his blades into the man's heart and twisted.

They? Noory thought about his phrasing as she trembled.

"I'm so sick of this shit," Nick said.

He opened his palms and both daggers vanished as mysteriously as she had seen them arrive.

Nick reached up to draw the sign of the cross on Brad's forehead. "You're not my problem anymore."

Noory exhaled. "Dear God," she whispered.

Chapter 3

Noory watched Nick walk outside the warehouse and send a text. She could only assume he was contacting someone to take care of the body. She couldn't help but wonder if it was John who he called every time something like this happened. How often *did* it happen?

He turned his head ever so slightly in her direction, and she tried to fade into the shadows, but then he started walking. Noory had to know what was going on with him, and maybe she could drag it out of John the first chance she got, but for now, she wanted to find out whatever she could for herself.

It was Noory's experience that the kind of people at a hole-in-the-wall bar in the early afternoon weren't exactly a bunch of go-getters, and this group was no exception. One man sat in the far-left corner with blood red lipstick smeared across his cheek as the woman next to him—with breasts hoisted high enough to smother her in her sleep—palmed a wad of cash and laughed a little too loudly at his jokes while 90s power ballads played in the background. Two other patrons were perched in front of the bar while Noory sat under the dim lighting watching Nick.

She didn't know if her interest was just raw curiosity, or their obvious shared passion to try and save these kids before they self-destructed, but after watching him drink deep for half an hour, she realized he might have been doing a little self-destruction of his own. After nursing her own beer that remained half full, she finally mustered the nerve to speak to him—hoping the liquor would have loosened his lips. She shoved her chair back, deciding to approach him before he drank himself into complete incoherence.

"Nicholas," Noory said, sliding onto the stool beside him. "How are you? I'm the manager from the shelter. We met earlier today."

"Yeah, I know." Nick turned to look at her with heavily lidded eyes. His thick, dark brown hair had fallen into his face. He ran a clumsy hand through it. "You can call me Nick."

"Okay, thanks. Call me Noory."

"Riiiight, Noory. Why do you follow strange men around the city? That's not safe, love." His voice was low and rough from the whiskey. It sent a wave of warmth through her body that she found shocking and soothing at the same time.

"What?"

"I know you saw me in the warehouse earlier," he said.

What would this man do now that he knew she'd witnessed what he'd done? "I was curious."

"Don't be. It'll get you into trouble."

"Do I look like someone who's afraid of a little trouble?"

Nick laughed. "No, but you should be."

She refused to argue with him. Half of winning a battle was choosing the right one to fight, and truthfully, she *was* a little more than rattled by what she'd seen. Living in the city and hearing about murders was one thing, witnessing one was quite another. Though she and her adoptive father had gifts that weren't exactly normal, Nick was clearly both supernatural and lethal. Despite that, she couldn't shake the feeling that he posed no threat to her.

He pressed his palms over his eyes as if trying to block an image only he could see. A few more shots, and she wondered how this millionaire hero was going to stumble his way home, superpowers or not.

"C'mon, Nick. Let's get you home. Should I call a cab, or is it close enough to walk?"

"Walk," he managed to slur out.

"Good, I'm thinking you could use the fresh air."

∞

The two walked down the Atlanta streets in silence, with Nick occasionally glancing at her. Noory noticed because she was watching him as well. He wasn't walking all that straight, and she feared he might stumble into oncoming traffic. Night had begun to fall, and headlights glared into their eyes, seeming to make him even more disoriented.

"Here," Nick pointed to what Noory knew to be the most expensive apartment building in the city. He nodded at the doorman, who either didn't notice Nick was drunk or was used to overlooking the vices of their affluent tenants.

The two got in the elevator and made their way to the eighteenth floor. After the doors slid open and he stumbled into the hallway, Nick leaned on Noory as alcohol emanated from every pore. "It's gone on forever, you know."

"What has?" Noory asked.

"Me, saving them. Sometimes not. I'm exhausted, Light." He looked at her with a sad smile.

"Light? You know my name means light."

"I do. I can see it, too. It's like a soft glow," Nick said, passing a hand over her head to indicate an aura around her. Noory wondered if he could see anything else about her but didn't dare ask. She was suddenly afraid to know.

"Now," she said, "how could it have gone on forever? You don't look like you're much older than me. You're what? Thirty?"

Nick laughed as he failed typing the pass code to get into his penthouse. "Third time's a charm," he said. The door gave a soft click, and Noory helped him inside.

She looked around at the open space and large windows framing the Atlanta skyline as the city lights twinkled in the night. The place was all polished dark wood floors and leather furniture, but she didn't see any pictures of family or friends. She led Nick to the couch, and he fell onto it as she sat down beside him. He looked at her.

"Do you hear them, too?" he asked.

"Who?" Noory thought she saw a glimmer of hope in his whiskey-brown eyes.

He placed his hand on the top of her head, warm and strong, if a little clumsy. He ran his fingers down the length of her hair, past her cheek, her neck, and dangerously close to her breast. The look of hope was replaced by desire for the briefest of moments before she marked the instant he withdrew back into himself. "You wouldn't believe me if I told you." Nick exhaled and sank deeper into the couch. She watched as his eyelids grew heavier.

"You'd be surprised what I'd believe, Nick." She leaned over and gently brushed the thick brown hair from his forehead. As she did, her sleeve fell back from her wrist, revealing a small tattoo of an "X" with a tiny hook on the top right corner. Nick's eyes opened wider in recognition before they rolled back into his head, and he began to softly snore.

Noory passed her fingers across the tiny hooked "X" and wondered if he had really known what it meant but doubted he would remember seeing it in the morning. She took off his boots before she removed her own and lay down at the opposite end of the couch. She thought of the day John had given her the tattoo. *"I am giving you this symbol so that if you ever need help and I'm not around, my brothers will recognize you and give you whatever you may need."*

Noory rubbed the small tattooed "X" again; it helped her think. Despite knowing what he'd done, she didn't fear him and was in no hurry to leave. Why? Fatigue enveloped her as she gazed out the large windows at the skyline and thought of Calista. Before drifting off, she said the one thing she'd wanted to say to Nick all evening—had he been in any condition to discuss it. Even though he couldn't hear her now, and it didn't matter anymore to anyone but her, she whispered, "I knew her too," before finally drifting off to sleep.

The next morning, Noory woke to find that Nick was still fast asleep at the other end of the couch. The room had gotten cold overnight. She looked around for a blanket and noticed one lying on the back of the couch. Unfolding it, she went to cover him before she left. As she pulled the blanket up to his chin, his arm shot out, and he grabbed her wrist without opening his eyes.

"Good morning, Light." She jumped as he smiled. Only then did he look at her and release her arm.

She tried to act unfazed as she sat back down on the couch to put her boots on.

"Hang around a while. I'll make you breakfast," he said as he sat up and rubbed his eyes.

"Thanks, but I've got to get to work."

Nick nodded. "All right, stay out of trouble," he said.

But as images from the warehouse flooded her mind, she knew it was too late for that. She had no intention of going to work.

CHAPTER 4

"John!" Noory called, walking into the old farmhouse without knocking. Though her adoptive father was a steely eyed police detective with a history and powers, few would believe, in his downtime he lived the life of a farmer in North Georgia. He had chickens, goats, sheep—Noory never forgot it because of having to scrape droppings off her boots every time she visited him. But John had told her long ago that the universe demanded one thing above all else, if one were to live with any semblance of sanity: balance. He balanced out the chaos of his inner-city law enforcement with a heaping dose of fresh air punctuated by manure.

God, why? Noory thought for the thousandth time as she wiped her feet on the mat while looking around for him.

"Good morning, sweetheart," John said as he entered the living room with a cup of coffee. He set his mug down and motioned for Noory to sit. She did and thought about all the questions swirling in her head. Where to start? Would he even tell her anything? Her knee bumped up and down, and she chewed the edge of her thumbnail.

"What's going on, Noory?"

"Who is Nick?" she blurted.

John answered quickly. "Nick is a good man wrestling with a lot of demons." He took a drink of his coffee.

"You're being vague."

"Not every story is mine to tell. Learning about someone is a privilege that must be earned. Though I wouldn't get too close to Nick. His commission is . . . a difficult one."

"I'm going to need more than that."

"Why? You have your path, and he has his."

"Like you have yours?" Noory tried to hide the bitterness from her voice as she thought of growing up with John for a father. He had taken good care of her. She knew he loved her, but there was always a distance there. She remembered trying to call him Dad once when she was a little girl, and he'd corrected her— "Just John," he would say with a smile and a pat on her head.

"Well, yes," John said.

"All right, Just John." She blinked back the tears threatening to form at the backs of her eyes.

His put-together demeanor vanished, and he set down his coffee. He clearly knew what she was referring to. "Noory, I . . ." He swallowed, propped his elbows on his knees, and studied his palms as if he might find the right words written there.

"I've watched your line live and die, live and die, live and . . ." He looked up at Noory with shimmering eyes, then past her into a history she couldn't fathom. "It hurts. Every. Single. Time. So, I thought it would be easier if—"

Noory screamed at him. "Easier on who, Just John?" She was taken aback by her own anger—anger that shocked her with its ferocity. She hadn't even realized she'd jumped up until she found she was standing, shaking. "You withhold."

"I give everything, Noory! My past. My future. Even my right to die!" Now he was the one raising his voice and getting to his feet.

"I saw someone get murdered last night! I don't need an ancient disciple right now. And I get it—I'm a grown woman, but I need my father."

The color drained from John's face. "What were you doing there?"

"So, you know about it?"

John nodded. "Justice can be messy. I'm not saying it's always okay for Nick to do what he did last night, but sometimes it can't be helped. My hands aren't clean either. There are people in this world that . . . I've seen people do things as foul as any demon would, and the scary part is there is often no entity to blame it on. Sometimes it's just a shitty human being."

Noory nodded. Her insides were a jumble of old hurts, new confusion, and a gaping wound.

"I think its best you stay away from Nick. There's nothing but heartache there."

She placed her palm over her chest. "There's heartache here too," she said, forcing the words past the lump in her throat. "He and I are in the same business when you think about it."

"You can't save him. I've tried. He has to untangle that knot on his own, baby."

"Baby." She sighed. "I was your baby."

A tear escaped the corner of John's eye and slid down his face. "Still are."

"I can't remember what Mom looked like." A sob tore loose from her throat, defying the strong front she wished to maintain before him. Her mother died when she was little. She only remembered flashes, impressions of her. Like something from a dream. There were precious few pictures of her.

He said nothing as he left the room and then returned moments later with a small framed photo. He handed it to her with shaking hands. "I keep it in my nightstand, always."

"I forgot her eyes were blue," Noory said as she ran her fingers across the smiling face in the frame. "I remember her hair being dark but always think of her eyes as being brown, since you told me she was Jewish."

John smiled. "I know several blue-eyed Jews." He reached up to wipe his eyes. "Not me of course."

Noory looked up at him and realized it was the first time she'd seen him cry. "I'm sorry about the 'withhold' remark. You did your best."

"No, you're right. I was protecting myself. It wasn't . . . it *isn't* fair to you. You should know. I should let you know me better. No matter how much . . . I can show you where it began."

She'd asked him his origin story. He wouldn't talk about it, except to say it was a lonely world when everyone you'd known was gone. He lifted his hand slowly with his thumb poised over her forehead, as if to bless her, then closed his eyes, and no sooner did his thumb touch her head . . .

Galilee, Israel, she heard John whisper in her mind. The rest she experienced clearly, as if seeing flashes of a movie.

A gentle breeze blew past them, carrying with it the salty air from the sea. Jesus had just told Peter of his fate. Peter, never being one to sit contemplatively and keep his thoughts to himself, couldn't help but ask, 'What of him?' He gestured to John.

"What is it to you if he should live until I return?" Jesus, the master teacher, answered.

∞

She opened her eyes to find a face as vulnerable as any she'd ever seen. A look she never thought to see on John.

He whispered in a haunted voice, "I still don't know why."

"Thank you," she whispered back, as if speaking too loudly might break the newfound bond of trust between them.

Noory looked down at the photo in her hand, took a deep breath, and closed her eyes as she tried to memorize her mother's face. She handed the frame back to John, but he refused to take it. "You keep it. I have copies."

Noory felt as if she were seeing this man for the very first time. She had always thought he didn't date because explaining who he was would be impossible, but she realized what she'd always known on some level: he was still in love with her mother.

∞

That night Noory lay in bed as sleep eluded her. She thought of her conversation with John and the anger she had carried for so many years—without really understanding it. The wound wasn't completely healed but the heaviness had lifted. She didn't know her father and barely remembered her mother, but John was always there.

She rolled onto her side and smiled at the picture of her mother on her nightstand. On an impulse, she grabbed the frame and kissed the smiling face. She lay there remembering being little and John throwing her into the air as she laughed. She never worried he'd drop her, not once. As her small arms flew out from her sides like a bird, she remembered turning her head ever so slightly and saw her mom there beside John and heard her laughter on the wind.

Chapter 5

Nick pressed his palms to his head as the familiar buzzing began. It swept through his mind as the center of his being was pulled toward a downtown hotel. He walked to the back entrance, placed his hand over the slot for the key card, which he didn't have, and concentrated until the mechanism gave a soft click. Once inside he stopped and listened again, then right, up the stairs, left, up three more flights of stairs, then two, before opening the door to a rooftop recreation area overlooking the city. Strings of lights crisscrossed a huge pergola illuminating the night and casting a glow over the modern outdoor furniture and large dance floor he guessed was rented out for parties.

He expected to see the teenage girl—her distress is what brought him in the first place—but he didn't expect to see Noory there confronting her and the man with her, who looked to be at least forty. They didn't seem to hear Nick come outside over the wind on the rooftop and the traffic noise from below. He remained out of sight, observing.

Noory shouted, "I've been worried sick about you! Ava said you snuck out of the shelter again. Then I see you running off with this guy." Noory pointed directly at the man, who wore a stunned expression that was quickly turning to anger. "And don't think I don't know what *you're* doing. She's a minor, jackass!" She grabbed Grace's arm and pulled her to her feet as the man yanked her back onto the couch.

"Blake!" Grace screamed.

"Get out," he said to Noory in a tone that indicated a slithering entity had taken up residence behind his cold eyes.

Everything in Nick wanted to rush forward and beat the hell out of this man, but he was almost certain he knew what Noory was—given the Templar's hooked "X" he'd seen on her wrist and her connection to

John. How she handled a malevolent being would likely prove his theory—if he could only restrain his urge to do what he did best for another minute or two.

"I'm not going anywhere," Noory said as she stepped into Blake's personal space.

Blake rushed at her as she shifted to the side and grabbed his arm while using his momentum against him. She hooked her ankle around his shin, and he hit the concrete but was back on his feet quicker than any human should have been, shoving her and throwing her off balance. She crashed face-first against a post holding up the pergola, leaving a gash above her eyebrow. Blake used the opportunity to drive his fist into her gut, doubling her over.

He grabbed a handful of her hair and yanked her head back. His voice had morphed into something unearthly like too much bass funneling through a speaker. "You amuse us, scion."

Nick's nails were leaving bloody crescents in his palms from clenching his fists in a barely restrained effort not to act, but he felt certain he was right about what Noory was: stepping in might actually make her angry. When Blake drew a knife from his belt, though, Nick could no longer restrain himself. He rushed from his hiding place ready to unleash hell.

Blake let go of Noory's hair, and as she pivoted sideways to kick him in the knee, he raked the knife across her thigh.

Grace screamed from where she sat frozen on the couch.

Nick grabbed the arm that held the knife and twisted it mercilessly around the man's back until he dropped the weapon. Blake spun around and threw him several feet before advancing on Noory once more.

Nick felt the energy on the roof shift before his body even hit the ground. When he looked up, he saw Noory had gone feral: she looked at Blake as a deadly smile made its way across her face while sweat and blood carved thin trails down her cheeks. She threw her arms out wide in smug invitation before crouching slightly, fingers curling. She was no longer simply defending Grace. Something ancient and wild had clawed its way to the surface. A string of lights hanging from the pergola above

Noory flashed brightly, then burst. Glass rained down to coat her hair like a fine layer of snow. The outdoor furniture began to slowly slide across the concrete in Noory's direction as energy coalesced around her.

Blake grabbed her by the throat, but Nick was no longer worried; he knew the man was toast. Noory snatched the arm that held her. The man screeched and began loosening his grip, barely able to hold on through the pain she was obviously causing him. Nick got to his feet and watched as Noory's hair fanned out from her face, her eyes narrowed, and he felt chills run up his spine as he heard her speak.

"You will release me." The voice was hers but sounded as if it were in unison with hundreds of other female voices, some with Hebrew accents, others Irish, Norwegian, all as fierce as her own.

The rooftop door opened, and Nick turned to see that John had shown up. He knew Noory must have called him to help.

"Oh, Noory," John lamented. As he watched her, grief and awe made their way across his face.

Nick knew John's mind was inside the same memory as his own: a memory of Noory's young, widowed, great grandmother, Sarah Solomon, wild-eyed and shoving Nick and John out of the way so that she could deliver the killing blow to one more Nazi, never sleeping, nor eating, just blazing a trail of vengeance that would never bring Levi Solomon back. The three of them had saved hundreds during that time, but Nick and John couldn't save her. Despite John's apparent hesitancy, Nick *wanted* Noory to embrace her power. In the short time he'd known her, he'd sensed it: a kindred soul. Best of all, she could help save those kids she cared about.

Then shame washed over him as he realized it may have only been that he was sick of being alone—the only killer on the block.

Noory squeezed the arm that held her throat even tighter, and Nick heard bones snap.

Grace stopped sobbing long enough to screech in terror and cover her face.

The man screamed in agony and released Noory, but she refused to let go as he sank to his knees. She kept hold of his broken arm, grabbed his hair with her other hand, and slammed her knee into his face. "Trash," she said, before throwing him into a grouping of tables and chairs. Fear had taken up residence on his once-arrogant face as furniture broke and scattered beneath his weight.

Noory swayed a little on her feet before lowering herself to the ground.

John started to make his way toward her but diverted to Blake, who was trying to get up. He walked over and kicked him in the ribs. "Stay down!"

Nick ran over to Noory and kneeled in front of her. "Remind me to never arm wrestle you."

Noory knocked a patio chair across the concrete as the unnatural strength still coursed through her body. "I don't like it, and I'm never using it again. It makes my veins burn, my head hurt, and I have to see inside their sick skulls, and I don't wanna know all that shit."

Nick knew, out of anyone in the world, he should be sympathetic but felt anger rising in him anyway. "Why the hell should you get to whine your way out of your commission? Nobody else gets to. You could be using that power to help these kids. You can't turn away and pretend it isn't your gift to use. You can't just ignore this." Noory didn't look all that stable, and he feared she might accidentally place her hand on one of the larger chunks of bulb fragments that lay scattered about. Nick picked up one of the more jagged pieces beside her and flung it away.

"I don't ignore it. I'm there day after day, listening to their stories. Helping them when they screw up for the thousandth time. Pulling them off rooftops when they sell themselves to some sick son of a bitch like that." She pointed to the man who John was placing in handcuffs. Blake screamed as John showed no compassion for his broken arm. "Besides, you wouldn't even tour the shelter when I asked you."

"I don't have to. I'm out there, giving up my life. At least you still have the right to die when this shit becomes too much. You'll be long gone when I'm still here dealing with it, day in, day out." Nick saw the horrified look on her face. He'd spoken of her life as something expendable, flippant, like it didn't matter to him, when it really did—much more than he even cared to admit. His mind screamed at him. *This is where you apologize, dumbass! Say something!* Yet when he opened his mouth, no words came.

"Maybe I don't want to be a killer like *you!*" she said.

Her words swept across his heart like an icy wind. He knew she had seen him in the warehouse the night he'd taken down Calista's killer, and she was still able to look at him, walk him home, and maybe even understand him. For the first time in centuries, light had crept in through the cell door of his soul. It was mercy from heaven, but now he knew . . . he was nothing more than a killer in her eyes. He'd been moments from apologizing. Now all he wanted to do was lash out. Like a train barreling off the tracks, he tried to stop himself, to no avail.

"I don't have the luxury of being a coward," he spat.

"Screw you!" She kicked him in the chest, but this time, it was weak. Nick looked down at the spot where her foot had landed and saw a bright red, bloody shoe print smeared across his white shirt.

When he looked back up, he saw that she'd gone ghostly pale and was having trouble focusing. Her jeans were soaked from the knife wound, which had bled more than he'd realized.

"John!" Nick called. He crawled a few feet until he could get behind Noory and ease her onto the ground before she passed out. Glass ground into his knees, but he ignored the pain. "Jesus, Noory," he whispered as panic crept into his voice. He'd said stupid shit about her death only to find that she might bleed out only seconds later.

John ran over and looked on in horror at the amount of blood still pouring from the gaping wound. Blocking Grace's view of what he was doing, John placed his hands over the laceration and begin concentrating as Noory tried to shove him away.

"No! Take me to the hospital," she protested.

"There's no time. Stop fighting me," John said.

Her protests ended only seconds later when her eyes rolled back in her head.

"She's out. Thank God," John said. He shut his own eyes and whispered under his breath. After several moments the wound closed under the faint glow coming from John's hands. He took Noory's wrist to check her pulse, and, seeming satisfied, placed her hand back down and patted it gently. "She'll wake in a minute. She's always been like that. Hates anything to do with her calling or mine."

"She's Catherine's daughter, isn't she?" Nick asked.

"Yes," John said without further comment.

Nick dared to glance at John's face and saw that he was far away, no doubt remembering Catherine. He had known John for over a millennium and Noory's lineage for almost as long. Though he and John had not been close in decades, he knew John had fallen in love with Noory's mother. Most things after that had become a blur of tracking, vengeance, and case after case of ouzo. Nick missed John terribly—though he sat right there beside him. It suddenly seemed so stupid that he couldn't just talk to him like they used to. But the chasm between them was wide, painful, and mostly, Nick realized, his own fault.

"John, I—" Nick began, before Blake interrupted them.

"Hey, Beloved!" Blake's tone was taunting as the entity he carried used the nickname given to John two thousand years ago taken from the saying, "The disciple whom Jesus loved." "My arm hurts. You're not going to heal me, too? You're holy, right? I said my arm hurts."

John gave an exhausted laugh as he rolled his eyes. "What an asshole." He stood, walked over to the man, and punched him in his already bloodied face as casually as if it were a handshake. "Shut up."

Noory woke and tried to get up immediately, but it was clear to Nick that she couldn't focus. "You're still lightheaded. Sit down for a while," Nick pleaded. He knew she was determined to make her way to Grace, who was shaking and staring in horror at the man she had arrived with. Noory sat for a few moments before trying to stand again. Nick helped her up and over to the couch where Grace sat.

"There was something *in him*," Grace said in a small, trembling voice. Mascara mixed with tears ran down her face in thick black rivulets.

"Yes," Noory said.

"How did I not know that?"

"Seriously? Did the dude have to be possessed for you to know you shouldn't sell yourself?"

"Easy, Noory," John said as he yanked Blake to his feet. "Nicholas, can you help these two get back home while I take him to the station?"

"Of course," Nick said, looking at Grace with sympathy.

John left, leaving the three of them alone.

"Grace, let's get you back to the center," Noory said.

"You're not my mother! Back off!"

Noory winced, and Nick couldn't blame her. She'd just gotten stabbed defending the girl and was in no mood for her smart mouth. Nick crossed his arms, looked at them, and laughed.

"What!" they both said in angry unison.

Nick gave a weary sigh, indicating they should already know what. "Neither one of you gets why the other is upset," he said, shaking his head. He pointed at Grace. "Noory's scared you're going to die, and she loves you too much to watch it happen."

He pointed at Noory next. "She knows how bad she screwed up and needs a damn hug right now, but you're too pissed for that."

They both looked annoyed by his analysis and now seemed allied against him. He opened the door for the two, turning his face to hide the knowing smile as they left the rooftop together. He'd given them a common enemy: him. *Whatever worked.*

Nick followed them out of the hotel and onto the sidewalk. Silence reigned on the way back to the shelter. Nick knew Grace was embarrassed, Noory looked ready to pass out at any moment, and he *really* wanted a drink.

After they settled Grace in at the shelter, Nick walked Noory, now wearing Nick's long jacket to cover the blood on her thigh, to her apartment. Once inside, he paused in front of a framed picture: a photo of John and Noory. John looked exactly the age he did now, maybe forty, but Noory looked to be about three years old. He hadn't known John had raised her. He thought again of the years they had barely spoken, except when John cleaned up one of Nick's crime scenes. Despite all the things he and his old friend didn't agree on, he knew his commission to save children was always common ground.

"Coffee?" Noory asked, pulling him out of his thoughts.

"Sure, but you sit. I'll take care of it."

Noory looked down at her ripped and blood-soaked jeans. "These have had it. I'll be right back."

He watched her go, half afraid she would collapse.

Nick heard the shower running, then saw her return later with her hair up in a knot and wearing fresh clothing. She sat as he placed a steaming cup of coffee in front of her.

Nick looked at his cup, wishing it was "Irish." He knew he had to address lashing out at her, but it had been so long since he'd even spoken to someone long enough to piss them off, much less apologize for anything. It made him realize how much he'd isolated himself and why he'd done it in the first place: relationships were too damn messy.

He ran his thumb over the pattern of the wood grain on Noory's old kitchen table as he gathered his thoughts. "I'm sorry for what I said on the roof tonight. Of course, you don't want to embrace your gift. If anyone understands, it would be me. I never should have called you a coward, either. In many ways, you're braver than I am. It's easier to fight, or even kill, than it is to care like you do." He remembered a time when he did, when everything went straight to his heart, but he had to stop when he realized it was ripping him to shreds.

"Thanks, but I never should have called you a killer."

"I am," he said.

"Not without reason. It's just . . ." She took a deep breath before continuing. "Tonight, on that rooftop. That man represented everything that I have to continually battle against to keep these kids safe. I wanted to destroy him. My veins *burned* for it. But if I let go once, will I let go again? When will it get easy? It might."

Nick rubbed a hand across his mouth before speaking, as if trying to hold in words that intended to escape despite him. "It never gets easy for me." His voice cracked as he spoke, and he wouldn't meet her eyes.

"I suppose that's a good thing then," she said.

"Well, it is, and it isn't."

Noory nodded and took a sip of coffee. "So, you know what I am then?"

Nick was grateful for the change of subject. "Yes," he replied as he sat up straight.

"John told you?"

"No, but I'm familiar with your lineage." He wanted to say more, to tell her he'd known generations of her kind, and that she was just as strong as any of them. He wanted to assure her she would be okay. But would she?

His hands shook as he remembered wading through centuries of blood and failure. He couldn't speak of Auschwitz, Treblinka, Belzec, the others. Could he even mention the Nazis he'd killed, and the truck-loads of human cargo he, John, and Noory's great grandmother, Sarah Solomon, intercepted before they'd reached the camps?

Could he tell her they'd been coated in so much Nazi blood that the people they had rescued were terrified of them and several ran in hor-ror? Could he tell her of his greatest failure—so tormenting that John had to wrestle a gun from his hands? He wasn't sure if he would even be able to die if he had succeeded. Then the guilt over trying to take the easy way out . . . .

"Nick? Are you okay?"

He saw her mouth moving, but it took several moments for his brain to process what she was saying. "What? Yeah, I'm good."

Noory stood and moved toward him, placing her palm against his forehead. "Are you feeling all right? You kind of zoned out on me for a minute. You're sweating."

"I'm fine, Light." He wondered what else he could say. *An abyss has opened in my head, and I'm falling into it.*

He could tell by the look on her face she didn't believe him. Her hand slid from his forehead to his cheek as she peered into his eyes. "You're not okay."

No, I'm not. "It's been a long night," he said.

Noory dropped her hand from Nick's face and returned to her chair.

He shook his head as if the act could loosen the bonds inside his mind. "Listen, I hate to say this, but the situation with Grace isn't over."

He watched questions play across Noory's face but felt grateful that she shifted her attention back to Grace along with him. "How so?" she asked.

"Evil people get these kids addicted, and then they follow their push-ers like the pied piper into slavery, but Blake had a whole other kind of malevolence going on. There's something more happening here. We can keep following her, hoping to get there in time when she makes another mistake, or we can find out who pulls the strings for the whole opera-tion. They'll be back for her."

"How do you know that?" Noory looked horrified.

"Well, she's obviously a good target: no family, no address, no ties, a history of abuse. She's a pretty girl, which makes human trafficking a sick possibility. She doesn't love herself enough to protect herself." Nick sighed long and heavily, as the weight of the ages rested on his shoulders.

"All true, but how else do you know it?"

"There doesn't need to be anything else. You know that."

"There doesn't need to be, but there is."

Nick hesitated, looking at Noory as she looked back, challenging him for the truth.

"She has a mark of destiny on her. She's ringing like a bell, and it didn't stop when Blake went to jail. There's more trouble coming for her."

"Explain and don't be all vague with me like John is. Spill it."

"Fine. You know John has special gifts, or you would have bled to death on the rooftop. So I have one too. I hear children in distress. It isn't a voice, though. It's more like a signal inside my skull that tugs at me, pulls my attention in their direction. It's hard to ignore. Not that I want to ignore it. I just . . ."

"It's exhausting," she said softly.

He cleared his throat and ran his palm across the back of his neck.

"Yeah. Anyway, they will come back for her, and when they do, we need to make sure we're there."

"I'm not sure how. She sneaks out a lot, and after us telling her she will need to answer questions in order to prosecute that asshole that bought her tonight . . . She knows a social worker will be on the way. I don't know how I will be able to keep her there unless I lock her up." Noory rubbed her eyes.

Nick could almost see the adrenaline that had carried her through the night ebbing away. "Is there anything that she always has with her?"

"Yes, she carries the same ratty old purse with her everywhere. It's like a security blanket. It's big, so it has everything she owns in it. A lot of them carry things like that in case they need to run."

"I have a tracking device we could place into the lining of her bag. Could you make that happen?" Nick asked.

"Yeah, I'll sneak back in tonight and do it."

Noory swayed a little in her chair. Nick's brow furrowed as he looked at her.

"I know I must look like hell, but it can't be that bad," she said with a laugh.

"You're pale. If you're going back out tonight, then you have to eat."

"I'm a big girl. Just go to your house and get your Bond-like GPS gadget for me, and I'll make a sandwich or something. It's fine, really."

"Huh, what's that?" he said, pretending he couldn't hear her before making his way to the kitchen to find something to feed her.

He heard her protesting from the other room. "Don't tell me to—oh, whatever. Even I'm too tired to argue."

Nick laughed as he shook his head.

After Noory had hidden the tracking system in Grace's purse and found and threw away a sandwich bag with five Percocet and marijuana inside, she sat in the silence and watched the girl sleep, marveling at how young she looked when her face was relaxed—when she wasn't gearing up for a fight against Noory, herself, the world at large . . . Sixteen years was such a short time to walk the Earth. Noory wasn't one for prayer, but for the first time in a long while, she bowed her head and begged God to protect this girl. She pled with God to make her strong enough to rescue Grace from herself.

CHAPTER 6

Grace gave a tight smile as an older man opened the door to the house where her boyfriend was staying. "You're out awfully late, aren't you?" he asked.

"Couldn't sleep." She ducked in and avoided eye contact with him.

"Ah, well, we're all night owls around here, anyway. Come on in. He's in the basement."

She found Elliot in the same spot she usually did, slumped over the box of wires he'd been tinkering with for months. She planted a kiss on his cheek. He hadn't even heard her coming down the stairs.

"Now, what is this thing again?" She asked.

He exhaled in frustration as he looked up at her. "Seriously, Grace. I love you, but you don't listen to a word I say." He watched as she dropped her giant bag on the workbench, rambled through it, and became increasingly frustrated when she couldn't find her stash. *Frigging Noory!*

"Tell me again. I'm listening," she said as she pushed aside a couple of large plastic storage bins and found the shoe box where she had hidden a stash that even Elliot didn't know about. She opened the box and got out her vape pen while leaning her bottom against the workbench.

"You know I don't like it when you smoke that stuff. It'll rot your brain. It literally kills your brain cells."

"You've got enough brain cells for both of us." Grace had been in awe of Elliot ever since they'd met in high school. He was an absolute genius. When she had told him some boys in her class had been teasing her, he'd hacked the school's system and placed unexcused absences and an abundance of "Fs" on their records. Grace snickered as the boys panicked. No one had ever looked out for her like he had. Now neither of them bothered with school. Grace couldn't abide being told what to do, and Elliot had been chronically bored in class—always complaining that he knew more than his teachers. These days he spent his time obsessing over the device he'd been working on. It frightened her. She watched, knowing his brain was frantically working, calculating. She just wanted him to hang out with her and talk—be a teenager. "You're almost eighteen years old. Relax a little." She offered him a hit.

"No, what I'm doing is far too important."

"I think it's weird. You're not going to control me with that box of wires, are you?"

She expected him to laugh, but he looked at the pen between her fingers, and she had her answer. "Well, the thing works through cell phones, right? I'll be the only person not using one. I don't want my brain waves altered by that thing," She pointed at the box and took another hit.

Elliot laughed. "Nah, you alter your brain in other ways. I told you I don't like that shit, now put it away." He got up and turned on a fan as she finished off what was left. She then grabbed a mint from her bag and popped it into her mouth as he came over and wrapped his arms around her, and they began kissing. She felt his arms stiffen as he moved to the side, grabbed something, and then backed up. "Where the hell did you get this?" He stood there holding a wad of cash that she knew he'd just retrieved from her bag.

"Stole it," she said as she leaned forward to make out with him some more, attempting to distract him.

"No, stop it." He swatted at her like a fly. "Grace, are you . . . are you hooking again?"

Grace hung her head while speaking. "I've told you before; it's not a big deal. I don't want to go back into the system, but I need money from somewhere."

"I can get money for you. You can even stay here with me. My foster father said so. He won't even report you to Family Services. He hasn't reported me."

"Doesn't something about that bother you?" she asked.

"Let me get this straight. You are in and out of that shelter because you don't want another foster family. I've found somewhere to live where I don't have to have another caseworker and you find something wrong with it. You cannot be pleased."

"It's just . . . when I'm around him . . . I don't know. It's a bad vibe. Anyway, I didn't have to sleep with anyone tonight to get the money. Noory stuck her nose in my business again, and two weird dudes showed up and the guy got arrested, and I got his money. That's it."

"But it wouldn't have been it. You would have done it. You've done it before."

"I did what I had to! You don't have the right to judge me!" Grace yelled, as she began shaking and trying not to cry.

"This is exactly why I have to get this device working. For people like you and me." He pulled her into his arms. "People have always forgotten us. They're too busy, just like my first foster father was—always gone, helping someone else, but once I get this thing up and running, we can fix that."

She knew better than to argue with him about it, and she was on thin ice anyway since he'd found the money. He began kissing her again, and they soon found themselves on the old hide-a-bed he slept on.

Grace had dozed off and when she rolled over, hoping to find Elliot there beside her, he'd already gotten dressed and made his way back over to the table to work on his project some more.

"This should be working!" he muttered.

Grace knew he was back in the zone and saw no point in staying if he wasn't going to pay attention to her anyway. She got up, grabbed her phone from her bag, and texted a friend to come get her. "Well, I've got to get going. Noory will be upset if I'm not back by the time she arrives for work in the morning."

"Okay, stay away from the weed, and if you need money, come to me. Don't be messing around with those old dudes anymore. I mean it."

"Fine." She leaned over to kiss him goodbye, but he barely looked up. He was already reabsorbed by the damn box of wires again.

She was halfway up the stairs when she heard him exclaim, "Yes!"

She turned to look at him once more and found the strange box had lit up in an odd blue glow that shone on his face, giving it an eerie cast that made him seem like someone else entirely. Though she loved him, her sudden urge to flee that sight had her running up the stairs.

When she reached the living room, she found Elliot's unofficial foster father on the phone. He stopped talking and placed a hand over the receiver. "Heading back home?" the man asked her.

"Yeah, a friend of mine is waiting out front."

"Okay, be careful. Go straight home."

"I will. I will." As she opened the door, she heard the man resume his conversation. "Yeah, she's heading back. Uh, huh."

Suddenly everybody's in my business! She rolled her eyes as she headed outside, hopped into her friend's ratty old car, and disappeared into the night.

CHAPTER 7

The next morning, Noory arrived at the shelter later than usual. She wondered how her assistant would react if she told her the truth: I'm late because I was stabbed saving Grace from a demon-possessed john on a rooftop and would be dead if it weren't for a two-thousand-year-old, faith-healing police detective. Instead, she told her assistant she'd woke with a migraine—she wasn't ready to try and explain things she didn't yet understand herself.

"Good morning, Ava," Noory said.

"Good morning. Feeling any better?"

"I'm getting there. Thanks." Noory immediately walked to the back to check on Grace. She was a late sleeper; she was surprised to find her bed empty and her bag gone. There was no one in the women's washroom either.

Walking back to the front desk, an uneasy feeling gripped her. "Ava, do you know where Grace is?"

"You just missed her. She acted like she had somewhere to be. That's a first. She usually wouldn't get up early for an earthquake."

Noory was out the door without another word. After seeing no one out front, she walked around to the side street, and what she saw sent a shock of adrenaline through her body.

"Grace!" Noory looked on in horror as she caught the briefest glimpse of the girl before the back doors of a van slammed shut and her bag spilled across the sidewalk as it pulled away. Despair sank in when she realized that there weren't even any license plate numbers to give the police. The GPS sewn into the lining of her bag would do them no good now, either. "Damn it!" Noory cursed as hopelessness gripped her heart.

"Noory!" she heard Nick call as he ran up to her. "Take a deep breath and close your eyes," he said with a sense of urgency.

"What?" She hadn't even realized Nick was in the vicinity.

"Just do it!" He said in a voice so startling and commanding that Noory complied out of confusion and the certain knowledge that she was at a complete loss to help Grace anyway.

Noory felt his warm arms wrap around her, followed by a sensation of being pulled into a breeze and carried away.

What's happening? Her thought was answered just as quickly.

We're following them, Nick spoke into her mind.

How?

You can decide to look, and you will see, but please don't scream— it will hurt my ears exactly as if they were still there.

What the hell are you talking— Noory saw they were flying together over buildings and screamed.

Damn it, woman!

Noory looked down again to see the roof of the van below them. When she peered at her own body, she saw the outline of Nick's arms around her waist, but they were no longer solid. She had seen some strange things in her time, but this was the most frightening.

Relax, Nick spoke into her mind as they descended through the roof and into the van.

They can't see you, he communicated to her.

Grace sat on the floor of the van looking stoned and confused.

Damn it, Grace. Noory grieved the girl's stupidity and her own sense of failure.

Just listen.

Noory complied as one of the kidnappers—whom Noory recognized as Blake; his arm miraculously healed—spoke to the driver about where they were headed.

"Find us a way around this traffic. We have to get to Savannah before the ship leaves or the captain will have my ass. Wait a minute . . ." Blake began sniffing the air as Noory had observed him doing the night before. "Something is here. Damn it! You were supposed to say the spell," Blake said in the preternaturally deep voice. "There is no barrier around this van!" His eyes began to glow. He narrowed them, and Noory heard a crackling as the man appeared to stick his head through some invisible field. "I see you," he said in a singsong voice. A shadow reached out of Blake and grabbed at Noory.

Nick jerked them both backwards as the van and those in it became a blur. Noory saw the roof of the van become smaller as Nick settled her on the terrace of a building.

"Breathe. Breathe, Noory. Come on," Nick said, giving her a gentle shake. Her head lolled back against Nick's shoulder. She felt one of his arms crisscrossed over her chest, the other across her waist. Her eyes popped open, and she saw the sky above her. Her head came up, and he released his grip from her chest.

The first breath was so painful she doubled over. She felt both joy and vertigo at being solid again. She stuck out her arm as she fell to her knees, disoriented. Nick went down with her, keeping his arm around her waist to make sure she didn't stumble forward and hit her head. His body curled over hers protectively. Noory felt his warmth cover her like a blanket.

"That always happens if you aren't used to it. Have a drink." Nick helped her sit down. Noory trembled as he pulled a flask from his jacket pocket. She hesitated for just a moment before she took a small drink. "Tastes like licorice."

Nick smiled and took a drink himself.

"What the hell was that, Nick? What *are* you?"

"You seemed shocked, but not as shocked as you should be. So, I assume you've seen some things in your time, too."

"Yeah, I've seen some things. You don't have to tell me your story, but I would like to know what just happened to my body."

"I took you into another dimension. It's dangerous to remain there too long unless you've crossed over naturally. I can travel quickly that way as well, speed of thought, that kinda thing."

"Oh, *that* kinda thing," Noory said sarcastically.

Nick laughed and took another drink before his expression turned serious again. "If they are headed to a ship, then this is most likely a human trafficking ring that smuggles American girls overseas. We have to get to that ship. Once she's on foreign soil, things get a lot more complicated."

"Maybe John can use what he knows from arresting that vermin Blake and find out who he works for. Maybe we could trace the ship from there."

"On it," Nick said as his thumbs flew across his phone, texting John.

After Noory made it to her feet and they were headed down the fire escape, Nick's phone buzzed. "It's a luxury craft called *The Chalice.*"

Noory gave a wry laugh as Nick relayed the message.

"What?" he asked.

"Nothing."

"Okay then. Time to go to Savannah and do a little recon. We'll be there hours before them. We can locate the ship. Maybe even board it and hide until they arrive," Nick said.

"Why can't we just pop back into the van like we did before?"

"We won't be able to do that again. Not in *that* van. You heard what Blake said about the barrier spell. That thing is sealed up like a drum by now. We can only hope they didn't do that with the ship."

"Well, I would imagine they would, right? Why wouldn't they?" Noory asked.

"They wouldn't if they are expecting people to board that are carrying entities inside them. The spell blocks travelers from other dimensions. Given their line of work, I don't doubt a few of them are hosts," Nick explained.

"*Hosts* . . . damn creepy word!"

"The creepiest." Nick lifted his brows as he said it, making Noory laugh a little despite the gravity of the situation.

Nick pulled Noory into the shadows of an alleyway and opened his arms to her. "All right. Ready?"

"For what?" Noory looked at Nick's outstretched arms in confusion.

"Ready to go to Savannah?"

"Oh, I see, we're taking the crazy train," she said.

"Always." Nick reached into his jacket pocket once more and opened the flask. "One for the road?" he asked Noory.

"No, thank you."

"Suit yourself." Nick turned it up for another sip.

Noory watched as Atlanta, then South Georgia, disappeared in a blur of pines, pecan trees, and highway. It seemed like only seconds before they landed softly on a cobblestone pathway behind a building and underneath a set of stairs. Noory had been to Savannah several times and knew right away that they were on the riverfront—which she would have loved under other circumstances. A stray cat saw them appear out of nothingness and arched its back before unleashing a hiss the likes of which Noory had never heard before.

Noory sucked in a deep breath as Nick gently rubbed her back. "You okay?"

"Yeah, it's a little easier this time."

Nick nodded but kept his eye on her until she looked steady on her feet. Noory watched the cat run off around the corner. "Even he knows this shit isn't natural."

Nick laughed. "Tell me what you really think, Noory." He instinctively went to his jacket pocket where the flask was before he caught Noory watching him. He quickly put his arm down.

The two walked out onto the riverfront as notes of "Moon River" carried on the warm, salty breeze across the water from a saxophone street performer.

Noory looked out over the river as the sun was setting in tones of deep orange, bright pink, and brush strokes of purple. The water reflected the soft colors, and the wave crests picked up the soft pink tones. Noory closed her eyes and breathed deeply as she said a prayer for Grace. When she opened her eyes, Nick was looking at her. She thought for a moment about how wonderful it might be to have someone to watch the sunset with. How it might feel if they were here for normal reasons—if they were just two people enjoying a romantic sunset.

Then again, she'd struggled with relationships and letting someone into her world, lineage aside. Even if she could trust them with her secrets, she didn't know if she was brave enough to trust them with her heart. When she'd ended it, the men she'd dated had walked away either calling her a coward or a bitch. She couldn't shake the feeling that Nick might read the vulnerability in her eyes. She glanced down at her hands with their chipping blue nail polish. When she looked back up, she saw Nick swallow hard, avert his eyes back to the river, and the gigantic, slow-moving barges heading toward the port.

"We'll find her. We're hours ahead of them," he said softly.

Noory thought of all the wonderful things Nick had done for kids. She didn't know how long he had been doing it. It must have been a while if those experiences had led him to drink. The feeling of helplessness was familiar to her. Her job felt so cyclical. She brought the kids in, helped them, encouraged them, got them jobs, foster homes, helped them get back into school, yet so many of them went right back to the streets, and it was enough to drive a person to escape into a bottle. She knew it wasn't just time she invested; it was heart and soul. She looked at Nick as the breeze coming off the river blew his thick hair across his forehead—he took it to heart, all the lives he couldn't save. She knew what it was like to care. It was maddening. It was why he drank, but she worried about him.

"Have you ever done the job without the liquor?" The question came out in a rush, and no sooner had she spoken than she wished she could gobble it back up and ask another way. His head snapped in her direction as he glared at her. He opened his mouth, then closed it again. "I'm sorry, Nick. I haven't known you long enough to ask that. Forgive me."

He looked back out at the river and rested one elbow on the railing while the other hand raked through his hair. "I've tried to, Noory. It's drove a wedge between John and me. We haven't been as close in the last few . . . John took me to an AA meeting once."

Noory listened intently as he shared a memory.

"Hi, my name is Martin, and I'm an alcoholic."

"Hello, Martin," came the soft reply from the crowd.

"Anyone new tonight?" The forty-something female facilitator asked.

John elbowed Nick, who raised his hand none too eagerly.

"Would you like to come introduce yourself?"

He shook his head and waved for her to pass him. She paused for a beat before continuing. "Well, we are pleased to have you here tonight. If you want to share in the conversation that would be great. If not tonight, then maybe next time."

Nick listened to one person after another share their struggles with alcohol: how it affected their wives, kids, jobs, even their dogs. Nick finally became annoyed and glanced at John before leaving.

Nick stood in the dark by John's truck. Once his old friend caught up, Nick said, "John, these people have nothing to do with me. They have no idea what it's like to live as long as I have with as much responsibility and failure as I carry. I can't relate to them. They can't know what it's like to be me!"

John paused; his expression unchanged. "You're so full of shit," he said calmly.

Nick felt as if he'd been slapped.

"No one gets out of this life unscathed. These people's problems aren't as different from yours as you might think. They are terrified of failing their families, their spouses. They're scared to death that no matter how hard they try they won't be enough. There is nothing new under the sun. We've just been in the game a hell of a lot longer than most."

"I'll thank you not to get all ecclesiastical on me, John."

"You want to believe that you are different, so you won't have to change. It's convenient. You love your crutch. I understand that. One day, you'll find a reason to stop. When you do, you'll be back. Until then, don't put yourself above these people. Life beats the shit out of them just like it does you."

After Nick finished his recollection, Noory said, "Yep, that sounds like John all right."

Nick laughed. "Yeah, that's Papa Bear."

"So, how old are you, Nick?"

"How old do I look?"

"Maybe thirty."

"Close enough. Let's go get some dinner," he replied with a sly smile. "I can hear your stomach growling from over here."

Noory started to protest but realized she had pried enough for one evening, and he was right: now that the nausea from riding on the crazy train was wearing off, she was getting hungry. The smells of seafood mixing with spices were wafting from the restaurants lining the riverfront. They followed their noses to one of them as the last notes of "Moon River" faded into the night air. She knew it might be the last bit of normal they'd be getting from this trip.

CHAPTER 8

The *Chalice* softly rocked in the moonlight as the ramp leading up to it bobbed up and down with the rhythm of the water.

"So, I imagine we don't just walk on board?" Noory whispered.

"Not so much, no. You ready?"

Noory took a deep breath. "Yeah, besides, I'm more than a little pissed. It might feel good to kick some ass right about now," she said.

"That's my girl!"

Normally, being referred to as "girl" would have felt like an insult, but it didn't bother her when Nick said it. Noory could tell by the moonlight that he was smiling. He held out his arms, and Noory moved into them and was shocked to find that she sighed as his arms wrapped around her. She was even more shocked when he didn't immediately shift dimensions but stood still for a moment just holding her.

"Please . . ." she watched Nick swallow hard before continuing, ". . . be careful."

Noory forced herself to look up at him. "You, too." Nick became transparent. She closed her eyes to keep from getting dizzy. A moment later, they were on deck.

Nick stood silent for a moment before speaking. "There are two guards on the opposite side. Let's take the stairs at the service entrance. I don't feel anyone waiting down there," he said.

Noory narrowed her eyes at Nick, wondering how he could know so much.

"I'll explain it later," he said.

They made their way below deck and settled in to wait for Blake to transport Grace on board.

"I still don't understand why we can't just wait on the van and grab her before she comes on board," Noory whispered.

"Because there was an armed guard with a semi-automatic positioned on the top of that building just as you turn into the parking lot and neither of us is bulletproof. Someone running an operation like this is going to cover his ass. Besides, if we're in here, we can both do what we do best," Nick said, lifting an eyebrow.

"Okay, yeah, I like that," Noory said. As much as she didn't enjoy leaning into her calling, she was ready to unleash hell on whoever had taken Grace.

A half hour went by before they heard voices and footsteps of people who had boarded. Nick pointed above him at the ceiling and moved his finger as the footsteps went off in different directions. He stopped and continued pointing at the northwest corner. "She's right there. That's where we have to go. Ready?"

Noory moved in close to him, and they were in the room where Grace was being held within seconds.

"Oh, Grace, no." Noory looked at the girl with black streaks running down her face. She looked right through Noory. "Let's get her out of here."

Nick nodded and wrapped his arms around them both.

"What are you waiting on?" Noory asked.

"Nothing. It's not working." Nick looked around frantically.

"Shit!"

A moment later Noory saw what Nick did. The walls were lined with a metallic type of mesh. "Dear God. It's a faraday cage," she said.

Nick looked at her and nodded slowly.

Noory knew about it from her engineering background. It blocked external static and could be used for testing and shielding in electrical engineering. However, she knew with sickening clarity its supernatural purpose here. Nick wouldn't be able to transport them out of the room now. They were stuck. The ship could sail around the world, and they would still be stuck in that room. John had explained a few supernatural things to her over the years, but the one that interested her most, as an engineer, was that if you needed to trap a nonhuman entity you get your-self a faraday cage. She knew for all intents and purposes going into the invisible dimension made them pure energy, and they wouldn't escape the faraday cage.

The door flew open, and Noory immediately drove her foot into the chest of the first man through the door. As he leaned over, she punched him in the throat. He fell unconscious as another man grabbed Noory by the hair, but Nick broke several of his ribs in one swift blow.

"Grace, come on!" Noory screamed as Grace just stared blankly at her.

Noory heard Nick fighting behind her as another man entered the room. Noory picked Grace up and flung her over her shoulder. Nick made short work of the final guard then helped Noory navigate over the unconscious men and soon they were out of the room and running down the hall. But they nearly ran straight into four men, all armed to the teeth and pointing their weapons directly in their faces.

"Make a move, and she'll be the first one to go." The man had his pis-tol lodged against Grace's temple. Noory gently sat Grace down against the wall. The man continued to hold the gun at Grace's head as he com-manded them to get on their knees.

A man stepped from the shadows. Noory's heart thundered in her ears. She'd hoped never to see this dangerous man ever again. It was her father, Jonah McNamara, and apparently, he was the captain of the ship. He spoke: "Make sure those two are too far apart to touch," he said, gesturing between Noory and Nick. He clearly knew about Nick's ability.

"Aye, Captain," a Latino man said to his right.

Leave, Nick. Go! Noory mouthed at him. He simply shook his head at her, almost imperceptibly. Noory realized that the ship was well away from the shore now. Soon they would be in open waters.

"Bishop Nicholas," the captain said with delight in his voice.

"Don't call me that," Nick gritted out between clinched teeth.

"Perhaps you prefer Santa Claus? Father Christmas?"

"Just get on with it!"

"With what? You don't know what I want," the captain said.

"You want me to throw this guy overboard?" One of the thugs asked.

"You would just be helping him escape. Know your prisoner before you decide on a punishment. This one will just pop up somewhere else. No, I have a gift for him. Elliot!"

A young man who looked to be in his late teens walked out of the shadows with an iron necklace in his hands and a wild smile splashed across his face. "Nice to see you again, Nick."

Noory watched as Nick's face went pale and grief stricken. Elliot turned to look at the captain. "He's here to save the world, but he couldn't save me."

Jonah laughed and clapped Elliot on the back. "That's because you don't need saving. You never did."

"He cleans up real nice, doesn't he?" Jonah gestured at the crisp white shirt, dress pants, and leather loafers Elliot was wearing. "Please present our guest with his fine jewelry."

Elliot took a large iron necklace and threw it over Nick's neck. "There, that's better."

"I'm sorry, Elliot," Nick said softly.

Noory thought she saw the briefest flicker of sorrow cross the Elliot's face before the hatred returned.

"Noory," the captain turned his gaze to her.

"I'd prefer it if you didn't speak to me," she said.

Nick turned a questioning look to her.

"Don't be that way, sweetheart." He ran his hand across Noory's head as she jerked away.

"I can't believe you would allow yourself to get caught over that one. She's not innocent, you know. Let me guess, she willingly went with my business partner when he approached her. She wasn't fighting or kicking. Blake wouldn't have had to rape her. You know that. So why in the hell are you risking your life for her?" His voice rose in frustration. "She's not worthy of someone of your caliber, your heritage, your powers. Can't you see that?"

Noory rolled her eyes.

"Okay, I see how it is. A little time below deck might do you some good. Miguel!" the captain said, motioning to a crewmember. "Take these two below; don't take your eyes off them," he said and motioned to Nick. "If that one gives you trouble, feel free to beat him." He lowered his voice before speaking again. "But if you touch this one, I-will-kill-you." With that, he opened his palm and gave Noory a quick pat on the arm. She felt something sharp pierce her skin seconds before she lost consciousness.

CHAPTER 9

Nicholas sat with the heavy chain around his neck as the ship rocked beneath them. He kept watch over Noory and an eye on the guard in the corner with a pistol at his hip.

Noory's eyes fluttered as the drug wore off. "Noory? Can you hear me? Are you okay?" Nick willed himself to remain calm, but he wasn't sure what Noory had been drugged with.

She groaned and held her palm to her head. Nick watched her look around until her eyes focused on him and the giant links of chain around his neck. "Nick? What the hell?"

"It's iron. It dilutes my ability to use my powers. Not only that, but there is also a spell worked into it somehow. I think your powers work differently because they are encoded in your DNA. You have to be contained another way."

Noory yanked at her own chains. "Damn it! What now? Did he drug me?"

"Yeah, he clearly knows about your gifts. Also, you beat the hell out of some of his crew. I guess now all we can do is wait on John to figure it out."

"Yeah, we would be lost without him, especially me," Noory said.

"You're not his, but he raised you, didn't he?"

"He married my mother before I was born, and then at the hospital he just signed his name to the birth certificate. I've been an Abramson ever since. How do you know that?"

"I saw the photo in your living room, and he may have warned me to stay away from you. He has some frustration over my *habit*," Nick said not wanting to get into that particular subject again. Anyway, he never told me the story. You have different energy. I could tell you weren't his blood."

Noory looked at Nick in confusion.

"When you live as long as I have, you learn a lot more about the subtleties of existence. People who share DNA carry a similar vibration."

"Like an aura?"

"Nah, it's a little different. Aura has colors connected to emotions and virtues—good, bad, in between, but blood . . . sings."

Noory crinkled her nose. "Ew."

"No, not really. All creation sings like notes on a piano," Nick said.

"You're weird," Noory said with a pained yet teasing smile. "Delightfully weird."

Despite the heavy chains around Nick, he couldn't help but smile. "I've learned a lot of things in all my years, but John has never told me your story."

He watched Noory turn her head from side to side, trying to relieve the tension in her neck. She stopped and locked eyes with him. "Well, we aren't going anywhere soon, are we?"

Nick looked at their shackles and the silent guard in the corner. "Doesn't look like it."

"The asshole captain is my father. His name is Jonah McNamara. You probably didn't have time to figure that out before they put the chain around you."

Nick whistled softly through his teeth. "I'm sorry to hear that."

"Yeah, I was too. He tried to take me one other time when I was small, and John damn near killed him."

"He's possessed," Nick said with certainty.

"Yeah, I know." Noory inhaled and soldiered forward. "He *attacked* my mother. Apparently, he thought he could use my special lineage to create some sort of super being to do his bidding. My mother died keeping me from him. John found her and tried to heal her, but it was too late."

"I'm so sorry. That's horrible."

"Yeah, it is. He doesn't define me though, you know?"

Nick looked at her with admiration. "I know." The ship groaned and popped as it rocked the two of them. The smell of rust and grease hung in the air but took nothing from the moment. "John might not be your father, but I do see him in you."

"God, I hope so," Noory said with tears in her eyes. "I don't even want to imagine what my life would be without him."

What little light illuminated the cargo hold glinted off the unshed tears threatening to spill over Noory's face. Nick held her eyes, aching to go to her and knew he would if he weren't bound. Shock raced through him. For the first time in centuries, he wanted someone. Needed someone. Maybe even had the audacity to believe he had something to give until he felt the weight of the flask against his chest. He couldn't drag her into his eternal chaos. He felt oddly grateful for the shackles. They allowed him to feel exactly what was inside him, this strange little spark, long dormant, with no danger of touching, getting closer. It was safer this way.

Noory lifted a shoulder and wiped her eyes as best she could on her sweater and squinted at him.

He squirmed beneath her scrutiny. He'd seen this look before and stared at the floor.

"Nick, do your eyes glow? It's like a very faint—"

Oh shit. "No, it's a trick of this weird dim lighting combined with the sedatives that asshole gave you."

"Okay. For a minute, I was going to guess you were a saint. Like one of those Catholic paintings that . . . never mind." She laughed softly. "I guess that doesn't line up, does it? Who is Elliot?" she asked.

"He's someone I failed miserably. He had been getting tossed around from one foster home to another because they couldn't deal with him. I kept getting pulled back into his circle. The force that directs me, well, it kept putting him in my life. I've learned not to second guess that, you know?"

Noory looked straight at Nick as she spoke. "Oh, yeah, I know."

"Anyway, I let him come live with me a couple years ago. I thought I could handle it. Besides, it would have been nice for once, *just once,* to see the payoff. Instead of just showing up to one tragedy after another, I could actually come home, maybe have dinner, and talk about how his day at school went. It was the closest I ever came to leaving the ouzo behind for good."

"But?" Noory asked, afraid to hear the rest.

"But, I kept getting called away when he needed me most. He had too much time alone to get into trouble, and then one day I came home to find the FBI at my door."

"What? For a kid?"

"Absolutely, yes. Elliot is a genius—which might be part of the problem. He doesn't have the maturity to handle it. Anyway, he'd been hacking into secure databases just for the thrill of it. Of course, they traced it to my house, and that was that. He already had a criminal history. He was taken to a juvenile detention center. I came to visit him, but he refused to see me. I've got the power to hear a child in crisis miles away. I can show up and kick the ass of a predator twice my size, but I couldn't save the child living under my own roof."

"I know wonderful social workers who have the same problem. It always shocks people when I tell them that. Why would he be with Jonah?" Noory asked, refusing to call him "Father."

"I would imagine he wants him for his ability to hack secure databases."

"For what reason?"

"I don't know, but we need to find out."

The door at the top of the stairs creaked open.

"Making yourselves comfortable?" Jonah asked. Nick wanted to beat the man so badly, it was a visceral need that almost became painful.

The man descended the stairs and kneeled in front of Noory, opened a bottle of water, and handed it to her. Noory drank it as she looked at him with pure hatred.

"Daughter, this whole thing could be so much easier if you would just join me."

Noory spat water in his face. He threw his head back and laughed. He took a handkerchief from his pocket and wiped his face. "And here I thought that with all the goodwill you have for those runaways, you were going to be a wise and loving creature like your great uncle." His eyes flashed a blood-red glow as he spoke.

"He got a little pissed, too. I recall a story about him flipping over some tables in a temple. Just sayin."

"You're every bit as capable of dying like he did too. Or worse, you could die like John."

"What?" Noory said in a cracked voice.

The man looked amused at her fear. He left the room with a warning: "Think it over, Noory."

Noory waited for the door to slam shut before turning to Nick. "Dear God, Nick, do you think John is dead?"

"No, he can't really die. He was killed in a sense, but only until his body regenerated. That's probably what he means."

The guard's head snapped up as Nick spoke.

"What? When?" Noory asked.

"Well, you know he's a Knights Templar, right?"

"Of course, that's why I have this tattoo. He gave it to me. They've been protecting my family's secret for ages."

"Well, many of them were burned at the stake. You knew that, right?"

"John fled though."

"No, he didn't. He refused to leave because he couldn't rescue his brothers, and it was their destiny to die there. He went to the stake with them, using his powers to soothe their fears as they marched to their end, allowing himself to be burned without the rescue of death." Nick squeezed his eyes shut and broke out in a cold sweat as he remembered wanting to flee from where he stood by in the shadows, watching the flames rise higher and higher but he'd promised John he would move his body to a safe location where it could regenerate.

If John could bear going through such a thing, then he could bear witnessing it, but the screams were unraveling him. They still did, even over a thousand years later. The bravery of John would give him nightmares throughout eternity. He took a deep breath and continued. "He was unconscious for a while and then slowly regenerated because he can't die."

"Mi Dios," the guard whispered from the corner as he crossed himself.

"Oh, John," Noory said as new tears streaked her face. "Nick, why would he keep that from me? He's told me so much about his past. Why leave that out?"

"He didn't want to hurt you," Nick spoke softly as if he were channeling how John might have felt about it.

"I can't imagine," Noory whispered.

Nick shifted as the leg irons creaked. Noory rested her head against the roughhewn wood of the cargo hold. "You're Saint Nicholas. Aren't you? I mean, I've seen you do all these things. Traveling at the speed of thought: that's why there are fables of Santa making it clear around the globe in one night, right? You've been spotted thousands of miles apart in minutes. I heard the rumors. I just didn't want to believe it. That would also make you the patron saint of sailors, right?"

He tilted his head. "One of my lesser known monikers here in the states, but yes."

The guard in the corner whispered, "Holy Santos."

Nick caught sight of it and didn't know whether to laugh or cry. Belief was precious, especially in the dark; he realized there might be hope for the captain's lackey.

Nick tilted his head toward the shocked guard. "His mind would really explode if he knew who you were."

"Probably didn't take you long to figure it out."

"Noory, great-great-great to infinity granddaughter of Mary. You're the granddaughter of James; grandniece of Jesus. No pressure there, right?"

The guard in the corner was now visibly trembling. He stood and walked slowly to them as Noory and Nick exchanged cautious glances. The man tucked his pistol into his waistband and kneeled in front of Nick. "Bless me, Bishop Nicholas, patron saint of sailors. Bless me, for I go to my certain death when I help you escape."

CHAPTER 10

Nick and Noory looked at each other, shocked and grateful for the turn of fate. But Nick hesitated at the guard's request. Noory watched conflict pass across the dark stubble of Nick's rugged face. She knew Nick didn't see himself as a priest. Nick asked the man his name.

"Miguel Delgado."

Noory watched Nick transform into clarity, confidence, and grace as he sat up straight and moved his hand in the sign of the cross over the sailor's forehead, chest, and each shoulder. "I bless you, Miguel Delgado, in the name of the Father, of the Son, and of the Holy Spirit."

Noory's breath caught in her throat as Nick began to glow. His grace lit up the dark cargo hold with the merciful light of a real saint. She thought of all the things he was: an alcoholic, angry and stoic, but no less a saint. A lump caught in her throat as she thought of her own fears: years of wondering why in hell *she* was who she was; she rarely prayed, certainly didn't trust God, and was often downright angry at Him. But watching Nick light up with the grace and peace of heaven made her believe that for the first time in twenty-five years she just might be enough, just as she was: made for her quest and on a quest that was made for her. A choking sob escaped her throat. She couldn't pull it back in and couldn't control it. She buried her head in her hands unable to look at the two any longer, unable to take any more of the blinding light that was paradoxically soft as the sunset over the ocean.

She felt Nick's arms wrap around her tightly as Miguel began to remove her chains. Nick helped her to her feet. She looked from Nick to Miguel. "We can't leave without Grace."

Once the ensorcelled irons were off Nick, his tracking abilities returned, and he looked up at the ceiling. "Damn it, she's back in the faraday cage! Even if we could get past it, once they reactivate it, we're trapped again."

"I don't care. Just help get me in there, and I will travel with her wherever they take her. They will eventually let their guard down, and then I can help her escape."

"That's awfully noble of you. But I'm thinking this whole thing is less about Grace and more about leading you into a trap," Nick said.

"Nick, your entire mandate is to help children. You should understand that I'm willing to risk it."

"I understand, but we don't know what they have planned for you once they take you wherever we're headed. We don't know what entities they've employed to deal with you. We don't—" Nick stopped and looked around. "Run! They're trying to trap us here!" Nick said as he grabbed Noory's hand and began racing up the stairs for the deck, with Miguel behind them.

The three of them stood at the railing as a low hum, like the sound of voltage running through transmission towers, got closer and closer to them. Though Miguel wouldn't be aware of it, Nick and Noory looked up to see what looked to be an inky black tarp. Nick quickly joined hands with Noory and Miguel.

Nick looked at Miguel with frantic eyes. "Where do you live?"

"Tumaco, Colombia," Miguel said with an edge of panic.

"All right. Don't let go!" Nick said as he looked behind him one last time to see the dark blanket just seconds from overtaking them.

Noory felt hot, sulfurous breath on her neck a mere second before they disappeared beyond the reach of the dark ones.

Moments later, they were in Miguel's village. He fell to his knees, gasping, while Noory looked on in sympathy.

Nick leaned over and placed his hand on Miguel's shoulder. "Just breathe. You're okay now."

"Gracias, Padre."

She followed Miguel's gaze toward a small house with a warm glow coming from the window.

Noory wondered what it must be like to have a family. Her heart ached for what she hadn't ever thought she might need until that moment.

Miguel slowly rose and turned to Nick. "Baby Jesus usually brings the presents to Columbia. Perhaps *you* will visit this Christmas?" Though Miguel smiled over his ironic question, there was sincerity behind it, a longing for absolution.

"Miguel Delgado, you are on my list," he said as he hugged the man. Miguel turned toward home without looking back again.

Noory knew, come Christmas Day, she would find Nick in Colombia.

CHAPTER 11

Nick and Noory were in his kitchen drinking coffee and deciding on their next move. She watched him as he worked around the kitchen, gathering ingredients. He'd offered to make her the best omelet she'd ever eaten. They were only a couple hours from sunrise and neither felt the urge to sleep as their bodies were still amped up on battle adrenaline while their hearts demanded they rescue Grace.

Noory couldn't help but notice how Nick's movements were fluid and sure. His mocha-colored shirt was rolled up to reveal muscular forearms. His six-foot-two size was perfectly proportioned in every way. She wondered if he'd always looked like this or if his commission came with such physical bonuses. Embarrassment overtook her as she realized that what she really wanted to know was if his "hotness" was God given.

"Something you want to ask me?" he asked.

She jumped. "Oh, for God's sake! You can't read minds, too, can you?"

He laughed. "No, you were just looking at me oddly."

"Do you mind if I ask how you came to be? I mean the supernatural part of it. Did you die or . . . ?"

Nick cracked an egg into the pan and froze as if he weren't sure he wanted to open that vault. Did it really scare him that bad to talk about it? Then again, her calling threatened to swallow her up daily. How could she not understand?

Nick took a deep breath and began. "It was the fourth century, and—"

"What century?"

Nick laughed. "Yep, the fourth century, as in three-hundred A.D.

Hey, John's even older than that. Why are you so stunned at how long I've been around?"

"Good point." She wanted to blurt out that he looked only a few years older than her and was gorgeous, but she realized it was just a matter of perception. She didn't see John that way because he was a father figure, which made him seem old and nonsexual. "Sorry, didn't mean to interrupt," she said. "Please continue."

"That's okay. I headed out to give the last of what I owned to buy freedom for a couple of young girls who were being enslaved by a man with a reputation for extreme cruelty, especially to his female slaves. A full quarter of the population of Greece were slaves then. They considered it a golden age, but damned if seemed that way to me," Nick said with an annoyed grunt.

"When I arrived, the owner told me that what I had brought wouldn't be enough. The girls were eight and eleven years old. They were emaciated and terrified. So, I offered myself in exchange for their freedom. He had a massive estate with dozens of horses. I was getting older but was still strong enough to tend livestock. He told me to come out into the field and he would show me around. I thought we had a deal, but when we got to the barn, he cracked me in the back of the skull. I remember feeling like my brain was about to explode. The next thing I remember was not being able to move as I felt blood running out of my ears, nose, and mouth. I saw the clouds move above me and felt my body being dragged through grass and dirt and into the woods. I heard digging that was steady and repetitive. I realized he was digging my grave."

"Dear God," Noory covered her mouth and fought the heat that was gathering at the back of her eyes and threatening to spill over. "Why in the world would he kill you when you offered to work for him for free?"

"Noory, the little girls were more . . ." Nick's hand went behind his neck as he uncomfortably searched for the right word. "They were more valuable to him than my services. So, he decided to keep the money and the girls and get rid of me." Nick looked down and realized he was burning the eggs and shut off the flame.

He continued. "I began saying my final penitence in my mind as I heard a buzzing sound in my head, and I felt my body being dragged into the earth. Everything went black as the dirt began to hit my face. For a moment, there was absolutely nothing: no thought, no sight, then a bright warm light washed over me, and I saw a kind old man lean over me. He gathered me into his arms and whispered in my ear: 'Hear the word of the Lord and live.' I felt my body surge with strength. Muscles that had become slack with age swelled. I felt my face tighten. I even felt my thinning hair grow back in. 'Guard my children,' the old man said and then was gone.

"By this time, I was covered in a thin layer of dirt. Anger rose in me, yet I felt none of the fear I usually did. At that moment, I had become aware of my invincibility. I felt like my legs were made of springs as I jumped into a crouch inside the grave. Gripped in my fists were two daggers that felt as if they'd always been part of me. Then I leaped at him and knocked him to the ground. Of course, I had not yet learned to balance my need for justice with my newfound strength. I had no control. He screamed as I started stabbing him, over and . . . over. It took me a moment to realize that he was dead. I've had to learn how to use my power wisely. You were born with your strength. You didn't have to relearn anything, but I learned the hard way how lethal my powers can be. Though, to be honest, I think it was that evil bastard's time to go."

"Well, I certainly wouldn't mourn that son of a bitch," Noory said, hearing the venom in her voice.

Nick laughed. "I didn't. I only worried about accidentally hurting someone in the future. I've broken some bones that I wasn't intending to, but truthfully, in most cases, it was merited. My commission includes going after those who hurt children. They tend to be hardcore evil. Most of the time there is no rehabilitation for them."

Noory thought of all the abuse she had seen in the children who came through the shelter. "I would agree with that assessment," she said.

Nick nodded. "Anyway, I sent home the kids who had family left. Some of them had nowhere to go, so they continued to stay with me. The older ones kept their jobs, and I paid them for their labor."

"Wait, you took over his estate?"

"I did. I had already found out that he had no relatives to lay claim. Before I approached the man, I'd learned all I could about him. And I couldn't go back to where I was from. The ones who recognized me wouldn't understand what had happened to me, and back then, people were a lot more paranoid and suspicious than they are now. I might have had to fight my way off a burning stake if I told them I had transformed like that."

"So, do you age at all?" Noory asked.

"Sometimes I think I may be aging a little but then later decide it's all in my head. When the miracle first happened, I thought that maybe I was spared just long enough to deal with the man I killed. The longer I lived there, the more I learned about him. Turns out he was a rapist and murderer; there was more than one body buried on his estate," Nick said with a grimace.

"I thought that since I'd dealt with him, maybe I would start to age again. I thought maybe God occasionally kept someone alive and gave them special gifts to deal with evil like that, but after a few decades I realized I wasn't aging, wasn't growing weaker, and every time I left the estate, I would feel my spirit being yanked toward suffering children. Part of me felt tempted to never leave the estate again. Not because I didn't care, but because it tore me apart. It was even worse for kids back then; there were no programs to help children, other than the occasional orphanage run by the church. Even that wasn't much by today's standards. If I stayed out of the proximity of suffering children, then I was okay. I realized I was being a coward, though, and I would end up dreaming of them. Eventually, I had to go, anyway. It wouldn't be long before someone showed up with a pitchfork, wanting to know if I was a witch." Nick laughed as he scraped the burned eggs into the trash.

"I handed over the estate to a young man who'd been there since I'd come. He had to have known why I was leaving. I'd been there for nearly three decades and that boy looked older than me. He'd been nine years old when I arrived. I went to Athens and began doing what I do now. I usually arrived in time to save the kids, but when I didn't . . ."

Nick looked frozen in place, but she guessed he was just frozen in time—inside a very painful memory. She had the urge to run to him and wrap her arms around him but feared damaging his pride. He looked fragile to her; like her arms might shatter him all together. For the first time, it occurred to her that Nick probably had post-traumatic stress disorder.

As if time had suddenly started again, he gave Noory a sad smile and grabbed the carton of eggs and cracked two new ones into the pan he'd reheated.

"Anyway, that's when I started drowning my failure in alcohol." He said it as casually as if he were talking about the weather.

"Even though you have gifts, you still aren't a god, you know? It sounds like you're beating yourself up for being human."

Nick exhaled and threw some chopped mushrooms into the omelet as he gathered his thoughts. "But I'm not human, am I?"

"You clearly have super strength and super intuition, but your emotions are very much human."

Nick sprinkled cheese over the omelet. "Yeah, it's kind of a cruel trick."

Noory agreed but had a new thought. "If your emotions were any different, you wouldn't give enough of a damn to use your powers to save them. You know? I'm not sure you can have one without the other and still do what you do. I think the heartbreak is a necessity."

"You may be right, but that doesn't make it any easier when all the memories gang up on me in the middle of the night."

Noory stopped just short of saying it might be better if she were there beside him at night, but she knew it would come out in a bawdy way, and she couldn't deny that was part of it. But as she looked at him and felt her heart breaking with the urge to heal him, she knew it was so much more than that. "I'm sure it doesn't," she said. "So, when did you meet John?"

"Not too long after I left the estate. A Monsignor I had known spotted me; he was elderly at that point, in poor health. At first, I was panicked. This man looked at me like he knew me. I tried to dodge him, but he sent a messenger after me and let me know he was ill. He sent a monk's robe for me to wear. That's when I knew that he knew, without a doubt.

He was sneaking me in to see him so that no one else would notice me. When I got there, he told me about John and begged me to speak with him. I was in a rough place—still trying to get through one day and on to the next. You would think that would make me want to seek him out, but it was John, for God's sake, a bona fide disciple." Nick shook his head. "Anyway, he eventually found *me*." Nick slid the omelet onto Noory's plate but seemed to be done discussing his past.

She took a bite. "You're right. You do make the best omelet in the world. Is this part of the superhero package?"

"Nah, just comes from being old as dirt," Nick laughed.

"At least you haven't lost your sense of humor."

"Listen, I really think we need to go through your father's . . . sorry. I think we should go through Jonah's house to see what we can find out. He took a boat, so he must have made some sort of plans. I can go alone if it's too much for you to deal with."

Noory stared at her plate as the idea of going into Jonah's house made her stomach clench. She tried not to think about the man, much less do something as personal as go into his home. Then again, the idea of not going felt as if she were letting fear control her, which translated to letting *him* control her. "Yeah, let's do it." Even as the words came out, she recognized the sound of empty bravado. Despite the amazing omelet, she felt her appetite vanish.

CHAPTER 12

After breakfast, they went straight to Jonah's home to look for clues where they might take Grace. At Noory's request, they had gone around John and used one of Nick's contacts to get Jonah's address; Noory knew John would try to keep her out of it. Nick had a sick feeling they would pay for that later.

Nick made quick work of the back door lock. Noory shuddered as she looked around Jonah's home. The walls were plastered with prayers for souls in purgatory, a page torn from the book of II Maccabees that was part of the Catholic cannon of scripture where the concept of purgatory was found. After a battle, the ancient Jews were praying for the souls of the dead. Another book rejected from the cannon, The Book of Enoch, lay open with names of entities responsible for teaching humans warcraft and spell casting: Azazel, Semjaza, and Amaros.

There were also books on physics: quantum theory, M theory, string theory, and parallel dimensions. And though he had an extensive collection of books on dark magic, he seemed to be obsessed with purgatory and alternate dimensions.

"What is he doing?" Noory asked.

"I honestly don't know," Nick said, looking both fascinated and horrified.

"Whatever it is, I can't see any connection to Grace or human trafficking." Noory continued going through drawers.

"I wouldn't be so sure about that, Noory. You wouldn't believe some of the things I've seen people use children for."

Noory peered up at Nick as he started to reach into his breast pocket for the ouzo but caught Noory looking at him and ran his hands across his face instead.

There were also maps with cell phone towers marked near major city centers.

"How does this," Noory said, tapping the map, "fit into all this other? Any theories?"

"I think the skin trade might be a front for something bigger," he said.

"Like what?"

Nick didn't answer right away but went back to the page torn from the book of Maccabees and ran his fingers across it. "A demon wouldn't need to possess a man to involve him in human trafficking. Man is evil enough to do that all by himself. I wouldn't go blaming a demon for it. This is bigger. I'm not sure what it is, but I think I know who we can ask."

"John?" Noory asked.

"No, a woman named Willow."

"Great. Let's do it. Where is she?"

"Purgatory," Nick said casually.

CHAPTER 13

"Purgatory? You know someone in purgatory?" Noory said.

"Well, most of us do, technically. And why in the world would this surprise you? I mean, you are a supernatural ass-kicking descendant of the Holy Family. It's cute that you still get surprised by things like this," Nick said with a wink.

Noory rolled her eyes while Nick laughed softly.

"Let's get out of here. We'll go speak to her from your apartment. I wouldn't do it here. There's no telling how many entities are attached to this place. It's a hellhole. Literally."

An hour later, they sat at Noory's kitchen table eating subs.

Nick asked, "So just how much did John tell you of what he knows? I mean, the man is a supernatural encyclopedia."

"After being around you, I'm getting the feeling that he's barely told me anything."

"Well, knowledge is a powerful and, often, dangerous thing. I think he's just trying to let you be as normal as possible."

"I do know what unicorns are," she said, smiling.

He laughed out loud and nearly choked on his lunch. "Yeah, the world would be truly freaked out to know the truth about those things. Dear Lord!"

"Hey, it isn't their fault!" she said defensively.

"No, but still, ew." He smiled and shuddered.

Noory punched him in the shoulder.

"So, how will this work?" she asked as she finished the last bite of her sandwich.

Nick pushed aside his half-eaten meal, picked up the rosary beads he'd brought, and rubbed them between his thumb and forefinger. "I'll do what I do when I travel. When you traveled with me, we were in the space where some people in purgatory dwell."

"Really?"

"Oh yeah, it's just another dimension. That's why I think that my friend there could help us. There are other people there, too, that communicate with each other. Someone punching their way through where they don't belong wouldn't go unnoticed."

"This is depressing. All those people stuck there..." Her lunch turned to a rock in her stomach.

"Oh, Noory, no. It isn't like that." He reached across and placed his hand on top of hers, absolutely shocking her with the gentleness and longing to reassure her she felt coming off him.

"It doesn't matter what you've heard. They aren't being punished. The Father isn't holding them there either. He wants them home, but a person can only accept as much grace as they allow themselves to accept. A person can't even be happy in heaven if they feel they don't deserve it. They are in purgatory trying to work out the things that keep them from walking into the light. They are learning, and when they are done and ready to receive grace, it will be waiting for them. It's waiting for them now. They just aren't ready. So, they watch and learn."

"Watch what?"

"How things play out with the choices they made. Everything is energy. When you think about a person, it is likely they were thinking of you at that moment. When you make a decision, you set a potential future in motion: a line of energy that radiates outward. Willow made a bad choice. She..."

Noory watched Nick take a deep breath and look down at his rosary beads.

"Her boyfriend had been beating her for years. She loved him to the point of obsession. He was the same way. It was very unhealthy. She felt trapped. One day, when it was particularly bad, she shot him, and then turned the gun on herself."

"Oh, dear God!" She put her hand over her mouth. Though she'd heard all kinds of stories at the shelter, some things still had the power to shock her.

"She's there understanding how her choice affected everyone, how she could have made a better choice, and how to love and forgive herself. Life had been pretty unkind to her. I knew her when she was a little girl in the 1920s. I exposed her parents' abuse and took her to live with an older cousin, but by then, a pattern was set in motion." He suddenly looked much older than thirty.

"I'm sorry. How long has she been there?"

"Since 1950, but that's in our years. Time expresses itself differently there. For her, it doesn't feel that long."

"Wow," Noory said.

"Okay, I shouldn't be long," Nick said as he sat the rosary down on the table and prepared to go.

"What should I do while you're gone?"

"Pray for her. It's all energy. The love will reach her there and help her accept the light. That won't necessarily help our cause in particular, but *I* would appreciate it." He gave her a soft smile.

Noory watched as Nick dematerialized. It gave her a shiver.

She seldom prayed because praying might make her responsible, accidentally showing a higher power that she wanted to take on some grand scion responsibility. She also didn't want to be associated with the horde of people who said, "I'm praying for you," then went on about their business as if it were enough. If only they'd get up off their knees and do something about it. Truthfully, every time she walked into the shelter, every time a kid showed up covered in bruises. "I'm praying for you," felt like one of the emptiest sentiments of all to her. But Nick was the most authentic person she'd ever met, other than John, and if he asked for prayer, she would honor it.

She grabbed the abandoned rosary beads and felt Nick's energy on them so strongly it was startling yet soothing. She'd never prayed the rosary before, the few traditions she grew up with, the ones John still practiced now and then, were Jewish, but just holding them had seemed to help Nick focus. She closed her eyes and thought about what she would need if she were in Willow's place. The words tumbled out in her mind: honest, bold, sweet, soft, and authentic. She knew Willow was likely a future version of many of the girls who passed through the doors of her shelter. Soon, tears began to streak her face.

Nick concentrated on Willow. When he opened his eyes, she stood before him, smiling. "Father Christmas," she said. A light radiated from her that he hadn't seen before. Suddenly, the light increased all around her, and he recognized Noory's energy enveloping her and had to concentrate with every ounce of his being not to cry. He'd never seen Noory's energy like this before: it was in its purest, loveliest, most Godly form, and it confounded, humbled, and mesmerized him.

A quick glance at his surroundings showed the faintest outline of a home with furnishings echoing the '50s, the time Willow would remember and mentally conjure—as any spirit could—as a sort of space for her time to be spent here on the other side, but they were fading, as if she no longer needed them. Her consciousness was letting go of its earthbound touchstones. He'd seen it before. She would move on soon. A good thing.

"Someone prays for me," Willow said softly as she placed her hand on the pulsing center of her being where her heart would be if she were in human form. "From what I understand, all those who knew me personally would be gone by now." She looked at Nick as understanding settled softly across her face. "Thank you, Bishop," she said.

Nick inclined his head.

Willow laughed as sparkling energy like diamonds slid down her face. Her supernatural form glowed such that it looked as if it would explode into shards of pure light at any moment. "I will be going soon, but first I do have an answer for you."

Nick hadn't asked her anything, but felt it possible that, since she was about to ascend, she could have gained the ability to communicate telepathically as those in the presence of the Creator did.

"A young woman named Grace has been here. Not only that, but we also spotted three others like her. I was shocked because she informed us, they needed to get back to their bodies. Of course, we have no bodies to return to on that side. She was asking about some SS officers with dark souls who we stay far away from. She also asked about a woman named Catherine—she means the scion's mother, but I don't think she knows that. Anyway, Catherine isn't here."

"So, she has already ascended?"

"No. I've asked around, and the collective memory on this side has no record of her *ever* being here."

"Did Grace indicate why she was asking?"

"Yes. She asked on behalf of Jonah, a man rumored to be inhabited by a dark spirit that has never had any intention of ascending either. He'd been waiting and watching for a way out or back from this place, and he found Jonah. There are several like that here—I and others like me stay clear of such beings. This is another reason why we're alarmed to see someone here who has a body to return to—she leaves herself open to having her body taken while her soul remains here. Jonah gave him that opportunity. If someone has found a way to send human messengers that still live, like Grace . . . I don't know what it is, Bishop, but if heaven has involved you and the scion, then it is very important. That's all I know."

"Thank you, Willow. That's very helpful. I won't be seeing you again, will I?" Nick asked.

"No, not here, but at another point, when your journey ends." Willow reached out and touched Nick's forehead with a shimmering, translucent hand. She was so close to crossing over that her spirit flowed around Nick with joy and love, the likes of which he'd not felt in hundreds of years. She kept her hand on his forehead while speaking. "Forgive yourself and allow your heart to open. Your purgatory must also come to an end."

Suddenly Nick heard a buzzing in his ears and memories began to flood his mind. Worse than that, they flooded his heart. "No!" he whispered as he tried to back away but only succeeded in falling to his knees. He looked up at Willow with pleading eyes. "Please, don't."

"Do not resist me. You helped me, now you *will* allow me to help you."

"I can't," he whispered.

"You can, and you will." Thousands of beings, starbursts of light, began popping up all around her. "You are loved far too deeply to be allowed to remain as you are." She looked at him with compassion but wouldn't remove her hand. She spoke with an authority he'd never heard in her before. "Let go, Father Christmas."

He gasped as 1942 slammed into him with the force of a hurricane.

"Give me the gun, Nicholas," John ordered.

Peace swept over him as John placed his hand on his head. He knew it wouldn't last, but it was enough to make him remove the pistol from his mouth. Sarah had gone to wash the night's worth of Nazi-killing from her clothes, leaving John and Nick alone in the old barn that smelled of moldy hay and a remnant of horse manure. The owners had long since fled the war-torn area. Nick had thought John was asleep. He should have known better. John knew all kinds of shit he shouldn't be able to know, asleep or not. He yanked the pistol from Nick's grasp.

"It's too much. I can't do it anymore," Nick sobbed.

"Of course you can. Sometimes existence is just putting one foot in front of the other."

"But you know what I did! Don't tell me you could be okay with living if you'd messed up as bad as I have. It's too much! I have to tell her! She thinks I'm a good man."

"She isn't wrong, Nicholas. But you don't get to hurt her to relieve your own guilt. Besides, she's unraveling. You know this. Promise me you won't tell her."

Nick looked at him as more guilt flooded his soul. John was holding them all together. The burden shouldn't have been squarely on his shoulders. Nick knew he should've gotten his shit together to help him. "I won't tell her."

When Sarah returned, she barely had the door open before she sensed it. "What's wrong?" She braced herself for more bad news as water plastered her dark hair to the sides of her face.

"Should you tell her, or should I?" John said.

Nick knew he meant the suicide attempt. "I didn't plan on telling her at all."

Though Sarah didn't yet know what they were talking about, Nick's tone made her look at him with hurt in her eyes. The three had been together ever since Sarah's husband died. When she insisted on spending every waking hour taking vengeance on Nazis, John and Nick had followed her into the fray, knowing anything less wasn't an option.

"Nick tried to take the easy way out," John said before leaving the old barn, pistol in hand. Nick knew he wouldn't see the weapon again.

Sarah began shaking with anger. "How could you? My people are being slaughtered. People who would give anything to have the power to save themselves, their families, and you dare try such a thing!"

She would do it, Nick thought. *All I have to do is push her.* It was shitty to hurt her that way. What did it matter now? He was damned. *But I promised John. I have to get out of this.* "There's something you should know."

Sarah looked at Nick warily. "What?"

"When we were in Warsaw," was all he had to say to watch Sarah's face transform into pain and caution. "You were away, taking care of your mother and—"

"I should have been there. He wouldn't be dead now. He knew better than to try to pull that escape off on his own."

She reminded Nick he wasn't the only one dealing with guilt. Cowardice covered him like an oily cloak. "No, it wasn't your fault. It was mine. Levi came to me, telling me he had a shot at getting an entire family out. He had solid intel. They were only going to send two guards to load them up. I told Levi I'd handle the guards." His heart began slamming against the cage of his chest. He watched Sarah hovering on the edge of hyperventilating. *If I stop now, she won't hate me. I can still salvage this. But this can all be over within minutes.* The relief at the very thought of being done with this life brought him a peace comparable to that of being under John's holy spell.

He pushed forward. "All they had to do was get out. The local population would have never reported them. But I was passed out drunk at the rally point. I didn't wake until I heard the gunshots. Levi, the parents, and three kids were mown down as they tried to run. Levi's faith in me was so complete that he didn't hesitate. When he didn't see the guards immediately, I'm sure he knew, just *knew,* that I'd done my job."

"Shut up, Nick. You're just trying to get me to take you out of your loop of existence. I understand. I've seen how it gives you migraines when we're near the camps, it's unlike anything you've ever had to deal with, but you really need to stop talking like this. It's painful for me. You're my friend. *Please* stop."

"I'm telling you the truth. Just end this!" he screamed at her.

"Hush, you're going to give away our position. I'm too exhausted to deal with more blood tonight."

"I've never lied to you. He's dead because of me!" The rafters of the old barn were shaking and dropping dust on them as he used the weapon of his voice to help end his existence.

Sarah looked up as a beam dislodged and landed a couple of feet away. "Stop it. Stop screaming."

"Even my voice is a force of death. I don't want it anymore!" He had one last shot at making her believe him. He reached into his pocket and took out the gold "chai" necklace—a Hebrew word consisting of two letters that, when put together, meant life. But all Nick could think of was death as he took it off Levi's neck before the guards had a chance to steal it for the gold. "I thought it was the one thing I could do for you, but it's been a year, and I'm too big a coward. It's been in my pocket all this time."

She reached out with trembling fingers to take the necklace. She slipped it over her head then stared at Nick with brown eyes turned black with vengeance. He saw the murder there. Now was the time. "Do it!" he roared as another beam crumbled and fell from the old barn roof.

She swept his feet out from under him. He didn't fight back.

He looked up as she pulled a knife from the folds of her skirt and lifted the blade above his heart as the rafters finally gave way, but not by

Nick's power. Her avenging demigod battle cry brought the ceiling down on them both, and everything went dark.

When Nick woke, he lay by the creek that he knew to be just south of the old barn. Someone had moved him from the debris. The first rays of morning light warmed his body as he rose slowly until he sat up. He looked down to find his shirt torn, damp, with remnants of blood that had been mostly washed away.

John sat a few feet away gazing at the sunlight reflecting off the water. Nick watched tears slide down his cheeks. His plan hadn't worked. And he had only succeeded in hurting Sarah and John.

He stood up and walked down to where he sat.

"You've revived," John said with an uncharacteristic emptiness to his voice.

"Yes. I thought if anyone could kill me and make it stick, it would be her. Maybe she wasn't really trying."

"No. She got you. Right through the heart." John handed Nick a canteen.

"Oh." He took a sip of water before speaking again. "Listen, I'll leave you two alone now. I don't see any way that I can be with you anymore after what I did to Sarah."

"Don't bother. She's gone."

"Gone?"

"Yes. I tried to stop her, but we only succeeded in hurting each other too. She'll be okay though."

"You said it yourself. She's unraveling, and what I did couldn't have helped."

"No, she'll be fine. She's pregnant. She will do whatever she must to protect what's left of Levi."

"I didn't know that." Guilt washed over Nick anew. He knew he wouldn't have done any of it if he'd known she was pregnant. "Doesn't matter. I shouldn't have done it, anyway. I'm sorry I broke my word."

"You broke more than your word. You broke my trust." He threw a stone into the water.

Maybe he should throw me away, too. "How do you do it, John?"

No clarification was needed. "You surrender. It's all anyone can do."

"You've never been afraid of the dark," Nick said with a shaking voice.

John looked at him with compassion laced with frustration. "Nick, you're not afraid of the dark. You're terrified of the light."

The creek before him blurred. A buzzing filled Nick's ears once again, and he lay at Willow's feet.

He lifted his head to find her watching him along with the multitude of lights, "a cloud of witnesses" that he felt only condemned him.

"But I failed so many of them," he said as he looked at them, recognizing the spiritual fingerprints of the souls.

Willow extended her hand and coalesced an orb of illumination into her palm. "In a universe of light, even death may bring forth beauty. Would you believe me if I told you that many of those you think you failed left your realm knowing love for the first time in their existence? Their spirits stood by, watching as you cradled their bodies and mourned for them. They had no idea anyone *could* care for them and hold them like they were precious. They entered this dimension feeling loved because of *you*. You did that." She leaned down and touched his cheek. "You did it for me."

She straightened, opened her arms wide, closed her eyes, and dissolved into pure light. A moment later she was gone, and Nick felt peace and joy in her wake.

He closed his eyes for a moment to clear them of the afterimages from the flash of light. When he opened them, Sarah Solomon stood in her place. She walked over to him, got down on her knees, and whispered softly into his ear, "Shalom, dear friend," before sending him back to the mortal realm.

Nick materialized at Noory's feet, gasping and sobbing.

"Dear God, what happened to you? Are you okay?"

"I'm fine. I'm fine," he said over and over again.

She knelt next to him, and pulled him into her arms, cradling him like a child as he lay his head against her chest. She used her sleeve to wipe his face.

"Thank you, Light," he choked out, feeling afraid she'd let go and terrified she wouldn't.

After a few moments, he pulled himself together and rose to sit in the kitchen chair facing her. He cleared his throat. "Sorry about that."

"Don't be." Noory stood back up and sat down in her chair. "I was just worried. Do you wanna talk about it?"

Nick had no clue how to answer. How does a person speak about something they can't even describe themselves: I was ganged up on by a deceased young woman and about a thousand souls I either saved or somehow saved by default? Shown my greatest failure for my greatest good? The other side is in a weird mood today? And was he ready to share his greatest shame?

She reached out to him. He clasped her palm like a lifeline thrown to a drowning man in the ocean. She spoke softly. "I'll be here when you're ready."

He nodded. She placed her hand on his cheek and closed her eyes. A jolt ran through him. Willow's words echoed in his mind, "Someone prays for me." He knew that's what she was doing. She opened her eyes and stared at him. He also knew, just knew, they stood on the edge of a precipice, both of them brave enough to peek over the edge, neither willing to jump, but nonetheless in awe of the beauty before them.

He turned his head until his lips met her palm and gently kissed her there. He said a prayer for her, too. *God, don't let me hurt her,* he pleaded, as a mental door slammed shut behind him—the one he was so sure he'd be able to walk through when the time came to let her go.

At last, she lowered her hand, and the absence of her warmth was a visceral thing that left him feeling hungry in a primal, emotional way. He knew it was in both their best interests when she got back to the matter at hand.

"Did it work? Did you find your friend? Was she okay?"

He could tell she was afraid to ask. Given his ridiculous return to this realm, she might have been thinking any number of awful things.

"I did. Willow has gone home."

"You didn't get a chance to speak to her, then?"

"Actually, yes. She gave me the information we needed first. Willow said Grace had been there and—"

"No!"

"Don't misunderstand. She isn't dead. It looks like Jonah has found a way to get someone into the other dimension without them technically dying. I don't know if he's using a spell or LSD or some other drug, along with his knowledge of physics or black magic." Nick rubbed his chin stubble as he thought. "Maybe getting these kids hooked on drugs isn't about the skin trade at all, or maybe that's only part of it."

"Oh, Grace. That girl has enough problems. We have to get her out of this. Why did he send her there?"

Nick looked away quickly. Noory knew the look of a man searching for a way to drop a verbal bomb, and it made her nervous.

"Willow said she came there looking for your mother."

"My mother?"

He nodded.

"So, it isn't enough to take her life? Now Jonah wants her soul?"

"No one knows why he's looking for her."

"He clearly wants to torment her because I won't join him."

"The good news is that can't happen."

"Why not? Grace got in and back out again. Why wouldn't my mother?"

"Well, because she isn't there. She never was."

CHAPTER 14

Noory said, "Well, I don't know much about purgatory, but I would assume there wouldn't be a way out unless someone like Jonah is involved and he's the one looking for her. So, she moved on then. That's good, right?" She knew in theory it should be good, but a part of her, a part she was suddenly feeling ashamed of, didn't want her mother moving on. Purgatory made her feel closer. Ascension . . . well that could be another star system or perhaps a reincarnation. That was just the point—no one really knew, and that made her seem even farther from her mother.

"No, there shouldn't be a way out, but Grace shouldn't have been able to get *in* either, and she did. You should also know that Willow says there is no record of your mother having ever been there."

"What does that even mean? She went straight to ascension? Straight to the big family reunion in the sky because of who she is?"

"I honestly don't know. I wish I had more answers for you. Although, from all my years studying these things, your DNA is the only thing that's different—altered from coming in contact with divinity—but your spirit is just like any other's: subject to growth and the laws of energy and transformation."

They were both startled when they heard a knock on the door. Nick got to his feet. "I've got it," he said. He walked over to the door and looked through the peephole before turning to Noory. "Be careful," he mouthed.

When he opened the door, Elliot stood there looking absolutely stricken. Ripped jeans and a t-shirt had replaced his teenage business-man ensemble. Noory watched Nick's reaction. She knew if he seemed worried, then she should be too. All she saw written on Nick's face was love, lined with sorrow. He turned to look at Noory as if asking permission to invite him into her home.

"Come in," she said, while motioning to a seat at the small kitchen table.

Elliot looked stark white as he sat across from her.

"I thought you all would've sailed halfway around the globe by now."

"No, as an act of trust, I'll tell you: he never even left the river. He was just luring you there," he said, pointing at Noory. I know you guys have no reason to trust me, but I didn't come here for me. Well, I sort of did. Anyway, it's Grace. Jonah sent her into purgatory one too many times, and this time when she came back, it wasn't her. Something took her place." He stared as his trembling hands. "We lost her over there somewhere, and Jonah doesn't seem to care. In fact, he likes the fact that whoever is inside her can answer his questions."

Noory suddenly felt swallowed up by the enormity of what they were getting themselves into. The very thing she'd been running from all her life was nipping at her heels. She realized, with sickening clarity, that she had no choice but to turn and face it.

CHAPTER 15

That evening Nick and Noory were back at Jonah's house but with a lot more to go on. They waited until Elliot said he would be gone, then quietly slipped in the back door.

"There has to be something else here," Noory said as they went through Jonah's things once more.

Nick pulled books from the shelves. "Looks like he's a history buff. There are lots of books here on World War Two."

A voice came from behind them, "Oh, I love history. All those repeating patterns. It's beautiful really." Nick and Noory both jumped as Jonah swiveled around in his desk chair laughing so hard at the looks on their faces that he was doubling over. He got up and came around to the front of the desk, and then leaned his palms back on the polished oak behind him with a look of casual indifference.

"My daughter is welcome here anytime she likes. However, it isn't proper for you to bring your boyfriend inside unless I'm home." Jonah looked at Nick with amusement. He clearly knew he was making them uncomfortable.

Nick watched Noory square her shoulders and heard her heartbeat racing as he felt her purposefully slow her breath to calm herself. He wondered what she'd do if she knew he could read her that closely. Maybe she wouldn't be too angry if she also knew how deeply he respected her for pushing past her fears and facing the thing that scared her the most and she understood least. She was stronger than she would ever know.

"You got here awfully quick," Noory said.

"Oh please, I never left the Savannah River. The shit I have to go through just to see my daughter!" Jonah said with exasperation.

"You've got me now. So, where's Grace?" Noory asked.

"I'll tell you if you do something for me," Jonah said.

"What?" Noory asked through clenched teeth.

"Lead my army. Look, I know you're a bleeding heart. So, I promise if you help me, I'll build you enough shelters to get all those kids off the street. Hell, we'll end homelessness together."

"There's always a catch. Your path thus far has included prostitution, drugs, and kidnapping. I'm inclined to not believe you," Noory said.

Nick said, "All right. I think we've heard enough bullshit for one day. I want to know why the hell Grace was in purgatory."

Jonah looked at Nick with smug assurance. "Oh, yeah. I nearly forgot. You're a slave to those kids too, aren't you? How appropriate. I mean, that is what your name means, right? Theodoulos? Slave of God. How's that working out for you?"

Nick didn't appreciate a man who had only lived a small fraction of the time he had acting like he knew what it was like to walk his path. He knew when he was being goaded though and forced himself not to take the bait. He steered the conversation away from the personal. "Mark my words. If you go messing with the souls in purgatory, you will unleash a shit storm on yourself. Those souls belong to the Father. He's gone to hell to retrieve them. Do you think he would back down from you?"

"Ah, so now the alcoholic Santa Claus suddenly has faith in the God he drinks to forget. Please." Jonah looked at Nick dismissively.

Nick tapped the bottle of liquor in his breast pocket. "This doesn't represent a lack of faith in God. This is on me. Just as the evil you're doing is on you."

"What do you think motivates man to great atrocities?" Jonah asked. "Many people would answer money or power, but those things can be obtained without bloodshed, given the right opportunity. No, what motivates people is fear. Fear wraps around the mind and squeezes until you are willing to give up choice, comfort, reason, and will. When people look back on the Nazi regime, they tend to see Hitler as a person that showed up and forcibly took Germany like a rapist in a dark alley closes in on a beautiful woman, and she is powerless to stop him."

Nick cringed at the imagery. He knew he used it to intimidate Noory and throw her off because of what he'd done to her mother.

Jonah continued. "Hitler was no rapist. The people of Germany welcomed him into their 'bed,' " Jonah made air quotes as he spoke. "They voted that beautiful bastard into office. They loved him. He was a fucking rock star! The German people did this. Why? He was their answer. He made sure no one went hungry, no one would take their jobs, and everyone would be safe, warm, and well cared for. Those people were traumatized after World War One. They'd lost pride and confidence in themselves and needed someone to soothe them. Hitler felt good in every way. The German people were in love. Head over heels. That sexy Casanova swept the Germans off their feet.

"Here we are again today. Terrorism is rampant, and people are powerless to stop it. Find me a leader that can fix this? Where is he?" Jonah said, as he slammed his hand down on the heavy wooden table. "Terrorism is an insidious weed. You can cut down what you see but it sends runners under the ground." Jonah gestured with his hands to indicate something slithering. He became more animated as he spoke. "The world is ripe once more. Paranoid. 'Give us a leader that can stop this!' You don't truly know who's going to show up on a crowded street and open fire. I can end it.

"This world is absolutely ripe for a strong leader. Our new savior will deliver us from terrorism, the war on drugs, nightclub and school shootings, and everyone will get on board because he will also save the whales, the environment, provide care for everyone, and no one will go hungry. It won't matter whether they're left side of the aisle, on the right, or sideways, they will get on board. Don't you see how much money we would have to feed the world if we didn't have to spend it fighting terrorism and drug cartels? This man will be the swift hand of justice with one hand and the benevolent ruler who feeds his gentle flock with the other hand. It works for everyone on every level. The people will love him!"

"You mean you?" Nick snarled.

"No, I mean them." Jonah turned a picture frame around on his desk. It was Elliot standing behind Grace with his arms around her. They both smiled at the camera. Jonah obviously had been luring Grace in for a while—like a predator.

" 'A child shall lead them,' " Jonah said.

Noory moved lightning fast as she grabbed Jonah by the hair and drove her knee into his nose. As he lifted his head, the heel of her hand made contact under his chin, causing his head to snap back, but the entity within him acted fast as well, grabbing Noory by the neck and lifting until her feet dangled.

Nick rushed forward, plowing into the man like a battering ram, which made Jonah drop her.

The voice that now came from Jonah was inhuman and so low that it caused the room to vibrate as it spoke. "You may be this vessel's daughter, but he can only hold me at bay for so long. Do not test me, scion." Jonah lifted his fist as if to strike out again, but Nick wrapped his arms around Noory, and they both disappeared.

Chapter 16

Nick and Noory landed on John's living room floor with Noory gasping for air and holding her throat. John was standing there as if he'd been waiting for them. Nick rolled her over and eased her hands from her neck to see the damage.

John shoved him out of the way. "What's going on? My spirit has been popping and crackling for the last hour."

"I'm fine," Noory croaked.

"Who did this to her?" John roared at Nick.

She had never seen this side of John before. It was startling. She ignored her aching neck and placed her arm on his shoulder to calm him. He got a closer look at her throat and saw bruises beginning to form. He reached out and placed his large hand gently over the injury. Noory protested.

"Hush," John said, brokering no argument from her.

She had to admit, it did feel better.

Ten minutes later, they sat at John's kitchen table and sipped coffee as the sun rose. John patiently listened to them recount the events of their capture, escape, purgatory, and visiting Jonah. She watched him scratch the thick dark stubble on his face and looked out his window at the new day and his livestock. A goat walked a few steps forward, leaned over, and raised back up with a mouthful of grass, roots and all.

"What I don't understand is why Jonah suddenly has an interest in me." she asked.

"He's tried to take you before. The interest isn't new." John tapped the table and stared off into space. "Okay, we know being descended from a womb that once held the Son of God has given you certain abilities: the strength, the insight, but what else?"

"I don't think there is anything else," Noory said.

John and Nick exchanged a look that annoyed her. It felt like this was one of those times when something was being kept from her for her "own good." It was irritating. "Well, could someone let me in on it, please?"

John took another sip of his coffee before speaking. "I've often wondered if the ability to communicate with the other side, call on the souls of the dead, and travel between worlds would extend to you as it did your uncle between his death and resurrection."

"As it did in my 'uncle'? Pft! Those are shoes I wouldn't attempt to fill. Besides, why in the world would God just leave a trait like that dangling in my DNA? I mean, I wouldn't want to misuse it. I wouldn't want to use it at all, but why leave a dangerous thing like that in our bloodline? We're just humans."

"Exactly right," John said, looking at her in a way that said it should click right about now, but it wasn't. "You don't want to use it. Why?"

"It's too much power for a human. People shouldn't mess with stuff like that."

"Right, someone who would misuse it would never say that," John said, smiling. "Someone is eventually going to need to go into purgatory and bring Grace back."

"I'm not good with running around disembodied. That's more Nick's thing."

"Noory, I can't take a disembodied soul anywhere," Nick said. "Using other dimensions as a mode of transportation is one thing; ferrying a soul out of purgatory is quite another."

"Look, I wouldn't send you there right now, anyway. You aren't ready. You need to arm yourself," John said.

Noory asked, "How?"

John took a deep breath before answering. "It's time to visit Scotland."

"Sounds fun, but how does that help us?" she asked.

"Well, I need a new kilt, and I want the best," John replied.

"Jews don't wear kilts," she said after drinking her last sip of coffee and rising to go get more.

"You don't know. *Anyway*, there's a relic there that can help you. I was hoping to never have to use it. We don't know for sure what it can do in the scion's hands, but you are in far too much danger now not to use it. I think it may be the only thing strong enough to separate Azazel from Jonah and subdue it."

"Holy hell!" Nick exclaimed. "That man is carrying Azazel?"

"Hello, anyone mind sharing with me?" she said.

"He's one of the Watchers from the Book of Enoch that was supposed to have introduced warfare to mankind," Nick replied. "That explains what he was doing with Enoch. It's not part of the accepted canonical holy books. People don't usually have it lying around their house."

John said, "Exactly. This thing is way too powerful to fight outright. It needs to be separated from Jonah and bound. By the way, why didn't you call me when you knew you were going after Grace?"

"Well, we—" Noory began.

"I'm not asking you, Noory. You didn't call because you knew I would make you wait and come up with a solid plan, and you are far too impatient for that. I'm asking you, Nicholas." John turned his ever-calm gaze to Nick, continued sipping his coffee, and waited.

She had seen John do that many times when she was growing up. It usually occurred when she'd done something John didn't approve of, and he knew she was squirming. Noory called it the "calm waiting." It was very effective. She hated it.

Nick finally replied. "If I keep involving you in things you can't easily explain to your superiors, you will end up losing your job and have to move again. I know you get tired of that scenario."

"I've made peace with what I am and what that means a long time ago, Nicholas. From now on, I want you to keep me in the loop. You have your mandate in this world. I have mine too," he said, looking from Nick to Noory.

Nick nodded. "Understood."

She looked at him as if he were caving to an overbearing author-ity figure, but deep-down she knew what happened when the girls she worked with had no positive male presence in their lives. It didn't even have to be their bio father. If she knew it, then Nick was sure to have learned that in all his years, too.

"So, this relic, are we talking about a full-out Indiana Jones-like scenario in order to retrieve it?" Noory asked.

"No, nothing like that. Just fly to Rosslyn Chapel in Scotland, and I will have one of the Templar brothers meet you there. I've not seen anything quite this huge in a good long while," John said.

"Every side trip we take delays us getting to Grace!" she snapped.

"Noory, this isn't just about Grace anymore. This is about the fate of everyone. I hate to say it, but Jonah's right. This could succeed; the world is ripe for it, and you are not equipped to deal with this on your own. You two almost got stuck on that ship."

"At least I would have been with Grace; they would eventually have to come ashore, and then I could have gotten her away from them."

"You don't go into battle unprepared like that. Besides, had you stayed, there's no telling what they would have done to Nicholas. He is a major threat to them. Do you think they would just turn him loose when they know he can rescue these kids and just blink them out of their grasp the second they move to an area unprotected by a spell? He might be immortal, at the moment, but he isn't invincible," John said quietly.

Noory realized with horror that John was most likely thinking of the time he was burned alive with the other Templars. It pulled down her wall of argument quickly. "You're right," she said, as she looked at Nick and realized she had been far too casual with his wellbeing so that she could accomplish her goals. For the first time in her life, it was occurring to her that the people she loved could be hurt—even the immortal ones.

CHAPTER 17

John, Nick, and Noory materialized amid the grasses and trees just outside the walls surrounding Rosslyn Chapel. The crisp night air washed over her with mingled smells of heather and peat, and a little sheep dung hovering just beneath it all.

A middle-aged man with wavy dark hair stepped from the shadows and into the glow of the light spilling over the walls from the illuminated chapel above. He wore a suit and tie and shook hands with Nicholas in a way that Noory had seen many years before. It was an ancient handshake shared by Masons the world over, but this one was a bit different, as these two men were also Templars. Nick and John spoke with the man for a few moments before motioning him over to Noory.

"Show him," Nick said.

She lifted her sleeve to reveal the tiny hooked "X" tattooed on her arm. The man nodded quickly and looked at her as a strange mix of surprise and reverence flashed across his features. Noory felt odd as the man inclined his head and said solemnly, "William, at your service."

As Nick and Noory followed John and William, she whispered to Nick, "Guess he thought the descendant of Mary wasn't quite what he expected?"

Nick chuckled. "Neither was your great uncle. I find with these types of things, if it's what you're expecting, then you probably have the wrong person. God works in mysterious ways, you know."

"Yeah, you would know. You're missing the belly, the white beard, and most definitely missing the jolly laugh."

Nick gave her a boisterous "Ho-ho-ho," but it sounded uncomfortable.

"Oh, God, Nick, no. Never do that again."

She watched him as he looked out at the darkened Scottish countryside. His hands shook, and she knew it was from his efforts to stay away from the liquor. She wasn't an alcoholic but understood the struggle of having the weight of heaven on your shoulders. She whispered without thinking, "I know you."

"Hmm?" Nick said, turning toward her slightly.

"Oh, nothing. Just thinking."

For the first time in her life, she felt understood. It wasn't an earth-shattering revelation, thunder from heaven announcing a potion to ease loneliness, but a quiet understanding of the human condition experienced by two not-quite-humans.

Noory, Nick, John, and William, the Templar brother, entered the chapel. She felt that her head was on a swivel. There were carvings everywhere: gargoyle faces, leaves, plants, flourishes of every kind. William walked them to a pillar with what looked to Noory to be winding vines.

"What does it look like?" William asked in his thick Scottish accent.

"Vines on a column," she answered.

"What else?"

She looked harder.

"Step back a bit," he said.

She did and let her mind relax, thinking that it might have been like one of those magic eye pictures from when she was a kid, where you had to allow your eyes to relax and a picture would coalesce. *Okay, I'm an engineer. I should be able to figure this out.* She laughed at herself a moment later when she realized her first thought wasn't that she should be able to figure it out because she was the scion, only because she was an engineer. After letting her eyes un-focus, she gasped when she realized what it looked like.

"It's a DNA strand," she whispered and looked around the room, suddenly afraid there might be others around listening.

"Precisely," William said with a smile. "It will allow you to retrieve what you seek if it recognizes your DNA."

"Can it see me?" Noory asked, feeling a little creeped out.

"No, but it can read your blood. It will need a sample. You'll need to place a drop on the column."

"I can prick you if you want," Nick said, reaching for his pocketknife.

"No worries, I brought my own," she said.

William laughed out loud as she reached into her waistband and produced a serrated knife. She took a deep breath, then quickly cut her palm. A thin red line appeared. "What now?" she asked William.

"I can't claim to know exactly how it works, but you'll need to place your blood on the column."

Noory placed her palm on the column as she wondered if the ground would shake or if she would hear voices. Instead, a panel slid open in front of her as stone ground against stone and dust drifted into the air. Inside sat an old chalice. It looked to be made of gold, or at least over-laid with it. There were Hebrew letters inscribed on it, but Noory only recognized one. In fact, it matched a piece of jewelry that she was wearing. It was a necklace, with a charm on the end, which John had given her. He said it had belonged to her mother; it was the Hebrew word for "light." She realized her name was engraved on the chalice. Whether it was coincidence or destiny, it made her cringe with a sense of respon-sibility. A responsibility she had never wanted and even doubted that it was hers to carry. She had dropped out of college and spent her time with runaways. It was one thing to want to help people, quite another to be taxed with scion duties.

"Noory, are you okay?" John's quiet voice broke through her con-flicting emotions.

"Are *you* okay," Nick said to John. "That cup must be bringing back some memories."

"A few," he said.

Noory looked at John. His eyes were distant. She found herself wish-ing she could look around inside his head and see the memory he was seeing of the last supper when they all drank from the chalice. Even if it were a happy memory at the time, how could it be in hindsight? When he caught her looking at him, he looked away.

"So, what do I do with it now? Do I drink from it? Is there some kind of ritual I should perform?"

William opened his palms and shrugged.

"Well, that was anticlimactic," she said with a nervous laugh.

William spoke with certainty: "You're the right person. That's all that matters. The rest will take care of itself."

"Okay then," she said, realizing William had more faith than she did.

"I guess we should get going," Nick said. They all walked to the entrance. Inside her backpack, the cup began to feel heavier than it had at first. She had a sudden desire to put it back where she'd found it. When she looked back at the column, it had closed itself and the blood had disappeared as well. All without making a sound.

CHAPTER 18

They said goodbye to William and made their way to the hotel in Edinburgh, where each had their own room. John barely said a word to them before heading into his. The chalice's reach was wide. Nick stood beside Noory's door before she walked into her room. Her heart pounded at the thought of being alone with the relic. She feared it.

"Noory."

She turned to look at him. "You're not alone," he said softly.

Good God. He'd said he couldn't read minds, but sometimes it felt as if he were.

She swallowed her pride and asked him for what she needed. "When we checked in, they said my room had two queens. If it isn't too much trouble, would you mind? I mean, if it isn't too weird." She looked down at the damask pattern carpet.

The next thing she knew, Nick's hand was on her cheek, and he stooped slightly to look into her eyes. "Of course, I will. It's okay."

She opened the door, and he followed her inside. Walking into a hotel room with Nick caused a rush of warmth to hit the center of her being, then lower still. As she looked at the bed, her mind raced with visuals of what they could do on it. She couldn't help but wonder if he was thinking the same.

He dropped his bag on the floor and sat down on the bed with a long sigh.

Amorous thoughts of Nick cooled when she sat down on the bed and pulled the backpack off her back and onto her lap. She felt the solid weight of the chalice against her legs. "I wish I knew what to do with this."

He smiled as he regarded her. "I have a feeling you'll figure it out exactly when you're supposed to."

"The bishop speaks with faith." She smiled up at him.

"The bishop is exhausted." He yawned so wide; his jaw made a cracking noise.

Nick went into the bathroom to change clothes and returned in an old pair of jogging pants and a thin gray t-shirt that was snug enough to reveal lean muscles beneath. Noory tried not to notice.

She changed into sweats as well and returned to her original position, clutching the bag.

Nick looked at her with concern. "Get some sleep, scion."

"It's Noory, just Noory."

"And that is enough," he said. He placed his palm on her head, and she felt a sense of peace—she realized it was no magic and had nothing to do with his gifts; it was simply because it was him. He leaned over and kissed her on the top of her head and then quickly, too quickly, went to his own bed, turned out the lamp, and rolled over to face the other direction without another word.

Noory watched him for several moments. Her body still hummed from Nick's touch. She knew she could no longer pretend he didn't affect her. A warm blush spread across her cheeks as she wondered what it would be like to slide into bed beside him. Would he ask her to leave? Would he turn over and give her the intimacy she had begun to crave from him? Guilt washed over her that she was thinking of her own needs and desires when Grace so desperately needed her. Or, as John had thought, the whole world needed her. She refused to think that far into it. Cursing her own weakness, she turned off her lamp and fell into a fitful sleep.

The dust swirled around her feet as she passed beneath the wide, spreading canopy of a terebinth tree. The sun beat down on her robe and a breeze blew across her face, bringing with it the sharp scent of cypress from a distance. There was something else that made her shudder: the tormented sounds of one who seemed lost, demented, and afraid.

The Messiah looked toward the tortured soul with purpose . . . and power. He did not hesitate. She noticed John looked a little worried.

The Messiah approached the demented man, whose head snapped up to look at him with an inhuman speed and deadly intelligence behind the eyes, reminding Noory of Brad on the hotel roof.

"What is your name?" The Messiah asked the man.

"We are legion. For we are many." Its voice was that of a chaotic chorus.

"You cannot continue to inhabit this man." The Messiah rolled up the sleeves of his robe.

The demented man looked around, eyes wild, panicked as he looked toward her, then John, but the Messiah shook his head and walked toward the man.

"No, please, Rabbi. Send us into this herd of pigs instead."

The Messiah casts the legion out, and they promptly went into the pigs. There were about two thousand swine who began thrashing and squealing. They could not bear the sensation. It became a near deafening cacophony. The pigs would rather die than carry the abomination. They raced toward the sea to meet their deaths.

Noory stared at her feet, frightened to look into the Messiah's eyes. Her heart pounded, her body trembled, and sweat ran down her face.

"James?" The Messiah said softly.

Why does he call me James? Noory thought.

"Fear not, brother. The same power you see in me, I give you and your descendants."

Noory realized with a start that she was reliving what her great grandfather had experienced on that day over two millennia ago.

"Noory, wake up." Nick sat on the bed beside her and smoothed the sweaty hair back from where it had become plastered to her forehead. "You're safe. It's just a bad dream."

She sat up, still gasping, as Nick looked into her frightened eyes. Despite his earlier hesitancy, he didn't restrain himself from pulling her into his arms. She allowed herself to relax against his chest.

"Want to talk about it?" he said as he gently rubbed her arm.

Noory felt a solid, cold weight in her palm and realized she was holding the grail as she slept. The backpack lay on the floor zipped up, just as she'd left it. They both looked down at the grail in her hands with awe and a touch of fear.

"The grail works. It works." She looked up at Nick with haunted eyes and quickly sat the chalice on the nightstand as if it had burned her.

Chapter 19

Noory sat at the small table in their hotel room with a full Scottish breakfast in front of her, getting cold. She pushed around the baked beans and blood sausage with her fork as she tried to muster the appetite for one more bite but couldn't. Since the dream, she had barely spoken. She stared out the hotel room window as the sun rose higher over Edinburgh.

"Are you okay over there?" Nick asked as he shoved a pair of socks into his duffel bag.

"Yeah, I'm good. Why?"

"You haven't said much."

She took a deep breath as she gathered her thoughts. "I have to summon an ancestral power that scares the hell out of me and separate this man from the dark entity inside him. I don't want to deal with *my father* at all." Noory looked back out the window and curled her knees up to her chest and hugged them to her. "When we were going through his house, he said something, or rather the entity said something, about Jonah holding it back because I was his daughter. This all felt easier before I heard that."

"You are afraid that if you separate the entity from him, it will force you to deal with the man. In some ways, it's easier to deal with the demon. They are evil; it's what they do. End of story. But humans are far more complex than that, aren't they?"

"They are. Grace has lied to me several times, willingly prostituted herself, and basically threw all the help I gave her right back at me. Yet I'll cross the ocean to save her because I know she does what she does because she's in pain. I'm afraid my . . ." She swallowed before saying the words again. "*... my father* may have a history that would somehow make it harder for me to despise him."

"You're comfortable despising him. It's easier. I don't blame you."

She looked at him, thinking there was a "*...* but you need to forgive him" or "but *...* something." It never came.

"I'm going to call John and let him know what's going on and work on our next steps, okay?" Nick asked.

"Sure," Noory mumbled.

Nick walked over to the small table beside the window and sat down across from Noory. "John says that we will need to bring Jonah here."

"So, when are we coming back?" Noory said as she continued to gaze out the window without looking at him.

"We aren't coming back to Scotland, Noory. We're doing it today."

Her head whipped around to face him. A look of stark terror held her face captive.

"No, I'm not ready for this," she said.

"John says it needs to be here because you will need to call on Leviathan to transport the entity back to the deep dimension. It's the only creature strong enough to contain it, and Loch Ness is the easiest place to call it forth."

If she hadn't been so frightened and emotionally burnt at the idea of dealing with her father, she might have found the situation somewhat comical: the Loch Ness monster was about to be called up to ferry a dark soul for them. Nessie was real, but no one had guessed that she was an interdimensional being, more spirit than flesh, but able to exist in either state. She was also spoken of in the Bible as Leviathan, but most people believed she was a whale or some prehistoric beast.

"John and I will sneak into his house and sedate him, and I will transport the three of us here. Once we get here, we will march him up to the top of one of the peaks surrounding the lake so that we can summon Leviathan, and we will separate him from the entity."

"What then?" she asked with a trace of panic creeping into her voice despite her best efforts to remain calm.

"We will need to go back home and have you go into purgatory, find Grace, and bring her back where she belongs."

"That's good, but what I meant was what do we do with Jonah after we free him? He's been possessed at least as long as he was pursuing my mother. That's at least twenty-five years. Will he even know how to function after he is free? He may be a drooling mess, and I'm certainly not going to take care of him," she said.

"No one would expect you to," he replied softly.

The two sat in silence for a while. Finally, his phone buzzed with a text from John.

"It's time for me to go." He walked over, kneeled in front of the chair where Noory sat, and placed his hand on her arm. "Are you going to be okay?"

She jumped at his touch. "Of course, why wouldn't I be?" she said in a much harsher tone than she meant.

"Okay," he said gently as he rose to his feet. "I'll be back as soon as I can. I'll come get you here first. I won't bring John and Jonah to the hotel room. We will meet them by the lake."

"Thank you." She reached out to Nick in a wordless apology for snapping at him.

He took her hand and gave it a small squeeze. "Always," he said before he shimmered out of sight, and her hand fell to her lap. The room suddenly felt cavernous and empty.

CHAPTER 20

The four made their way up the steep slope to summon Leviathan. No one thought it a good idea to materialize out in the open. It was also wise to limit Jonah's time between realms while he carried the entity. It might invite a warring entity to sense his presence and follow him back out, or worse, help him escape.

Jonah whined and fought against being captive. His strength was ten times that of an average man, but John had made a drug cocktail that suppressed the entity. Still, his complaining was wearing everyone down. The entity knew what to say to push everyone's buttons.

"Stop whining, Jonah, before I go back on my policy and rip your throat out," John barked.

"Harsh words coming from the Beloved."

Nick tried to suppress a laugh as he remembered finding out who John was so long ago. "Beloved" wasn't necessarily the word he would have used either. John wouldn't suffer fools for long. As they hiked, he thought back to their meeting many centuries before.

Nick knew he was being followed again. It was the same strange man that he'd seen the week before. Only this time he knew it was no coincidence. Nick took another drink and stumbled into the Parthenon, hoping his shadow would just leave him be. Though he was sure someone who bothered to climb the Acropolis to follow him wouldn't back down so easily.

"Bishop of Myra," the man called.

Nick squeezed his eyes shut and exhaled in annoyance. He knew the formal address could only mean one thing: he was being followed by the Beloved.

Nick took another drink before answering. He leaned against an ancient column as the Parthenon seemed to sway a little beneath him. "So, now I'm being followed by a collector of holy relics. With the Monsignor's dying breath, he told me to come find you," he said as he looked up at John. The sun backlit his dark, wavy hair, giving him an otherworldly glow. Nick laughed, thinking of the habit of artists to draw halos around those they considered holy. Recently he'd heard the rumor that the Nicholas legend, now a few hundred years old, might even earn him sainthood. He laughed again at the thought of a halo around his drunken head.

"Does something amuse you, Bishop?"

"Amuse me? I am the product of a divine comedy! You are too; though you can't seem to find a sense of humor about it."

"There's nothing humorous about squandering your commission, Bishop."

"Stop calling me that!" Nick said with a roar that shocked himself.

John stood steady as a rock, unflinching. This annoyed Nick even further, making him want to take another drink. Yet for the first time he felt a sense of embarrassment about it.

"I won't call you Bishop anymore."

"You won't call me anything anymore. I'm leaving."

"No, you're not. Hear me out, Nicholas."

"No," Nick said as he rose to his feet, unsteady.

John placed his hand on the back of Nick's head, and a rush of peace flowed through him. Peace had always struck Nick as something that would be soft like a summer breeze, but instead, it hit Nick like a hurricane and made the back of his eyes sting. Nick had grown so used to anguish that he felt the peace might kill him.

"Don't touch me," Nick screamed as he took a swing at John and missed.

John didn't miss with his own punch. His fist contacted Nick's face, and he hit the ground. His earthenware jug of liquor skidded across the stone and then shattered as it hit the wall.

"Dammit!" Nick said, as he rubbed his jaw, still feeling the imprint of John's knuckles.

"Now, get your ass up and stop sulking," John said.

Nick got up. "I can't do this! I'm not like you!"

"You're more like me than anyone else alive today," John said as he sat down and leaned against the pillar. "You may say you hate your commission, but you love the people you serve. It's a good thing you're so adept at turning a little money into a whole lot because I happen to know you give away nearly everything you make just to buy children out of slavery."

"So?"

"So, that means He picked the right person. The only way to get through it is to embrace it. If it didn't break your heart, you wouldn't be the right person for the job."

"What's in it for you, Beloved?"

"Immortality stretches itself out long and lonely. It would be nice to know there is at least one person I won't have to watch get old and die. I could use a friend, Nicholas, and so could you."

Smelling the freshwater of Loch Ness far below them, Nick looked at John and watched as a swirl of emotions crossed his face. He realized Noory wasn't the only one who would have a hard time dealing with Jonah once he was free of the entity. John and Jonah had been friends once, long ago.

The sedative was wearing off Jonah to a dangerous degree. He had stopped stumbling and had begun radiating a powerful energy once more. Nick was sure John and Noory could feel it, too. Yet he knew they were all a little afraid to encourage her to use the cup. As long as they had lived, they had never witnessed anyone use it. At least, not one completely mortal; John was there the first time it was used. Still, Nick trusted that Noory wouldn't let her fear endanger them as well as Grace, who desperately needed her help.

Noory kneeled and unzipped her backpack. Nick had told her that if she were scared, it would be best to do the exorcism quickly. She pulled a bottle of water from her pack and poured some of it into the grail. As Nick watched her drink from it, he suddenly wondered if the grail had any actual power at all—that perhaps it was only a catalyst to unlock what was already inside her. He remembered an old Cherokee proverb: "We can only be what we give ourselves the power to be."

She put the grail back into the pack and stood, looking at Nick. "I can see . . ." she whispered.

"Are you okay?" John asked.

Noory squinted. "Oh, my God! That's infrared!" She put her hands up to her ears. Nick realized she was likely hearing what they couldn't as well.

Behind her, the entity became cockier: "Unbind me, and I'll just transport us all to that cliff you intend to throw me from. Besides, we all know you can't do it. You don't have the guts to end me. Your father is in here."

Nick realized the entity was stepping up its game as it felt its time growing short. He observed lines of power coming off Noory like heat waves rippling from a hot desert road.

"I've grown tired of this," Noory said as the surrounding rocks shook, sending cascades of small stones tumbling down around them.

"The scion speaks with a voice of thunder but fears her own power," Jonah said.

"It is not *my* power to fear or doubt." Noory spoke as the power circulating in her body began building, now causing a slight wind to appear to be swirling about her. Her hair blew back from her face and her eyes moved like an animal's, alert to every movement and shift.

Nick both respected and feared her. He missed his Noory. He cringed as he realized he thought of her as his. She turned to look at him as if she'd read his thoughts. Their eyes met, and Nick searched deep within them, looking for Noory, her human side. It was there. There was something else there, too. A well of feeling. *Dear God*. He almost stumbled. It was for *him*. It slammed into him. He felt it calling to him in a raw, pure, unfettered, and vulnerable way that was at once frightening and reassuring. The power she possessed didn't bother concealing it on her behalf. It wrecked him, made him happy, made him hungry.

They trudged on for another half an hour—though Noory's steps were somehow lighter in the throughs of the grail's power— before Noory announced, "We're here."

Nick observed they had made it to the top of a hill with a great view of the lake but farthest away from the most populated area.

"Kneel," she said, looking at Jonah without a trace of emotion but with unabashed authority.

"So, my own daughter orders me around like—"

Noory flicked her hand out toward Jonah inhumanly fast. "Close your mouth, beast," she commanded.

Looking at Jonah, Nick found himself both horrified and amused. Jonah tried to speak but his lips were stuck together. He looked around in panic.

Noory casually walked to the edge of the cliff. Nick resisted the urge to run forward and grab her. He had to trust the power in her knew what it was doing though.

"Leviathan, rise." She didn't need to yell to be heard. Her voice rippled out from her like a sonic wave and permeated the surface of the water.

Moments later, there appeared to be a bulge coming up from the water, smooth and oily. The massive dark head finally broke the surface and roared. Nick looked at the interdimensional creature, spoken of in the scriptures and spotted frequently in Scotland, but never to be pinned down as it traveled between realms.

Nick wondered if they were the only ones able to hear and see it. If not, he was pretty sure the resulting stories would be met with the same skepticism as tales of aliens or ghosts.

Noory simply stood on the cliff and gazed at the creature for a couple of moments. It became still and silent, as it seemed to communicate with her telepathically.

She turned to face them. "Leviathan has agreed to transport the darkness below."

Nick and John stood a few feet from each other and exchanged a look. He knew they must have both been worried about Noory having to face her father when they were both human.

She advanced toward Jonah as the force of her earlier command wore off, and he opened his mouth again and wailed. "No! No one told me Leviathan was part of the deal. I've been deceived! You are no descendant of James. You are a frail little girl without the confidence to face me. You are afraid to love, afraid to live. You are only happy when you are a hero to those burnouts from the shelter. You're no different than your mother! Easily defeated. I could snap your bones—"

"Noory! Command him to be quiet before I hurt this human beyond repair," John said while he clenched his fists so hard his knuckles turned white.

"Don't get me started on you, jolly old Saint Nick. You're in love with the scion and are terrified that a drunk such as—"

Nick had already become consumed with rage and ran at the creature.

"I told you to remain silent," Noory said as she extended her arm toward Jonah and lifted him into the air by the throat, though she stood five feet away from him. Nick crashed into the power Noory had encased Jonah in and hit the ground.

Though Nick didn't need it, John walked over to help him up. Nick knew he was developing feelings for Noory, but it was quite another thing to have the father of your object of affection to blatantly ridicule you about it in front of her. Nick knew John felt sympathy for him— which wasn't helping.

She opened her palm and dropped Jonah in a heap, then turned to Nick and spoke softly, leaving the voice of thunder behind momentarily. "He taunts you so because the beauty of your soul burns his eyes." He knew the power of the grail would only allow her to speak the truth—and she was no liar to begin with. His eyes filled with tears as John reached over to grip his shoulder.

Noory turned back to Jonah as the beast struggled against the unseen chains holding him. "Beast, it is time for you to leave this vessel."

Jonah began trembling as Noory advanced toward him with her hand outstretched. He opened his mouth and screamed as the ground shook beneath him.

In the air, a soft hum began to build and grew louder by the second. Nick heard the air crackling. Dark clouds formed overhead, blocking out the sun. The wind picked up and began to howl. Jonah's body arched, and he appeared to be having seizures as Noory's power began to pull the entity from his human form.

Nick fought the urge to stand with Noory and protect her but knew this wasn't his battle, and he worried about actually harming her if he interrupted the process or broke her concentration. Noory had it in her to defeat the beast, but Nick worried about the emotional damage this whole thing was having on her, not only because this man was her biological father, but because the grail itself might damage her somehow.

Noory began speaking in an archaic language, then suddenly, oddly, she simply said, "Leave him."

Everything grew silent, and Jonah collapsed to the earth. He lay on the ground staring straight into the darkened sky. His chest rose and fell, and Nick noted that Noory seemed to register, without emotion, that Jonah had survived the process.

Leviathan moaned deeply, as there, clenched between the giant's jaws, was a dark writhing formless shadow. Oozing oily darkness dripped down Nessie's teeth until an additional chomp drew it further into her mouth, sending a ripple across the water. The sound caused a large chunk of the cliff to fall into the loch before the creature sank back into the depths, taking the entity with it.

The wind abated, the clouds began to thin, and Noory exhaled long and slow. Nick ran forward to put his arm around her as she looked ready to collapse. John was on his heels as he raced to her.

Noory looked up at Nick with exhaustion and vulnerability painted on her face. For once, she didn't try to hide any of it from him.

"Oh, Noory," Nick whispered. She leaned on his shoulder. "I'm proud of you, Light," he said as he kissed the top of her head. He steered her away from the pathetic pile that was her father.

She looked over to John and weakly gestured at her father. "I can't."

John nodded in understanding and went to deal with Jonah. Nick led her out of earshot, sure that she didn't want to know what John said to him.

∞

John had asked Nick to use his powers to transport him and Jonah. Noory wasn't ready to know where. Neither mentioned it to her. Later, Nick took the grail back to Rosslyn Chapel to sleep for what they both hoped was forever.

Nick stood in the middle of their hotel room in Edinburgh. "Ready to go home?" he asked.

"Yeah. Let me grab my bag." Noory looked around but didn't see her bag anywhere.

"I hope you don't mind. I sent our bags home ahead of us. The sun is setting over the ocean right about now. I thought you might like to see it on our way back."

He opened his arms in an invitation for her to step into them. For a reason she couldn't trace, the action brought tears to her eyes. She bit her lip, nodded, and stepped into them.

There was nothing but a vast ocean below them, yet she didn't worry he'd drop her. The sky that met the water was painted with orange, pinks, red, and even a touch of purple, a natural miracle. There was something healing about it. He must've known. As they crossed the Atlantic, Noory didn't think about Jonah or Leviathan. She didn't even think ahead to going home and retrieving Grace. She knew they would handle it when they landed. Now, she simply laid her head against Nick's chest and listened to his heartbeat as he held her close, and she drifted into a space between the madness into a gentle peace.

Chapter 21

"So, this should be fairly easy," Noory said. "I'll go into purgatory and tell her it's safe to come back, and she shouldn't be hard to find since the others there will know she's different, right?"

Nick listened to her with a deep concern carved into his features. "Yeah," he said.

"Don't look so freaked out, Nick. After casting the crazy out of Jonah and speaking to Leviathan, this should be cake for me."

Nick looked from Noory to John and back.

"What?" she asked.

"I can't shake the feeling that a plan as huge as bringing about world domination, while crossing the boundaries of purgatory to do it, would ever just fizzle out this easy," Nick said.

"I don't think crossing the Atlantic, retrieving the Holy Grail, and calling forth a legendary beast to transport a demon to the underworld is easy," Noory mused.

"I would feel better if I were going instead of you," Nick said.

John said, "Then there would be no backup if something goes wrong. I can't get in by myself. I share your concern, Nick, but I really think this is the best way."

She laid down on John's couch and smiled nervously up at the two of them. "So, will I just disappear like Nick or . . ."

"I don't think so," John said. "I believe you'll go in the same way Grace did. From all the research I've done through the years, you're human with some altered DNA. Whereas Nicholas has been purposely, fundamentally, changed."

"So, my body will stay here. I don't know if that's better or worse. Okay, now you two have got to stop staring at me. It's weird."

John walked into the kitchen, but she knew he was listening, anyway.

Nick sat in John's favorite chair a couple of feet from her.

"I'm not even sure how this works," Noory said with a nervous laugh.

"Well, when I go, I sort of picture my body fading into the other realm like something heavy sinking below the surface of a lake."

"Creepy."

Nick laughed. "I think if you just take some deep breaths and hold your intention in your mind, you can do it. I've believed for a long time that you could do this. If the situation goes south, please don't do your tough girl thing where you don't ask for help."

"I don't know what you're talking about," she teased.

"Liar," he said. "Be safe. I'll be right here waiting for you."

Without turning to look at him, Noory held out her hand. Nick squeezed it, then she closed her eyes and began breathing deeply.

A few minutes went by and then Nick felt the energy in the room change. An emptiness permeated him. He knew Noory's spirit had left the mortal realm. He reached for his flask and took a sip before remembering John was in the kitchen and slid it back into his breast pocket. John walked back into the room to hold vigil with him.

An hour went by, and Noory still hadn't returned. "Shouldn't she be back by now?" John asked. "You've been there many times. Isn't this taking too long?"

"I don't like any of it to begin with, but maybe Grace's spirit is confused, and Noory is trying to explain what happened," Nick said, trying to soothe John's fears as much as his own.

Suddenly, Noory's midsection arched up off the couch as her face contorted in pain.

"Damn it, John! What's happening to her?" Nick asked as he tried to stop the panic rising inside him.

Nick dropped to his knees beside the couch and began calling to her: "Noory! Noory!" Nick called repeatedly as he feared the worst.

John began praying and intermittently calling to her, "Please come back, baby."

Nick took a deep breath as a plan formulated. "I'm going in after her. I might not be the one to retrieve souls, but I can go find out what's going on."

John walked over to Nick and placed his hand on Nick's head. Nick felt the familiar wash of peace, even though John was clearly fearful for Noory. He still had the gift inside him, untouched by grief, steady and strong. Nick realized with a clarity fueled by adrenaline that what John had was something he wanted, needed: to become more than a barely surviving saint.

Nick closed his eyes, and John's hand fell to his side as Nick disappeared from view.

Nick looked around at a world that was very similar to the one he'd just left, but everything looked much more fluid. If he concentrated, he could see energy lines running everywhere. A soul sat to his left, a black man about thirty years old. He watched the lines, touched one, then sat back and observed where it went. After a few moments, he turned to look at Nick.

"You're different," he said looking at him with curiosity. "Souls pop into this realm all the time, but the Earth sticks to you. Are you in a coma? Asleep maybe?"

"No," Nicholas said.

The man walked forward and touched a line of energy in front of Nick and watched it run swiftly into the past. "Well, I'll just be darned! Saint Nick! Somehow, I pictured you just a bit more jolly."

Nick gave a wry laugh.

Pictures appeared all around Nick as the man observed the rescue of thousands of children of all ages and races, all around the world. Nick cringed as he saw the times he succeeded and the times he failed and grieved. The man looked at Nick again with a golden tear of pure light in his eye. "How may I serve you, Saint Nicholas?"

"I am looking for a woman named Noory. She's on a mission to retrieve a soul who isn't supposed to be here."

"Yes, word has spread like wildfire. Even those who have been here the longest say that they have never seen a misplaced human soul land here, not like that. 'Let God sort em out,' is a fairly flawless philosophy. Sure, we get the occasional sleeper or wandering coma patient, but these souls aren't completely lucid and haven't passed. They find their way back. The Creator doesn't make mistakes. So, it stands to reason a human, or a lower entity, found a way to punch a hole into this realm. We observe lower entities now and then, but they aren't allowed to interfere. So, what's going on?"

"As far as we can tell, a madman looking to bring about the Fourth Reich, if you can believe it," Nick replied.

"I can actually. I've been here a while. It's pretty hard to surprise me anymore."

"I'll bet," Nick said.

"My name is Roy. Let's go find your friend, Bishop."

The two stood in the middle of Peachtree Street in downtown Atlanta. In this realm, there was no traffic, just an eerily empty street. Souls occasionally walked past. Some glowed brighter than others. Now and then a soul would appear; a barely glowing form that seemed a bit lost. It only took moments for one of the brighter souls to come forward to guide the other.

Nick thought of Noory, her energy, her laugh. He called to mind the very essence of who she was and then sent his awareness out in search of her.

"Feel anything?" Roy asked.

"Yeah, let's take a right on MLK." Nick felt a tug on his spirit that was unmistakably Noory. He smiled to himself, recognizing that he would know her essence anywhere. It was both reassuring and frightening to realize she'd branded him in such a way.

The two walked on. "Something feels off, Nick," Roy said.

"Yeah, I'm getting that too." The two looked up the street and saw a black fog curling out from under the doorway of an old TV and computer repair shop.

Nick turned to Roy. "I thank you for keeping me company on my journey, but you need to stay away from this. I will not put you at risk. I don't know exactly what's in there, only that I believe it has my friend."

"I will not leave you. It is my calling to battle the darkness, just as it is yours," Roy said.

Nick looked on as the spirit form of the man in front of him coalesced to show Nick his earthly calling—Roy wore a priest's collar. "I was killed in a robbery after administering last rites to a dying parishioner at Grady Hospital," he said. "I walked outside the hospital and was confronted . . ." Roy shrugged. "I gave him my wallet. He shot me anyway."

"That explains the glow," Nick said, smiling. "If you're sure about this—"

"I am."

"Good, I could use the extra energy."

"At your service, Bishop," Roy said.

Nick cringed as he did most of the time when he met Catholic or Episcopal clergy. They knew the Saint Nicholas story—that he was once the Bishop of Myra. Very few knew that he still lived or what his life had been like since. He looked down, suddenly feeling inadequate. "It's just Nick." It wasn't just because he'd broken his celibacy oath in hopes that the touch of a woman would ease the loneliness that had settled deep within his core, it hadn't. It was more than that. A bishop should've been able to cope with his commission with far more grace than he had.

Roy moved his hands in the energy field around Nick, reading the lines coming off him and stretching into the past. "You're in love with the woman you seek. You're an addict. I see who you are, and I still call you Bishop. You must own it if you are to face whatever creeps behind that door. Besides, our father does not make mistakes. He chose for your commission to last for millennia. He either didn't know what he was doing—" Roy laughed out loud at the statement "—or he chose a flawed vessel on purpose." Roy reached out and placed his hands on either side of Nick's shoulders and looked into his eyes. "Own it, Bishop. Own it."

Father Roy and Bishop Nicholas slowly opened the door of the small shop. The place was an absolute wreck. TVs were thrown against walls and lay in heaps. They observed a torn wooden floor that looked as if something or someone had been dragged into the back room. Nick had a flash of Noory struggling against oily black tentacles as she dug her heels into the old wooden floor, unwilling to surrender.

Father Roy looked at Nick and said, "I see your vision of Noory. That's just one explanation for these marks."

Nick had observed Roy getting brighter by the moment. He was close to ascending and was now communicating telepathically, perhaps without realizing it.

They both came to the door as swirls of black smoke curled around their ankles and began to creep up their legs. "You ready for this? We can't have this mess here interfering with purgatory. It's too important, for everyone. This has to go," Roy said.

As Roy spoke, Nick acknowledged that though his main purpose for coming was to rescue Noory, the even bigger issue was keeping this realm pristine so that souls could continue their development and move on.

"I'm ready," Nick said.

"I know you are," Father Roy said.

Nick felt a tug at his heart over the priest's words spoken with the reassurance of a man who was born to bear the title "Father." He hoped at some point in his existence he had given at least one of the children he'd rescued, even half the reassurance that Father Roy provided him in the last few minutes.

"Don't worry, Bishop, *you have*," Roy said. "You have over and over and over again." The priest showed him memories stretching back over a millennia of Nick rescuing children and the safety and reassurance they'd felt—some of them feeling a sense of security for the first time in their brief lives.

"You did that, Bishop. *You.*" He pointed at Nick and held his gaze. "Let's go." Father Roy gestured for him to open the door.

Nick tried the latch but felt energy on the other side, pushing back against him. He knew with absolute certainty that Noory was behind the door. Thoughts of her being held by the creature were so upsetting that Nick felt a growl emanating from him unbidden. He lifted his leg and kicked the barrier—a vexing combination of solid and spirit. "I'm both of those things too, jackass," he murmured as the door splintered.

The sight they both took in on the other side was horrifying. Noory was stuck to the wall with the oily black tentacles pinning her down. The entity wasn't just dark, it was a void that contained a well of despair, rage, and fear. It gave off an effect of not wanting to look at it, but not wanting to look away either, like a terrible car accident on the side of the road. It opened its mouth and screeched at Nick and the priest. "Mine," it screamed.

"You don't belong here, beast," the priest announced.

The beast swiped at the priest with large black talons that went right through him like fog. It reacted with rage when it couldn't get a hold of him.

The entity cried, "Her father failed me. I will not fail. I will find my way into this vessel and rule with the combined power of glorious beast and scion. I will be unstoppable." With that, the beast slammed itself against Noory. Sparks flew as it met a wall of resistance.

"She has a physical form on this side as well. Why? No one foresaw this." Nick looked at Noory's pained eyes and realized this had been going on for a while; the light inside her was dimming. He also saw that she held four other spirits inside her: Grace and the three other teens from the shelter that Jonah had used to hold the SS officers. He didn't know she had such an ability. She probably wasn't aware she possessed that capability until the moment she needed it.

Father Roy grabbed his hand. A surge of energy shot through him. "Send that thing back to hell, Bishop."

Nick cringed as the monster seemed to sense what they were planning and threw itself at Noory with even greater force. She screamed as sparks flew from her once more. He wasn't sure how much more she could take before she lost her hold on her earthly body and the beast took over. Even more bothersome was that they might lose the four teens along with her.

Nick gave a long, low, guttural battle cry as white-hot energy came from him and slammed the monster against the far wall.

Father Roy looked at Nick with shock. Nick sensed what had happened. When the father had joined hands with Nick, he'd found out who Noory truly was—a descendant of James, the brother of Jesus. The beast gained its senses once more and came at them again.

"I am attacked by a drunken Santa and a puny priest who died hating his father. You are no match for me!" it roared.

The priest laughed. "This is what they do, Nick. They remind us of all our faults. They try to break us that way. We accept what we are here. We don't run from it."

Nick closed his eyes and thought of Noory, John, and every brave soul he'd ever encountered along his heartbreaking journey through life. He let go of the priest's hand and ran at the creature, cloaked in light and courage. The entity screamed and thrashed as Nick tore at him with his bare hands. His power shot through the monster like lightning, ripping and tearing until he was thrown back again. The creature retreated as it swirled near the ceiling, out of reach except for the tentacles still pinning Noory to the wall. No doubt repairing itself for another round.

Nick called upon the two blessed daggers as streaks of blue light arched through the darkness. The beast fell back to the ground and Nick severed the creature's limbs, but the victory was short lived. They repaired just as quick, and Noory was still stuck.

Nick was shaken as he turned to the priest. "I don't believe we can defeat him. I'm not giving in. I'm just saying that we have to do something else. Will you bless me, please?"

"Of course," Father Roy said as he drew the sign of the cross on Nick's forehead.

Nick walked over to Noory, held her hand, kissed her on the cheek, and whispered something into her ear that made her start sobbing.

Then Nick approached the creature. "You can't have the scion, but I'm offering you the services of a blessed saint: my knowledge, my insight, my immortality, my gifts, but you must let her go first, and the souls she carries with her get safe passage back."

The creature looked at Noory, then back to Nick. "Agreed," he said as the tentacles around Noory slithered away, and she fell to the floor.

Nick spread his arms wide and began saying the "Our Father" as the beast slithered onto him. Bit by bit, he experienced his own being compared to the beast and he understood a profound truth, perhaps too late; there was a good man inside worthy of protecting. He tried to hold that part of him in some sacred space as the beast drove the light from his eyes.

Father Roy ran to where Noory lay crumpled on the ground, more frightened and exhausted than at any other time in her life. She watched the spirit before her gather its energy into a solid form so that he could hold her upright.

Nick turned to look at them as the beast took hold of him and distorted his blank expression into a feral smile. It sickened Noory to see *her* Nick turned into such a creature. She searched for him inside, just as he'd searched for her when she was "taken" by the grail. She thought she saw a faint spark, but it was just as quickly snuffed out, as if the beast sensed that she'd found it.

"What did the bishop say to you before he surrendered to the beast?" Father Roy asked.

"He said, 'I love you,' and that I would need to destroy him."

Chapter 22

Nick, controlled by the entity, exited the repair shop with inhuman speed.

"I have to go find him," Noory told the priest as she swiped at her eyes with a dirty and torn shirt sleeve. "He'll be heading to the mortal realm."

"Okay, but you're not going alone," he said as he helped her to her feet.

"You can't come with me," Noory said.

"I've been told different," he said with resignation.

"But you're so close to ascending." Noory reached out and gently placed her hand in the light that emanated around him.

"That's exactly why He's sending me. He says you'll need me."

"So, you have a plan?" Noory asked hopefully.

"No, not at all, but if He's sending me then He does, and I've come to learn that is enough," he said, smiling with a self-assurance that was almost contagious enough to make Noory believe everything just might be okay. Almost.

Once more, Noory felt the couch beneath her and was glad to be back, yet deeply grieved. Her eyes popped open with a start as she felt the four souls she had sheltered within her immediately break free. She made a mental note to confirm they were where they were supposed to be—back in their bodies and not sharing space with dead SS officers. Father Roy stood beside the couch, surveying John and the living room.

John was startled but didn't seem surprised that Noory had brought a glowing priest back from purgatory with her. He rushed forward and gathered Noory into his arms. "Where's Nick?"

Noory couldn't meet his eyes. She turned to look at Father Roy as the lump in her throat prevented her from speaking.

"The bishop allowed the beast to take him instead when he realized it was moments from breaking through her defenses," Roy said. "He sacrificed himself."

John staggered backwards into the worn leather chair beside the couch. "Oh, Nicholas," John whispered. He closed his eyes and retreated deep within as Noory realized he was praying for Nick.

"Whoa," Father Roy said as he lifted his hand to feel the energy emanating off John, a gift Noory assumed he'd brought back with him. "Who is this man?" Roy looked closely at John, as if to see through a veil that he felt certain concealed something important.

Noory laughed softly. "If you thought I was a surprise, wait till you hear who *that* man is."

"Oh, sorry," John said after he ended his prayer and rose to introduce himself. He grasped the priest's hand. "I'm John."

Father Roy gasped as if John had burned him, but he didn't let go of John's hand. He looked deeply into his eyes and quoted the scripture that had begun John's journey long ago: "What is it to you if he should live until I return?" the priest said with awe and wonder in his voice.

"Pleased to meet you, Father . . ."

"Roy," the priest said.

"Has this one told you who she is?" John asked.

"Uh, yeah," he said slowly, still sounding a little awestruck.

"If you were brought all the way back here, there must have been a very good reason for it. I haven't seen someone come back in this fashion since . . . well, ever. Nick was brought back, but he had not died long enough to even make it to purgatory. This is unique. Any theories?" John asked.

"I feel that I'm here to help Nick," the priest replied.

"In what way?" John asked.

"No idea, John, but I was sent; so, there is a reason. I'm sure I'll know exactly when I need to," Roy replied.

Noory could tell hearing Father Roy eased John's grieved spirit. She was thinking Roy wasn't just here for Nick.

Noory wrapped the blanket around her tighter, trying to banish the cold from her. The contact with the beast had the effect of making her physical body feel chilled to the bone. An hour had passed since they'd returned, and her shivering had only subsided a little. What John was saying now certainly didn't make her feel any warmer.

"He must be stopped. The problem with him inhabiting Nick, other than the obvious, is that Nick can hear the souls of vulnerable children. I'm not sure that gift will cease just because he is . . . inhabited," John said.

"I won't kill him. I won't do it," Noory said.

"Hopefully, we won't have to," John replied.

"What do you mean, *hopefully*?" she challenged. "He's been your best friend for centuries! How could you even consider such a thing?"

"Noory, I love Nicholas. He is my brother. I would exhaust every other option before I would do such a thing, but if the creature starts using Nick's gift in order to track down and use the vulnerable souls of children, then I will do what I have to do to protect those kids. That's what Nick would want. You know that."

"Stop talking about him like he's dead," Noory said.

"You know it's what he would want," John repeated softly.

A wave of nausea hit Noory as she realized John was right. Instead of dwelling on it, she shifted the subject to something else that needed to be dealt with. "Well, for now, we should probably go over to Jonah's house and make sure Grace and her friends are no longer speaking German."

John, Noory, and Father Roy walked into Jonah's house cautiously. The smell of cigar smoke hung thickly in the air. Noory was quietly explaining to Father Roy about the shelter she ran and how she knew the kids.

"The shelter isn't that far from the Atlanta diocese. I'm familiar with it. You've got a good sense of commitment for one so young."

It startled Noory when he called her young. She was twenty-five but felt the emotional exhaustion of one much older. She'd been working at the shelter in one capacity or another since she was thirteen.

"So, the man that lives here is the one that took the kids captive and figured out how to exchange souls?" Roy asked.

John took a breath as if he were about to answer for her. Talking about Jonah always made her uncomfortable. But a shift had taken place after she'd driven the demon from her father. Noory only thought of him as pathetic and, at times, pitiable even. She also felt an ease around Father Roy and that made her not mind his questions.

Noory answered him herself. "Yes, we believe the plot has been in motion before I was even born. Jonah used my mother in order to create me, hoping the scion DNA combined with his would breed someone that he could control and help him reach his goals, but John raised me after Jonah killed my mother. Once we drove the demon from him, John put him away." For the first time, Noory wondered where John had sent him but still wasn't quite ready to ask. She continued, "Without the entity, he is just a pitiable soul trying to figure out what to do with the rest of his life." Noory put her ear against the basement door and listened.

"Do you hear them?" John asked.

"Yeah, the door is reinforced, two dead bolts." Noory turned around and motioned for the priest to move back. John already knew to get out of the way.

The door held fast as she kicked it, but the frame around the door splintered under Noory's strength. One more kick, and it caved in.

"Ah, I see the scion has supernatural ass-kicking skills. That comes in handy," Father Roy said with a laugh.

Noory looked at the priest with shock.

John just laughed at the expression on Noory's face.

The trio walked carefully around the door that was wedged in the stairwell as the smell of cigar smoke got even thicker. They all stopped as they heard pounding on a door a few feet away.

"Back away," Noory instructed those inside. Another couple of kicks and they stood staring at four bewildered teenagers as dust billowed out around them.

Grace stood with a cigar hanging out of her mouth.

John looked at her curiously and asked her a question in German.

"Huh?" she looked at him bewildered, clearly not catching a word of it.

"Good, you're back," Noory said with stark relief. "Now give me that nasty damn thing." Noory yanked the cigar from Grace's mouth and stomped on it. "Good Lord."

"Franz liked them," Grace said softly as she simply stared at Noory.

Noory braced herself for the usual disdainful, you're-not-my-mom-tirade that Grace was prone to launch into. It never came. Grace dissolved into tears and fell into Noory's arms. One of the boys in the room was also in tears, one was trying to act unaffected, but the shaking was giving him away, the other seemed almost catatonic.

John went back home to get ready for his shift with the Atlanta PD, feeling that he could keep an eye out for Nick at work just readily. However, Noory had known him long enough to recognize that John also liked to retreat into his work because it helped him think and put everything into perspective.

Noory and Father Roy took the teens back to the shelter. They spent a few hours talking to the kids about what had happened. Noory had thought they might be damaged permanently, but, oddly, it seemed to have the opposite effect on them. The young man named Jason was asking Father Roy about becoming a priest. He was determined to "battle darkness." Grace seemed completely transformed from a rebellious pain in the ass to a humbled and contemplative girl who wanted to go back to school. The other two seemed like they might be okay as well, if not a little more cautious of "stranger danger."

The sun was going down as Noory and Roy stepped out of the shelter and back into the noise of the Atlanta streets. Noory realized with a jolt of fear and grief that now that the kids were safe, she had no choice but to turn her attention to the issue of what to do about Nick, and it was a heartbreaker.

CHAPTER 23

"How about we buy you a waffle before we take you back to John's place?" Noory asked.

"It's been so long since I've experienced hunger that I almost forgot what it feels like," Roy said.

"Great then, waffles it is. So . . ." Noory proceeded cautiously, realizing that he might not want to talk about it. "When did you pass, in the earthly sense?"

"July in 2000. So, what year is it now, like 2001 or 2002?"

Noory worried about shocking the man's psyche, but he was going to find out sooner or later. "It's 2022."

"Huh, I always wondered if time moved differently on the other side. I majored in physics before I joined the priesthood," Roy said.

Noory laughed softly.

"What is it, Light?"

Noory's eyes filled with tears as he referred to her the same way Nick did. "Oh, I just like how you approach the unexpected." Noory thought back to the way he had reacted when he found out who John was and didn't seem rattled by what she was either. He simply held a delighted curiosity for the new surprise's life—as loosely defined as it had become for him—brought him.

"Let's hang a left here," Noory said, thinking of a place that made breakfast food at any hour.

A man passed them, raised his hand, and said, "Father," casually and moved on. Beside her she heard Father Roy's breath hitch and come out quickly, almost panicked. Noory realized the man they'd passed had worn a Roman collar as well.

"Are you okay?" Noory asked.

"Yeah," he said, lending no further explanation.

They slid into a booth with well-worn but cozy seats, and the waitress handed them huge, laminated menus. They spoke little as they looked over the menus. Noory supposed one needed time to gather their thoughts after returning from the dead. After being suspended against a wall by a demon, she supposed she did too.

"Well, I'm not sure maple syrup can smother trauma, but I'm about to give it a shot. How about you?"

Father Roy laughed. "It's worth a try." The waiter showed up, and Roy ordered, then stared over Noory's shoulder, eyes unfocused.

"A waffle for your thoughts," Noory said. She suddenly felt sympathy for him having to pop back into the world of the living after already having accepted his death. She felt a little guilty as she realized she hadn't thought of it before because of the collar. "Everyone thinks a priest will just magically be okay no matter what, don't they?" Noory said, breaking him out of his trance.

Roy smiled. "Sometimes they do, Light. Yes," he breathed.

The waiter brought two cups of coffee. Roy poured a generous amount of creamer into his cup and stirred it. "I knew that man on the street . . . before I died, he was my boyfriend."

"Ah. I see. That's an Episcopal collar you're wearing there." Noory wondered if he'd be happy to know he and his boyfriend could've gotten married if they were together in this day and time, or would he be sad to know he'd passed before that opportunity was even an option for them?

"Indeed. The thing is: he didn't recognize me out there. I mean, I know it's been a while, but we don't continue aging over there. So, I should look the same to him. It's not like we were mere acquaintances. We'd been dating for years."

"I wonder if being on the other side has such a profound effect on the body that it changes what people see. I mean, after Christ rose, his disciples couldn't recognize him at first. Would there be a picture of you online? It would be interesting to see if there is a physical difference. This may sound weird, but have you looked in a mirror since you returned?"

"No, it never occurred to me. On . . ." The priest paused and looked around to see if anyone was listening. "On the other side, we spend our time in spirit form unless we need to show ourselves. I'll be right back."

Noory guessed he was headed to the bathroom to look in the mirror.

After a few minutes, he returned. "Nope, looks the same to me," he said.

"Maybe something is happening at a molecular level while in another dimension that changes the perception of those whose eyes haven't gone through the same changes," Noory offered.

"Like if they spent some time on the other side, they might recognize me?"

"Exactly, like having to be on the same frequency. Like tuning a radio," Noory offered.

The waffles arrived, and Noory loaded hers down with butter and syrup. "I'm sorry."

"Huh?" Roy said.

"Well, I imagine it was painful for the one you love to not recognize you."

"Or maybe it's for the best. It might turn his life upside down if he suddenly thought I was back." Roy stopped and took a sip of coffee. "You know, he wasn't even considering the priesthood when I passed."

"Do you think your death was the catalyst?"

Roy looked out the window into the night. "Maybe . . . maybe." He drank more of his coffee, then set the cup down again. "I'll think about that later. We've got to get Nick back."

She didn't want to badger the priest, but she hoped Father Roy was the key to getting him back. She felt helpless.

"Do you mind if I ask why you might have been sent to help us retrieve Nick?" she asked. "I know we have to remember that Nick probably can't control this thing's action." Noory felt a shiver as she remembered the way the entity had looked at her with that feral smile. It wasn't just deranged; it was also intelligent and calculating. "I didn't spend the last several years protecting and helping these kids just to forget about them because I . . . I care for Nick."

"I think the reason I may be here has to do with my personal history as well. I think, like most things He orchestrates, this may have a dual purpose. It may be part of my trying to understand my own journey. My father was an alcoholic. I hated that man, and I believe that was the main reason I needed to gain understanding in purgatory, which I'm grateful for. It isn't a punishment like some folks think. I'm happy to be unburdened from the grudge that had burned in my heart for decades. I'm being delivered, not punished."

Noory smiled. "That's how Nick described it."

"He's a smart man, much smarter than he will ever give himself credit for. When I met him, I understood some things about my father in mere moments that had escaped me for years. My father was such a severe alcoholic that he couldn't hold a job. I watched my mother cry as they threw our belongings out onto the lawn when we were evicted. We couldn't even find my father to tell him we didn't live there anymore. I have very few memories of him being sober. I had seen him as a worthless human being. That took root and then I ignored it. I didn't even pray about it anymore. Meeting Nick and seeing all the beautiful things he had done for these kids for centuries, despite being a severe alcoholic, helped me realize my father had worth too. I just felt abandoned and couldn't get past it."

"Father issues: I know a thing or two about that." Noory gave a wry laugh and went back to her waffle.

After getting Roy settled in at John's house, she went back to her own apartment to sleep, but mostly stared at the ceiling thinking of Nick. She intermittently thought of the warmth and security of his arms around her tight as the sun set over the Atlantic, before her thoughts betrayed her and circled back around to the moments after the entity overtook him and gave him that twisted, feral smile.

∞

The next day, Noory met with John and Roy to make a plan.

"Why can't I just use the grail again? It worked on Jonah, and he had a very powerful entity inside him that had hold of him for many years," Noory said.

"Nick invited it in. He made a deal with it. Exorcisms are for those that don't want the entity. He might even fight you over it for fear that it would leave him and go straight back to attacking you again," John said.

"There has to be something," Noory said.

"There is. We just have to find it," Father Roy chimed in.

John took a deep breath and slapped his thighs in resolution before standing. "I think I know exactly where to find what we need."

"Where? Let's go," she said. Her eagerness to help Nick made her feel like everything was moving in ridiculously frustrating slow motion.

John walked over to Noory, placed his hands on her shoulders, and leaned over to kiss her forehead. "For now, I just need you to trust me, daughter. Okay?"

Noory's eyes filled with tears despite her best efforts to hold them back. It was the first time John had called her "daughter." He'd told her she was "like a daughter," but never just his "daughter." She hadn't realized until that moment how much she'd needed to hear it.

CHAPTER 24

John sat in his pickup truck outside the monastery and couldn't even manage to pray. He gripped the steering wheel until his knuckles turned white. He didn't want to go in, but Nick needed him. Everyone did. For years, he'd wanted to see Nick free of the alcoholism, but he knew that if he'd had Nick's flask right now, he would have taken a drink.

"You're too old for this," he said to his reflection in the rearview mirror. He laughed at the irony; most people meant that statement in the reverse. He meant it to scold himself for being two thousand years old and afraid to go face a weak mortal, but then again, this was no ordinary mortal. He forced himself out of the truck.

John walked around to the back entrance of the monastery. They all knew him well enough by now. Two of them even knew his secret. The others knew he was well-respected by the abbot and sensed something about him, if only a subconscious niggling in the back of their minds. Before he reached the back door, he found a moment of grace. The abbot was out tending his bees. "Brother Patrick!" John called as he approached.

The old abbot had bees swarming about his gloved hands and netted face. He walked away from the hive, took his hat and gloves off, and laid a gentle, aged hand on John's back. "Beloved." The man smiled gently up at John.

John marveled at Patrick's ability to read him. He knew it was a vain thought, but he often wondered if God had put Patrick—and others before him—on the earth just so that he had an occasional confidant, a father figure, in the mortal realm. It would hurt intensely when Patrick finally passed.

"I'm okay," John said.

"You aren't, but that's okay too. I can see that you'll feel much better as soon as you get this over with." He glanced at the one window that belonged to the underground rooms of the monastery. Patrick walked with him in silence the rest of the way. He knew who John was here to see. He'd been counseling the man since he arrived.

"All shall be well," Patrick said as he drew the sign of the cross on John's head.

The abbot turned to go as the huge guard named Brother Thaddeus stepped forward to shake John's hand. Thaddeus was 6'5" with a shaved head and combat boots beneath his robe. He also had a SIG Sauer strapped in a pistol belt around his waist instead of the usual rope belt with a rosary hanging off it that the other brothers wore. He owed his vocation to John.

After returning from Iraq, the former Marine had joined the Atlanta PD. John couldn't help but notice the Templar cross tattooed on the man's shoulder. Not long after, he'd began talking religion with John and had mentioned his desire to live the monastic life but felt that he couldn't handle forever silencing the warrior side of his spirit. John had almost choked on his lunch when the man mentioned his love of history, particularly the Knights Templar. That's when John realized he had the perfect place for Thaddeus. Only John and a select few knew of what lay in the monastery's basement just outside the Atlanta outskirts: the criminals whose crimes were "supernaturally motivated" were sent to a special prison where they could receive the help, or containment, that mainstream penitentiaries couldn't offer.

"How've you been, John?" Brother Thaddeus asked.

"I've had better days. And you?"

"Actually, can't complain. I suppose you're here to see him," Thaddeus gestured to the fifty-something man curled up on a cot and hugging his knees to himself.

"Yeah, unfortunately," John said.

Thaddeus slapped John on the back before turning back to his post.

"Beloved!" one prisoner taunted from a nearby cell as his eyes flashed red before going back to normal and a forked tongue darted out to test the air. The lower entities always called him that to make it clear they knew exactly who he was. It was usually a type of challenge.

Thaddeus reached through the bars, quick as lightning, and grabbed the "man" by the neck. "Don't make me have to come in there, Bob!" Thaddeus said in a deadly tone.

"Bob? Really?" John said, smiling for the first time since arriving.

"Why not?" Thaddeus said, shrugging. "It's a classic, and his demonic name is unpronounceable to the human tongue."

John turned to face the man he'd come to see. "Jonah, we need to talk."

The man slowly looked up at John with haunted eyes. He'd been there ever since Noory had driven the entity from him. John had asked Nick to bring them straight to the monastery. The transformation that had taken place in the last several days was shocking. Gone was the cocky arrogance from before. The man in front of John was a frightened, empty shell. Within John, a war waged between sympathy and pure, raw anger. The hands that had taken Catherine's life now trembled without ceasing.

A hollow, pleading voice came from the cell. "John, why didn't you just kill me?"

"I've asked myself that a few hundred times," John said as the exhaustion of the ages descended on him. "Even after you raped Catherine, I thought there might be hope for you, Jonah. I didn't think you would have done it if it weren't for the entity."

"I let the entity in. You had a power around you I thought made Catherine love you. I thought if I had that same kind of power, I would have a chance with her, but once I let it in, it took over. I wasn't strong enough to hold it back."

Despite John's anger at the man, his next words came out almost unbidden. "Noory says that the entity told her you were holding it back, keeping it from hurting her."

"I did all I could. I never wanted to hurt her. She is so much like Catherine." Jonah rubbed his fists across his eyes as if trying to banish painful memories.

"Damn it, Jonah. Every time I try to hate you, I just find one more reason to pity you." John felt a little sick that maybe he subconsciously looked for those reasons in order to justify his own mistake of not killing Jonah as soon as he discovered what he'd done to Catherine.

"It's because you're good, John. You are a force of light in this world. I'm glad you raised Catherine's daughter. I can't even bear to call her mine. She should have no relation to someone like me."

John knew they would simply go in circles, rehashing the past. He knew he needed to get what he came for and leave, but their history was hard to ignore. "I need to know what the entity has planned. I find it hard to believe that this plan started and stopped with you. There must surely be more players involved in something this big."

"There is, John. It goes much further than me. I was simply the one to awaken it. You'll need to go to Argentina. The Fuhrer fled there. You probably already knew the US lied about him killing himself in the bunker," Jonah said.

"Yeah, I knew."

"There's an estate near Bariloche where he and a few of his men hid and a tunnel coming off the house. Inside the tunnel is a relic that was intended to help them establish the Fourth Reich, but the SS never found a way to unlock it. It has a protective spell around it. The entity believed it could help the Nazis succeed if he could find someone powerful enough to release the spell. I don't know exactly what it is. The one who inhabited me didn't even have all the details. It just knew that it was to gather the SS officers from purgatory and go find the relic. Perhaps if you destroyed the relic, all this will stop. I don't know."

"Is there another entity controlling the first? When you were inhabited, did you report to someone?" John asked. He didn't want to say out loud what had happened to Nick. He knew the few prisoners that were held there were in for other things. But there was no way to know what messages might take place between realms or what unseen thing might be listening.

"Azazel was to bring back another dark spirit from purgatory named Amaros."

John knew immediately, from everything Noory had told him, the spirit that had tried to inhabit Noory and finally took Nick was the same one Jonah spoke of. Perhaps it thought it could use Noory to unlock the protective spell around the relic.

Jonah continued. "Azazel had made a deal long ago to bring Amaros back, but he had no plans to follow through. He hated him and even had a plan to destroy Amaros if he ever got free, so that he could be the leader of the Fourth Reich. Azazel wanted to shape the world in his image."

"Is there a way to destroy Amaros?" John asked.

"The one that inhabited me knew an archaic spell that would bind it to a human and when the human was killed, the entity would not be able to escape the shell of its body. Both would die. The human would journey on to whatever afterlife it was headed to before, but the entity would cease, forever."

John felt despair set in. He wanted to free Nick, not destroy him. "Can you tell me the words?" John hated asking. Once he knew them, he had the responsibility to use them to destroy Nick and the entity.

"I feel them in my memory but only a being who could read them would be able to get them out. They are useless to me."

"But if there were an entity in you, it would be able to recite them?" John asked.

Jonah's eyes grew wide with fear.

"No, I have no intention of bringing one to inhabit you. I'm just trying to understand," John replied.

"Not just any old lower-level being would know it. Only the ancient and powerful," Jonah added.

"Huh." John stared at the wall behind Jonah as he thought of what this might mean for Nick. "Thank you for your cooperation, Jonah."

"I have no reason not to. Other than being way too jealous of you and Catherine. "I'm not going anywhere, if you find you need to ask me anything more."

John started to ask him if he needed anything then reminded himself what the man had done. Instead, he just nodded and walked away.

On the way out, John did a doubletake as he passed one of the prisoners in the next to last cell. He had a thick metal chain around his neck, and his cell was clearly a faraday cage.

"Brother Thaddeus?" John called.

"Yeah?"

"What particular power are we guarding ourselves from with this one?" John gestured to the man with a long, scraggily beard who sat cross-legged, reading a book.

"Oh, that one can move through walls and even travel into parallel worlds briefly. Get this: he even killed a guy in this world, journeyed into a parallel dimension and brought back a version of the one he killed and simply replaced him so he couldn't be charged with murder. That fella went insane, which is how this one landed here. He's been with us for ten years now," Thaddeus said.

"Huh," John said.

"Everything okay?" Thaddeus asked.

"Yeah, just thinking."

"Are we getting a new resident?" Thaddeus asked.

"Let's just say I hope it doesn't come to that." John slapped Brother Thaddeus on the shoulder and headed back to his truck with a lot to think about.

CHAPTER 25

John left the monastery and reported for his shift. It was an overnighter. Though he didn't have to work them anymore, he liked to stay abreast of what was happening at various hours. And truth be told, he was hoping to run into Nick—though he got a little nauseated at the thought. He hated the notion of looking at his friend and seeing evil look back at him through eyes that had once beheld innocence in its purest form and offered his own lifetime and again to rescue the helpless, but he knew it was inevitable. He would eventually have to deal with Nick . . . one way or the other.

John walked out to the street in uniform and looked at the Atlanta skyline. It was an overcast night, and the lights coming off the skyscrapers reflected against the clouds, obscuring any stars or moonlight that might peek through the haze.

"Please, don't let me mess this up," he prayed quietly as his own inadequacy washed over him. He listened to the street noise he'd heard so often that it had become like the hum of a refrigerator, ever present yet quickly unnoticed, but tonight the traffic, horns, and distant laughing, yelling partygoers sounded like a symphony. There was an unexpected peace to it. "Thank you," John whispered before heading back into the precinct.

Noory yawned and stumbled into her living room. After searching for Nick to no avail and then tossing and turning, she hadn't gotten to sleep until three a.m. She got the feeling he wasn't even in Atlanta and wasn't sure how she knew, except for the emptiness in her heart that felt like a chasm. After coming home, she'd lain in bed thinking of Nick, trying not to think of him, meditating, giving up, walking around the apartment, then finally falling into a very light sleep that felt like no sleep at all. She needed to get to work and help Ava with the books. She also had to check on Grace. It looked as if she might go to live with an aunt and finally get off the streets.

She rolled out of bed and immediately cracked her little toe. "Damn it," she yelled, leaned over, and rubbed her pinky toe as it throbbed. She glared at the coffee table with a vengeance before thinking: *Coffee, hell yeah!*

She put in one of the tiny cups and listened as the device steamed and heated like a small dragon whose mandate it was to deliver comfort and clarity in steaming mugs. "You rock," she said to the cherry red bringer of caffeine as the cup began to fill before it suddenly stopped, and the little screen told her it was clogged. She took the small pod out and slammed it down on the counter and looked around for the small paperclip that she used to unclog the spigot. She rubbed her eyes and growled at no one in particular and contemplated if an eighth of a cup of coffee would be enough to wake her up since the paper clip had disappeared into another realm. She thought of Nick again, slumped against the counter, and sighed.

A knock at the door jarred her out of her spiral. "What!" she yelled, knowing she shouldn't be allowed to converse with anyone until she'd had at least two cups of coffee.

She opened the door and tried to look welcoming bur failed miserably as John lifted his eyebrows and smiled. He read her like a billboard. It was annoying and comforting.

"You haven't had your coffee yet, huh?" He smiled and held out one of the two lidded paper cups he carried.

"You know me," she said, taking the drink as she glared at the coffeemaker as if it should be jealous that she'd moved on after it had failed her. They sat on her couch and each gulped caffeine.

"Up early?" she asked.

"I worked an overnight," John replied.

"Haven't been home yet?"

"No."

They sat in silence for a few moments, knowing why he'd worked all night, for the same reason she'd been out last night.

"He's not in Atlanta," Noory said.

"No, I couldn't feel him either. I think I know where he is, though," John said as he pulled out three plane tickets to Buenos Aires. "We're bringing Father Roy. He believes he's here to help Nick. He may be here to help me, too. I've enjoyed having him at the house. It's strange knowing Nick has that thing in him," John said with a faraway look in his eye. "For nearly all my life, he's been a type of constancy while everything and everyone else changed around me. Anyway, I think we may find him in Argentina."

Noory read the tickets. "Yeah, among all the World War Two memorabilia we found in Jonah's apartment were lots of research on SS officers hiding in Argentina, Nazi assets there, all kinds of things leading to Argentina. It makes sense. We're leaving tonight then?"

"Yeah, I think it's the next logical step. My contact told me about a relic there left by the SS unit that was in charge of looking into the supernatural on behalf of the Furher."

"Sounds creepy."

"That's because it is. Then again, some might find me creepy when you think about it," John said.

"You are creepy," Noory said, laughing. "All right then. You guys will come get me on the way to the airport?"

"For sure. Okay, I'm going to head home and catch a couple hours of sleep." John got up and walked over to the door and paused before turning back around.

"And?" Noory asked, sensing something heavy en route.

"Noory, I know you have feelings for Nick."

"Of course, he saved my life."

"He did, yes, but that's not what I mean. All I want to say is please remember that the being within him will use your feelings for Nick against you if you let it. They manipulate. That's how they work."

"John, you don't think I know that? I know I'm only twenty-five and that seems young to you, but don't forget, I've seen a lot."

"Yes, but I've also seen the way you look at each other. You love him, and I don't want to see that used against you."

Despite Noory's agitation with John, she knew he spoke the truth. "I'll be careful. I promise."

John hesitated for a moment, obviously fighting the urge to say more, but to his credit, he simply smiled. "Okay, see you this evening, kiddo."

After John left the apartment, Noory sat at the table finishing her coffee and found herself smiling at the idea of seeing Nick again. She felt warm all over till she remembered the last time she'd seen him. A shiver ran over her as she remembered him taking the entity on her behalf and the moment he turned to look at her.

CHAPTER 26

The three of them landed at Ezeiza International in Buenos Aires and rented a car. John had been to Buenos Aires before and pointed out a few landmarks as they drove. "You'll notice a lot of European architecture here. This gorgeous building to our left is the Barolo Palace. It's an office building now but very interesting inside. The builder was a fan of *The Divine Comedy,* so there are sections of the building dedicated to hell, purgatory, and heaven."

"Lower rent for the office spaces in hell, right?" Noory asked.

John just turned and looked at her, deadpan.

Noory snorted in whimsical derision when John mentioned *The Divine Comedy.* Though she knew it was Dante Alighieri's poem about a man's journey to God, she couldn't help but feel that her whole life was a divine comedy at the moment. John also pointed out the beautiful jacaranda trees that were in full bloom with purple flowers now that it was November, the Buenos Aires springtime, but it was lost on Noory. The jet lag and worry for Nick were tugging at her.

It was almost lunchtime and even though they were exhausted, they went out to eat, as their room still wouldn't be ready for another couple of hours. Noory stumbled into the restaurant, and they were led to a table. She looked around, feeling a little confused. "It's like we're in Italy here," she said to John.

"Yeah, many of the restaurants have Italian-looking décor. Buenos Aires is a real melting pot.

The asado, a type of barbequed beef, was delicious. Though Noory didn't think she would be able to eat, she managed to in spite of her worry. She couldn't help but picture her and Nick together in this beautiful city but forced herself to snap out of it each time her mind would drift.

The three of them made small talk over lunch but worried about what they would find when they caught up with Nick. When lunch was over, they made their way to Alvear Avenue, to the Recoleta area where Noory's head was on a swivel: there were many old mansions that had been transformed into five-star hotels and embassies. Noory had spent most of her life in Atlanta. This trip was reminding her of just how little of the world she had seen. Her mind drifted once more to the possibility of seeing it with Nick. She had a feeling if she could just get a warm shower and a decent nap she would be in better control of her wandering mind and emotions. Her wish was granted when they made it to their upscale hotel room that John had paid for.

"This trip is difficult enough for us. I thought we might as well have a nice place to stay," John said as Noory and Roy looked around the large suite in surprise. There was a nice sitting room, a bathroom, and two bedrooms, one with two full size beds and another with a queen.

Noory smiled at him. "Thank you."

He nodded. "You look tired, sweetie."

"I am," she said with a jaw-cracking yawn. Noory grabbed her toiletry bag and clothes and took a hot shower and slipped into her sweats. She was concerned she would lay there the entire time worrying, but her adrenaline from fretting during their flight, instead of sleeping, was finally starting to ebb. She drifted off to the sounds of Father Roy and John discussing their plans for that night.

That evening, they got back into their rental car and drove to Bariloche, a beautiful city surrounded by mountains and lakes with a quiet town at its heart. If she wasn't in such turmoil over Nick, it was a place that would evoke serenity on any other day. It was even the kind of place that made her think if she found Nick, they could just hide out here and forget the rest of the world and all their responsibilities.

They parked their rental down the street from the estate where the relic was supposed to be; they didn't want to surprise anyone. Noory looked over at John as they trekked through the woods: Patagonia cypress and coihue, so different from home. They both felt it: Nick was nearby. John had no shortage of contacts around the world and had no trouble finding out that the estate had been rented for the last couple of months but was now unoccupied due to some extensive rewiring. He'd even got permission to be on the property as long as no one went inside.

They reached the house, which reminded Noory of an old ski chalet, where they split up, and fanned out, looking for depressions in the ground. Ideally ground penetrating radar would have made the work much easier, but John was convinced that Nick was already there and would guide them right to the relic. It really became more about finding Nick.

Noory had been walking for about ten minutes when her breath caught in her throat, making her cringe at her own weakness. Nick was right ahead.

He leaned over, brushing the leaves away from a depression in the ground. She wondered what lay below it, but she had the feeling he knew. The light of a bright full moon, filtered through the trees overhead, lending his normally rugged, tanned skin a ghostly look, while the nighttime forest gave Noory the feeling of being wrapped in a cone of privacy, even though she knew that John and Father Roy were nearby.

"Hello, Light," Nick said softly without looking up at her.

Common sense told Noory that she should call for John and Father Roy, but the sound of her name on Nick's lips made her banish the thought as quickly as it had come. Bristling at the idea that she should have to call in a couple of men to save her, she knew she wasn't just an ass-kicking supernatural descendant, she was also a strong woman, even without the powerful lineage.

"So, who am I really speaking to here?" Noory asked, refusing to let her feelings for Nick rule her.

"It's me, Light. I can keep this monster at bay."

"Then why are you in Argentina in the first place?" she asked.

"I want to know what this thing is looking for so I can stop him." Nick rose and turned to face Noory.

Noory was excited for a moment at the idea that Nick might actually be able to control the entity. He had lived for nearly two millennia. If anyone could control such a thing, it would be him or John. She also knew the deceptive nature of evil; how it often convinced those it used that they were doing something noble.

Nick moved closer, and Noory swallowed hard as she saw that Nick's shirt was unbuttoned halfway down his chest, framing his muscular build and small patch of dark chest hair. As he neared her, his eyes grew hungry. His chest rose and fell quicker as he took his time gazing at her body. He drank in the sight of her like she'd never seen him do before. Like no man had done before. There had always been a hesitancy coming off him in the past. Now there was a raw yearning that excited Noory in a way that both frightened and thrilled her.

Before she could analyze the situation any further, he closed the space between them in two long strides and took her into his arms, immediately pressing his body to hers. His mouth took hers as a groan escaped him. His kiss was fierce with desire as Noory slid a hand into his unbuttoned shirt. Her hand roamed across his firm chest, and she felt his body push against her in response. His mouth found her neck and made her insides melt. She'd dreamed of touching him in this way more times than she cared to admit. She realized she'd spent so much time trying to deny it that when she released it, she barely had the power to keep it in check. His mouth slid up to her ear as he rasped out: "Don't give up on me, Light."

Tears sprang to her eyes as she heard John's words of warning echoing in her head mingled with Nick's own words from just before he sacrificed himself, saying that she would need to kill him. She shoved the thought from her mind as best she could. Nick's hands were helping her forget as well. As his mouth found hers again, his hand covered her breast. His palm and fingers were warm even through her t-shirt and bra. She hated admitting it, but she knew if John and Father Roy weren't around, she would let him take this as far as he wanted. She felt herself free-falling as an imaginary door slammed behind her: the one that would allow her to turn around and pretend she didn't love him.

Had the entity set him free from his inhibitions toward her? She was ashamed to know that part of her was grateful to whatever force had released him from his hesitation. Still, she searched his spirit as best she could, looking for traces of the entity. He stiffened in her arms. "It's me, Noory," he whispered breathlessly.

John shouted, "Take your filthy hands off my daughter, beast."

"Damn it," Noory breathed. She turned around slowly, holding Nick's hand. "John, no!" Panic made her voice shake as she saw, with horror, that John was pointing his pistol at Nick. She knew he couldn't be killed from a bullet but there were things that could be done afterwards to keep his body from being able to regenerate. She cringed to think that John was capable of planning such a thing for his friend—a friendship that had stretched through the ages.

"Noory, step away from him," John ordered.

Her throat had gone dry with fear. All she could do was shake her head and stand firm.

"Noory! Damn it! Use your head, girl! He has the damn anti-Christ inside him! He's using you," John cried.

"First of all, I'm not a girl. I'm a grown woman! I will not let you hurt him and don't talk to me like I'm a teenager that just snuck out of the house."

"Wake up, granddaughter of James. Niece of the Messiah. I wouldn't need to treat you like a rebellious teenager if you would stop acting like one. Now move while I deal with this," John shouted with grief lacing the edge of his anger.

"No." Noory said as she firmly planted herself between Nick and John.

"Noory, an entity raped your mother. Do not kid yourself that it couldn't happen to you," John said with a voice that held generations of pain.

Nick stepped out from behind Noory putting several feet between them. He spread his arms wide. "John, I would never hurt her. Jonah was merely a weak human with an urge for power. I'm no weak human, and I could do without the power that I do have. You know that."

Noory heard the hurt in Nick's voice, but the boldness was somewhat new. There was an undercurrent of pride that didn't sound like Nick. Noory had to admit that the entity was emboldening him. She had a feeling that if Nick made it out of this situation in one piece, he might, oddly enough, take away a trait that could serve him well.

"I love you, brother, but I will do what I have to save these people. I've been fooled before. I won't allow it again," John said.

The two were looking each other in the eye, sharing some mutual understanding, a history that she didn't fully know, that made Noory feel like a complete outsider.

"I know," Nick said as he exhaled the burden of ages and whispered," I love you too, brother."

John cried as he began a prayer. Noory realized it was a prayer for the dying.

Terror overtook Noory as she realized Nick was allowing John to execute him. For the first time, Noory's power couldn't help her. She was glued in place.

Chapter 27

Nick felt the entity within him rage and roar, but he kept his feet planted. Every muscle strained with the effort as the entity demanded action from him. It didn't want to let go of his mortal form or his power. Father Roy stepped out of the shadows. "You won't touch this man," Roy said in a tone that suffered no exceptions as he stood between the two men.

John said, "He's my brother. I love him. I cannot imagine my life without him, but you aren't thinking straight, Father. This man is dangerous! People like you and me are here to make the hard decisions."

"With respect, John, I know you have two thousand years on me, but you have to trust that if He sent me back knowing exactly who I am, how I think, my opinions and beliefs about everything, then He knew I would react this way as well. And you have to trust that if He allowed Nick to take on this beast, then He had to believe Nick is strong enough to deal with it. He's placed more faith in Nick than we have. We have to trust in that."

John walked up to the priest without warning and plowed the butt of his pistol into the side of Father Roy's head, but John found himself on the ground from the momentum of his swing. His arm had swung right through the priest as he shifted into spirit form and back into solid form once more.

"No, I didn't know I could do it either," Father Roy said as everyone stared at him in shock. "I assume you carry cuffs, John?"

"Yeah," John said as he accepted his defeat, shook off the disorientation, and reached for the zip-tie cuffs in the pocket of his light jacket.

Father Roy took them and cuffed Nick. "I know a man of your power can escape these. The point is, as long as you don't, we can trust you. Deal?"

Nick nodded, unable to say more as he contemplated whether he should be happy or sad about not escaping the mortal realm. He looked at the moonlight shining on Noory's hair and thought she looked like an earthbound angel and decided on the former.

As they left the woods, Nick worried about the damage he'd caused. He noticed John wasn't looking at Noory for fear she hated him. Noory wasn't speaking to John. Nick knew it was hard for Noory to open her heart. The second she did, John tried to shoot the object of that affection. Nick couldn't look at John because he couldn't bear to see the distrust in his eyes. For centuries, they were all each other had had.

For once, he wanted to bring joy, to be something close to the idea of Saint Nicholas.

Not a chance.

That evening, the four of them shared the suite in downtown Buenos Aires. Noory had her own bed. John had the other room. Nick took the fold out couch, and Father Roy told them he required almost no sleep. So, he sat on the small balcony overlooking the city. John noticed that sometimes he appeared to be talking to someone and would give off a slight glow. Roy offered no explanation, and John didn't ask for one. He never felt a need to explain himself to the guys on the force when they caught him praying and didn't think Father Roy had to supply an explanation for whatever communication he had with the other side either.

John listened at the door to make sure Noory's breathing was deep and steady. He'd lived so long that he knew when one slept, woke, or pretended to sleep. He walked into the common room and sat on the fold out couch next to Nicholas.

"I'm sorry, Nicholas," John whispered.

"I know," Nick said softly. "For what it's worth, I don't hate you for it. Throughout the ages, people have had to make hard decisions for those they love. If anything, I admire you for it. I don't know if I could have done the same."

"You've done what you've had to do for centuries. You are a noble soul, Nicholas Theodoulos, but I messed up with Catherine in a way that I will never fully recover from. She died because of me," John said.

It was a sunny day in Piedmont Park, where they sat on a blanket and the wind blew Catherine's chestnut hair off her shoulders. Her laughter filled his mind like music. He reached for her hand, thinking he might finally have the courage to love her. He'd had such courage only three times before. It always ended the same. She would eventually grow old and have to leave him. He'd tried leaving her alone, but they were drawn to each other in a way that hurt them more to be apart than it did to be together. It was a familiar dance for him, but new to her. His attraction to her made him feel weak, but he'd lived long enough to understand that love was always a risk.

"What are you thinking, John?" Catherine asked.

"Nothing," he replied.

"Just be here . . . now." She got up on her knees and slid in behind John. She ran her hands down his shoulders, his arms, and then leaned over to whisper into his ear. "I need you," she whispered.

John leaned back into her embrace, tilted his head, and smiled as she closed the distance between them and kissed him passionately. He reached his hand around the back of her neck and sighed as her dark hair fell about him.

But one thing kept him from being able to truly relax. "We have to tell Jonah," he said, interrupting their reverie.

"I can always count on you to drag the logic into our magical moment," Catherine said with a sigh.

"It's what I do." John smirked. "He and I have been friends for a very long time. I owe it to him to tell him the truth. He's loved you for a while. He's going to wish that he never introduced us."

"It makes me feel a little queasy. I don't think he will take it well.

John thought of the day Jonah had introduced them. Jonah was a brilliant museum curator. He and Catherine met when he'd brought the collection of Middle Eastern artifacts to Atlanta to the exhibit at the Fernbank Science Center and Catherine's mother had only told her she was the scion just a few months before and she had the urge to connect to her past. Jonah had been researching the descendants of James; he'd gotten very close to the truth but refused to speak of it among his peers—all brilliant historical researchers who might laugh him out of academia for his theories. He asked Catherine out for coffee. They became fast friends, and she'd eventually confided the truth to him.

He already knew who John was because they'd worked together recovering an artifact that had special interest to John. It turned out to be half of an engraved pot that John's father had made for him. He didn't mind it being in a museum but had no intention of it winding up in some greedy thief's basement, slowly molding and decaying away. Jonah knew the two simply had to meet. John had kept up with the scion lineage and had even been close to some of them, but in general, tried to keep his distance unless they needed him. They were a link to his past. In some ways, the only family he had, and it hurt too badly when they passed away.

John listened to the children playing in the park and thought of how timing made all the difference. He knew that if he'd met Catherine when she was a child, he wouldn't be attracted to her now. That's how it worked with him. He couldn't shift gears once he viewed himself as a father figure to them, but he'd met Catherine when she was almost thirty and it felt like someone had punched him in the gut the second he laid eyes on her. She was strong, wise, and had a confidence about her that was intoxicating to him.

"Jonah is one of only three people who know the truth about me. We've been through a lot together." John thought of their time in Lebanon when the bombs were falling around their ears as they huddled in a ramshackle hotel in Beirut. They'd gone through a special kind of hell to track down the thief who had stolen the pottery. Fourteen hours of wondering if the next bomb was the one that would end one's life, at least for Jonah anyway, had the effect of bringing people closer. "I'll tell him tomorrow morning."

Catherine nodded and bit her bottom lip like she always did when she was worried.

"I'm sure it will be fine. He's a reasonable man," John said.

"Yeah," Catherine said as she nervously plucked at the grass. "He's just been sort of weird lately, ever since he started working on that exhibit that he's taking to Boston."

"Oh, you mean that Third Reich thing?"

"Yes. He showed it to me. It creeps me out, John. He's a little too into it. Did you know Hitler and a bunch of his SS were into black magic? I mean hard core, crazy stuff?"

"Yeah, I knew that," John said.

"Of course you did." Catherine laughed. "Do you know how annoying it is to be with a man that you can't ever tell anything new to?"

"No, I don't know. Tell me. Show me," he said, raising his eyebrows in challenge and thinking if she only knew how he found something new and amazing about her every day, she wouldn't say that.

She complied by pushing him to the ground and straddling him.

"Catherine!" John scolded as he looked around the park to see if anyone watched.

"There's the two-thousand-year-old morals, right there," she said. John sat up as she laughed at his embarrassment.

"It will be fine." John took her hand and pulled her to her feet, and they left the park.

Nothing was ever fine again.

Nick said quietly, "I know. Jonah was your friend at one time. You hoped that he could be delivered from the entity. You spared his life. I know that's why you feel you need to kill me. You only wish to protect Noory, and maybe you're right. I can feel the thing pushing and pulling at me. I believe I can control it, though."

"She's so much like her mother," John said quietly. "The strength. The confidence." John swallowed hard against the lump in his throat. He'd pushed thoughts of Catherine away so often that it felt both good and frightening to speak of her.

Nick ran his bound hands over his face and took a deep breath as he rubbed his eyes.

"You're still hearing them, aren't you?" John asked.

"Yeah," he said in a strained voice.

John knew the voice and look well. Nick was trying to tune out the tug in his spirit that came when a child was in danger nearby.

"It's an infant. Female energy. Very fragile."

It hurt John to see Nick suffer. He had to constantly remind himself of how Jonah had deceived him, but children were suffering. The Creator hadn't thrown a switch and shut the mechanism down when Nick had taken on the entity. He was still hearing them. John thought that there should be a failsafe that took away heavenly gifts when there was potential to use them for dark ends, but he realized for the thousandth time in twice as many years that he wasn't the CEO of heaven and it wasn't his job to understand anything, only to do his part.

"John, you can hold me at gunpoint the whole time. I won't resent it. Just please, let me go help her," Nick pleaded.

John exhaled and nodded. "Let me tell Father Roy what we are doing."

"Thank you," Nick said.

John looked at Nick and wondered if he were making a fatal error. He said a prayer as he walked out onto the balcony to find the priest.

CHAPTER 28

John stepped out on the balcony and took a deep breath of the night air. It was just past two in the morning, and they could still hear the late-night partygoers on the street below. John looked at Father Roy, who glanced up as if he'd been expecting him.

"A child needs help," John said. He placed his hand behind his neck and rubbed at the tension he held there. "I'm going to go out with him."

"You're worried about whether you can trust him. That's understandable. You trust the man though," Father Roy said it as a statement. Not a question.

"I don't trust the thing inside him, but I do trust the man. He has his flaws, but if I'd had to live my entire existence seeing what he has . . ." John said, feeling his heart ache in sympathy for Nick, for God only knew how many times throughout the ages he'd known him. "Would you like to come with us?"

"As much as I want to see how his gift works, I think the two of you need this time together," Father Roy said.

"Look after Noory for me?"

"Of course," Roy said as he turned his gaze back toward the Buenos Aires skyline.

John walked back inside and cut the zip ties off Nick's wrists. Nick massaged the red lines gouged in his skin and said, "Thank you, John."

John nodded and tapped his pistol beneath the thin jacket.

"Understood," Nick said without a trace of animosity.

Nick exited the building and immediately turned left. John couldn't help but think that Nick reminded him of an animal that was on the scent of something.

At the end of the building, Nick stood for only a few moments as he briefly closed his eyes, then turned right and crossed the street. An old apartment building stood in front of them with crumbling stucco and broken fire escapes. He heard a couple fighting from one of the open windows. Music poured from another as laughter drifted through the night. Nick reached up and ran his hands through his hair as he struggled to drown out the sea of humanity in the bustling city.

"Around back," Nick said suddenly.

John followed as the thought of Nick fleeing seemed less and less likely. Nick was as consumed by his quest as John had seen him be so many times before.

Without hesitation, Nick climbed up the side of a large garbage dumpster and disappeared over the side.

"Nick?" John said as he heard lots of banging around. Moments later, Nick was climbing back out with a bundle wrapped in a dirty blanket.

"John, she's not breathing! Call an ambulance!"

Nick unwrapped the small bundle and began breathing into her tiny nose and mouth at once.

Summoning the Spanish he and Nick had learned long ago and supplemented with modern slang, John dialed 911, which fortunately was the emergency number in Argentina too. After a quick conversation, he ran over, reporting, "They're on their way."

Nick had a wild look in his eyes, as if the fate of the entire world rested on reviving the girl. "John, help her, please!"

John placed his hand gently on the tiny girl. He noticed she was a couple of months old. This wasn't a stillborn hidden by a frightened teenage girl. Luckily, she was still warm enough that he knew she hadn't drifted beyond the reach of his healing. The tiny heart started beating again, softly, gently. The breath of life filled her small lungs, and she began to cry weakly.

Tears spilled from Nick's eyes as he picked the baby up and held her close to keep her warm. "Dear God, sweetie. Who did this to you?"

John couldn't help but think Nick would make a wonderful father, though perhaps he knew far too much of the dangers in the world to be brave enough to let that happen.

The ambulance and police arrived just a few minutes later. John did most of the talking. As a police lieutenant in Atlanta, he knew all the right things to say.

It was almost three a.m. when the two finally headed back to the hotel.

"I'm going to call her Sophie," Nick said with a smile.

"Still naming them, huh?" John asked.

"Yeah, it helps. The first Sophie died in Spain, 1743. She was almost one. She was already dead when I got there."

John's heart broke inside the cage of his chest. He couldn't tell whether he hurt more for those who had lost their lives or for Nick, who had to see their faces before he fell asleep at night. He was a haunted soul. John briefly put his arm around Nick and directed peace and healing toward him as he always did. For the first time in over 1600 hundred years, for the briefest of a second, he felt Nicholas recoil from his touch, as if burned, then pretend it hadn't happened.

John broke out in a cold sweat.

The first rays of sunlight began filtering in through the window. Before John even opened his eyes something felt off. He reached for his pistol, and his eyes popped open as his heart rate kicked into a racing rhythm; the gun was gone.

He got up and looked around frantically. Noory and Nick were both gone, too. He might have thought they had just snuck off to be alone together, but the absence of his pistol told a different story. Father Roy had left as well, though it was hard to believe that Nick could take him. All he had to do was collapse his mortal form and he could avoid any restraint, any violence. John had learned that when he'd tried to knock him unconscious.

He chastised himself for not putting Nick back into restraints before they'd gone to sleep, but truthfully, if the entity wanted out, it was strong enough to break the zip ties. He'd tried to shoot him the night before and in a few scant hours he'd let down his guard enough to just fall asleep as if the man didn't have an antichrist demon in him. John briefly considered that Nick had had him under some sort of mind control but then felt he was just using it as an excuse for sloppy work; he knew better.

John's head whipped around as he heard the doorknob start to turn. He had a speech ready for Noory and a swift kick in the ass for Nick scaring him. It was neither.

"I brought breakfast," Father Roy stood in the doorway with two bags. "You okay, John?"

"Noory and Nick are missing," John said.

"They were here when I left," Roy said.

John rubbed his face. "This is bad."

Chapter 29

"Where are we going?" Noory asked.

"Back to the estate near Bariloche," Nick said. He looked around the dim hallway to make sure they were truly alone. "Ready?" He opened his arms for her to travel with him. She didn't really like the way the interdimensional traveling felt. It was especially frightening now that distrust niggled at the back of her mind. But her need to know what he was after overcame her fear, and the sight of him welcoming her into his arms appealed to the side of her that had heat spreading to all the right places.

She stepped into his arms with a shudder—a feeling as if she were crossing a great chasm on a bridge that crumbled behind her as she went. She was never one for prayer, but she whispered a small, desperate one as she closed her eyes, aware of the dampness behind her eyelids and the dryness of her throat as she swallowed hard, and they faded into oblivion.

After only seconds, she felt they'd regained their earthbound forms, but everything was completely dark, and she felt a presence in the darkness. Her next thought was even more frightening: What if they were stuck between realms? "Are we trapped?" she asked.

"No love. We're in a cavern." He whispered the words into her ear, and even in the black and with the fear of not knowing what was going on, she felt her desire for him rise. She got the feeling he knew it, too. Before letting go of her, he grazed his lips across her neck. Though his arms were no longer wrapped around her, he kept her protectively close.

After pulling a flashlight from his jacket, he moved the beam across the floor as if he were looking for something. It finally landed on a couple of battery-powered camping lanterns. Noory realized that he'd already been here. He hadn't mentioned it to her. She hoped he had told John but got the feeling he hadn't.

He handed her one of the lanterns. "Stay close to me. There's something in here," he whispered.

"I know. I feel it too. Any idea what it is?"

"Probably something left to guard the relic," he said. "It's a little too aware of the fact that you're a woman. I can feel its intention."

A low growl came from Nick. She'd never heard him do that before and realized it was a threat to whatever lurked in the darkness, but it made Noory wonder who to be more afraid of, whatever was in there with them or whatever was inside Nick. Dropping his lantern, he shoved Noory behind him and reached into the darkness inhumanly fast. She heard something slam against the wall.

"You won't touch her!" Nick said in a deadly tone. "She's mine."

She initially felt a thrill at what Nick had said to the creature. After all, she wanted to be "his." She wanted to be his in ways that made her blush even when she was alone. At the moment, though, the words felt wrong to her, and she couldn't piece together why.

Noory hadn't heard the being say anything and wondered how Nick had heard it. She could only guess it was a heightened sense that the entity had given him. She lifted her lantern to see what Nick had pinned to the wall. It had a human form, male, looked to be in his twenties, dressed in jeans and a t-shirt, yet it had violet eyes that flashed when the light hit them. The pupils were shaped like that of a goat. When he trained his eyes on Noory, the lust they gave off felt beyond threatening. It only glanced at Nick who had the thing pinned with one hand. It couldn't take its eyes off Noory. Its long tongue came out and licked its lips.

Nick had had enough. "The hell you will," Nick said through gritted teeth. He pulled the creature into the darkness beyond Noory's lamp, and she heard a loud squeal, then a crack followed by a thud. She knew the thing was dead.

Terror rushed through Noory. Her mind raced to understand why she was afraid. She knew that sometimes it became necessary, especially when dealing with lower-level entities, to destroy them. She knew, without any doubt whatsoever, that the goat-eyed demon had every intention of raping her. No doubt. No remorse. His intention would have been clear to a regular mortal, but to her heightened awareness, it came off him in waves. She knew Nick was simply saving her from the lurid brutality of the demoniac creature.

Yet something about the encounter bothered her. She realized what it was as Nick turned to face her: the killing came too easy to him now. Nick, her Nick, was a man of conscience. He did what he had to do to keep the children safe. Sometimes that meant violence, but his reaction to it now felt off. Too easy. She couldn't help but feel that it was changing him, bit by bit. How long before Nick became unrecognizable? It was the first time she'd held any sort of sympathetic insight into what might have happened to her father. She had to remind herself that Jonah had taken an entity willingly, for selfish reasons. Nick had done it to save her life. It was different, but the results could end up the same. Her eyes burned again. She moved her lantern to arm's length, hoping that Nick wouldn't see her crying.

It was no use.

"Don't be scared, Noory." He reached up and brushed tears away from her cheeks. "I won't let anything hurt you."

Each word hit Noory like a punch. He might defeat a thousand enemies threatening to hurt her, but she knew at some point, he wouldn't be able to save her from himself.

"I'm fine," she whispered.

"I know. I know you could have beaten the hell out of him yourself. It just feels good to look out for you now and then." He leaned over and kissed her forehead.

She wondered if the next kiss was the kiss goodbye—when Nick would no longer be Nick. She scolded herself for getting emotional and forced herself to move on to the larger picture: how much did he know and how much the entity might keep from him? "What are we here for, Nick?"

"Honestly, I don't think I will know until I see it. It's an ancient relic. I'm figuring this thing out on a need-to-know basis."

"Isn't that awfully convenient for the being inside you? It could lead us both into a trap."

"Noory, I have control over this thing. Please trust me."

He squeezed her hand, and she wanted to believe. She wanted to believe so bad that her heart ached from the effort of it, and that was the problem. She shouldn't have to try so hard to believe. *Why didn't he bring John with us?*

"I can feel the energy coming from this direction," he said.

The tunnel branched off and Nick took a left.

She said, "We should have brought John with us. He knows a lot about old relics."

"Well, The Beloved has lost faith in me as of late."

"What did you say?" Noory asked as her heartbeat ratcheted up enough to make her chest hurt.

"Huh?" Nick asked.

Had he called John "Beloved" before?

They stepped over rubble and stumbled their way forward. It looked as if someone had collapsed the tunnel on purpose at some point. Her engineering skills told her this didn't look like natural decay.

There was a faint, whitish blue glow in the distance. When they reached the source, Nick had to move rubble off it. Noory worried about the tunnel becoming unstable as heavy chunks of concrete were tossed aside. No normal human could have done it. It would have required heavy equipment. Nick seemed unconcerned about collapse. He was working frantically. Just when she was about to stop him for fear it would all come down on her head, he stopped.

"This is it," Nick said. He kneeled down and ran his hand across the faintly glowing box.

"Can you tell what it does?" Noory asked.

Nick ran his fingers across the ancient engravings as if reading Braille.

"Wow! Interesting," he said. "This thing sends messages. Nowadays it would be through radio waves or basically anything picking up a signal from a tower. It works subliminally. It's ancient, so I can only assume at some point we had more technology than we thought. The writing that I *can* read is Egyptian."

Noory thought about the implications of that and shuddered. "This is bad," she said.

"Or good, depending on how you use it, right?"

"No! I think you get into some debatable free will issues. We need to take this thing to John and let him figure out how to destroy it."

He turned to face her with a look of exasperation. "Dear God, Noory! I'm seventeen hundred years old. You don't think I can figure out the right thing to do with this?"

"I didn't mean to offend you, Nick. It's just that you have to remember you have something inside you. You need to be cautious."

"Cautious!" He got up and was just inches from her face in mere seconds. Noory sucked in her breath. "Do you understand the amount of restraint I've had to have? All the things I've had to keep him from doing? Not only that. He's amplified my own desires." With that, he grabbed her around the waist and pulled her to him so roughly that the wind was almost knocked from her. He shoved her against the concrete wall and began kissing her with a fierceness that made her knees buckle. He pushed his pelvis against her and reached down and pulled her thighs up so that she had to wrap her legs around him to keep from falling to the ground.

Noory's mind screamed at her to knock the hell out of him. He'd always treated her like a lady before. She somehow knew that if the being suddenly left him, he'd be ashamed of handling her in such a way. Yet . . . she wanted him. She wrapped her legs around him tighter and pushed her hips up and forward with a moan that made Nick smile against her lips. Then, for reasons she couldn't explain, she had a thought that made her stop what she was doing and break out in a cold sweat: she remembered what Jonah had done to her mother while he had a beast inside him.

"What's wrong, Noory?" Nick said, breathing heavily.

"We can't do this anymore until we've found a way to get that thing out of you."

He ignored her comment. "You want me too. I can feel it." He looked at her with hunger clearly written across his face.

"I do, but I want it to be just *you* from now on. Not you with a demon riding shotgun. That's just how it has to be, Nick."

He nodded, set her back down, and took her hand, pulling her forward toward the relic. He'd shifted gears so fast she could barely keep up.

"Look at the words on the side here. I could read some of them, but not all. Do any of them seem familiar?" he asked.

"I don't know any of the ancient languages."

"Just give it a look and see what you think," he encouraged.

Noory leaned down, hating the way the relic made her feel. Whether it was just paranoia over what it might be or an actual sense of evil coming from it, she couldn't tell. As she moved her lantern closer, a strange sensation came over her, and her mouth began to move. She tried to stop the words from coming out, but she felt compelled to say them. Noory didn't recognize the language, yet she instinctively knew she was releasing some sort of lock or spell that kept the thing dormant. Wind swirled around her even though they were closed in the tunnel. It was only a sentence but enough to know once the words were out . . . it was too late. She fell back onto her butt, then leaned over and vomited.

Nick took the box in one arm and Noory in the other and they faded into the in-between. Within a second or two, they were on the streets of Buenos Aires in the alleyway outside their hotel. Noory tried to slap at Nick's arm around her waist, but she was falling. He caught her as she fought nausea and dizziness, and she knew she couldn't make it up to their hotel room. She just wanted to see John—more than any other time in her life. She wanted a father to tell her everything would be okay because right now, she couldn't believe it.

Nick kneeled in front of her. She took a swing at him as sickening clarity made her feel stupid for trusting him. She cracked him in the side of the head despite being too weak to make it hurt him like she wanted to.

"You used me," she sobbed.

Nick sat back up, rubbing the side of his face. "I did what I had to do to save us all, Noory. We can use this to help the kids. Just think about what it can do. We can program it to stop kids from making choices that get them killed. Don't you want that? We can program it to stop rapists, child molesters, people who beat their children senseless. Noory, you've only had to deal with the horror of humanity for twenty-five years. Imagine having to live it every damn day for seventeen hundred years!" he spoke with a grief in his eyes that Noory knew was one hundred percent Nick.

"I know you hurt beyond anything I can ever imagine, but that thing is dangerous. The beast inside you is convincing you it will help you end your misery. Nick, it's using you. It will use that device to hypnotize people and bring about the Fourth Reich. That's what it wanted since the very beginning. Please, just let me take it to John. You trust John; you always have."

"That man tried to kill me, Noory! Do you have any idea how bad that hurt?"

"You know why he did that, and we can't escape the fact that you used me. You lured me there; knew I would trust you because I love you." After the words were out, Noory looked around frantically. Her brain caught up a few seconds later, and she understood why. She'd just admitted her feelings to Nick, and she wanted to run, escape, especially after being used. But it was too late. Too late to take the words back. Too late to avoid being used. So, she continued. "Then when I got there, you tricked me into reading that inscription without telling me what it was. That's the nature of evil. That is not the Nick that I . . ." Noory tried to stand but collapsed again. She didn't know what that thing had done to her brain, but the vertigo was so intense she couldn't get her balance.

Nick wrapped his arms around her and whispered: "Remember that I always love you."

The next second they were standing in the hotel room with John looking at Nick like he was about to try and kill him again.

Father Roy looked at Nick with love . . . and grief. Nick set Noory down on the bed.

Noory's look of shock and betrayal wasn't lost on John. "What did you do to her?" John said in a deadly tone.

Nick took John's pistol out of his jacket and set it on the coffee table.

"She's fine." Nick said. "Sometime later you will wonder about last night; saving Sophie wasn't a trick." A tear ran down his cheek, and a second later, he vanished with the relic in hand.

Chapter 30

Noory stood in the shadows of Nick's penthouse building, waiting for him to come out. He'd been leaving every night for the last week, around eleven or twelve. She followed him as he did what he always did: he saved children. She'd watched as he pulled a fifteen-year-old boy off a bridge and sat there talking to him until the sun came up. That was all Nick. She knew an entity wouldn't give a damn about that. She watched him rescue a young girl from an abusive boyfriend who'd beaten her in an Atlanta alley. He then walked her to the shelter Noory ran. Every single night, he rescued them. If he'd been using the device to do what he'd said, then there wouldn't be anyone to rescue. Noory wondered if she had gotten through to him, but every time she tried to let him off the hook, she chastised herself. He'd deceived her.

John had already been through his apartment and could find no trace of the relic. He had explained to her he could put Nick away in the monastery so that it would be unlikely he'd be able to use his powers, much less the device. However, he held off hoping Nick would lead them to the device. Nick had left Argentina in seconds. It took them a full day to get home. So, he'd had plenty of time to hide the device. Noory wondered if he was waiting on someone or something else to arrive. She also knew the other reason John held off imprisoning Nick was Noory's insistence that they could save him. Father Roy echoed that sentiment and often kept watch with Noory through the cooling Atlanta nights. She enjoyed his company more and more.

"Something's on your mind, Light?" Roy asked as they followed Nick through Piedmont Park.

Noory smelled fall in the air. The trees gave off a different scent when they changed colors, and Noory wondered if it was her scion senses or if everyone noticed it. She contemplated if Roy would even know the answer to what was on her mind.

"If John could imprison Nick, then why did he try to kill him?" She said it all in a rush, not knowing just how deeply the question disturbed her until it came out.

Father Roy breathed in deeply and exhaled before answering. "John's a police lieutenant, Noory. He's learned to see patterns. He had the sickening experience of seeing evil close and personal. When Jonah killed Catherine, it was the worst thing that had happened to him in all his two thousand years. If he lives another two thousand, I don't think he will ever truly get past it. He couldn't take the idea that it might happen again. He knew if he imprisoned Nick, you'd be able to get him out. So, he thought the very best way to protect you and ultimately protect him from being haunted by another fatal mistake was to end Nick. He knows that Nick's soul would be safe. Ultimately, I'm not sure John could have pulled the trigger, though, or do what he'd have to do after to make the death 'stick.'" Roy shuddered.

"I didn't know you knew much about his history with my mother."

"Living with John has been a real privilege. As a priest getting to meet an actual disciple . . . it's mind blowing, but not only that, I'm glad he feels like he can talk to me. It often must be a lonely existence for him. He has you, of course, but there are things he might not want to burden you with or feel comfortable discussing with his daughter."

Noory nodded. Although she would like to think John could tell her anything, she knew he had a need to protect her feelings and his own, for that matter.

"I guess I still don't understand why he doesn't imprison him now. He knows lots of archaic knowledge. I think we could find a way to make the entity tell us where the device is," Noory argued.

"He doesn't do it because of *you*. He knows that you have to come to it on your own or you will rescue him. You're a woman in love."

"But I'm not stupid," Noory argued.

"No one thinks you're stupid. We just know what love can do," Roy said with a smile.

"You were that head over heels with your boyfriend?" she asked, hoping she wasn't crossing a line or tearing open an old wound but at the same time, feeling like he might have a burden to release as well.

"Indeed, I was. Jeff was, is, he corrected . . . everything beautiful."

Noory looked at this man, a powerhouse of light, love, and strength. "You are everything beautiful, my friend, and I'm so glad you're here."

Father Roy smiled, then dabbed at the corners of his eyes. "Thank you, sister."

The two walked on in silence. Finally, they found Nick sitting on a park bench talking to some poor, stoned, weeping teenager. If there was evil in the man, she couldn't see it.

The next day, Noory was at work yawning a jaw-popper from following Nick night after night. It felt good to be back at work. In the day-to-day of running the shelter, she could almost pretend that everything was normal again.

"You wouldn't be so exhausted if you would get some sleep instead of stalking your boyfriend every night."

Noory jumped when she realized who it was.

Nick noticed her surprise, and his smile widened, revealing dazzling white teeth against his sun-kissed skin and dark hair. The suit and tie he wore appeared to be immaculately tailored. She couldn't help but notice that he looked healthier and more rested than ever—despite the fact that she knew he was out all night, every night. That's when it hit her. She hadn't seen him drink since he'd taken the entity. She couldn't believe she hadn't noticed before. He had always drunk as he tracked down his charges. He leaned in close, and she noticed that the aroma of the licorice-smelling ouzo no longer clung to him as it had done before. She cringed, realizing he was more attractive than ever.

Anger welled up inside her that he'd had the nerve to refer to himself as "her boyfriend" after the way he'd used her. She wanted to scream at him that she wasn't his girlfriend, but she knew Nick was still in there somewhere and couldn't do it.

"What do you need, Nick?"

"A date. A colleague of mine is throwing a party this Friday night, and I want to be with the most beautiful woman in the room," Nick said.

Though she wanted to say no, she also wanted to jump across the desk into his arms and was afraid he would ask another woman to be his date. But she also knew his statement didn't make sense. Though Nick was a wizard for making sound investments, he really didn't have what anyone would call "colleagues." Something was up, and she felt that it might have something to do with the endgame that the entity was working toward.

"All right. I'll go."

"Excellent. I'll pick you up at seven. It's a black-tie affair, so you might have to lose the nose ring and combat boots. You know I dig them, but . . ."

"Hey, I can be elegant. Don't underestimate me," she said with a smile.

"Oh, I never do." He kissed her quickly on the cheek. Before reaching the door, he turned back around. "I almost forgot." He reached into his pocket and pulled out something small and threw it to Noory. She plucked it out of the air. "Tell John I found his little bug. If he wants to know what I'm doing, he can just come ask me."

CHAPTER 31

Noory stood in front of the full-length mirror and studied her reflection. She had chosen a classic little black dress and her hair was in a sophisticated side bun. It felt wrong to be this excited for a night out with Nick, but she couldn't help herself. She'd missed him terribly, even though she knew he wasn't entirely himself, to say the least. However, she had been smart enough to tell John she was going out with Nick and to reassure him she would keep her phone on her so he could track her GPS signal.

When she heard the knock at the door, her heartbeat hammered like a metronome gone berserk.

Nick stood in the doorway, speechless for several moments. She knew he had never seen her out of her street clothes before, but she didn't think she looked *that* good. Noory felt her cheeks turning a bright crimson as he stared.

She couldn't look away from him either. His suit brought out his old-world sophistication. Ever since she'd known him, there was an undercurrent of something regal that Noory couldn't quite describe but made her want to be near it, to understand it, to love Nick as she traced it to its source.

He held out his arm to her. "My lady," he said, as if reading her mind.

They rode to the party in Nick's Lexus. The proximity to him was making her stomach do flip flops but she tried to remain cool-headed. She focused on feeling the energy within the car: it was Nick, and it wasn't.

She realized they were heading into Buckhead, where many of the nicest homes were in Atlanta. They drove up to an enormous house and Nick handed his keys to one valet as another opened Noory's car door to let her out. Nick came around and took her arm once more, and she was very aware of the warmth coming off him. Again, she chided herself not to let him get to her, but her feelings had become a runaway train. The more she fought them, the more insistent they became.

The two walked into the ballroom, and Nick immediately waved at a man who appeared to be in his late forties. He was tall, good-looking with a little grey starting to appear at his temples, but most of all, his air of confidence made him stand out.

"Robert, good to see you again." The two shook hands.

"This is Noory," Nick said.

"Pleased to meet you, Noory," the man said as he gently shook her hand. "I'm Robert Billings."

"Likewise. So, what business are you in?" Noory said, feeling weird about snooping but also realizing it was an ordinary thing to discuss at a party such as this one. She felt a twinge of irritation coming off Nick, but he'd brought her there knowing she would be inquisitive.

"My company builds cell phone towers. What do you do?" he asked.

"I manage a homeless shelter for teens and young adults downtown."

"Ah, you're doing the Lord's work," the man said with a smile. "My company donates a certain percentage of profits to charity every year. Do you have a card or something for me?"

"Of course." Noory reached into her clutch and retrieved a card. Despite the circumstances, she felt a thrill at the idea of being able to get better supplies for those who came through their facility.

Robert looked at her card and slid it into his breast pocket. "Well, you two enjoy some drinks and hors d'oeuvres. Nick, you and I can talk a little business later?"

"Sure, sounds good," Nick replied.

Robert gave him a nod and left them, calling to more newly arrived guests.

"Nice place," Noory said, shifting to small talk.

"Yeah," Nick said in his usual unimpressed way that made Noory smile.

They stepped out onto the balcony. The music drifted out, making the crowd noise less intrusive. Nick bowed regally as if they were in at a palace a couple hundred years earlier. He stood up straight and offered her his hand.

She took it; he pulled her close, and they began dancing. Noory started to argue that she couldn't dance, but Nick was so good at leading that it didn't matter. She just moved as he did.

"This is what heaven is like: no one needing either of us. Just you and me and the moonlight."

Noory sighed deeply and went on his fantasy with him. "We dance, drink champagne, eat tiny quiches, and someone else takes care of them."

"It could be that way, you know," he said.

"Maybe the part about eating the tiny quiches, but I don't think the rest of it would work. That's not reality, Nick." She knew why he'd said it and didn't want to walk down that road. "You look very handsome tonight."

"So do you, Light." He spun her around unexpectedly and she felt a little lightheaded. "There's something I need to apologize for," he said.

"What?" Noory asked, though she could think of a few things right off the bat.

He looked down at her body, then lifted his eyes without lifting his head. "I think you know what for." The action made her blood sizzle and rush southward as she rubbed her thighs together. *Damn.* She began to think his apology might need an apology. "I didn't have a lot of control when we were in Bariloche. I thought I did, but when I think back on the way I grabbed you and . . . well, don't get me wrong, I enjoyed it. I just want to treat you with the respect you deserve."

"Well, I mean, there is a time and a place for that sort of thing. I didn't hate it," Noory said with a wink.

Nick laughed. "Yeah, true enough," he said with a sly smile. "It just isn't . . . or wasn't . . . ."

"It wasn't you. The entity was driving you. That's why it feels wrong in hindsight," she offered.

"Yeah."

"But there are also times when you have an instinct to defend the thing inside you, don't you? I'm not trying to be accusatory. Just, you know, real," she offered as she cringed at the idea that she was offending him.

They both stopped dancing as she awaited his response. "Sometimes I do, and I know I have to be careful about that."

His honesty surprised her. He took her by the hand and walked her over to the balcony that overlooked the sprawling garden below. Beyond it, the moon reflected off a large pond. "Perhaps our heaven will be just you and me living a normal life. We'll get a little house somewhere where we can walk to a coffee shop on Saturday mornings to get your caffeine fix."

"Your first thought was for my habit. I appreciate that. Or perhaps you really don't want me to be grouchy in this daydream," Noory said.

"That's part of it, yes," he said with a laugh. "Nah, I just want to make you happy." He pulled her to him and kissed her forehead, her eyelids, and then delicately rubbed his thumb across her lips before kissing her softly, then pressing their foreheads together.

This was Nick, her Nick.

He put his hand behind her neck and kissed her again with the same longing he had shown in Argentina but with a wholly different presentation that made her feel loved, respected, cherished. "I love you, Noory," he whispered.

"I love you, too, Nick." She pulled him to her and wrapped her arms around him, feeling that if she could just hold him like this, she could keep him safe from the beast inside, from anything. The magic ended when they heard a few women chatting excitedly as they came out onto the balcony.

Nick squeezed her hand and leaned over a little to catch her eye. "It's going to be okay. You'll see."

Noory squeezed back. "And I'll be here," she said as she lifted their entwined hands to show him she was still holding on.

As soon as they walked back in, Robert called to them. "There you are. Feel like talking a little business now?"

"Of course," Nick said.

"Noory, let me introduce you to my wife, Jacqueline, and her friend, Ellen."

"Pleased to meet you," the two said cordially.

"They can keep you company while Nick and I talk shop."

Noory hoped her agitation at being left to gossip with the women while the big, strong men talked business, wasn't showing. She smiled and nodded. "Great," she said.

Nick squeezed her hand, obviously knowing she would find it annoying to be handed off this way. It spoke of how well Nick knew her and made her feel even closer to him.

The two went into Robert's office as Noory sat in the waiting area just outside the door with the other two women. They drank cosmos and made chitchat until the other two got bored. "Noory, I think we're going to go on out here, ignore the carbs, and see if there's any more of those mini quiches wrapped in the puff pastry. Wanna come with?"

"No, thanks. I'm going to kick off my shoes for a bit and wait on Nick."

The two women nodded and left as Noory sighed in relief. She wanted to get a handle on who Robert was and what they were saying to each other that couldn't be said in front of her. Noory walked around the well-appointed room with a leather couch and chairs. She looked at the pictures on the walls and various plaques acclaiming Robert's success.

Noory continued walking around the waiting area, trying to learn all that she could. When she passed the window, she saw something move out of the corner of her eye. She doubled back to the window and looked out but saw nothing.

"Sounds good, Nicholas," Robert said as he slapped Nick on the back while they exited his office.

"Sorry, Noory. Did my wife leave you in here all by yourself?" Robert asked.

Noory had to grit her teeth to keep from telling him she was a grown woman who didn't require a babysitter. "Oh, I'm fine. It was a nice break from the noise."

"Well, feel free to stay and enjoy the party. It was lovely to meet you, Noory," Robert said.

"Likewise," she said.

As the two exited the room, Robert went to pour himself a scotch from the small cart beside his desk. When Noory glanced back, he tipped his drink at her and winked. The action made her skin crawl, though she couldn't say exactly why.

"Ready to get out of here?" Nick asked when they got back to the party.

"Oh yeah," Noory replied with relief.

The valet brought the Lexus around as Noory's mind spun with questions. There was a lot she wanted to ask Nick, but if she were to gain his trust, she couldn't be too suspicious. But Nick also knew she wasn't one to hold back.

"You're awfully quiet over there, Light," Nick said.

"Yeah, I'm just tired."

"No, you're just worried and maybe a little suspicious," Nick replied.

"Can you blame me?"

"Nope. You don't like Robert, do you?"

"I do not," Noory replied.

Nick smiled. "He's a little misogynistic. I knew you would pick up on that."

"Yeah. So why are you in business with him?"

"I may as well tell you. If I don't, you and John, and possibly Father Roy, will bug my apartment, follow me, and snoop until you figure it out anyway, right?"

"Pretty much, yeah."

"We're figuring out how to hook up the device we recovered to a cell phone tower," Nick said.

Noory struggled to keep the emotion from her voice. She felt her body go numb as her worst fear was realized. "So, you're going through with it?"

"I am. We can have that normal life."

"No, we can't, Nick."

Nick's voice became heavy. "How many times have you lost?" he asked.

Noory struggled not to sound defensive. "What's that supposed to mean?"

"It means you've never tried with all your heart to save one of those kids then found them lying face down in a pool of their own blood and knew it was because you failed them."

Noory swallowed hard. "Yes. I failed Calista."

"Jesus. You knew her?"

"Yes."

He pulled up to Noory's apartment and cut the engine. They sat in silence for a long while.

"Listen to me. That was my failure, not yours," Nick said with a tone of voice that conveyed if he could make her believe it by sheer force of will, he would.

"It isn't always on you. I didn't find the right words to say to her. I couldn't get through." She opened her mouth to speak again, but the words were choked off by the lump in her throat. She felt Nick's eyes on her and wanted to take him upstairs to her bed and drown in him, entity or not. But she knew it wasn't the best of reasons to take him there.

"Why didn't you tell me that night?"

"Well, you were . . ." She didn't want to say it. She knew it would be one more thing to feed his self-loathing.

"I was drunk."

"You were crushed."

"You were hurting too, but I couldn't be there for you because I was too busy throwing a pity party."

"After seventeen hundred years, could I fare any better with it? I'm not sure I could."

"I wasn't there for you. I won't fail you again."

"Good. Then don't mess with this device. There's something wrong with it. If you didn't have the entity inside you, you would know that."

Nick sighed and shook his head. "Except for that."

They sat in silence for a while. Noory knew there was nothing she could say at this point to change his mind. Nick finally got out of the car and went around to open Noory's door. They walked up to her apartment in the same uncomfortable silence.

Noory unlocked the door, but Nick made no attempt to enter. He pulled her to him and held her tight. "I love you."

"I love you, too," she whispered.

"Always will," he said as he kissed her forehead.

Despite his words, she already felt him slipping away. Grief filled her heart as she worked hard to keep from crying.

She stood and watched him walk down the hallway and into the elevator, where he simply looked at the floor, unwilling to meet her eye.

Noory hurried to her apartment window and looked out at Nick's car on the street below. Like a child longing for comfort, she watched him walk to the car, silently hoping he would come back up. Come back to tell her he had seen reason. *At least turn around and look at me.* He didn't. She turned aside before he opened his car door, not being able to take watching him get inside and drive away.

CHAPTER 32

Nick walked to his car parked just outside Noory's apartment. He felt a hollow spot where his heart was. "You don't need her," something deep inside whispered. Yet just before he reached for the car door, he felt a soft longing, pure, unconditional, bloom inside his chest like a warm summer breeze. He turned around to stare up at Noory's window to see if she might be looking for him, too. The curtains fluttered as if she'd just turned away. His heart ached to see her face there. Maybe she'd had enough.

He started his car and drove down to the next light just in time to see something disappear around the corner, with claws hanging from what looked like human hands. Nick followed it, worried that it might have been creeping around Noory's apartment. He heard the familiar call of a child in distress. Thinking it might have had something to do with what he'd seen; he parked his car on the side of the road, got out on foot, and began following the call. It got stronger and stronger till it seemed to be all around him. That's when he saw her. It was Grace. According to Noory, she'd been doing well at her aunt's house. So why in the world was she out here?

He heard her laughing with a friend. They had just come out of a late movie, but the tall being was creeping around them, stalking them. It had an uncanny way of blending into shadow, almost becoming shadow. He watched it observe them as it clicked its long, sharp nails together. He could feel its desire to pounce.

Nick faded into the in-between realm and came out behind the creature. He grabbed it and pulled it back into the other realm and emerged with it four blocks away in an abandoned lot.

The being looked around confused as its eyes flashed, revealing orange irises, long eyelashes, and sharp cheekbones. It took a swipe at Nick, and he grabbed it by the wrist before its talons had the chance to take half his face off. He punched it in the side of the head.

"Who sent you?" Nick demanded.

"Fuck off!" the creature snarled.

Nick punched it in the gut as the creature took another swipe at him. This time, his sharp claws drew blood across Nick's chest. Despite the initial sting, within moments, the pain subsided. "This was my favorite suit, asshole!" Nick said. Fueled by the adrenaline rush of pain, Nick punched the creature several times until it doubled over.

"Who sent you?" Nick demanded again.

"None of your business," it snarled.

Nick thought of what the creature was planning for Grace and her friend; the way the creature had clicked its razor-sharp claws together as it watched Grace; it was pure bloodlust. The thing intended to kill her and enjoy it. Then Nick thought of what he'd said to Noory just a half hour ago about whether she'd ever seen one of the kids face down in a pool of blood. He almost vomited at the idea that it would happen again. The idea of Noory's heart breaking at Grace's death would've been nearly as reprehensible as the act itself.

He felt anger at himself that he'd been compelled to ask her such a question to begin with. As he pummeled the creature before him, he found that he'd come to a point where he couldn't tell the difference between beating this creature to death and his own inner monster. He wanted them both gone. He looked down to find the thing was barely conscious. He kneeled on the ground and grabbed it by its gelled black hair, "I will ask you one last time. If you don't answer, I'll finish you off," Nick said between gritted teeth. "Who the hell sent you?"

"Robert Billings," it croaked as it spit out two of its pointed teeth.

Nick took hold of him and, together, they disappeared.

Nick checked first to make sure Robert was alone in his office then burst into the mortal realm without preamble and slammed the entity down, face first, onto Robert's desk. Nick kept its head pinned there as Robert jerked back in shock.

"You sent this piece of shit to kill one of Noory's kids. Never pull anything like this again, or I will take that device you want and disappear. You know I can."

"First of all, it's bleeding all over my desk. Please remove it," Robert waved his hand as if it were a mere nuisance.

Nick ignored him.

"Second, we need to ensure that woman of yours understands exactly how much this device is needed. That's why I sent Damascus. And third, you need me every bit as much as I need you," Robert said and took another sip of his scotch.

"The hell I do!" Nick said with a deadly laugh. "You're not the only man with cell phone towers. Hell, for that matter, it could be a radio station or TV. My options are endless. Yours are not."

"You know I work for some very important people," Robert bragged.

"Can I get up now?" the creature sputtered.

"No!" Nick said as he tightened his grip.

"Keep in mind that I know where your girlfriend and everyone she loves lives," Robert said smugly.

"This is uncomfortable," the creature whined again.

"Shut up!" Robert and Nick said in unison before the creature lost consciousness and slid to the floor.

As he hit the ground, Nick flew across Roberts's desk, knocked him out of his chair, and pinned him to the floor. A low growl came out of Nick, and his eyes rolled back in his head for a moment as a low voice that rattled the furniture in Robert's office came from Nick's chest. "I am Amaros, and my host demands cooperation of you. Do not test me." Amaros sent images to flood Robert's mind that were so frightening he couldn't move or speak.

Nick shook his head as if to clear it. He looked around, realizing he had missed a few moments. He didn't want Robert to see his confusion. He knew, no matter what had happened that it would be in his best interest to stay in control until he walked out the door. When the man looked at him in stark terror, he knew the entity likely had shown itself. He knew nothing short of that could have rattled the cocky bastard.

"Stay away from Noory and anyone she loves, or I will come for you." Nick promised.

Robert nodded, and Nick saw a terror there that told him he need not worry.

But as he appeared back in the parking lot where his Lexus was parked, he did worry. He worried a lot. He couldn't help but be grateful that something had happened to scare Robert enough to guarantee Noory's safety and the safety of those around her, but the fact that it had taken him over so easily scared the hell out of him.

CHAPTER 33

John heard a knock at his door as he and Father Roy watched reruns of *The Simpsons*, which John thought was endlessly hilarious due to Bart's hijinks.

John opened the door and was surprised—which didn't happen very often to one who was over two thousand years old. Nick stood there with blood splattered over his shirt, which had clearly been ripped by claws. But it wasn't the shirt that bothered John. It was the fear painted on Nick's face.

"Don't worry, it's my blood," Nick said, apparently thinking John was scared it had come someone else.

"Do you need a first aid kit?" Roy asked.

"It's okay. I'm almost healed up by now," Nick said with a nonchalant shrug that John could tell he didn't feel but had said for their benefit.

John caught Roy looking at Nick with sympathy, anyway. It astounded John how the man always seemed to be in Nick's corner. It was gentle and humbling to the man in him, no doubt threatening to the beast within Nick. But Nick was no fool. He and the entity both knew there was a power to compassion like Roy's that was often lost on the foolish because such power often showed up in things no one would deem powerful: the mother who gives her time, sleep, energy, and patience to her child, the father who works two jobs to provide for his family and never complains, the priest who leaves the beautiful embrace of eternity to assist a hopeless alcoholic. It was the reason John never truly tired of mortality, these moments of blinding beauty.

"Do you want to talk?" John asked as he motioned for Nick to come in.

"No, I just want to be here . . . for a while."

"Good enough," John said as he put an arm around his friend. For a moment, Nick seemed to fight to hold back the relief John knew he felt at his healing touch.

John gave Nick one of his shirts to replace his ripped and bloody one. The three talked little but watched TV until John and Nick eventually fell asleep.

At some point during the night, even Roy dozed, and Nick had gone.

Roy and John had coffee and watched the sun paint the sky for a brand-new day.

"You would think someone as old as me would know what to say to him," John said as he rubbed a hand across his stubble.

"Sometimes there isn't anything you can say, John. It's just a matter of being present."

"Well, that's all I have right now."

Roy lifted his cup with a reassuring smile. "And that is enough for now." He looked out at the sunrise with a peace that invigorated John's exhausted mind.

CHAPTER 34

That afternoon, Noory sat at John's kitchen table telling him and Father Roy about what she'd seen at the party Nick had taken her to. "There were photos of cell phone towers, years-old commemorative photos. There was an enormous map on the wall of all the towers he'd built. He's taken photos with governors and congressmen," Noory said. "This dude is seriously connected."

"What's the name of his company?" John asked.

"Second Sight Communications."

John set his coffee down. "This is worse than I thought. I was thinking this was just Elliot and Nick trying to find a local tower to hook this thing up and create a safe radius to give Nick a little peace of mind, but Nick is involved with Second Sight now. He has a device with the ability to send subliminal messages to the entire country. It means this thing is bigger than all of us. These people aligned with Robert are everywhere, Noory. The highest levels of power with one agenda: to create a utopia. *As they see it.* It sounds great, but it comes at the price of free will. It rarely works because there will always be some who won't want to get on board, but with a device like the one Nick has . . . We have to find that thing."

"Wait. I thought Jonah's agenda was to bring about the Fourth Reich. Why are we talking about some utopia now? Aren't those two totally different things?" Noory asked.

"Well, no, not really," John said.

Roy nodded in agreement with John. "The Third Reich was a utopia if you were on that side of it. These people convince themselves they're doing a just thing. That's what's so insidious about it."

John continued. "When Jonah carried Azazel, the idea of dominance expressed itself the way it did because Azazel was the influencing force behind the rise of the Third Reich. It was a formula that worked. Once it infected Germany, it started oozing beyond its borders. Now that Azazel is gone and Amaros is in the driver's seat, the way he intends to accomplish his goals is different, but it's really the same thing. Second Sight is a far more dangerous route, too. It's already set up on a global scale, has been for a while. They're all selling the same utopian idea. Did you get any idea why Nick was meeting with that particular man? There must be a reason Second Sight is using him."

"Robert is in the business of building and maintaining cell towers. Their plan is to use Nick's device to send a signal from the towers. And these things are all linked . . . No, this is crazy, John. We're grasping at straws here. I don't want to be one of those unstable people who sit in their basement at night thinking they see weird patterns on different websites and start building a bunker and stockpiling dehydrated eggs. That's bonkers."

"They're not all crazy, Noory," John said softly as he looked over at Father Roy.

Roy's suspicious look wasn't lost on Noory.

Noory rolled her eyes. "Oh, Lord, not you, too!"

Roy looked at John. "How does she not see the irony?"

"I don't know. She's always been like this," John said, smiling.

"Like what?" Noory asked.

"Your father here is two thousand years old," Roy began. She liked that he always called John her father without thinking twice about it.

"Two thousand and some change," John said with a laugh.

Roy smiled. "Yes, and some change. You are the great granddaughter of James, and your boyfriend is Santa Claus."

"Yeah, so?" Noory said in all sincerity.

Roy threw his hands in the air and looked at John again. "How do you put up with this?" he asked John.

"It's the siren song of normalcy," John replied. "We oddities have all heard its alluring call at one point or another."

Roy laughed. "Noory, if your life is possible, then why in the world wouldn't some of those 'crazy' conspiracies be true? You've gotten far too used to being weird!"

"I'm not weird. You're the one that's only a step above zombie status. You're weird." Noory accused.

"Exactly! That's my point," Roy said. "That's why it shouldn't seem at all strange to you that there are people in this world plotting all kinds of shocking things for any number of nefarious reasons."

"He's right," John said. "Second Sight has been around for ages. It's the perfect time for it to come to fruition. People are terrified for some very valid reasons: economic collapse, terrorism, global warming, and dictators with nuclear arsenals at their disposal. Pick your poison. People want an answer, a hero. Now's the perfect time."

Noory couldn't help but concede. "And Nick is the perfect person to help them. He's tired of fighting," she said softly.

Roy and John both turned to look at her. Clearly neither expected her response.

"What can we do?" she asked.

"I hate saying this, but I think you need to stay close to Nick until he leads you to the device. Maybe even let him believe you're on board," John said.

"I don't like deceiving him," Noory said.

"I know, and I don't like you being around him right now. But I think this thing just got bigger than all of us," John said. "Above all, you must always assume he's tricking you again. Don't be led by your emotions." John swallowed hard before continuing. "It could get you killed if you do."

"Yeah, you're right," Noory said, hating everything about this plan but not having a better one.

CHAPTER 35

Noory stood on the ledge of the office window, listening to the conversation in the room. The dark of night and heavy drapes concealed her from those inside the office. She eavesdropped through glass that had been opened only a couple of inches to let in the cool night air.

"Look, Nick, we need to make absolutely sure she's on board. We've worked way too hard for the scion to wreck everything now," Robert said.

"Don't worry. I've got that under control," Nick said with a confidence that made Noory want to smack him, but she knew that kind of self-assurance would make him more likely to confide in her. Either that or he knew she was listening, and he was trying to mess with her.

"Besides," Nick added, "Noory wants what we all want. That's why she runs that shelter. She's brilliant. She could be anything she desires, but she does it because she's trying to make a better world where people aren't suffering like they do now."

Robert continued. "Let's hope so. Besides, Damascus has confirmed that the priest we saw you with is definitely the same one that died years ago. That means the scion brought him back. That's the kind of security that we want to be able to offer those that sacrifice so much for our cause. There's no limit to what a person will do for us if even death is no longer a threat."

"Are you sure? Back from the dead seems like a stretch, even for someone as powerful as the scion," he said.

"Yeah, we're sure. Damascus is brilliant with research and the occult."

Noory felt hope rise when she heard Nick was trying to lead them off Father Roy's trail. She knew it meant that he was still loyal to them, still trying to protect them in some way.

"I don't want that slimy little Damascus anywhere near Noory and her friends from now on. I warned you about that," Nick said. "He has too much unbridled blood lust."

"Don't worry; Damascus knows you will kill him. I've informed him I would kill him first though if wanders near them again."

Noory wondered exactly what Nick meant by saying he didn't want this Damascus anywhere near them "from now on?" The cool night air blew at Noory's back. Along with it came an uneasy feeling that made the hair on the back of her neck rise. Someone or something was behind her. Worse, they had to be floating in midair. She calculated her situation. She was two stories up. If she fell, it wouldn't be a problem for her like it would for most people, but she knew a scuffle might blow her cover. She decided to be direct and turned her head only slightly. "What are you?" she whispered with authority.

"I am Damascus, ancient and brilliant, and you are busted, scion." With that he grabbed Noory by the waist and flung them both through the window. The glass shattered, and Noory managed to turn her face away and pivot her body so that only her right arm was cut. The two landed hard on the office floor.

Noory realized Nick didn't look as shocked as he should have, but when he saw the being that shoved her through the window jump on top of her to restrain her, he moved so fast she couldn't track him with her eyes.

He had Damascus by the collar, leaning him backward over the broken window frame. "Keep your hands off her unless you are ready to die."

"Forgive me, Amaros. I didn't realize she was with you," Damascus rasped out.

Noory sprang to her feet. She caught the look on Nick's face and realized it matched the horror she felt inside at the idea the one they called Damascus didn't even recognize the man before him as Nick, but as Amaros.

Robert was clearly annoyed at the scene unfolding in his office. "Nick, drag his ass back into the office before someone sees you. This is a respectable neighborhood, not the Wild West, for God's sake! Besides, I can't have you killing him. He's very helpful to me."

Nick pulled him off the windowsill and casually tossed him back in the office. Damascus' eyes flashed an unearthly orange and the energy he gave off said that he would hold a grudge for a very long time. A low growl emanated from his chest.

Robert looked at him and shook his head in warning, which seemed to calm the beast. Noory realized with a sickening lurch that Damascus had claws that were slowly retracting back into his human-looking fingers. She cringed to think he could have sliced her face off if he'd been let loose.

Nick frowned at the blood trailing down her arm and dripping onto the floor. He leaned over and whispered, "Are you okay?"

"Yeah."

Robert said, "I thought this one was on board. We can't have her playing both sides, Nick."

Noory was deeply annoyed that Robert didn't address her directly. She whistled through her teeth and waved her hand to get Robert's attention. "Hey, I'm standing right here."

"Noory just likes to know what she's getting into. She won't blindly follow anyone. She's smart like that." Nick winked at her.

Noory knew the conversation was calculated on Nick's part, and he was answering for her because he wanted to steer the conversation in a way that she might not understand because she didn't have all the information, but she still planned on giving him hell about it later.

"She's either with us or must be destroyed," Robert said in a casual tone.

Nick's head whipped around to face Robert. Then he looked at Noory with an unreadable expression. "Maybe she is, and maybe she isn't, but if you lay one hand on her," Nick said in a deadly tone, as he turned back to Robert, "I *will* kill you."

Noory watched Nick narrow his eyes at Robert. She knew he didn't miss the fact that Robert had shoved his hands in his pockets to try to keep everyone from noticing how badly they were shaking. His words were pure bravado. He feared Nick or what was in him.

Robert managed to regain his composure. "Don't forget you need us, Nick."

"I don't give a damn who you are or what you have. Noory is non-negotiable."

"Well, you damn well . . ."

"Okay, that's enough of the pissing contest," Noory said. "I know what you're trying to do, and besides the fact that you're a raging misogynist," she said, pointing at Robert, "I agree with Nick. This will benefit everyone. I've seen way too many kids beaten within an inch of their life, hooked on drugs, and even dying. I didn't agree at first, and I still don't like that I was used to begin with. So, from now on, I expect to be kept in the loop." She looked from Nick to Robert as they both nodded. "Maybe this thing was just waiting for us to find it when the time was right. Maybe humanity has finally reached a tipping point, and it's time to do something about it."

Chapter 36

As they left Robert's Buckhead estate, Nick looked Noory over, taking in the black boots, pants, and sweater. "Well, does my sexy spy need a ride home?" he asked, laughing.

"I'm parked down the street, but I wouldn't object to dinner," she said.

They got in the Lexus, but before pulling away, Nick gently took Noory's left arm and pushed up the sleeve. He was afraid she might need stitches. The simple act of lifting her sleeve took his mind to a deeper, more erotic place. He had to work to calm the beast inside him. He knew she was right to refuse his bed until the beast was gone. Maybe it could never be gone without forfeiting their deal, in which case it might take Noory, and that was forever off the table. He slowly pulled her sleeve back down.

"See, it's just a few scratches. Besides, I heal quickly," she said.

"But you aren't immortal," Nick said with an edge of sadness. He turned his attention back to their destination. "Where to?" he asked as he started the car.

"Maggie's," Noory said smiling.

"You got it."

The two found a quiet booth in a downtown hole-in-the-wall restaurant that served the Southern food Noory loved. They both placed their orders, and Nick reveled in the normalcy. After the situation they had just left at Robert's house, it felt good to just be together like a regular couple. They had come to an unspoken agreement not to talk shop, at least for a little while. All Noory's problems seemed to flee as she dug into a plate of fried green tomatoes and fried chicken. She caught Nick staring at her.

"What?" Noory mumbled with her mouth full.

"Your face lit up when the food arrived. It's cute. I really like this Noory."

"Not the others?" she asked.

He looked at her over his coffee cup and fought down sultry thoughts of more Noory than he could handle. "All of them. Every square inch. I just want you to be happy. You deal with a lot. I hate that I'm one of the things that causes you grief," Nick said softly as he watched steam rise from his coffee.

Noory knew she couldn't lie to him and say that wasn't the case. "I'm just glad you're in my life. You're worth the worry."

Nick munched on a piece of bacon from his BLT and wondered if that was true.

After they'd eaten half their meals, Nick felt the familiar buzz in his spirit. It would slowly build until he couldn't ignore it anymore—a child was in trouble. He managed to put it off long enough for Noory to finish her food and for him to eat some of his. After this many years of it, he could read the severity of the signal.

Noory leaned over and quietly asked, "Is it happening again?"

"Can't get anything past you, can I?" As the words left his mouth, he suddenly thought that she would be angry at him for not telling her about the attempt on Grace a couple nights ago, but he knew it would just worry her. He almost felt a weight slam down on his shoulders as he realized keeping the attempt on Grace from her might be the first of a whole host of things he would end up needing to keep from her the longer the entity had him. He shoved the thought away as he pulled a wad of cash from his wallet and threw it on top of the check as they both slid out of the booth.

"Can I come with you?" she asked when they got outside.

Nick knew her cooperation at Robert's house was for show, but realized working together might help her see all they could accomplish together and, just maybe, seal the deal on her being on board about the device. "Yeah, sure. Who couldn't use a hot blonde to fight all their battles for them?"

The two drove a few minutes before pulling over and heading out on foot. It was a cool crisp November night, and the air funneled between the skyscrapers, creating a wind tunnel. Nick took his jacket off and handed it to her. She wrapped herself in it, then looked at him and smiled. So much love and trust looked back at him, maybe more than there should be. If he could choose one moment to stretch out forever, this one just might be it. He held up a palm for them to stop walking. "Left," he said after standing at an intersection for a few seconds.

After walking another block, he stood still and listened for a moment more. "This way."

They both made their way up a fire escape. Nick hated the way it rattled through the night air. It called far too much attention to them. "Damn it," he said. "We have to go through a window."

"Wouldn't be the first time tonight," she said with a laugh.

Nick quietly checked to make sure the window wasn't locked, then slowly lifted it as it creaked on the way up. "Stay behind me," he said as she followed him through.

It was a small, sparsely furnished apartment. They heard voices coming from another room. Noory readied herself for a fight, but instead they turned into a room across the hall from the voices. When they walked into the dimly lit room, Noory froze. On the bed lay a boy of maybe twelve dressed in a pair of shorts with his wrists tied to a headboard and a gag in his mouth. When he saw them, his eyes opened wide.

Nick told her, "Untie him. Take the gag off last. He may not know we're on his side."

Just like at Rosslyn Chapel, Noory had a blade with her. She cut through the ropes holding the boy while quietly reassuring him. Nick stood guard by the door.

"Get him out to the fire escape while I deal with these guys."

Nick waited a few moments then looked out into the dimly lit hallway. He motioned for them to cross into the living room.

They had nearly made it to the window they'd come through when a man yelled behind them, "What the fuck?"

"Go!" Noory shoved the boy onto the fire escape as one of the men grabbed her from behind. She elbowed him in the nose without turning around. As his hands went to his bloody face, she spun around and kneed him in the groin. The anger for every abused kid she'd ever counseled in the shelter welled up inside her, and she put everything she had into the strike. He hit the ground, wailing in pain. Noory felt no sympathy as she kicked him in the face, knocking him out.

A viselike grip closed on her throat. Another man began dragging her backwards. Despite her extraordinary strength, he managed to pull her into the room where they had found the boy. On the way in, she saw Nick holding his own with two men, unable to help her. She saw stars dance before her eyes and realized that if she passed out, anything could happen to her. She heard a shot fired from the living room but knew she couldn't lose her concentration as the man shoved her on the bed.

As soon as she was free of his grip, she kicked him in the face. It didn't slow him down, and the look in his eyes was wild. She realized he was probably extremely high. He was huge, all muscle. She began to feel something she rarely ever felt in battle: fear. He plowed his fist into her face several times, making her ears ring. On the third blow, she could see blood on his fist. On the fourth blow, her lights went out. The last thought running through her head was, "Damn it!"

In the living room, Nick lay on the floor unconscious as blood poured from a bullet wound in his chest.

CHAPTER 37

When Nick woke, he felt someone going through his pants pocket and pulling his wallet out. Without thought, his arm darted out, lightning fast. He snatched the thug by the hair on his head and smashed his face through the glass coffee table. The noise alerted the man who had shot him. He walked over to grab Nick, but when Nick sprang to his feet and faced him, the man froze. His mouth moved, but no sound emerged. Nick heard words coming out of himself from Amaros: "Frail, worthless human," it said to the shooter. "You have damaged my host." Nick swatted the man like a fly, sending him into the wall as drywall buckled and crunched. The thug slid to the ground. The low voice emanated from Nick's chest once more. "Where is my mate?" He stomped from the room with one purpose in mind: finding Noory.

Nick found the door to the bedroom locked. It took only a second to kick it down. When he found her tied to the bed by a man who was stripping her, the being inside him raged with an indignant possessiveness that another creature had taken its property. The human in Nick was horrified at the blood caking Noory's face, her sweater and bra torn open, breasts exposed. Noory groaned as she began to regain consciousness.

When the man saw Nick, he went for the gun tucked into his waistband. Before he could reach it, Nick raced forward and grabbed him. With inhuman strength, he broke his neck and watched him crumple to the ground. The entity receded now that it neutralized the threats.

Noory gasped and sputtered as blood clogged her nose.

Nick took out his pocketknife and cut through the restraints binding her. Grief assaulted him. "I'm sorry. I put you in danger."

Noory turned her face to him, but her eyes remained unfocused as she struggled to breathe. As soon as she sat up, blood poured from her nose.

Nick buttoned his blazer she wore to cover her exposed skin and pulled her into his arms. "Please forgive me." As he cradled her, he heard sirens in the distance and remembered the thug had dropped his wallet before he knocked him into the wall. He didn't want to leave it for the police to find. He picked up Noory and went into the living room where he retrieved his wallet, dipping her low as if in a dance, and then opened a portal for them.

"What about the boy?" Noory choked out as they materialized in Nick's penthouse.

"He ran. They always do in that situation. I can't blame them," he said.

"Those men might go after him again."

"I know at least two of them won't," Nick said.

"I can walk," Noory said.

"I know," he replied, but didn't put her down. He carried her into his bedroom and laid her down gently. "How does your nose feel?" he asked.

"Still throbs like hell, but I can feel it healing already."

"Good," Nick almost choked on the word. Her nose was clearly broken. Seeing her like this was warping his insides. He got up and walked into the large master bathroom and turned on the hot water to start filling the sink. He wet a washcloth. His hands shook as he felt the warm water run over them. He expected to eventually lose her to old age but losing her in such a way as he could have tonight had never even occurred to him. It only strengthened his resolve to go forward with his plan. He walked back to the bed and began gently washing the blood off Noory's face, neck, and chest. It had even run behind her ears.

He said, "That really went south. When I go out on those calls, it's pretty rare that there's more than one assailant, but I have run into this scenario several times over the years. I should have been more careful. If you would like, I can take you to John's house or bring him here to heal you." The last thing he wanted to do was face John. He knew he would immediately blame him, but he would do it for Noory.

"No, I want to stay with you tonight. He'll just give us a speech and get mad at you."

"I would almost welcome it," he said.

"Nick, you know I've beaten the hell out of men that size before. I've lived downtown for a very long time. I've gone into crack dens and pulled kids out of there and faced down people like that several times. It was just the perfect storm: too many of them, one, or all of them high, and I lost consciousness. I may be the strongest woman in the world, but if I'm knocked out, then no amount of strength matters." Noory reached up and stuck her finger through a blood-soaked hole in Nick's shirt. "But maybe you need John's healing more than me."

"No, I'm fine, now." He grimaced at the amount of blood soaked up by the washcloth.

"A nosebleed always looks worse than it is," Noory said nonchalantly.

"No, it *is* as bad as it looks. Please don't try to downplay this for my sake. Don't do that. I mean it." He gently lifted her hair and wiped behind her ears, then leaned over and kissed her there, gently. "I'm sorry," he whispered.

"Well, now it's my turn. Stop apologizing. I mean it," Noory said sternly. "This is a situation I would have put myself in any way, without a thought, and you know it."

Everything in Nick wanted to make the argument that this was exactly why he wanted to get the ancient device online as soon as possible, but he kept silent, knowing it wasn't a good idea to use her pain as a chance to make his case. He exhaled as he looked at her. "Your lip is swollen and bruised. You'll have a black eye in a few hours." He felt anger rising in him again but tamped it down for her sake.

"Yes, and by this time tomorrow night, they will be almost healed. It's not a big deal," she replied.

"Stop saying that!" Nick got up and rinsed out the washcloth, then retrieved one of his soft black t-shirts from his chest of drawers.

When Noory went to take the blazer off, she whimpered in pain. Nick noticed and bit his tongue to keep from making a big deal out of it. He helped her get out of her ripped sweater. And although her breasts were completely exposed, Nick didn't look at them anymore than he would her arm. Any other day, he knew it would have been a chore to tear his eyes away. Not on this day. He eased the t-shirt over her head, guided her down onto the bed, and pulled the covers up over her.

After getting Noory some water and pain reliever, Nick changed into his sweats and thought of climbing into bed beside her, but he wasn't sure if she would want him close after what she had been through that night. "I'm going to go sleep on the couch, Light." He leaned over and kissed her on the cheek.

"Please don't leave me, Nick. I mean, would you mind just lying down beside me?"

"Only if that's what you want."

"Please," Noory's voice cracked, and he felt his heart shatter. It hurt but also felt good to know that entity or not, it couldn't stop him from feeling.

Nick grabbed a t-shirt and sweatpants for himself, changed out of his bloodied clothes, turned out the lamp, and climbed in bed behind Noory. She seemed to sense his hesitation and rolled over until she was just inches from his bare chest. He pulled her close, wrapping his arms around her, and she laid her head on his chest. He was afraid to turn his body to face her, afraid she would feel his erection. It wasn't a problem until he got into bed with her. He felt ashamed of wanting her when someone had just tried to rape her. He stroked her hair until he heard her slow, steady breathing. Before long, he felt himself relax into peace. Night after night he had lain in bed, worried he would lose her. Thinking he should be strong enough to let her go, that it would be safer. Now that she was here beside him, he knew he couldn't let her go. She was his peace.

An hour later, he woke with a start, remembering something that had been lost in the chaos of battle. Amaros had spoken through him, saying Noory was his "mate." He realized with sickening clarity that this was part of what caused Jonah to do what he did. It wasn't hard to trace the line of disaster leading to Noory's creation. Jonah already had feelings for Catherine. Then the longer he was Azazel's host, the more the two lines blurred, and given the fact that Azazel had an agenda to create Noory anyway, before long, it probably felt like the next logical step for Azazel to claim Catherine. He remembered Amaros feeling fury that a human would attempt to take what was his host's, and therefore his, by default.

Nick reached behind him to the nightstand, grabbed his rosary beads, and said a prayer from the very depths of his heart. As he did so, he felt the entity within him recoil. The fear was subtle but there. It didn't stop him from praying, "You created me. You made me. You've got to help me," he whispered to the darkness before he drifted off, holding Noory, and his rosary, as they slept.

The next morning, Noory sat on Nick's sofa, wrapped in a blanket and drinking a mug of coffee while he cooked breakfast. Her swollen lip hurt a little every time she took a sip. As predicted, she had black eye. She had always healed quickly. If she went to bed with a bruise, it would be nearly gone by morning. This time was different. She had never been beaten that violently before.

She looked out the window at downtown Atlanta and thought of all the misery out there. Her bruises reminded her of the almost paralyzing fear she had felt the night before. It was rare for her to experience that kind of abuse. She was nearly always on the other end, dealing out justice, the hero, the strong one. The city even looked different, too, as if it were an open maw of evil and danger just waiting to consume. She understood Nick's position like never before. She also understood the victims like never before. She looked over at Nick as he moved around the kitchen. He seemed to feel her watching him, and their eyes locked.

"Are you okay over there?" he asked.

"Yeah."

He looked at her a moment longer before turning his attention back to the bacon. The skepticism in his eyes told her he didn't believe a word of it.

A moment later, they both jumped when someone began pounding on the door.

"Shit!" Nick murmured. "Bet I know who that is. John must have heard about what went down at the apartment last night and realized it had my mark on it." They both looked toward the big dark oak door with a sense of dread.

Noory felt completely overwhelmed. "I'm not ready for this. Nick, I'll go to your room until you have a chance to explain what happened. If he sees my face first, he might throw you out the window and ask questions later."

"That's probably a good idea," Nick agreed.

After Noory fled to the bedroom, Nick opened the door and John barged in, followed by Father Roy.

"Where is she?" John said, obviously struggling to keep his worry and impatience in check.

"She's just fine, John. She's in the bathroom. She'll be out in a minute."

"I'd prefer her not stay here unless you're married, but since she's too old and modern for me to enforce that and you clearly—"

Nick cut him off, feeling a little offended. "John, I'm almost as ancient as you are. My values are not that different from yours. I would rather she and I be—" Nick stopped, realizing that Noory was most likely eavesdropping and wouldn't want him discussing her love life with her father. "It's not what you think."

John wouldn't let it go. "Look, I don't want her spending the night with you while you have that thing in you!"

John's words hit Nick like ice water, but he understood. "It's not like that. She needed help, so she stayed here."

"Help! What the hell happened, and why didn't she come to me? I was called because her car was towed at three a.m. near Buckhead. She didn't answer her phone, and then I hear that some crack den downtown has two dead males in it and two who were seriously wounded. Whoever broke the neck of the three-hundred-pound tower of muscle had to be supernatural. The other man was thrown into a wall so hard they think he died instantly."

"Please, John, Father Roy, let's have a seat and talk."

John and Father Roy sat down on the big leather couch facing the large windows overlooking the Atlanta skyline. The morning light slanted in through the glass and shown off the polished dark wood flooring. Nick sat opposite them in the chair and tried to calm himself out of respect for John and Noory. "Last night, Noory and I went to dinner. While we were out, I heard a child calling. Noory wanted to come with me. In most cases, there is just a child dealing with one sick bastard, but when we got there, we found a twelve-year-old boy and four crackheads."

He continued, "Noory and I have fought off that many before. Anyway, she just got the child out of there when all hell broke loose. The boy took off running. Noory nearly kicked this one guy to death before another grabbed her from behind and dragged her into another room. They shot me in the chest . . ."

"Are you okay?" Father Roy asked with a look of shock on his face.

"He's fine," John said with annoyance. Nick couldn't blame him. If he were on the other side, listening to the conversation, he would want John to shut up about himself and get to the part where he found out Noory was okay, too.

Nick said, "Thank you, Father. I'm fine. Anyway, the man beat Noory pretty bad. She passed out, and by the time I made it in there, he had Noory tied to the bed."

"What?" John yelled as he jumped to his feet. He was so upset that Nick braced himself for John to attack. John rarely let his emotions go unchecked like this, but Nick wasn't completely surprised given that it was about Noory. "This is why I don't want her here."

"I understand," Nick said softly. "He didn't rape her, but maybe it *would* be best for her to stay away."

Noory burst into the room. John took one look at her bruised face and turned to Nick, livid. "How could you let this happen?"

"John, stop it, right now! I'm a grown woman. You can't keep me from him."

"Noory, you lost consciousness and were almost raped. I've never seen you so badly beaten before," John said.

"I'm fine, and I've gotten into lots of fights that you don't know about. I've pulled kids out of crack dens and beaten the hell out of their pimps. I've had several black eyes over the years. You just didn't see them. All that happened *before* I met Nick, and it wouldn't stop if he were out of my life, either. In some ways, I do exactly what Nick does, just to a lesser degree."

"Then it needs to stop. Noory, you are not immortal, and this man is going to get you killed."

Noory snapped, "John, I am not Catherine!"

Everyone froze as the implication of what she had just said sank in. Noory felt grieved that she had just said the most hurtful thing possible to her father and possibly to Nick as well; because it was like saying that she knew John now thought of Nick as if he were Jonah. The silence was deeply oppressive.

"I'm sorry, John. I shouldn't have said that," Noory murmured. "But Nick didn't *let* me get hurt. Nick killed the man that did this to me."

Father Roy winced. He hadn't been around Nick long enough to understand that there were times when it was inevitable.

John said, "Noory, I understand you love him. He's a wonderful person, but he isn't safe while thing has a hold of him. It's causing him to make bad decisions. Don't forget how he used you to retrieve that device in the first place. *That happened.* I would like you to get your things and leave with us. Please, Noory."

Nick felt sorry for her. He knew she was being forced to choose between the two people she loved most in this world, and he loved her too much to put her through it any longer. "Noory, it's okay. You should go with him. He loves you, and he's worried about you. If I had a daughter, I would do the same."

"Thank you, Nick," John said. "I appreciate your understanding. Noory, I'll give you a few minutes to say goodbye to him."

She looked at Father Roy, who was smiling. He already knew she wasn't going.

Noory walked over to John and hugged him. "I love you, Dad, but this is my life."

"I love you too, baby. I'm sorry to have to do this." With that he turned and spoke to Nick. "She's been playing you. She's only been pretending to be on board with this stupid plan of yours. She can't be trusted. If you keep her here, she will thwart you at every turn."

Noory looked back at John with betrayal written all over her face. Then she seemed to brace herself for Nick to be angry with her.

Instead, Nick said softly, "John, don't you think I already know that? I'll take a Noory that's deceiving me any day, over no Noory at all. I'll always know that if she's playing me, then in her heart, she would have a very good reason for it. I may not be able to trust her actions, but I will always trust her heart."

"I only wish she could trust yours," John said sadly. He walked to the door without another word.

The door shut as Father Roy stood and faced Nick and Noory. "He loves you, Nick. Please don't doubt that. He just wants to protect his daughter. He is always on your side. Call me at John's if you need me. Either of you. I'm here for you." He leaned in and drew the sign of the cross on both of their heads.

"Look out for my dad, please," she said to Roy. Tears dripped down her face. It was clearly the worst confrontation she'd ever had with John.

"You know I will, Light."

After Father Roy left, they stood in silence for several moments.

"Why do I feel like I just lost him?" Noory asked as she stared at the door with grief etched in her features.

Nick laughed softly. "You couldn't lose him if you tried, Light."

CHAPTER 38

Noory called in sick to work, not wanting anyone to ask questions about her bruises. Nick had helped get her car out of the impound, and she drove to her apartment while he went back home. Her instinct was to curl up on Nick's couch and let him take care of her all day, and he would have. She knew a shift had occurred in her after the attack the night before. The world was suddenly completely foreign. Gone was the invincibility and cocky kick-ass attitude. It had been replaced with hesitancy and fear. She didn't like this new version of herself.

She walked into her apartment and looked around like a visitor; things seemed somehow different, but she knew she was the one who had changed. She began wondering if she should get another deadbolt for her door. When she arrived home before, she always walked in with a list of things she wanted to get done, for the shelter, for the kids, for herself. Today she felt frozen in time with no direction.

She wandered into her kitchen and made a cup of coffee. It was the great stabilizer for her. Today she could barely taste it. She sat and replayed the events of the night before over again in her head, trying to find some sense of what she could have done differently to save herself and keep Nick from getting shot. She knew Nick only thought of what had happened to her. His getting shot was barely a footnote in his mind, but for her it loomed just as large as what the crackhead behemoth had done to her. By the time she picked her coffee back up, it had grown cold, and she was shocked to see that an hour had passed.

She poured the coffee down the drain and reached up to her hair to feel blood still caked on her scalp from the night before. Her phone began ringing, making her jump. Grace was calling. She wanted to pick it up but was too overwhelmed to talk to her. She felt sick when she realized it was the first time she would ignore a call from her, but it was also the first time she felt she had nothing to give. The call went to voicemail, then rang again almost immediately. Her fear that something was terribly wrong won out over her emotional exhaustion. "Hello," Noory managed, her own voice sounding foreign to her.

"Well, thank God. I've been trying to reach you. You weren't at work; you weren't returning my texts. Are you okay?" Grace asked.

"Of course, I am," Noory said feeling weird over the role reversal that was underway.

"Good then. Let me in. I'm standing outside your door."

Noory panicked, knowing her bruises weren't healed well enough for her to see anyone. "Grace, I'm not feeling well. I don't want to get you sick. Let's meet for lunch in a couple of days," Noory offered.

Grace persisted. "Stop dodging and let me in."

Noory fell silent as she tried to think of another way to get rid of her.

"I'm not leaving." Grace knocked on her door to let her know she really was camped outside her apartment.

"Fine. Just give me a minute or two to get decent." With that, Noory ran into her bathroom and grabbed a tube of concealer. She began to frantically dab it over her bruises. When she had a solid layer on, she stepped back to look at the finished product. The bruising was much less noticeable, but she had a feeling a girl like Grace wouldn't miss it though. She decided if Grace pushed the point, she would just tell her the truth: that she was helping a child escape some thugs—though she planned on leaving out most of the hard-to-explain supernatural components of the story. Though that was almost silly, Grace had been back and forth to the other side several times already. Noory sighed at her own reflection and went to the front door, hoping to get this over with as soon as possible.

"Hey girl. Come on in," Noory said, trying to sound upbeat, though it rang false even to her. She cringed when she turned away from Grace to shut and lock the door.

"Yeah, hey," Grace said. She stared at Noory for longer than Noory was comfortable with.

Damn it! Noory thought, knowing there would be no getting out of a grilling. "Have a seat." Noory gestured to her small kitchen table. "Can I get you something to drink?" she asked.

"Black coffee," Grace answered.

Noory retrieved a cup from the shelf and tried to think of anything to fill the awkward silence but failed.

"I've never seen you with injuries before," Grace blurted out.

"It wouldn't be the first time I've gotten involved in one of your lives and took a few lumps. I'm sure it won't be the last," Noory said as the smell of fresh coffee filled the air.

"This is different," Grace said.

"How's that?" Noory asked, playing dumb.

"Vulnerability is rolling off you in waves," Grace said.

Noory's hand shook a little as she sat the coffee down in front of Grace. The statement Grace made reminded her of something John would say. The way John read her so effortlessly. The Grace who Noory had always known didn't have that kind of insight because she was too wrapped up in her own drama to perceive the world or anyone in it with so much discernment. "What?" Noory asked, even though she knew exactly what Grace meant.

"Noory, you may have a hard time believing this, but I knew you were in danger. I was awakened last night, out of a dead sleep, with an overwhelming fear for you. I knew without a single doubt that you had been hurt," Grace said. Her voice held worry, but it also held something Noory had rarely heard in it before: confidence.

"Well, like I said, Grace, these things happen in my line of work. You know that."

Grace didn't give an inch. "And I told you; this is different."

Noory sat down opposite the girl, wishing that she had made herself a cup of coffee as well: since she suddenly had no idea what to do with her hands as Grace watched her.

"Why is it different?" Noory asked. She found that now she wasn't just trying to dodge Grace's line of questioning but wanted to open one of her own to find out what had brought about this change she was seeing.

Grace took a drink of her coffee. "Maybe because I'm different now, and I can finally see that you are, too."

"How so?"

"Ever since I came back from purgatory, I sense things and know things about people that I shouldn't know," Grace answered.

"Oh," Noory said as she pondered the possibility of what Grace was suggesting. Her mind also delved into the physics of it, as she remembered her conversation with Father Roy about why he couldn't be recognized after spending so much time on the other side. "Do you know if any of the others are experiencing things like this?" Noory asked.

"I don't think so. Thomas and I hang out a lot since the ordeal. He's the one that wants to become a priest now. Anyway, I told him about it, and he didn't mention feeling any different. Well, except for the sudden urge to become a priest and spend the rest of his life celibate," Grace sneered and rolled her eyes at the idea. "I told him he could be an Episcopal like Father Roy, but his family is Catholic, and he plans on going full-on cold turkey."

For the first time that day, Noory smiled as she saw how Grace twisted up her pretty face in distaste over Thomas' choice.

"Anyway," Grace continued. "I've thought a lot about it, and I think I know why it's just me. Jonah sent me in to find Franz and his minions, but as soon as I found those weirdos, I saw them cross between our world and this one. It was as if my body became some sort of bridge that they traveled along." Grace shivered.

Noory felt sympathy for Grace's ordeal as she remembered the shakiness she had felt after she returned from purgatory.

Grace continued. "I was there the longest; they used my body as a conduit, which didn't happen to the others. Also, I poked around in one of the journals that Jonah kept in his lab. When he was first experimenting with me to find out how to get me across the border between our worlds, he let me flatline. He didn't do this with any of the others. He didn't get the dosage right until he found the guys."

Noory felt bile rise into her throat as she realized how he had used

Grace as a lab rat and could have easily ended her life permanently. Her anger at him experienced a renewal.

"I think it caused some permanent sort of change in the way my brain is wired," Grace said. "The next couple weeks were no fun at all. I would feel fear, anger, depression rolling off complete strangers I passed on the street. I would start crying without realizing it. I used to think most people were generally happy, and I was the only miserable one, but damn, Noory. Did you know how unhappy most people are? It's shocking. People are frickin' miserable!"

"That's quite a revelation, huh?" Noory asked.

"Well, yeah! Anyway, I knew something was wrong with you. I just knew it, but I think there is more. You aren't . . . right. I mean, you are very different. In my memory, I see you glowing. Which is strange because the memories I have of you even before my brain went all whack-a-doodle have you giving off a glow. It's as if my brain even went back and pulled the curtain off of something I always knew was there, that my eyes had seen, but my mind couldn't yet process it, so my brain told me it wasn't there. I knew something was up, but when I went to mass with Thomas it got worse. There is a statue of Mary there. When I looked at her, I saw your face superimposed on hers for a moment. It freaked me out! I wasn't even high that day."

"That day?" Noory was glad she wasn't drinking coffee because she knew she would have shot it through her nose when Grace said she wasn't high "that day."

"Sorry, old habit. I haven't been high since. Well . . ." Grace began, then stopped as if there was a half-truth going on.

Noory lifted her eyebrows and stared at Grace, waiting for a second confession.

"I admit to drinking a little a few days after I got this gift. It was exhausting listening to everyone's emotions. People are exhausting, Noory. Did you know that?"

Noory laughed out loud this time, and the irony of what Grace had said apparently wasn't lost on her either. They both burst out laughing.

"I can't believe you went to mass!" Noory said as she wiped the moisture from her eyes after laughing so hard.

"I know. It's bonkers! But I was hoping that Thomas would go and realize how boring it was and see that he was making a mistake."

"Wait a minute," Noory said. "Why would you care whether or not he gives his life to the church?" Noory gasped and looked at Grace slyly as it all came together. "You like him! What about Elliot?"

"No," Grace protested.

"Liar," Noory shot back, good naturedly.

Grace changed the subject. "Why would I see your face on a statue of Mary? I mean, look at you?" Grace gestured to Noory, who knew one explanation would be that Grace saw her as a mother figure sometimes, but she damn well wasn't telling her that.

"I know, right? I'm a wreck," Noory said laughing.

"You're dodging the question, Noory."

Noory took a deep breath and exhaled. "Okay, this is just between the two of us. Got it?"

"I'll always have your back after what you've done for me," Grace promised.

Noory was taken aback by the maturity and sincerity in the girl's voice. She had transformed in more ways than one. "Mary is like my great grandmother to infinity."

"Oh, my God! Well, you don't look like a Jew!" Grace said.

Noory laughed. "Well, technically I am, since all my mothers, going *all* the way back were, but as to the skin tone, I get your meaning. Every once and a while, as I am told, the people in my lineage get the urge to return to the Middle East and our line gets a bit more olive-skinned."

"Yeah, Jonah told me that he was your biological father and he's fair-skinned," Grace said.

Noory nodded.

"Ugh! I'm sorry. I shouldn't have mentioned that. I felt your spirit get agitated. *John* is your father. More so than Jonah ever would or could be."

"Yes," Noory said with a soft smile. She couldn't help but think how hard it was to believe Grace was only sixteen. She had changed so drastically.

"He glows, too, but you already knew that, didn't you?" Grace said. "You weren't surprised when I told you that you glow. Are you psychic, too?"

"No, actually. I'm not. I sense things more than others and—"

Grace cut in. "And you kick ass. I mean, like seriously, so. I remember that day on the roof and distorted snippets of being on the boat. It's beyond what you should be able to do. Isn't it?"

"Yes," Noory said nodding.

"Then why are you beat to hell today?" Grace slammed her hand down on the table and stood, looking around. "You're in danger. Something wasn't right about what happened to you the other night. You should have been okay. Something was messing with you. Why else would I have been woken up for it? It's like you said, you've been through shit like this before."

Noory stood and placed her hand on Grace's arm to calm her and get her to sit back down. She had the look of a wolf about to start sniffing a trail like a predator.

Grace complied. "Something's going on. Will you tell me?"

"I can't," Noory replied.

"You won't because you think you're protecting me. I will only get half-truths from you the rest of the evening, but that's okay. One day you will call upon me for a favor."

Noory smiled at Grace trying to sound like a mob boss, but the girl just might be right. Having a powerful psychic in her corner couldn't hurt, but damned if she would involve her any more than she had to.

"Well, I got stuck with the boring gift. Why can't I be an ass-kicking super chick like you? God should have known I would much rather have that!"

"What is it they tell kids in elementary school? 'You get what you get, and you don't pitch a fit?' " Noory mused.

"I always did hate that little rhyme," Grace said.

"Me too!" Noory said with a yawn.

Grace walked over to her and reached out her hand. "You've got blood caked in your hair." Grace gently touched the side of her head. "Take a shower and get some sleep. I love you," Grace said quickly before nearly running for the door.

"I love you, too, Grace. Please tell your aunt I said hello and let's get together in a few days and have lunch. You've got a lot to talk about."

"So do you," Grace said. She stopped with her hand on the door handle, turned around, made eye contact with Noory, and spoke. "A leap of faith is coming your way."

"Okay," Noory said, not quite sure what to do with the information. "I'll watch for it."

Grace continued. "Be very careful in the next few weeks; everything is not what it seems."

"It never is," Noory chuckled, hoping she was coming off as indifferent for Grace. She had a feeling she wasn't fooling her, not anymore.

CHAPTER 39

After Grace left, silence permeated Noory's apartment. She sat there, astounded at the transformation in the girl. Seeing how other people have to march forward despite their own fears and sorrows had transformed Grace like no pep talk, punishment, or positive reinforcement ever could. She couldn't help but think Grace was doing better than she was right now.

Minutes later, she stood in the shower washing her hair and watched the soap suds hit the tile floor. The foamy white bubbles had pink swirls of blood mixed in them. Noory had seen lots of blood before. She didn't understand why she would take it so hard now, but as she watched the bloody soap make its way down the drain, her own frail humanity washed over her, and she sank to the tiled floor and cried until her throat was sore and the water had turned cold.

She got out of the shower and put on her old, warm robe and sat on the bed listening to the silence when she saw the light blinking on her phone. Nick had texted her four times. "How are you feeling?" the latest one asked.

She paused with her thumbs poised over the keyboard. The truth would make him feel worse and wouldn't help her, either. "I'm fine," she texted.

"Can I bring you some dinner?" he asked.

She wanted to see him again. Wanted to curl into him and forget everything. She loathed her own weakness but the need for him was too intense. "Sure," she typed out.

She looked at the clock and realized it was almost seven. Between meeting with John and Roy, getting her car out of impound, and the time she'd been at home, she hadn't realized how late it was or even noticed that she hadn't eaten a thing all day.

When she opened the door, Nick smiled softly and held up a couple of classic brown bags with small grease stains soaking through. She knew he was thinking it would cheer her up if he brought something fried in greasy deliciousness. It also wasn't lost on her that he was checking out her bruises.

"See, they're healing up," she said as she closed the door and locked it behind him.

"They do look much better than this morning," he said as he took the food out of the bags and laid it on Noory's kitchen counter for them.

She smiled as she saw he had brought more fried green tomatoes and fried chicken. Her stomach growled, and she looked up at Nick and realized his presence was making her feel even better than the food could.

"Hungry?" he said, laughing at her growling stomach. "Have you eaten anything today?"

"No." She rubbed the hooked "X" tattoo on her wrist, which always helped her think. She wondered just how much to confide in him.

Nick looked at her with concern as he pulled out a chair for her. "Have a seat, Light."

They ate in silence for a while. She knew they both had a lot to say but were hesitant to unpack any of it.

She finally broke the silence. "Nick, I'm willing to truly explore the possibility that you might not be completely wrong about this device."

"Oh?" Nick asked as his eyebrows rose in surprise.

"I've still got some reservations, but I don't want anyone feeling like I've been feeling all day."

"I think you're still coming down from last night. The adrenaline dump from something like that can really do a number on a person physically and emotionally. You're going to feel better in a day or two," he said.

"I hope so," Noory said looking out the window with a thousand-yard stare. "Will you stay with me tonight?" she asked in a timid voice.

"Of course, I'll stay with you. Whatever you need."

∞

After dinner, exhaustion overtook them both, and Noory led them to her bedroom. Nick took off his shoes and shirt and laid down beside her. She curled up close, and he wrapped his arms around her. This was where she was meant to be.

Despite John's warning, she couldn't imagine herself with anyone else, ever. She also believed that just lying beside him would not be enough. He stirred a hunger in her that went beyond mere attraction and lust. Of course, that was there to a degree that made her toes curl, but it went so much deeper. He obviously knew what it was to dedicate one's heart to see another go free; to put his own life on hold because he couldn't bear to see someone else suffer. And she knew he would understand, without question, the hunger to have that one person be there to give her back all that her heart had been pouring out. To have another fill that emotional void that had been torn into them for as long as they could both remember was what she wanted.

She could see in his eyes that he longed for it, too. Her hands slid across his bare chest and started rubbing slowly then propped up on one elbow. She leaned over and kissed his collarbone and grazed her lips across it.

Nick groaned softly. She ran her fingers through his hair and planted soft kisses on his lips. He wrapped his hand around the back of her head and deepened the kiss until Noory's insides melted. His tongue searched her mouth with longing. He reached his other hand around her back and pulled her down over him as she reached between them and opened her robe so that her body was pressed against his. She only wore panties, no bra. A warm current ran through her as her naked breasts pressed against him. There was no hiding his erection from her. He growled as he arched his hips, pressing his length against her through their clothing.

"Nick," she moaned, feeling almost possessed by the need to take him inside her.

He wrapped both arms around her and rolled her over until she lay beneath him. He kissed her neck hungrily, then stopped. His breathing was heavy as he clearly struggled to get himself under control.

She could feel the tension overtake him. "What's wrong?" she asked breathlessly.

"We shouldn't do this, Noory. Not tonight."

Noory felt her cheeks burn. She knew Nick was from a totally different time, where women who opened their robe and jumped on top of a man—whether or not they were in love with him—were considered whores. "I see. I offended you or you don't want me," she whispered.

"Oh, God. Noory, no! I want you so bad I ache. I've felt that way since the day I met you. I've never been with a woman I felt this way about. I couldn't allow it, couldn't feel it, until you." He rolled off her with what seemed like a herculean effort, like it was the last thing he wanted to do. "I just think that you may be doing this because you feel a little . . . vulnerable." He looked worried, perhaps about offending her. "You also had told me you didn't want to be with me like this until I was rid of . . . it," he said. He sighed and grabbed one of her throw pillows to put over his lap.

Noory closed her robe, before he could see her again. She felt exposed now in more ways than one. But his words rang true, and she knew what needed to be done to get past the oppressive feeling of vulnerability.

She sat up and scooted back against the headboard next to him. "Next time you go out on one of your missions, I'm coming with you."

"What?"

"I need to make sure what happened last night doesn't have any power over me," she said.

"I don't know if that's such a—"

Noory interrupted him. "I know. You're afraid I'll get hurt, but I need this, Nick. Last night took something from me. Before it takes anything else from me, I have to face it. There's only one way to get it back. I have to go out there again. Besides, you said it yourself; last night was just a fluke."

"Okay, but you have to promise me you will leave if I ask you to."

"Sure," she said, chewing on her thumbnail.

"Liar. I'll drag you away caveman style if I have to," he said, sounding like he was only half-joking.

"Hmm, I kind of like the sound of that." Noory said to diffuse the tension.

"Damn, woman. Someday . . ." he said, looking at her with hunger in his eyes. He rolled over and punched his pillow as if to release some frustration before he turned to face the wall. She had a feeling it would be a frustrating night for them both.

CHAPTER 40

Noory put on her black tank top, leather jacket, dark wash jeans, and boots. She looked in the mirror and smiled. She had nervousness in her gut more intense than she was used to, but she was ready to go out and face the beast. She was on a mission to retrieve her courage, her fire.

Nick had texted her to let her know he heard "the call" and would be on his way to pick her up. She met him on the sidewalk, not wanting him to waste time coming up when he was on the trail of a child that needed him. She got in the Lexus and Nick began driving until they were on the outskirts of town. "I would just portal us there, but I don't have an exact location. We'll drive until the signal gets stronger."

They drove into a really nice neighborhood that defied any stereotype of abuse being solely associated with low income.

They found the female child they'd been tracking sitting on the back porch of a three story, four-car garage, new brick home. She was sobbing, shaking, and having a hard time catching her breath. When Noory started toward the little girl of about six years old, she realized the child wasn't upset because she was being physically hurt. The girl's spirit was calling out because the man inside was beating her mother senseless. It was easy to hear just standing on the back porch. Noory looked in the window and saw the sick scene unfold.

"Won't the girl be afraid if we approach?" She looked at Nick in his black jeans and boots, black leather jacket, well, he often dressed like her, and his looks weren't exactly soft either. They were more beautiful, smoldering danger than kid friendly.

"No. Adults perceive me as frightening. The little ones never do. It's part of my gift." He walked up to the little girl, who didn't even flinch as Nick placed a hand on the top of her head as if blessing her. She recognized it as the same thing John did with Nick. What *was* John doing when he did that? One day she would have to ask him.

"I'm going to text a social worker friend of mine for the girl." His fingers flew across his phone, and then he simply walked into the house through the back door. There was no need to break in. The woman inside had blood running down her face as her husband, she presumed, just kept coming at her.

Noory leaned over and whispered to the little girl. "Don't worry, we're here to help your mom. What's your name?"

"Madison," she said in a trembling voice.

"Everything is going to be okay, Madison." The girl wiped her eyes and watched Noory walk into the house.

Nick had shoved the man into another room so that the girl couldn't witness anymore. Noory helped the woman to the couch. "Is anything broken?"

"I don't think so."

Noory placed a comforting hand on the woman's arm then got right to the point. "Don't let that asshole smack you around like that."

From around the corner the man came roaring at Noory. "Bitch, you don't even know me." Nick looked at Noory and did the game show presentation hands to let Noory know he was all hers. After all, that was what she'd come for.

He took a swing at Noory. She blocked his arm with her right hand and before his eyes could even focus, Noory punched him square in the face. Now he had a bloody nose to rival that of his wife's. He grabbed his face with a look of absolute shock and attempted another swing at her, but she sidestepped it and the heel of her hand snapped out and broke a couple of ribs. He leaned over and grabbed at his side as Noory shoved his head into the door frame. She watched the man wobble slightly, then slide down the door casing before crumpling to the ground.

The woman on the couch stopped crying and looked at Noory with wide eyes. Noory sat back down next to her without needing to catch her breath.

"Who are you?" the lady asked.

"I'm Noory."

"Damn, right you are," Nick said as he winked at Noory and grabbed the tiebacks off the curtains to restrain the man in case he woke up before the police arrived.

Noory grabbed a towel from the kitchen, wet it, and handed it to the woman to clean her face before heading outside to be with Madison. Once they were outside, the woman opened her arms, and the frightened girl ran into them.

"You know, you can learn to defend yourself." Noory reached into her pocket and pulled out one of her business cards. Let's talk about it. There are some people I can refer you to."

After the police arrived, Nick gave them a plausible sounding story about he and Noory just passing by when they heard the commotion. They explained that the man had come at Noory, and she had told the officers she was a martial arts expert, which wasn't far from the truth as she had taken kung fu for many years. They didn't need to know about the superpowers to believe her, and it wasn't the first time they had been called out to the house. The man went to jail via the hospital, and the social worker had arrived to file her report and make sure the little girl was okay.

"Feel better?" Nick asked smiling after they got into his car.

"Very much so, yes," Noory said.

"Glad to hear it." Nick reached over and took her hand. "I'm proud of you."

"Thank you," she said. "You know, it never occurred to me that you would get a call about a parent being the one abused."

"Well, it stands to reason. Watching your dad beat the hell out of your mom or vice versa, for that matter, *is* child abuse. It's truly shocking how many couples don't see it that way."

"Good point. How do you know the social worker?"

"Oh, that's become a necessity. I can't just take a child from a home no matter what brand of crazy is happening. I have to have somewhere to take them. She actually thinks I'm a sort of psychic. That was the only way John and I could think of to get around explaining my powers. We were lucky to find someone who would believe that. It's been extremely helpful."

She heard her phone buzz again and groaned. It was John. She read the text silently: "He can't be trusted. Open your eyes." Before that it was, "I'm worried about you. Call me."

"Who is it?" Nick asked.

"John," Noory said as she removed the back of her phone, took the battery out, knowing he couldn't trace her without it. She stuck it in her back pocket. "That's like the tenth message in the last few days. I'm tired of him stalking me. I'm a grown damn woman."

"Whatever you think is best, Light." He kissed the top of her hand.

"You usually defend him."

He turned to look at her and simply shrugged.

She felt a little queasy.

Chapter 41

Noory sat behind her desk at the shelter, looking online for the best deal on new sheets for the beds. It had been a while since anyone had donated and despite the fact that she knew Nick would buy them if she mentioned it; she felt odd about turning him into a wish-granting genie.

"John's here to see you," Ava called from up front.

Noory took a deep breath. She missed him terribly but didn't want to talk with him about Nick anymore. She knew how it would end. "Send him back," she replied.

John was already approaching her office. "Hi, Noory."

Despite herself, she felt a lump in her throat. She loved him.

"Hi," she said as she swiveled her desk chair around to face him. "Have a seat."

John sat on the old orange couch opposite her desk. "Listen, I came to let you know—"

Given the look on his face, this wasn't going to go well, but then, suddenly, his face softened.

"I've come to let you know that I used to carry you around on my shoulders. I remember your laugh before the weight of the world descended on you. I remember when you lost your first tooth, taking you fishing, your high school graduation. I've come to tell you that I love you, and I miss you."

"I love you, too, Dad."

"I promise I won't track you through your cell phone anymore if you at least give me a way to stay in touch with you. It's killing me, sweetie."

Noory suddenly felt terrible about what she had done.

"I'll put the battery back in." She knew her coworkers needed to reach her, too, and while there was a certain freedom to it, she knew she wasn't being fair to anyone.

"I shouldn't have said what I did to Nick the other day. All I wanted was to protect you. I've never had any children of my own. I was never brave enough to cope with having to watch them grow old and die while I continued on."

Noory had always wondered if he'd had children, but it always felt like snooping to ask him. "Not brave enough? You're the bravest man I've ever met," she said.

John shook his head and continued his line of thought. "Honestly, I'm not even positive that I have the genetic ability to have children. When I met your mother, I thought I was finally ready to try, though. But before I had the chance to . . . well, you happened."

John smiled, and it looked to Noory as if the sun had suddenly come out on a cloudy day.

"I was there the day you were born. You came out kicking and screaming. Defiant and lovely," John laughed softly. "And you haven't changed since. The moment I laid eyes on you, I swore to myself and to your mother that I would protect you. Noory, you are mine, not a possession but a piece of my heart, taken from my very own being. Genetics be damned. You're my little girl," he said as his voice cracked.

Noory wiped her eyes with her shirt sleeve. "I would be lost without you, Dad. Everything I am I owe to you."

"I can't claim responsibility for the superpowers. They came from James."

Noory watched that familiar look pass across his face as his mind traveled back in time, further than anyone would or could ever believe.

"Well, I guess it would have come from Mary, really, but all of it begins with Him," John said.

"Not to be blasphemous here, but I disagree. I believe what I am, even my powers, come from you. Without you, what would I have made of my power? If you hadn't raised me and Jonah did? I was born with certain powers and qualities, but *you* made them worth having in the first place," she said.

John couldn't speak for a moment. He opened his mouth and lifted his hand as if he might try but then looked at the floor. She knew he was struggling with his emotions and decided to let him off the hook. "You came here to tell me something, though. I promise to listen without getting defensive."

"I appreciate that," he said. "I've been looking into what happened to you and Nick last week. There's a CCTV set up just outside the building where it happened. A couple of days prior, a limo pulled up to the building, and I traced the plates back to a company that does a lot of chauffeuring for Robert Billings. I can't say for sure that it means there is a connection between a limo at a downtown crack house and the ambush that you two walked into the other night. I can only say that it's a little strange and you might want to consider that this man could be pulling more strings than you think."

"I wouldn't doubt it," Noory admitted. She twisted her mouth in disgust. "I don't like him."

John smiled. "There's my girl. Any closer to figuring out where that thing is?"

"No, not a clue. I've got my eyes open though."

"I know you do." John walked to her, leaned over, and gave her a kiss on top of the head. "I've got to get to work. You don't mind if I text to check on you now and then, do you?"

"No, it's fine. I didn't mean to worry you."

John paused as if he wanted to say more. Noory could tell that he was biting his tongue so hard it was probably bleeding by now, but whatever it was, he kept it to himself.

She watched him walk out, thinking how she would love to confide in him that she was beginning to think the device might not be all bad, but she knew he would lose it all over again. It felt good to have him back.

As he walked out the door and out of her sight, a horrible feeling curled around her heart. She felt fear that she might be making the wrong decision. But when she thought of all the little ones like Madison who wouldn't be sitting out on their porch crying while their moms were beaten, all the women who wouldn't be raped . . . How could she refuse to stop it when she had the power in her hands. But if she went through with it, would John ever look at her the same? Would she lose him? She felt lightheaded, took a deep breath, and waited for it to pass. It didn't. She was overcome with nausea and had to sprint to the bathroom. She couldn't help but think if it were the right decision, then why did it feel so wrong?

CHAPTER 42

Meeting with John had been a kind of wake-up call. Part of her realized that her recent acceptance of Nick's plan had a lot to do with being damn near raped by a crackhead and Nick getting shot. She knew if she were to be true to herself; she had to learn more about what she was getting into.

She'd had a nagging question ever since Argentina: why in the world did she automatically started reading the spell to unlock the device? The more she thought about it, the more she wished she had someone to ask about all of it; someone who was an expert. That's when she realized her biological father *was* an expert. She went back to his house to search for answers. No way was she ready to see him face to face, but from what John had said, he knew nothing specific about what lay in the tunnel in Argentina. She hadn't told John or Nick about going to Jonah's house again. They both wanted her loyalty, and she didn't want to hurt either of them.

She didn't find any answers about the device itself and didn't think she would, but she thought there might be something there that would lead her in the right direction. In a file cabinet, she discovered notes about Jonah's old colleague Dr. Darius Davis and found that he and her father had been close and that the man still taught at the University of Georgia. She called him immediately—before she lost her nerve—and asked him to meet with her. He seemed interested, especially when she'd told him she was Jonah McNamara's daughter. She hated using that information to get his help, but it was a necessary evil, literally, in this case.

Noory was thankful for the drive east to Athens. It gave her time to think. A few of her high school friends had gone to UGA while she had gone to Georgia Tech. They had probably graduated since and moved on to graduate school, work, family. She felt no jealousy, though. She loved the feeling that she was helping people. If she helped Nick get the device up and running, they could do even more.

She thought about it as she walked across the UGA campus. Leaves fell around her and helped soothe her nerves somewhat. Though she had gotten her confidence back after patrolling with Nick, she knew she still wasn't quite herself. She also knew that she was playing with fire. Nick wasn't the same man that she had fallen in love with. Sometimes she looked at him and felt that he was barely there. It was him, but it wasn't. She loved him for wanting her even though he knew she had been playing him for information. How could she turn him away? He had only taken in the entity to save her.

She was so lost in thought that she had entered Baldwin Hall, home of the archaeology and anthropology faculty, and was searching for the correct office number before she knew it. Dr. Davis was a professor of archeology with a specialty in religious artifacts. She had also done some research on him and found that he spoke several languages, including Hebrew and had a familiarity with ancient Aramaic and Greek.

She found the right office but felt frozen as she stood there staring at the nameplate beside the door, unable to decide what she was hoping to hear. Part of her wanted Dr. Davis to say that the device came from some benevolent tribe of people she hadn't heard of. The other part of her wanted him to confirm what she had thought in the beginning and tell her it was definitely evil and then she could just focus on finding the damn thing and destroying it. She also thought, for the first time, that something must have been wrong if she felt she couldn't tell Nick where she was.

Her hand shook as she knocked on the office door.

Dr. Davis opened it and smiled. His bushy white eyebrows and kind smile set her at ease. "Pleased to meet you, Ms. McNamara. Come in."

Noory felt a wave of anxiety wash over her when the man used her biological father's name. "It's Abramson, actually."

"Mrs. Abramson. Well enough. Have a seat."

Noory realized he thought she had married into the name Abramson. She didn't push the point.

"I worked with your father in Cairo during the nineties. He was a brilliant man. I was sad to hear he left academia."

"Yes, that was before my time, but he seemed happier then, from all I've heard."

"Well, tell me about this mysterious artifact of yours," he said.

Noory handed him the sketch she'd made. She had always been a fairly good artist. It seemed easier to draw it than try to explain it to him.

He put on a pair of reading glasses and examined the image. "Interesting," he said as he lifted those wild white eyebrows once more. "How in the world did you come across such a thing?"

"A friend of mine found it in Argentina. This may sound strange, but something about it feels . . . off," she said, knowing it was a gigantic understatement, but the actual story was a bit much for anyone to swallow.

"Hmm," he said as he scribbled some notes on a legal pad. He then walked over to a large, overstuffed bookcase and grabbed an old volume with a cracked spine and peeling leather cover. He opened it gently and pored over the pages while making more notes. He was so into what he was doing that he seemed to forget she was in the room. The man didn't come up for air for at least ten minutes. She was thinking she might try clearing her throat to get his attention.

Finally, he said, "Well, there's a good reason this feels strange to you. This has marking in both Hebrew and ancient Aramaic. I'm impressed that you were able to remember all of this after looking at it only once."

"My memory is somewhat photographic," she said. As a child, it had taken Noory years to realize that not everyone could do what she did. When she was taking a test in school, she would simply see pages of her textbook in her mind. For her, studying was just a matter of reading the text. If she had read it, then she didn't have to memorize it in the usual sense. She would just close her eyes for a few seconds until she saw the right page. Of course, that wasn't all. What happened in that cave was burned into her brain.

"Lucky girl," he said. "The closest that I can interpret this, the inscription claims that it was built by Azazel. He was one of the Watchers from the book of Enoch. As legend has it, he brought warfare, knives, armor, etcetera. to mankind and paid the price for it along with several others. Semjaza and Amaros are also mentioned here."

Noory shuddered when she heard the name Amaros.

"Semjaza and Amaros are both associated with spell casting. This inscription here," Dr. Davis said, pointing at her sketch, "speaks of influencing someone to do your will, like hypnosis. The other side speaks about corrupting or defiling the descendants of the holy one, but through means of trickery and hypnosis. The word they use is more similar to "trance" because they wouldn't have had the reference of hypnosis. So basically, if you believe in this sort of thing, it is a dangerous device that has the power of hypnosis and claims to even have the power to control holy people or their descendants. Or maybe holy things since who knows who a holy descendant would be," he scoffed. "There's also a symbol here representing eternity. So, perhaps it means to control them forever."

Noory grabbed the edge of the table as the room began to spin.

"Are you okay, dear?" Dr. Davis asked. He went to a small refrigerator and grabbed a bottle of water for Noory.

"Yeah, I'm fine. Thank you." When he used the word trance, it became clear to her why she had just started reading the spell off the relic to unlock it while she and Nick were in the tunnel. It had put her in a trance. After that, all Nick had to do was coax her to try and read it. Amaros knew that's what had to be done, and Nick did it.

Dr. Davis opened the bottle and handed it to her. "I've never seen anything quite like this before. You said it belongs to a friend of yours?"

"Yeah, he comes from an old Greek family that has an extensive collection. When he showed it to me, it kind of gave me the chills. I just had to know what was so strange about it," she said with a laugh as she tried to keep things light *and* keep the note of hysteria out of her laughter. She wasn't sure whether he bought it and worried that he would question her, thinking it was a stolen artifact.

"I wouldn't worry about it. It's probably an old fake from someone who was interested in the occult or perhaps looking to sell something to someone without the knowledge to know they were being taken for a ride."

"Yeah, you're probably right. I appreciate you making time to speak with me," Noory said, setting the bottle on his desk. She suddenly felt claustrophobic in the old office. She just wanted to be alone so she could drop her mask of being okay.

"You're most welcome, my dear." The man rose and went to open the door for her. "If you ever get your hands on that thing, I'd love to take a look at it. Even fakes can be interesting. Some of them are ancient and have a story to tell as well."

"Will do," Noory replied.

"Please tell your father that an old friend says, 'Hello,' will you?"

"Of course," she replied as she felt sweat making its way down her back. "Thanks again for your time."

Noory walked back to her car in a daze. She was grateful for the cool fall air. The sweater she had worn that morning didn't seem warm enough when she left home, but it had become stifling.

She got in the car and checked her phone to find messages from both Nick and John. Both wanted to know how she was doing. She had a strange feeling they both knew she was up to something. Noory wanted to talk to each of them for different reasons. Another part of her didn't want to talk to either because she knew she was caught between them.

At least now she knew exactly what needed to be done.

CHAPTER 43

It was three a.m. as Noory made her way through the crisp Atlanta night. Robert Billing's alarm system was a joke. She had it disarmed in no time and slipped in through the same office window she had been thrown through by Damascus a week ago.

She stood in the room and reached out with her awareness to sense if anyone was around, then made her way to Robert's laptop. He hadn't even been cautious enough to shut it down before going to bed. If it were password protected, it wouldn't do any good if the thing never went to sleep. She searched through his files for only a few minutes before she found his latest project. He was building a tower in South Georgia. It didn't take her long to see a notation at the bottom indicating that Nick was part owner. Next, she opened his calendar and found that he was to meet Nick that Saturday night at the new tower. This would be her best shot at getting close to the device.

Noory wrote the information on a scrap of paper, put everything back the way she had found it, and slipped back out the window.

"Why do you have to do business so damn early in the morning?" Damascus froze a few steps inside the doorway and sniffed the air like a wolf tracking prey.

Robert looked up from his computer. "What's wrong with you?"

"Did you have the scion over here last night?" Damascus asked. He walked to the window, still sniffing the air, then made his way over to Robert's desk.

"No, I haven't had her over since you two crashed through my damn window last week."

"Well, she was here." Damascus sniffed the air again. "I'd say it was only a few hours ago, actually. Yeah, she was here around three or four this morning."

"Are you sure?" Robert asked.

"Oh, yeah. No doubt about it. Her scent is fresh."

Robert's fingers flew across his keyboard as he checked his browser's history. Noory had erased it, but it didn't matter. There were searches missing that he had made before going to bed; they were gone too. "Damn it. That love-struck Santa Claus is going to end up screwing us all!"

"You gonna change the startup date of the device, then? I'm sure she knows now," Damascus said.

Robert scratched his head and rolled his neck around, trying to loosen the gathering tension. "No, I don't think so. Let her show up. Maybe this is what Nick needs in order to understand that she is going to thwart us at every turn. She can't disappear into another realm like Nick can. Let her climb that tower. There won't be anywhere for her to run from there. Perhaps it's time for me to deal with her. Consequences be damned. My brothers have made it clear to me that if she doesn't get on board, I have orders to finish her. She's too much of a liability."

"Yeah, but you're forgetting about the crazy factor. That fucker damn near killed me. My teeth are just starting to grow back in, and with Amaros in him, he dampens my strength and contains my fire power," he said as he spread his palms and a small fire erupted between them.

"You don't need to be there," Robert said.

"He'll kill you!"

Robert couldn't lie to himself; he was afraid of Nick. More to the point, he was afraid of what Nick had inside him. He shivered as he remembered Amaros threatening him, flashing images of his worst fears come true. "My brothers and I believe in what we do. I'm willing to die for it . . . if I have to." Robert's hands shook as he walked over to the small bar and poured himself a scotch.

"Pft! Everyone believes their cause is noble. I'm a long-lived being,

Robert. Trust me. It's all cyclical vanity. Whether your cause succeeds or fails, another will rise. Don't throw your life away for this. Reschedule it."

Robert looked at Damascus. "Remember, I have a boss to answer to as well." He finished the rest of his scotch and poured himself another.

CHAPTER 44

Noory listened to muffled car horns in the city outside her apartment as she drank a cup of coffee, which was intended to calm her nerves. It wasn't really working. After returning from Robert's office, she had tried to sleep but tossed, turned, and cursed for hours. Her phone vibrated again. It was Nick texting. "Everything okay?"

"Yes, just had a hard time sleeping last night," she replied. Now that Nick carried the entity, he was popping and crackling for two. She had the feeling he knew when something was off or when she was starting to doubt. A knock at the door interrupted her thoughts.

Annoyance washed through her as she stomped over to answer it. Before she turned the knob, she felt a slight tingle in her spirit. Something felt off, but she also got the feeling it wasn't dangerous. Her instincts made sense when she looked through the peephole. It was Damascus. Nick would hate that she was about to open the door for this guy. Creature? But he was sure to bring information, and she doubted he would knock on the front door if he were there to kill her.

She opened the door and found him looking around the hallway, clearly paranoid. Sunglasses hid his oddly colored eyes, and his claws were currently retracted. He looked fairly normal. "Can I come in?" When she hesitated, he added, "I'm actually here to help you, believe it or not."

Noory didn't believe him but stepped back for him to enter without answering. Though she truly didn't believe he meant her any harm—at least not during this visit—she still placed herself between him and the door, just in case.

He removed his glasses and looked at her. He was clearly worried about something. "Listen, Robert knows you were in his office last night."

"Oh, really? How?" She figured there was no sense in trying to lie out of it.

"I smelled you," he said it as if it were the most natural reply one could offer.

Noory wrinkled her nose. "Oh, ew."

"No, you smell pretty good. It's like bergamot, cassia, and . . ." He paused for a moment. Noory smiled because it actually seemed important to him. She realized she might even like him if he weren't a murderous demon. ". . . and vanilla."

"Hmm, good to know."

The two sat in awkward silence for a time.

"I don't want Robert to succeed in hooking up this jackass device," he said in a rush.

"Oh, I didn't expect to hear that."

"Yeah, well, he might not need me anymore if everyone does what he says," Damascus said.

"Does what he says? I thought it was just something to plant a hypnotic suggestion to keep people from killing each other and making shitty choices."

Damascus laughed sarcastically. "No, that thing can be programmed with any suggestion."

Noory felt nauseated and angry at herself for ever coming close to believing it was a good idea. She knew Robert must have been involved in things going south at the crack den—just as John had suggested—because it had caused her to get on board with their plan.

"Besides," he continued. "I want you to succeed in destroying it without Robert having to interfere and destroy you. If he kills you, Amaros will tear Robert apart."

Noory couldn't help but notice that Damascus' voice shook as he spoke. He was genuinely terrified of losing Robert.

"You love him," she blurted out. She could not keep the wonder from her voice. Robert was such an ass that she struggled to believe that even a demon could find him attractive.

Damascus exhaled in frustration. He nodded but didn't speak about it. "Anyway, after Robert found out you knew about when he was meeting Nick to get the device online, he changed the schedule. He's going to meet him tonight at six. It shouldn't take long. I'll text you when they arrive back at the estate. If you get there before twelve hours passes it won't have time to send out any actual programming. Hooking it up to the tower is one thing. Programming it to do its thing is another. I want you to go get that stupid box and destroy it. Burn it, throw it in a volcano. I don't care. I'm sick of the damn thing. It's getting in my way. I've heard them say it has the ability to protect itself, but I get the idea that's only on weaker minds. I think the scion could retrieve it if you stay focused."

He rose to go but then added, "Because you are doing something for me, I'm going to give you a little tip. Amaros will kill Robert if he tries to hurt you. Robert is about as afraid of Amaros as he is of his boss. *Almost*."

"His boss?" Noory asked.

"Yeah, Robert answers to a very powerful man. This thing goes way deeper and further back in time than you would believe. He knows he can't fail, and he knows you stand in his way. He plans on killing you when you show up, and then I will lose Robert when Amaros kills him. What I'm trying to tell you is that Amaros is very possessive of what he thinks belongs to him. If you don't separate him from Nick, he will eventually take over. Even one as strong as Father Christmas won't be able to resist him forever. He will get more and more possessive until you won't be able to leave his sight. He will eventually kill *you* in order to end his misery. I've seen it before."

Noory felt her blood run cold. She knew he was right because she had seen it before, too. She had seen so many women come in beaten from being with possessive men. *How could I be so damn stupid?*

"You love him," Damascus said softly. "It won't be easy. Hell, lock yourself in somewhere if you can't stay away from him. I've lived a long time, and I can tell you it won't end well. And if someone like me is doling out advice, then you know it's bad," Damascus said.

"What about you? I don't exactly think Robert is good for you."

"Pft. I tried to kill your friend, and you are concerned about me? You humans crack me up. That's just the point, though: Robert is human. I can handle him. Amaros is something else entirely. He scares the hell out of me, and scion or not, he should scare you, too."

"What do you mean you tried to kill my friend?" Noory asked.

"Yeah, I didn't think Nick would tell you." Damascus pointed at Noory. "He's already hiding shit from you. Robert sent me after Grace so that you would see how awful the world is without that stupid device. Don't worry. Nick caught me, knocked out a few of my teeth, beat me unconscious, brought me back to Robert, and threw my bloodied ass on his desk and threatened to kill him. Amaros actually showed up and scared Robert so bad he nearly went catatonic on me. He needed me that night," Damascus said softly. He shook his head as if to clear away the memory, got up, and headed for the door. "Don't tell Robert I was here. I will cause trouble for you if you do."

Noory stopped him before he could leave. "Now here I thought we were on the same page, and you have to go and threaten me. Don't be an ass. I won't rat you out. At the moment, we need each other," Noory said as she turned around to open the door. "And by the way, if you go near Grace or any of my kids again, shit's going to get a little too real for you, too."

"Understood," Damascus said with a wink. "What the hell could I do, anyway? Amaros would find fifty different ways to kill me. I hate that creepy son of a bitch," he said with a shudder.

Noory shut the door behind him and tried to calm her racing heart before she walked over to her apartment window to watch as he crossed the street. He waved without turning around. Noory couldn't help but think that if God worked in mysterious ways, then sending a demon to save her life had to be one of the most mysterious.

CHAPTER 45

The fall night air was biting as it whipped Noory's ponytail around. She was grateful for the wind, hoping it would cover any noise she might be making in case Damascus had been wrong or somehow mislead her about Nick and Robert being done installing the device. Robert wouldn't sense her coming, but Nick certainly would. She kept climbing the cell tower. Even though the device was installed, she wasn't sure if it was already up and running. She didn't know if she could disconnect it if it was. Even as an electrical engineering major with a knack for understanding how things worked, it was ancient technology. Some sort of spell might even protect it.

She began to think not telling John was a grave error. He would come closer to being able to understand the ancient ways than she would, but even though she'd made peace with John, she was genuinely afraid for Nick. She knew Nick was changing more and more every day. It wasn't just the wind stinging her eyes, as she wondered how long it would be before Nick disappeared completely.

She looked behind her as she realized she was about three quarters of the way up. Heights didn't concern her, but the lightning in the distance did. She reminded herself that she wasn't immortal like John and Nick.

She reached the top, pulled herself onto the platform, and looked around. It wasn't long before she spotted something that seemed out of place. The device was tucked in where it could be missed if someone hadn't seen it before. But it wasn't just a matter of seeing it, she could feel it. It felt as if it were calling to her, and she caught herself staring off into the distance as her mind relaxed. She shook her head to clear its grip. *Focus, damn it!*

The device was hooked up to the tower via an interface that Robert had clearly designed himself to patch into the downlink with just a few wires. She walked over to it and quickly disconnected them, but the artifact felt as if it were whispering to her. It made her fearful, like she wanted to put it back, run away, and forget about it. Instead, she hefted it. For the second time, she wished she had asked John to come. She was beginning to understand his frustration with her. She whispered a prayer for strength. If the last few weeks had taught her anything it was that she had to admit she needed help now and then.

Without warning, Robert appeared on the platform with Nick. He looked a bit rattled, and Noory knew it must have been the first time he had traveled with Nick in such a way. She realized that the device must have had some sort of alarm attached to it. *You knew this could happen,* she reminded herself. She stood stock still with the device in her arms as Robert looked at her with a mixture of anger and malice. It was the look of a man with nothing left to lose.

"Oh, Noory, no," Nick said with grief and disappointment in his voice. "Hand it to me."

Noory stood on the edge of the platform with the device. She knew she couldn't just hand it over to them. After all her running from being the scion, here she stood risking her life because she *was* the scion. It would have been ironically funny if she weren't afraid she was about to die.

Robert advanced toward her. "There's nowhere for you to run. You are not immortal, little girl. I don't care what your lineage is. This whole thing is bigger than you."

Noory knew if she handed it back to him, she might never get it back again.

Nick walked over to where she stood and tried to reason with her. "Hand it to me, Noory. I would never do anything to hurt the innocent. This device will free us from having to constantly run from one crisis to another, patching everyone up, hoping they stop making the same stupid mistakes. Please, open your mind a little, Light."

"This thing violates free will, Nick. This is antichrist crazy shit! How do you not see that?"

"I'm not arguing with your girlfriend anymore," Robert said as he pulled a pistol from under his jacket and aimed it at Noory.

Noory knew if anything would force Nick to decide, this would be it. Time seemed to slow as all her senses closed in on one solitary thing: Robert's index finger as he began to pull the trigger. He wasn't waiting any longer. Noory held onto the device tightly and turned without another second of thought and jumped, not knowing if she would fall to her death, not knowing if Nick would follow. Faith alone accompanied her over the ledge, and the ground raced up to meet her as she fell.

CHAPTER 46

"Ooof," she huffed as Nick landed on top of her and knocked the breath from her lungs. They had both landed on what felt like a mattress. The device tumbled to the floor. Noory realized he had jumped with her and transported them moments before hitting the ground. His arms were still wrapped around her.

"Sorry, are you okay?" Nick asked.

She felt his warmth covering her and though she was having a hard time catching her breath, she realized she really didn't want him to get off of her, but he did anyway. She inhaled and knew he'd bruised a few ribs when he landed on her. "Ouch!"

"Oh, God! Did I break something? I've never jumped between realms while moving that fast before. The only thing I could think of was to land on my bed to cushion the fall. Do you want me to go get John to fix you?" Nick asked.

"No!" Noory said horrified at the thought of John finding her on Nick's bed. He might think the bruised ribs were caused by something else, punch Nick, and ask questions later.

Nick reached over to turn on his bedside lamp.

"You left with me," Noory said as hope filled her heart.

"Of course. I wasn't going to let that asshole shoot you."

"If you think he's an asshole, then why are you working with him?"

Nick sat back against the headboard and took a deep breath as he ran his hands through his thick hair. "He can help me get my life back. He can help us both get our lives back, but he won't trust you anymore. I'll have to figure something else out."

Noory sighed in exasperation. "He's part of Second Sight. I don't think that's a blacklist you'll easily be able to get off of. I'm afraid they'll hunt you down and do what they have to to get this device."

"He's not the only man who can help me get that thing out there."

"You're not going to stop, are you?" Noory asked with defeat clear in her voice.

Silence fell between them.

"What if I just walk out of here with it?" Noory asked.

"That won't happen, Light," Nick said with resolve and an edge of danger in his voice.

"Don't call me that again until we can get that thing out of you," Noory said softly. Noory rose, knowing it would do no good to try to take the device. Not when Nick could just wrestle her for it and jump into another realm.

Noory stood at the bedroom door feeling a deep sense of grief for the Nick that she used to know. "Thanks for saving my life tonight."

"Always," Nick said. Before she could get to the door, Nick moved like a blur, grabbed her wrist, and spoke with a voice that was huskier than usual. "Don't go." He pushed her gently against the wall and held her eyes as his lips found hers and began kissing her hungrily. She knew in her heart that it wasn't her Nick, not really. She knew she had to tear herself away for good.

She pushed at him and met resistance. "Nick, please, let me go."

She knew, she felt, that he had no intention of letting her go until he saw the fear in her eyes, and the Nicholas deep inside him fought its way through layers of Amaros that were slowly smothering his light. "Go, Noory. Go quickly and don't come back."

It wasn't anger over the device she saw written on his face when he spoke, it was absolute fear.

Noory left without looking back.

CHAPTER 47

Robert Billings sat in the waiting room of the high rise looking out the window at the Manhattan skyline. Despite the half bottle of antacids he had swallowed on the flight over, he still felt bile crawling its way up his throat. He'd failed. From standing on the brink of making all their dreams come true—dreams that were decades in the making—he had failed them all. He knew he could lose everything for this.

An administrative assistant walked out. She wore a sleek business suit, with her hair in a ponytail and a professional mask of confidence. "Mr. Billings?"

"Yes," he replied as his own nerves coiled around him tightly, making him feel like his necktie was far too tight despite every effort to breathe deep and find a soothing place.

"Follow me," she said.

Robert rose like a man heading to his execution. He pulled a handkerchief from his pocket with a shaky hand and wiped at his face where beads of sweat were forming. The assistant opened the door to an office that held at least ten different monitors. Most were following the large news outlets like CNN, MSNBC, and Fox. Others were following news agencies from several other countries. He watched as Arabic, Hebrew, and Japanese scrolled across the screens. Below them sat a large desk made mostly of Plexiglas, all sharp angles and sleek modern design. A woman who appeared to be perhaps forty, with chestnut hair pulled into a demure side bun, shrewd blue eyes, a black suit, and long legs that ended in at least three-inch heels, sat behind the desk, talking on the phone. She glanced up and said goodbye in French to the caller on the other end. She looked at Robert with a stern expression and let silence hang in the air.

Robert began to feel that perhaps she was confused about who he'd come to see or why he was there. "Excuse me, ma'am, I'm looking for the head of Second Sight."

The woman laughed loudly. "Would you say that if I were a man? Heaven help us. The power of the penis rules us all, doesn't it?"

"I'm sorry. I didn't mean to cause offense."

"Oh, Robert. What are we going to do with you?" She stood and came around to stand in front of him. "We need to talk about what went down on that cell phone tower."

"I failed, plain and simple. Despite my partner being inhabited by the being that shares our goals, he is still swayed by his girlfriend. When she took the device, I tried to shoot her—" Robert watched as the woman's mask of complete control cracked for the briefest moment; her eyes widened slightly before she reined it back in again like the flipping of a switch— "but the damn fool girl jumped off the tower and her boyfriend, Nick—I assume you know of his gifts?" She nodded her head curtly.

Robert went on. "He had to have grabbed her and transported them to safety because I combed the ground around the tower, and there were no bodies. I'm given to understand the scion can survive what an average human can't, but we had the device interfaced at about a twelve-story height."

"Were you given orders to shoot this woman?" she asked.

"Not directly, no. I was told that my life depended on getting the device up and running, though. It motivated me. How else was I supposed to interpret that? I will not let some young punk girl get in the way of all that we've worked for."

He found himself flying across the room and landing against the far wall with a thud. His abdomen ached from having the woman's designer heel damn near thrust through his body, and his head rang from bouncing off the wall. He fought to catch his breath, finally inhaling to find an array of body parts screaming in protest. He looked up as the woman grabbed him by the collar, yanking him to his feet until her face was mere inches from his.

"That girl has more courage and resolve in her little finger than you have in your entire worthless body. You will never, ever threaten her again. Are we clear?"

Robert stammered to find his voice again. "Yes, of course, Miss . . ."

"Abramson, Catherine Abramson," she said. "Now get the hell out of my office!"

Chapter 48

Noory cut the engine and sat in John's driveway as the first rays of dawn backlit the ridge of pine trees running across the back of the pasture. She could make out the small shapes of various sheep and goats. For a moment, she envied their simple existence. She had been up all night agonizing over what to do about Nick. She still wasn't completely sure, but she knew she couldn't handle it alone anymore.

"You can do this," she whispered to the silence. Still, she couldn't move. She thought again about Nick as her fingers went to her mouth, and she remembered the way he had kissed her. The way he made her feel things she thought she never would or even could. She was well aware that part of her was a vault that no one could breach until Nick. Tears stung her eyes as she thought of him feeling betrayed by her.

Before her agony could fester any longer, the front door of the small farmhouse opened, and John walked out onto the porch, looking as if he might have been up all night too. When she saw him, she couldn't get out of the car fast enough. She felt like a kid again.

She fell into John's arms, weeping. "It's time. I don't think we can trust him anymore."

"I know," he whispered in the same sad voice.

John led her inside to the kitchen table and poured her a stout cup of coffee as she used her shirt sleeve to swipe angrily at her eyes. The two sat in silence for several moments, watching the steam curl from their cups.

"Where's Father Roy?" Noory asked.

"Out walking. He has one foot in this world, one in the other. He talks to the other side. When he's out in the fields, he can feel freer to do that, I think."

"I think Nick truly believes that he is doing the right thing, but to me, it's become pretty clear this thing is just convincing him he is. He's found a way to justify everything."

"They always do, sweetie," John said.

"There's just that small part of me that still worries I'm doing the wrong thing. Why can't God just tell me directly? It would be so much easier," Noory mused.

"No, it wouldn't. Trust me," John said.

The back door opened, and they both heard Roy stop to wipe his feet before coming into the kitchen.

Roy walked in and stood in the kitchen as he gazed at Noory with a look of profound sympathy and compassion. Roy repeated exactly what Noory had said to John moments earlier: "It's time." He pulled up a chair beside Noory and held her hand. "Have faith, Light. Nick is profoundly loved by his creator."

John held a sad smile on his face as he watched the two of them.

Noory shared her story about everything that had happened the night before, including the fall from the tower. John looked at her in horror, but to his credit, did not give her a speech about neglecting to call him first. She'd already told him she knew she'd made a mistake by going without him.

Finally, John spoke. "I'll call Brother Thaddeus. He can help us make sure we secure Nick without incident."

"No, I will take down Nick," Noory said. "As burly as that man is, you know I'm stronger. Besides, Thaddeus will smack Nick senseless and ask questions later."

"Not if I ask him not to," John said. "Besides, you are speaking of Nick like he's helpless. He isn't—that's why we are apprehending him. I've seen what happens when he catches someone hurting children. I've seen him beat a man unconscious in half a minute. Not that they didn't have it coming."

"Still, please let the three of us handle this ourselves. Then we can take him to Brother Thaddeus," Noory said.

John looked over at Father Roy to get his input. He nodded at John.

"We're all in agreement then," John said.

The three sat in silence for a while, mourning a decision they never wanted to make. Then they made a plan.

Noory paced back and forth in her small apartment and occasionally glanced back at her bedroom where she knew John and Father Roy waited. She felt nauseated, and her hands trembled no matter how many deep breaths she took. When the knock at the door finally came, she jumped, and a shot of adrenaline flooded her body so strong her chest hurt.

"Hello, Light," Nick said as he walked in.

Noory cringed.

"I'm sorry, you asked me not to call you that. I can't help it. That's what you are to me: the only light that doesn't hurt my eyes, but you really should stay away from me."

She closed the door behind him and fought back the tears. She tried to compose herself before turning to face him, but it was no use.

"Thanks for coming," she said.

Nick looked at her, clearly perplexed. "What's wrong, baby? I mean, other than this grand disaster we find ourselves in."

She began walking to her bedroom, and he followed like she thought he would. Before they reached the door, she turned to face him not caring that John and Father Roy would hear every word. "I love you, Nick, with all my heart, body, mind, and spirit. You know that, right?" She couldn't stop the tears from spilling over any longer.

"I love you, too, Light. Always," he said softly as he reached out to wipe a tear from her face.

She pulled him to her suddenly, wrapping her arms around him tightly as she whispered into his ear: "Please don't hate me."

John moved silently from Noory's room and threw a thick iron chain around his neck. The iron would keep him from being able to escape into another realm. He spun quick as a blur and grabbed John by the throat as he roared in an unearthly voice, "Why does the Beloved insist on stopping me? You've been cursed to walk the earth while everyone around you dies. I will bring a better world for these people—these sheep that you love."

Noory grabbed Nick in a choke hold as Father Roy rushed forward and administered a powerful sedative into Nick's arm. He loosened his grasp on John. She pulled Nick to the ground. John grabbed handcuffs from his pocket and put them around Nick's wrists and ankles as Noory held him down.

Nick's human side appeared to gain control once more as a look of horror spread across his face. "Oh, God! John, I'm sorry! I didn't see it coming, or I would have stopped him. I didn't mean to hurt you," Nick pleaded.

"I know, Nick. That's why we have to contain you," John said while doing an admirable job of keeping his emotions in check.

Noory wasn't able to do the same. "I'm sorry, Nick," she said through tears, while still making sure he was restrained after his last outburst.

"Please don't cry, Light. You're doing the right thing."

Father Roy stood by, making sure no one hurt Nick, just as he'd promised. He handed John the second syringe with the strong tranquilizer, in case the entity surfaced again. The moment Nick saw it, the entity within him rebelled once more. If Noory wasn't sure there was a problem before, now she had no doubt. It had clearly been calculating odds of escape. It flashed through Noory's mind that being inhabited was like a computer constantly running a program in the background, even though the user went about his business as usual. Nick would have understood that John was drugging him to keep the entity from being able to fight him. It was only the entity that saw chances of escape diminishing.

In a split second, he had broken both cuffs and was going for John again. Noory smacked Nick in the back of the head hard enough to knock him unconscious. John quickly emptied the syringe into his arm before he woke again. He restrained Nick's arms and legs once more.

John had worn his uniform so that no one would think it too suspicious that he had an unconscious man thrown over his shoulder. Even though it was nighttime, they knew it might still raise questions. John loaded Nick into his squad car. He knew he could always claim Nick was passed out drunk if anyone asked, but they tended not to when he was in uniform. Father Roy sat up front with John and Noory sat in back with Nick.

Noory leaned over to kiss his forehead and cradled his head in her lap for the entire half an hour it took to reach their destination. They pulled up to the monastery under the cover of darkness.

John took Nick from the van and hoisted him over his shoulder. Brother Thaddeus met them by the back door.

John turned to Noory. "It might be best if you stay here, Noory. I swear to you, I'll make sure he's okay. No harm will come to him. Isn't that right, Thaddeus?"

"If he don't try to kill me, I won't try to kill him," Thaddeus replied with all sincerity.

"John!" Noory exclaimed, clearly worried about Thaddeus' answer.

"Brother Thaddeus, will you please assure Noory you understand that Nicholas has been a faithful servant of God for centuries, saving thousands of children from harm and death at the hands of some of the most disgusting evil one could imagine, and that you understand he took this entity in order to save my daughter's life, and that you would exhaust all other means of restraining him at your disposal before harming him?" John said in a tone that demanded compliance. It was also a tone that said he'd been Thaddeus' superior at the Police Department as well and they already understood one another.

Brother Thaddeus walked up to Noory and took her hand. "I did not mean to seem flippant. I will do anything and everything at my disposal to contain him before I would harm him. I give you, my word."

"Thank you," Noory said, pleased with his vow.

They all turned to go inside before John stopped Noory once more. "Noory, there's something I haven't told you. Not because I was keeping it from you, but I got the feeling you didn't want to know. Your father is in here. This is where I brought him after you drove the entity from him."

"Oh," Noory said in a small voice. "Listen, I think I have to go in anyway. I need to see where they're going to keep Nick. If not, I'll picture something worse than what it really is. Besides, I think I may need to see . . . Jonah. I don't like thinking that I'm avoiding anything."

John nodded as he shifted Nick's weight on his shoulder. "I'm proud of you, Noory."

Noory smiled as they all walked in together. Brother Thaddeus led the way.

Red eyes flashed in one of the cells. A voice that sounded half-snake spoke as it approached the bars and started to reach out to her. "Well, well, this incarnation of the scion is particularly juicy. Maybe—"

Noory grabbed the being's wrist and twisted it back until it screeched. "I'm in no damn mood for bullshit tonight. Open your mouth again, and I will break it!" she said through clenched teeth.

"You're no fun," it said before slinking back into the recesses of his cell.

Father Roy couldn't help but smile. "That's how it's done."

John placed Nick down gently on the cot. The furnishings were sparse, but Nick would be warm enough, well fed, and safe until they could figure out how to separate him from the entity. Nick was coming around a little.

"Noory?" he called through a drug-induced haze.

Noory knelt down beside him and smoothed the thick, dark brown hair off his forehead. "I'm right, here, Nick."

"I thought I was strong enough, Light. I'm ready to die and be done with this life. My only regret is leaving you."

Noory realized his confusion. "Nick, no one is going to kill you. You're in a holding cell; the one in the bottom of the monastery."

"You make it worthwhile."

She kissed him gently on the lips.

"We need to activate the faraday cage now, Noory," Brother Thaddeus said.

"Don't worry, Nick. We will figure this out. It's going to be okay."

Noory left the room, and John and Father Roy went in to speak quietly to Nick. Noory walked a few steps away to give them some privacy. Her eyes were drawn to a trembling creature in the corner of a cell several yards away, hiding its face in its hands. None of the cells touched for fear that the entities might use this to their advantage. Sympathy was the first thought in Noory's mind. She'd thought anyone here, except for Nick, of course, would be a vile thing like the half-snake demon that taunted her on the way in. But the creature huddled in the corner seemed out of place—a simple, weak human. She walked a little closer, and the trembling creature looked up at her with haunted, fearful eyes.

Noory's breath caught in her throat as she realized who it was: Jonah, her father. When he noticed her, his eyes grew wide with terror. At first, she thought it must have been because he was remembering the fierceness of her when she separated him from the entity at Loch Ness, but then she registered sheer guilt, remorse, and shame on his face and knew that it was much worse than simple fear. What he had written on his face couldn't be removed as easily as fear. She knew that it was etched on his soul, and any hatred she had for him vanished. She wasn't ready to accept or necessarily forgive him, but she was done hating him. She walked up to the bars of his cell. He opened his mouth to say something, but his mouth only moved like a landed fish. As she turned away, he managed to finally say, "I'm sorry."

"I know," she said softly without anger.

When she turned around again, she realized that John and Roy had left Nick's cell and Nick was sitting up watching her. He'd seen the exchange between her and her father. He mouthed, "Are you okay?"

"Yes," she mouthed back to him. She brought her palm to her heart and whispered, "I love you." He smiled back with genuine joy and placed his hand over his heart as well: "I love you, too, Light."

They all turned to leave. Before the door closed behind them, Brother Thaddeus smiled gently at Noory and said, "I promise."

CHAPTER 49

She crept along the fire escape without a sound. With the stealth of a cat, she blended into the night rather well; her dark hair, black turtleneck, black pants, and boots completed the walking shadow ensemble. She couldn't quite see into Noory Abramson's window, so she crept out onto the thin ledge that circled the building. That's when she saw her. Her breath caught in her throat and despite herself, her vision clouded. She cursed herself for her weakness.

She knew the wisest and safest choice for everyone would have been to stay away, but she had to check. What she'd heard from Robert Billings at her Manhattan office had shaken her deeply. Deeply enough to risk everything just to make sure Noory was okay. Her usual informants had gone quiet. *What if that idiot Robert was wrong about Noory escaping? What if she had fallen to her death?* But Catherine knew from her own experience there was a very good chance she might have even survived the fall under the right circumstances. Still, images of Noory lying mangled on the ground haunted her.

She swiped at her eyes with her sleeve and went back to memorizing her face. Seeing her in person was so much different than seeing her in the pictures she retrieved from social media and Noory's phone. She'd had a hacker doing that for years. It told her daughter's life story in images. No one was happier about the invention of the iPhone than she was.

"My baby," she whispered.

She sensed him before she heard him. She knew it was a man because the wind had brought his scent to her: musk, woodsy deodorant, and beneath it all a hint of sheep and goat dung. He was a shepherd. *Dear God, it can't be. One thing at a time. Please.*

He spoke softly but with authority. "Slowly, back onto the fire escape and put your hands where I can see them," he said.

Catherine exhaled in frustration. "Damn it!"

"Good. Now slowly turn around," he said.

She acted as if she were about to comply but then at the last moment, before he could get a good look at her face, she grabbed the railing and jumped two stories and landed on the ground in a crouch. As soon as her feet hit the pavement, she started running. John ran after her. She knew the one advantage he had was that he knew these streets very well, especially the ones around Noory's apartment. Noory's phone wasn't the only one she'd hacked. Every night he was on duty, he drove by Noory's place just to make sure no one was creeping. This time, someone actually was.

After being pursued down three different streets, she ran into an alley that eventually dead ended. She stopped and looked around, realizing her mistake. All she had wanted to do was make sure her daughter was okay and get back to Manhattan unnoticed. Now she had to deal with John. It was a worst-case scenario. Catherine felt a rising panic. She imagined several possibilities of what to say to him. She'd pictured this moment with John over and over again in her mind, with so many outcomes. Somehow, she didn't envision being chased down in an Atlanta alley. She'd thought there might be a café involved and hopefully fresh coffee. *Coffee,* she thought, knowing it would soothe her nerves right about now.

"You've got nowhere to go. Get your hands up and turn around. I will not tell you again," John said.

She knew John wouldn't kill her. He might shoot her in the leg, though, and she wasn't in the mood for that. She turned around slowly with her hands up.

John lifted the flashlight to her face. She couldn't see his expression but felt certain, even though she looked older, though not as old as she should, that it would all coalesce for him in a few moments. She knew the very moment it did because his flashlight wavered. He was shaking, and it broke her heart.

"It's going to be okay, John," she said softly.

She heard a tortured sound escape his throat as if he'd tried to speak and the words were constricting his throat before they made it out. "Catherine?" he finally managed.

"Yes. It's me," she confessed.

The next thing he did took her completely by surprise. He put his flashlight away, grabbed his handcuffs, walked over to her, and pulled her hands behind her back before she could even realize what was going on.

"What are you doing?" she asked.

"You've been gone for almost twenty years. I thought you were dead. I deserve some answers, and you will not leave until I get them." He shoved her forward. She tried to turn around and look at him, but he pushed her head back around to face forward. He was either so angry at her he couldn't bear to look at her or he was crying and didn't want her to see him. She knew either could be true. Or both.

When they got to the car, he let her sit up front with him. "Talk."

She dared a glance at him. He looked straight ahead, keeping his emotions in check. "I heard what happened to Noory on the cell phone tower. She's taken the battery out of her phone. I can't track her anymore."

"I told her to after the incident. At least for a while."

Catherine nodded. "I was scared that my informant was wrong about her surviving the fall, or the leap, as I understand it. I had to make sure she was truly okay. She's such a beautiful girl, so tough. You've done a fine job raising her, John." Catherine had a lump in her throat that was downright painful, but she couldn't deal with letting even a little emotion out for fear that the entire dam would burst.

John spoke with anger. "How are you alive, Catherine? I mourned you! Noory cried for you for months and months. Damn it! She was only five years old when you died, but I see now you just left us! How could you do such a thing?"

"John, I did die, but the ashes my mother had were not mine. They were switched with an unclaimed body. But I couldn't go home, and I couldn't come back to you and my baby either. It wouldn't be a stretch at all to say I was simply brought back to hell."

She was crying now and angry that she couldn't contain it. He reached to his pistol belt and fished out the key to the handcuffs. He reached over as Catherine turned to the side. He unlocked her cuffs and gently slid them off her. "Please don't run yet, Catherine."

"Thank you. I won't. Not yet."

"How were you brought back? I did CPR on you even though you were already cold when I got there. I checked your pulse over and over again, but worst of all, I could feel it; your spirit was gone." John didn't bother hiding the fact that his voice was cracking with emotion as he appeared to relive the horror of finding her that day.

"With all my heart, I want to tell you what happened, but I cannot. Please don't keep trying to find out. I stayed away to protect Noory and as much as I . . . love you. I have to keep that story to myself if Noory is to stay safe."

"No, Catherine. That's bullshit!" The anger was back, and Catherine knew he went with it because it was easier than the despair of all the missing years.

John put the heel of his hand to his head. "I'm sorry, Catherine. I just mean that Noory and I have encountered so much, especially lately. If we've learned anything, it's that there are ways around things. You just have to dig your heels in and look for it. There has to be a way that you can—"

"You don't think I tried every angle I could to get back to my family?"

John reached over and gently wiped her tears away with his thumb. "Of course, you did." He met her eyes. She wanted to drink him in when something seemed to dawn on him. "You should look a little older than you do. You would be fifty this year. Yet you look maybe forty or younger. Why?"

"I'm sorry John. I cannot tell you. If it were up to me, I would tell you everything. I would *crawl* into your arms and never, ever leave." She hoped the conviction in her voice was unmistakable, so he'd know she wasn't feeding him bullshit. "You're the love of my life." She reached up and grabbed the hand that was wiping her tears and kissed the palm of his hand as she closed her eyes and remembered their passion and love. "I'm going to need to go soon. Please know that I love you. I've waited so long to tell you that. I've repeated it in my mind a thousand times."

"Stay with me, Catherine. I'm still your husband. There has been no one since you. It's okay if you've . . . It's okay. Just stay with me. If it's only for a night. Let me remind you what we had together," he pleaded.

"You don't have to remind me, John. I've never forgotten. I've gone to sleep every night thinking of you, but I've done things, the things I've had to do to fulfill my end of the bargain, to buy Noory's freedom."

"What?"

"If you knew, you wouldn't be able to look at me the same anymore."

"Yes, I would. Have some faith in me. I still believe in you."

Catherine started looking around, checking every shadow. She closed her eyes and whispered, "No."

"What is it, love?" John said with a depth of concern that made her want to run away with him forever. It had been so long since someone, anyone had spoken to her that way.

"John, I have to go. They watch."

"No! Who? Don't do this to me. Not again. I can protect you. Stay."

"No. You can't. If you don't let me out of here, Noory will get hurt. Don't make this harder than it has to be."

"No, we can find a way to protect her. Whatever it is."

"Damn it, John! I know the lengths you would go to keep her safe. I'm her mother. Please don't stop me from doing the same. You have to trust me."

John grabbed her face and kissed her with years' worth of longing. She felt her insides melt despite the dire circumstances. She returned the kiss with equal passion.

"Promise me you won't stop trying to get back to us. Swear it, Catherine."

"I swear it, John. I haven't stopped yet, and I never will."

She opened the door and started to get out. He grabbed her wrist. "No."

"Do this for our daughter. I beg you," she said looking around with urgency.

"Find a way to let me know you didn't get hurt tonight," he said.

"I'll try. I promise."

He let go of her wrist and watched as she ran down the street, took a left, and vanished, breaking his heart all over again.

CHAPTER 50

O n a lonely Atlanta night, John slammed his hands against the steering wheel of his squad car in frustration and then cried until he was completely exhausted.

When no more tears would come, and the silence became oppressive, he let loose on heaven: "How could you do this to me?" he whispered to the silence. "How could you do this to *her*? I've done what you've wanted. All these years . . ." he said, as the weight of the ages hung on every word. "I've been a good man. How could you withhold this one thing from me?" It was the first time in more than two thousand years that he turned to the heavens in anger. He had stoically pushed forward for so long. He thought he was beyond the bitterness and anger of existence, past looking to heaven and whining about life being "unfair," but he knew this was a reminder that he was no better than any human walking the earth; he had just been at it a little longer—just as he'd once told Nick during one of his pity parties. Now he had to eat his own words.

His first thought was that he wanted to go talk to Nick. Nick was a man who understood loss on a deeper level than anyone he'd ever known, but he was in the basement of the monastery literally battling his own demon. Nick could also help him understand what might be happening to Catherine, since it sounded like Catherine had given up her life to buy another out of slavery as well, only it seemed Catherine's servitude was still going on, whatever that was. That was the maddening part of it; he didn't know what it was and couldn't help her if he didn't know. If Nick were here, they'd make a plan. They'd go over possibilities. He'd never felt so truly alone in all his existence.

He sat there for another three hours in the off chance that she would come back, that she might decide to run from whomever or whatever had her so afraid and he could somehow save her, but she never returned.

∞

John walked into his house knowing that there was no chance of him being able to sleep. Father Roy sat at the kitchen table with two steaming cups of coffee.

How does that man always know? John wondered.

"Have a seat, John. You look positively spent."

"I positively am, Father. Rough night at work."

"Nah, this is personal," Roy said as he casually took a drink of his coffee.

John rubbed his eyes. "How do you know these things?"

"Energy. It's all energy. Also, your eyes are red."

John was torn between annoyance that the man read him so readily and gratitude, because tonight he felt completely wrecked, and deep down he didn't want to carry this burden alone—though he didn't want to discuss it either. Before he could think about it or find a reason he should be embarrassed to ask, he said it: "Will you pray for me, Father?"

"Always," Father Roy said as he rose and drew the sign of the cross over John, then gently placed his hands on either shoulder.

Tears began running down John's face while the priest silently prayed.

After a few moments, Roy sat back down and looked at John. "I have been told that there is a plan at work in your life. Whatever happened tonight is not a surprise to Him."

"Well, it shocked the hell out of me! Any chance you know what this plan is?"

"No, I just knew that when you were gone tonight, something crucial was transpiring, and I felt in my spirit that it was part of a bigger plan. When we are out somewhere and run into someone we haven't seen in a while or the phone rings and it is someone we were just thinking of, that's no coincidence; that's part of the plan. We when say to ourselves,

'Now what are the odds of that?' That's when there is, for sure, a plan. And if there's a plan, then it means we aren't in it by ourselves."

"Do you know what happened tonight?" John asked.

"I do not."

John's eyes suddenly felt heavy, and he only had one thought in mind: sleep.

Roy said, "Sleep well," to John as his friend walked off to bed, barely awake at that point. He didn't tell John, but he had mostly prayed he would be able to sleep.

He looked like he could use it.

CHAPTER 51

I t was two o'clock in the morning as Damascus watched Robert lay
on the couch in his office, cringing in pain every time he moved. He
came through his open window and landed on the floor in a crouch with
the grace of a panther. Despite the fact that the man often behaved as
if Damascus annoyed him, he knew Robert was often impressed with
him but wouldn't dare show it. Tonight, he could be a sight for sore eyes.
He wanted Robert to be able to count on him, to be reassured he was
in his corner. He always came when Robert called, and although that
sometimes made Robert lose respect for him, on a night like tonight, he
needed that kind of security.

"You don't look well," Damascus said with deep concern.

Robert forced himself to sit upright, grinding his teeth together to
keep from yelping. Damascus rushed over to help him sit up. "I'm *not*
well. I've failed."

"You are afraid the Second Sight will not allow you to live?" Damascus asked.

"No, I think if they were going to kill me, they would have done it
when I went to answer to them in Manhattan. They roughed me up, but
it seems they've decided to let me live; although I'd be shocked if they
call upon me again."

Damascus knew that Robert Billings wasn't used to failing. Everyone
wanted the man's help. He was well respected, but such a failure could
seriously injure his reputation. This was Damascus' fault. He'd helped
Noory succeed—something Robert could never know. Now he had to
help clean up the emotional mess his actions had caused, but it was
worth it. He'd gotten what he wanted: a Robert who needed him.

He took a shot at cheering Robert up. "You still have all your holdings, though. You have a nice life here." Damascus gestured around the room, indicating how well Robert lived. He didn't bother mentioning Robert's wife. She was inconsequential to them both.

"But it isn't enough," Robert roared and held his abdomen. "I wanted to be part of something greater. After I gained all my wealth, I was hollow. Do you know what that's like? To have no greater purpose?"

"Yes, I certainly do," Damascus said softly. He took a chance and sat down next to Robert. "There are other causes in this world, perhaps better causes, that would be lucky to have a man of your caliber on board. Hell, start your own cause if you want to." Damascus briefly patted Robert on the leg, then braced himself to be cursed for it.

"Thank you, Damascus."

He grabbed on to the morsel of sincerity like an oasis in the desert. "Let me know how I can help you, Robert. Anything."

"I don't know if there is any help for me. Amaros told me if I came after that damn punk-ass girlfriend of his, he would kill me. I tried to shoot her. I may be dead before dawn."

Damascus felt as if he'd been punched in the gut. He couldn't bear the images that flashed through his mind. A plan began to form. As much as he feared Amaros, he feared losing Robert even more. "I've been thinking a lot about the situation with that prick Amaros. He's formidable, no doubt. However, I am ancient, and my memory is long. For centuries, there has been a rumor that there is a spell written in an archaic language that only a few of us know. This spell could trap Amaros in whatever vessel he inhabits, bind it to the human, and when one dies, they both die, even Amaros."

He noticed a glimmer of hope in Robert's eyes. "Do it then. Wait, why in hell didn't you do it before?"

"Because the only demon that I can think of who would have the spell memorized was driven from his host recently, but it occurred to me yesterday that there is a possibility that the human host may still have the words imprinted in his memory somewhere. It is doubtful he would be able to speak them himself. It isn't like learning a modern language; the mind has to be wired in a certain way to understand it, but if I could see into his memories, then all I would need to do is get inside him, access the memory, and say the spell."

"Try it then!" Robert said.

Damascus started to tell Robert how dangerous it would be for him to do it. He could get stuck inside the host, trapped by the ancient magic. He could accidentally destroy himself in the process. He opened his mouth to say those things then closed it quickly. Given what he knew of Robert up to this point, the man wouldn't give his safety a thought. He would just want to save his own ass, and though Damascus knew that was the deal, he couldn't bear to have Robert confirm it. He kept the risk to himself. Damascus rose to go, even as he hoped that Robert would grab his arm before he could rise from the couch and tell him to stay. He'd done so before. This time, he didn't. "I've got work to do then," Damascus said.

As Damascus began to climb out the window. Robert rose to his feet with great effort. "Damascus," he called.

Hope rose in his chest as Robert called to him. "Yes."

"Do be careful, please," he said with sincerity.

Damascus nodded and smiled softly. "At least try to get some sleep." A moment later he vanished out the window and into the night.

CHAPTER 52

For once, Nick was free. Between the faraday cage and the iron necklace, he couldn't hear the voices. He was glad of it and miserable about it all at once. The anxiousness was gone, but so was the joy of knowing he'd helped someone who couldn't help themselves. He had a cot, a lamp, several books, a pen, and paper, and a small toilet and sink in one corner of the cell.

He'd learned that the burly monk, Brother Thaddeus, had been told his story and John had made sure he knew Nick was a friend but that the entity within him couldn't be trusted. Thaddeus kept him company, often asking questions and talking well into the night of history and the role he and John had played in it. Thaddeus had become a true, if cautious, friend to Nick.

Nick asked questions about Jonah. Thaddeus informed him that the man barely spoke. Without the entity, he was pathetic. Nick agreed, but no one was sure what to do with him yet and not entirely sure that he wasn't still open to negative spirits. They all knew once one became open to it, the likelihood of it happening again was higher. Thaddeus had told Nick that John and Patrick had spoken at length about what to do with Jonah but neither felt right releasing him just yet, and he was still guilty of rape, murder, and kidnapping, even though it was a malevolent being that had used him.

Nick still felt the entity within. It frustrated Amaros to be trapped and it was frightened that someone might learn how to send it back to purgatory or worse. It made suggestions to Nick about how it might escape. Brother Thaddeus was smart enough to stay farther than arm's length from the cell even though he and Nick had become friends.

Nick had thought of talking with Jonah several times. He understood how the entity made justifications for what it desired, how it manipulated and amplified Nick's own desires, using them against him to get what it wanted until the lines between its desires and Nick's were so blurred that they were barely distinguishable anymore. He also thought of how it must have been difficult for John to see the transformation in Jonah after knowing him as a true friend and brilliant historian. It made him realize how difficult it must have been for John to have to go through it again with him.

It was the fifth day there when Nick turned to find Jonah staring at him, deep in thought. Nick nodded, and Jonah looked away quickly.

Damascus parked down the street from the monastery under the cover of night and wandered into the woods surrounding it. He found a spot not too far away, spread a blanket on the ground, laid down, and began breathing deeply. He knew the basement prison was guarded, and he wouldn't be able to just walk right in, but he knew that didn't matter either. His body didn't actually need to go in there anyway, only his spirit. After a few minutes, he felt himself break free from the shell of his body and moved swiftly toward the prison before he lost his nerve.

Once inside, he found both his targets. He also found an obstacle. A faraday cage surrounded Nick. It would make it impossible to get Amaros out of Nick and get Jonah back in there with him, for Nick to, hopefully, destroy him. Jonah had nothing left for this world as it was—this wasn't the first time Damascus had visited his target. By his estimation, he was doing him a kindness. Damascus traced the energy of the cage, found where the switch was and used his concentrated energy to short circuit it.

"What the . . ." Brother Thaddeus had noticed the hum of the cage had stopped, and he worked quickly to re-energize it. Damascus didn't think the monk would be able to do it in time, though; he'd fried it so well it would need to be rewired, but still he worked quickly.

Noory's father lay on his cot, looking frail. Damascus knew it would make him easier to inhabit in his weakened state. He descended upon the man and settled in. There was little resistance, as Jonah was far too used to sharing space with another being. Damascus was happy to know the man hadn't awakened, making it easier to rifle around in his mind without resistance. It wasn't long before he found what he was looking for. To his surprise, there was not only a spell to destroy Amaros but also one to call it forth. Apparently, someone else had the same thought he did: that they didn't necessarily want him killed in just any host. They wanted to choose in case he ended up in a host who was valuable enough to save. This was a bonus.

He had not told Robert, but he was hoping he wouldn't have to kill Amaros while he was still inside Nick. He liked Noory, which he realized was ironic given that he and the scion should have been natural enemies, like cats and dogs, and he knew killing Nick would destroy her. He realized it might have been that they both loved the wrong person. Whatever it was, he was thrilled to know he didn't have to take out Nick in the process; besides he thought the man was way too beautiful to damage. He also knew it was risky. When he inhabited Noory's father, he would need to pull Amaros out of Nick, say the spell to call him into Jonah, and get out before Amaros turned on him.

He fished around inside Jonah's mind, looking for something else: the absolute will for redemption. When he found it, he knew Jonah would say the spell for two reasons: he wanted the redemption that giving his life would bring. He was a broken man with few options left in this world, and he could now read the archaic language, which he would, by default, share Amaros' knowledge of, whether it wanted him to or not. Damascus felt certain Jonah would say the spell, and if he didn't, Damascus would whisper the words into his ear. And this time, once Amaros was bound to Jonah, with an optional exit plan, Jonah would waste no time taking it.

Nick's sleep was deep but troubled that night. The entity within him was more agitated and restless than ever. In his dream, it screamed at him to awaken to no avail. Nick felt almost as if he'd been drugged. Each time he swam near the surface of consciousness, he'd dream of the same old man who had appeared to him so long ago when he had been snatched from the jaws of death and given his commission, and he'd fall deeper into sleep.

When he finally woke, he found Jonah standing over him, speaking an archaic language into the dim lighting of his cell. The other denizens of the prison caterwauled and pounded on their bars as if they sensed what was happening and they craved the potent entity being coaxed free of its host.

Nick wondered briefly how he had gotten in before he felt a tug deep within himself, as if something were refusing to let go and sinking its tentacles in with all its might. Then, finally, a snap as he felt the darkness exit his body. He wept with relief at the thought of no longer having to constantly work to suppress it.

"I need you to destroy me, Bishop Nicholas," Jonah said as sweat ran down his face. Nick realized Jonah was now carrying the burden of having to suppress it. "Destroy me, and it will die with me. I learned from carrying Azazel how to bind Amaros so that it must die with me. The two were ancient enemies."

Nick's mind raced to understand what was happening. Jonah was making the same request of him he had made of Noory when he first took in the entity. "I don't know that I should, Jonah."

"Please, I beg you. It won't let me destroy myself. I tried over and over again after I . . . hurt Catherine."

Nick looked at Jonah with a well of sympathy he'd never felt before. He couldn't imagine hurting Noory like that and having to live with it.

"Please, let me do this for my daughter. I need to give her one noble memory of me. I need redemption, Bishop," Jonah said, now gritting his teeth to keep the being in check. It had been hard enough for Nick to suppress; now it was back in one fully human. Nick found an odd admiration that Jonah was able to do it. That he was willing to do it was a type of nobility and irony. He'd taken it on once to get what he wanted. Now he'd taken it on to offer his very life for someone else.

Sweat ran down Jonah's face. His fists were clenched. Nick could see Jonah starting to lose his grip over the entity.

"No matter what you have done, I don't know if Noory and I could be the same after—"

Jonah resumed speaking in the archaic language that even one as ancient as Nick couldn't understand. Nick realized the constant hum of the cage had ceased and knew that nothing contained Amaros anymore. Even the door had opened under his power. The words themselves had some kind of power. Nick was glad he couldn't speak them. He had heard long ago there was a language that carried such force. He knew now that they were in Jonah's head from when Azazel had inhabited him and only another entity capable of speaking them could look into his mind and read them. Even though it could be destroyed, now that Jonah had spoken the words, it was also speaking a language capable of releasing very powerful magic; nothing could contain it.

Nick watched panic contort Jonah's face. "I see what he's planning! Destroy it or it will kill every last brother in this monastery," Jonah begged quickly before the entity silenced him again. Jonah pressed onward with a resolve that made Nick admire him. "Now, will you tell me you can't?" Jonah asked with a frantic look distorting his face so that Nick could no longer tell Jonah from the demon.

Nick knew that even if Noory never understood, he had to stop it. As strong as he was, he feared he was still no match for it. He'd carried it long enough to know.

He felt nauseated as he realized by the feral grin on Jonah's face that he'd lost control entirely. It was now Amaros that spoke. "You can't and you know it. You love her too much. It has made you weak. You said it yourself: You 'can't destroy this vessel,' " it mocked.

"But I can," Brother Thaddeus said as he pointed the SIG Sauer at Jonah's temple and pulled the trigger. Jonah crumpled to the floor. The captives in the surrounding cages shrieked and wailed, maybe sensing the death of one of the most powerful entities to escape purgatory and wondering whether their own dabbling with the dark powers would seal their death sentences as well.

Nick looked at Brother Thaddeus in startlement. He hadn't even realized the monk had been there. Thaddeus holstered his weapon and reached into the folds of his robe for a small bottle of holy water. He handed it to Nick and whispered, "Last Rites, Bishop? I think Jonah earned his redemption. I'll call John and inform the abbot," Thaddeus said with an impressive amount of control.

Nick nodded as he kneeled beside Jonah and felt no trace of the entity. He pulled his blanket from the cot to contain the spreading pool of blood as he began the final ritual to bless Jonah into eternity.

Damascus drifted up through the ceiling into the cool night air, over the treetops, then down, lower still, until he settled back into the space of his body lying on the forest floor.

CHAPTER 53

Catherine Abramson came back home to her Manhattan penthouse after a long day at work. Her heels clicked softly across the marble floor as she immediately made her way to the bar to pour herself a drink. She yanked the cork from the half-drunk bottle. The cork slipped from her fingers and rolled under a space beneath the heavy bar that was too tight for her to reach under. She simply leaned over and picked the table up with one hand as the glasses and bottles rattled. Her mother hadn't told her she was the scion until well into adulthood. Until then, she had always wondered why everyone else was so damn weak. She'd never once in her life asked a man to open a jar for her or hold a door.

She poured the red wine and drank deeply. After seeing John only once, she had come back home to find her life even emptier than usual, her duties more distasteful. She walked over to her balcony doors and opened them to let the cool night air in as the Manhattan skyline twinkled before her.

She emptied the glass, walked back over to the bar, and sat it down. Someone knocked at her door, and she sighed in annoyance. She punched the buzzer. "Yeah?"

"It's Neal. Boss has a message for you."

She opened the door. "What? I told you I don't like you showing up unannounced like this. I don't want to have to tell you again. You could have just called with the message."

He walked in, over to the bar, and picked up the bottle of wine she'd just opened, read the label, and sat it down. "The way I see it, I can show up any damn time I please."

"You don't have anything to tell me. Get out." She walked over to the front door to open it for him. Before she could reach it, he was already blocking her path.

"I'm not going anywhere. I had a taste long ago, and I intend to get more." He leaned over and ran a fingertip down the side of her face. She remembered the vulgarity of their first encounter. She had not been back from the dead long and was fragile and needed his help. He took advantage of her in exchange for giving her information about some very bad people who intended to harm her daughter. Since then, she'd worked her way up to the presidency of Second Sight—if she had no choice but to work there, she may as well be at the top—and the stupid son of a bitch worked for her now.

The feel of his finger on her cheek enraged her. She hated remembering the vulnerability of her past, and he brought it all back like being swept away by sewage. She grabbed his finger and broke it.

He screamed, shook it a little, and then it was good as new again, just like she knew it would be. Still, causing him pain felt good.

"That's all right. I like it rough," he said.

She wanted to break his neck but realized he might enjoy it too much. "There are other ways to hurt you. You can't survive everything, and you know it."

"Yeah, that bitch boss thing won't work on me anymore. You have a boss too, you know, and I have information that just might make you want to cuddle up with me tonight," he said with a smug arrogance that was beyond irritating.

"No, you don't. Leave." She stepped around him and headed for the door once more.

"I know you were in Atlanta. I know you met with the Beloved."

She stopped as ice water snaked through her veins. He had her attention. She didn't turn around as he continued talking.

"I knew one day you would slip. I can make it worth your while to spend a little time with me or I can make one phone call and . . . you know."

Before another word crossed his lips, Catherine had him by the neck as his feet dangled. The sound of her heels across the marble floor was now like the vengeful thunder of a titan at war. "No one threatens my family." She tore through the penthouse, building momentum as she kept him suspended, and flung him off the balcony without another word and watched as he sailed across the night sky and slammed through the window of an accounting firm on the other side of the street.

She walked back inside and closed the balcony doors behind her.

CHAPTER 54

Noory stuck her hands deep into the pockets of her sweatshirt while she walked into the woods of the cemetery that the monks managed. It was a natural cemetery: no manicured lawn, no headstones, and only simple flat stones throughout the forest to mark the graves of the departed. Below the earth, the bodies were only in shrouds or simple pine boxes. Their bodies would feed the surrounding forest. Noory felt a peace as she knelt beside her father's grave. His life had become a wreck for him and everyone around him. There was a certain joy in thinking that he would return to the earth and cycle back around into something beautiful, perhaps the trees that now had their roots already deep in the earth. The ground would renew his body, and she trusted that a power even greater than she could renew his soul.

It was well into fall now. She was surrounded by all the rustic colors as a gentle early morning breeze blew and leaves swirled around her and landed on the fresh red Georgia clay atop her father's resting place. She knew she was grieving for something she never had but couldn't help but love him for giving Nick back to her and the rest of the world. "Thank you," she whispered.

They had buried Jonah the morning after he'd died. It had been a simple ceremony with only John, Nick, Brother Thaddeus, and Father Patrick—the monastery's abbot. Father Roy had stayed away in case the monks had asked questions about him. He realized he might be a bit much for even his fellow men of the cloth to accept. Nick had held her hand as they lowered Jonah into the ground. He was a strong, constant comfort to her that day, but she had not heard from him since.

Despite the peace she felt over her father's fate and what should have been a happy ending now that Nick was free, loneliness settled over her like a fog. It had been almost five days since Nick had gone home, but he hadn't visited her or even called. On the third day, she broke down and called him in case he thought she was mad at him for his actions while he dealt with the entity, but he didn't answer. She wanted to talk to John about it sooner but was a little embarrassed for him to know how much it bothered her, but she couldn't wait anymore.

She got back into her car and realized that she also grieved for Father Roy. He'd clearly been sent here for Nick. Now that Nick was saved, why would the powers that be keep him from crossing over? Even though she wanted to go see John, she also was afraid to. She hated the idea of walking into John's house and having him confirm was she already knew: that Roy was gone, but she was not one to put off the inevitable. The quicker she dealt with it, the quicker she could move past it. As usual, John waited for her on the front porch with a cup of coffee in his hand.

"Thanks," she smiled and walked in. They sat at the kitchen table in silence, sipping their coffee.

John was the first to break the silence. "I've already been to check on him. A few times actually. He's fine. You know, in case you were wondering."

Noory smiled. "It's confusing."

"Nick loves you," John said in a tone that meant she ought to already know that.

"It certainly doesn't feel like it."

John sighed.

Noory narrowed her eyes at him. "You know something."

"Look, he didn't want me to say anything, but as soon as the entity left him, he started drinking again."

"Damn it," Noory said as unexpected tears filled her eyes. She hadn't realized just how much she had wanted to believe he would stay sober.

"Noory, the good thing is, he's grown. He wants to get clean. I've never seen him so determined to do it. He's never had the will before, and the reason is *you*."

"But why won't he talk to me about it? He has to know ignoring me is hurtful."

"He wants to deserve you," John said.

"That's silly. He doesn't have to be perfect for me."

"Yes, he does. No one's good enough for you," John said, smiling.

She smacked his arm. "Oh, stop it."

"He just needs a little time," he said.

"I get it. It's just that Jonah's gone, and that seems odd, even though I didn't know him that well. Nick's incommunicado, and Father Roy's disappeared. It's just . . . I don't know."

John smiled. "Well, you got two out of three right." John pointed out the window.

Noory looked out and gasped. She set her coffee on the table, ran off the porch, and didn't stop until she reached Roy, as he was halfway back to the house.

"Noory!" he called with a huge smile.

"Why are you still here?" She wrapped her arms around him and couldn't stop tears from welling up in her eyes yet again.

He returned the hug and laughed. "I know! I didn't expect to be! After I heard Nick was free, I kept expecting to return from where I came, but it hasn't happened yet. I can only assume I'm not done."

"Good!" Noory smiled broadly before realizing what she was saying and what that might mean to Roy. She bit her lip and looked up at him sheepishly. "I mean, maybe bad for you, though. I guess you probably wanted to go."

"I'm content to be wherever I'm supposed to be. There's a reason for all this, you know."

"Maybe you can tell me what it is," Noory said.

Father Roy motioned for her to come closer as if he were going to tell her a secret. He whispered into her ear, "I have no idea." He laughed. "But that's okay. It's enough to know that there is someone who does know." He put his arm around Noory, and they walked back inside, where John was making breakfast for them.

∞

While Noory set the table for breakfast, Father Roy handed John his mail.

John flipped through until he saw a plain envelope with no return address. He opened it curiously. It only contained two words: "I'm okay. C" Just knowing she was out there and okay filled his heart with joy. He worried, of course, and there was also the matter of what it would do to Noory when she eventually learned her mother had been alive all this time, but he decided, if only for the morning, to simply find joy in just knowing that she still lived.

John smiled and slapped Father Roy on the back, good-naturedly. "I feel like having some breakfast, Father. You hungry?"

"I'm starving," Roy said.

John smiled. "Are you hungry, Noory?"

"Yeah," she said. "What's that look on your face?"

"What? It's nothing."

"Oh, it's something, John Abramson, and you're *gonna* tell me," she teased.

He smiled and dropped his head, feeling almost embarrassed, like a kid again, in love—how in the hell he remembered what that was like he had no idea. "Someday," he said to Noory. "Someday."

CHAPTER 55

Noory followed at a distance. It occurred to her he might sense her. She knew Nick was a thousand times more intuitive than the average human. However, he looked like he was struggling just to keep his head above water. He was pale, sweating, and shaking. Noory closed her eyes briefly and prayed for him. He stopped walking for a moment and looked around. She quickly ducked into the shadows.

She knew he had been trying to detox. He hadn't returned her calls and now she knew why. He didn't want her to see him this way. She knew he would never understand that she knew this was him at his strongest, most courageous. He was trying to face the world with his own power—the simple human kind, nothing supernatural about it. Noory loved him for it, deeply, soulfully. She wanted to run to him and lend him her strength.

Nick slipped into the side door of the Church of the Sacred Heart. Noory knew there was an AA meeting held there twice a week. She wanted to wait there until he came out. For that matter, she wanted to go in with him and hold his hand. Yet, she knew Nick wouldn't want that. She did make her way back to his penthouse.

She sat on his couch with her boots propped up on his coffee table when he returned an hour and a half later. "Isn't breaking and entering above the scion?"

"What was it you once told me? 'When it comes to sacred things, if it looks like you think, then it probably isn't the real thing?' Something like that?"

"I can only hope that's true, love." Nick raked a hand through his hair while looking beyond miserable. He was trembling.

"You might want to head back home. This could get ugly. I'm no ordinary drunk, you know. I've been at it for centuries. Apparently, the entity was keeping me from feeling the effects of detoxing. Now that's gone. Well, I picked up the ouzo just long enough to try to make the symptoms go away and . . . whatever. It's hard. I'm three days in, but you should go until I've got a better handle on this. I'm an irritable pain in the ass right now."

Noory rose slowly, all the while praying he wouldn't send her away. She walked over to where he stood in the kitchen. "No." Noory reached out for his hand and led him to the couch. She sat down on the far end and threw one leg up and pulled him down in front of her and wrapped her arms around him, pulling him back against her. "It isn't just the alcohol you're weening off of, is it?"

He exhaled deeply. "No," he said. "Narcotics too. There's a doctor near Cabbage Town that leaves a prescription pad at reception. You just give her the money."

"I'm proud of you," Noory said softly.

"Don't be. I'm not sure I can do it."

"I'll be here either way."

Nick shook in her arms as she gently brushed the thick brown hair back from his clammy forehead. "So, what finally brought you to this? Why stop now?"

"A few reasons. When I met Father Roy, he saw all these amazing things in me. I wanted to live up to what he saw."

"But he met you as an alcoholic. He saw the beauty there even with the addiction," Noory said.

"Yes, he did, but I would like to feel worthy of it. Spiritually speaking, I know there are doctrinal reasons to argue anyone's worthiness, but as a human . . . I would like to believe that I've earned it. But that isn't the only reason, the main reason. I want to deserve you."

She could barely speak and hoped he wouldn't turn around to see the tears threatening to spill over.

"Please, say something. I'm hanging by a thread here," he said.

She felt sick that he would think for even a moment that she didn't feel the same depth of commitment to him. Though it went against every instinct that she had cultivated over a lifetime, she sat up and pulled his arm so that he would turn to face her.

She let all the vulnerability wash across her face. She realized she could do no less when Nick lay in her arms shaking and fighting for his sobriety. "You saved my life, you went through hell with me, you gambled your immortality for me, but that isn't why I love you."

"Why in the world, Light?"

"Because you are you, Nicholas Theodoulos, and I believe you were meant for me."

Noory stayed with him until he drifted off in her arms.

Chapter 56

Noory had texted that morning that she was coming by around noon to try to get him to eat something. He knew it was now or never. After waking up to find her gone after she held him close—nothing wrong with that, she had to get to work—but the pain of her absence hit him so hard in his vulnerable state; it reminded him he wouldn't be able to bear losing her to time. So, he made a plan to stop this relationship. Shut it down. After that, he would move far away. He would have to. John would be ready to kill him for hurting her.

Noory knocked once, then walked in. The smile on her face quickly vanished once she saw them on the couch. She didn't move. She didn't speak. It was all he could do to keep from crying. His chest constricted. He could barely breathe. His brain screamed at him to stop this. Instead, he smiled up at Noory and pulled the prostitute closer to him.

The blonde woman looked at her in amusement. "Something we can help you with honey?"

The smell of ouzo permeated the air. Nick was disheveled, with lipstick smeared across his cheek. He looked up at Noory with a smile on his face.

"I see you have a type." Noory said, gesturing at the woman's blonde hair.

He watched anger and hurt wrestle for position across Noory's features.

Noory turned to go. Nick said nothing as he heard the door click shut with what sounded to his ears like a gunshot but was no more than the closing of a door.

"Thank you, Bianca. Please leave," he told the woman as he handed her a wad of cash.

"You sure that's all you want, honey? This is a lot of money, and you are slammin'. I'm more than happy to make you forget your troubles for a while, and you are most certainly a man with troubles."

"Yeah, I'm sure. Please take this with you." Nick handed her the bottle of ouzo.

Bianca slipped the bottle into her bag. "I realize this is absolutely none of my business, but why do you want to hurt the girl like that?"

"Because she's better off without me. It's for her own good."

"No, you clearly love her. I think it might be for your own good . . . or misery," she said as she shook her head. Bianca pointed at Nick. "*You* are a masochist. Why the hell people insist on being miserable always eludes me. I do what I like," she said with a seductive wink.

Nick reached into his wallet once more and pulled out a hundred-dollar bill. "Here," Nick held out the money to her.

She reached for it curiously. "Want me to make you feel better? Seems a little counterproductive to your self-flagellation but okay."

"No, just paying you for the therapy," Nick said.

Bianca put the money in her purse. "What a waste," she said giving Nick one last once-over before she slowly walked out the door. She looked back a final time in invitation.

He waved goodbye, and she finally shut the door.

CHAPTER 57

Noory finished trimming the hooves of a white sheep she had nick-named "Baby Doll," for the way she sometimes appeared to be bat-ting her eyelashes.

"Good job," John said. He inspected the hooves and gave Baby Doll a pat before she sauntered off.

"Where's Sampson? I might as well give him a trim while I'm here," Noory said.

John sat on the stool across from Noory, took the files from her, and set them to the side.

"You've been here for two days now. When are you going to tell me what's going on?"

"Nick's an asshole," Noory said.

"Well, sure," John said with a laugh, "but you knew that going in."

Noory began brushing the dust off her clothes with a vengeance, hoping that John would just go away. She loved him but hated the vul-nerability she was feeling. Part of her also didn't want John to hate Nick when she told him what had happened. Then she wondered why she was protecting him. He certainly wasn't protecting her. "I caught Nick with a prostitute. It also smelled like he's been drinking again. He worked so hard to get clean."

John exhaled in frustration. "Damn it! I'm sorry, Noory. I really thought he was going to kick it this time. The drinking doesn't really sur-prise me, but the hooker does. He's never, ever been one to hire them. He's seen too many kids get pulled into sex work and never leave. Are you sure it was a prostitute? Never mind, the point is, forget about him. You deserve to be happy. He's just hurting you."

"He saved my life."

"That doesn't mean you need to be in a relationship with him."

"I know that," Noory said, trying not to sound irritated but failing. She stood up and started putting things away.

"Okay, okay." John rose and watched Noory straighten up the barn. Even though she wasn't his, it pleased him to see that she'd become like him in at least one aspect: she'd found the peace he did in leaving people behind to care for the four legged. He started to walk away before another thought hit him that brought tears to his eyes. Maybe she just wanted to be near him.

"Noory?"

She turned around, looking exhausted, angry, and grieved all at once.

"I love you, baby."

"I love you, too, Dad," she said with a pure, sweet smile that reminded him of when she was little riding on his shoulders through the fields.

CHAPTER 58

Nick lay on his couch as the sun rose over Atlanta and the first morning rays slowly made their way across the floor, catching dust motes as they lazily traveled to some arbitrary destination. Nick's head pounded, not from drinking, just misery, but he felt too despondent to get up and take something for it. He also felt that it was a fitting penance for who he was and what he'd done. His head pounded even harder as someone began banging on the door.

"Go away!" Nick yelled.

"Don't make me break it down, Nicholas!"

"Shit," Nick said, knowing it was John, and he was clearly pissed.

Nick rose to his feet and paused a moment until the room stopped spinning. Nick opened the door with a pit of fear in his stomach. It didn't matter that he and John had been friends forever, didn't matter that he could blink himself into another realm; he knew John would want to beat his ass over hurting Noory, and he could tell by his tone that John knew what had happened.

John looked at him with undisguised disgust. "Noory has been at my house for the last two days trimming sheep hooves."

Nick felt a stab at his heart at the very mention of her name. It was a visceral thing that almost made him double over as if punched in the gut. John looked at him curiously.

"Stop reading me," Nick said as he squeezed his eyes together and pinched the bridge of his nose.

"I wouldn't need to read you if you would stop acting a fool and let someone in. You love her."

Nick nodded but wouldn't make eye contact with John, who moved to the kitchen. Nick watched him return with a glass of water and a couple of pain relievers for his head. "If you needed to disconnect from her, you should have talked to her. You shouldn't have done it the way you did. That was brutal. I really want to beat your ass for that, but it would only add to the masochistic trap you're in." He handed Nick the water and pills.

Nick cringed as John used the same word Bianca had. He hated feeling he was that damn transparent. "I had to do it the way I did. I needed to hurt her enough to be done with me. For good," Nick said and then popped the pills into his mouth and washed them down.

John leaned over and sniffed. "You haven't had anything to drink in quite a while," he said as a statement. "I don't think you slept with the prostitute, either."

"No, I didn't," Nick said softly.

John walked over to the large bank of windows. He turned his face to the near blinding sunrise and let the light wash over him. "The Creator's ways are not our ways," he said softly.

"No, they are infinitely more painful," Nick said.

John couldn't disagree after seeing Catherine again, but this wasn't about him. "Painful, like what you did to Noory?"

"One day she will die, and I will be alone again," Nick said as his voice cracked, and he hid his face in his hands.

"So, you deny yourself joy because it won't last?" John asked.

"So have you," Nick said, remembering further back than Noory's mom to a woman John had met in the mid-seventeenth century.

"I have, yes, and I regret it."

"But when you let her go, you kept yourself from having to watch her age and die. At her death, she would have grieved over knowing she had to leave you in such pain. It wasn't just about your pain, but hers too," Nick argued.

"I still regret it. She married, but she wasn't in love. She lived but had no spark. Do you really want to do that to Noory?"

"I'm not strong enough, John."

"Yes, you are. Stop hurting my daughter. Stop hurting yourself." John left without another word.

Chapter 59

It was her fourth day at John's farm. Every day when she got off work, she tried to go back to her apartment, but found herself hopping on the freeway and heading north, and as much as Noory had enjoyed spending time with him and Father Roy, she was beginning to hate feeling paralyzed by her own fear. Every time she thought about going back to her apartment, she got depressed. It was the first time in her life that she had truly feared being alone, and she resented it.

The horse she'd been brushing scraped a hoof across the barn floor in annoyance when he noticed that she'd stopped. "Screw this!" She threw the brush down, went inside to get her keys, and was headed to Atlanta within a few minutes.

Noory knocked on Nick's door. He didn't answer immediately, but she felt him in the apartment. "You know I know how to get in there. You may as well go ahead and let me in," she said, knowing he was just a few feet away, on the other side of the door.

Fear danced through his veins. He'd gone to great lengths to keep her away from him. He'd even hurt her to do it. Cruelly so. Then there was the advice to avoid relationships for a year while getting clean, which had never been a problem when he'd tried sobriety before. For him, there was a greater question: did he deserve the light? His sponsor, Brother Thaddeus, one of the few people who both knew the truth about him and had been through the program himself, a short list indeed, had spent most of their time talking with him about his issues with worth.

"I'll break it down," the Light herself said from the other side of the door. She sounded just like her dad. He was shocked to find a smile briefly flash across his face—it had been so long it nearly hurt. His somber countenance returned when he realized he was about to fail in the promise he'd made to himself. Nick opened the door and motioned her to come in.

Noory looked frustrated as she spoke. He could tell she was about to let him have it. She'd earned the right. He closed the door and braced himself for it. "You've spent over seventeen hundred years wishing God would deliver you, help you, something. Did you ever consider that this," she said, slapping herself on the chest, "may well be how he does it? I'm here, Nick. You've spent your whole life helping everybody else. For God's sake, let me help *you!*"

He put his hand behind his neck and took in a ragged breath. "I didn't want to drag anyone into my mess."

"Damn it, Nick! I'm already part of this. I have been long before I met you."

He sank into a chair and covered his face. Noory walked over and knelt in front of him. He knew she was smelling for the ouzo, again, just like John. She slowly reached up and pulled his hands from his face. "You haven't been drinking."

"No."

She leaned forward slowly until their foreheads touched.

"Oh, Light," he said. "When I look at you, that's what I see, and it's almost too bright to behold."

"That's because you need to come out of the dark more often."

As Nick looked at her, all his resolve and determination to push her away began to melt like snow under the sun. He felt like a fool to ever believe he could stay away. "Maybe I do." Nick freed his hands from Noory's grasp and gently took her face into his hands and kissed her lips softly. It was his first kiss when he wasn't half drunk or "inhabited." It was his first kiss as just him, in . . . it had been so long he couldn't even remember. His heart was laid bare, open, vulnerable, and . . . free. Nick nearly wept with relief over the close contact. He couldn't recall what it was like to be this close to anyone who wasn't dying or trying to kill him.

His armor cracked for a moment, and that was all it took for his gentle and passionate nature to crawl out into the light of day and enfold Noory like wings. He pulled her into his lap and kissed her like a man finding water in the desert. Noory moaned softly as he swept her into his arms and took her to his bedroom.

He laid her down gently on the bed. He hoped she'd find this Nick a sharp contrast to the one who had shoved her against the wall in Argentina and ground his hips against her. He would forever regret letting himself touch her while Amaros was part of him.

"I remember how I was before," he said. "I'm sorry if I hurt you or offended you."

"I was more upset by the prostitute than what happened with us in the cave." He heard her heart kick up to a gallop, and she couldn't look him in the eye.

"I never slept with that woman or had another drink since I've started rehab. I paid her for her time, and she left not long after you did."

He heard her pulse slow to a less-erratic rhythm.

"Oh, good. No, not that easy. You can't push me away like that anymore. No more of that. You can't start a pattern of hurting me every time you get scared and want to hide. You have to run *to* me, not away from me."

"Running to the Light. Now that's something," he said as he walked through a door he'd long feared. On the other side it was beautiful, terrifying, and as he looked at Noory he decided, worth the risk. "And you're right. I've been extremely unfair to you. That stops today."

He lay beside her, propped up on one elbow as he brushed hair back from her face. "I'll be honest with you. Sobriety is rough, and I can't promise you it will be easy from here on out, but I swear to try for you and myself," he said.

"That's all you can do," Noory said. She pulled him down to kiss her.

He returned the intensity that she gave and moaned. "Dear God. I want you more than my next breath."

Noory stopped kissing him.

"What's wrong, Light? If you don't want to . . ." Nick began.

Noory laughed. "Oh, make no mistake about it. I want to. I just wonder if I'm doing something wrong. Every time someone calls you Bishop I wonder if I'm doing the wrong thing here."

"I've come to realize that we all have a calling in our lives. I intend to fulfill my calling no matter how it breaks my heart, but I don't have to be a bishop to do that. At one time, it was just right for me, and I walked that path. Now, I'm just Nick, and I love Noory Abramson."

As he kissed her, he put his hand on the small of her back and pulled her hips to meet his. Lust shot through him like a bolt of lightning. She wrapped a hand around the back of his head, deepening the kiss, and pressed her pelvis against his erection with a whimper. Her answering body drove him to urgency. He rolled her onto her back and placed his weight on top of her, covering her as he nudged her legs apart with his knees. She wrapped her arms around him as he brushed his lips across hers, softly at first, then parted her lips with his tongue, exploring her mouth, thrusting deeper, mimicking what his body craved. When moving on top of her through their clothes wasn't enough anymore, he raised up until he was straddling her. He unbuttoned her top, planted kisses between her breasts, and made a trail down to her navel. Nick looked up at her with heavy-lidded eyes as he began unbuttoning her jeans. She helped him shimmy them down her legs, and he threw them onto the floor.

Noory sat up and tipped onto her knees, then slowly lifted her head. The hungry look she gave him told him he didn't need an ancient devil inside to want to press her back down onto the bed and do wild things, but he controlled the beast that was comprised of him alone as she pulled his shirt off him. She ran her hands over the hard muscles of his chest and abdomen as Nick closed his eyes.

He whispered into her ear. "You've got no idea how many times I imagined . . ." He put his hands over her breasts and then slid his hands inside the bra cups and groaned. "I need to feel you. You might have to help me with this. I haven't been with a woman since bras were invented."

Noory pulled back and looked at him with shock.

"Well, I don't sleep with prostitutes, and I don't like women to get involved in what I do. Is my lack of lingerie knowledge a problem?" he asked, looking away from her for a moment.

"Absolutely not," she said with a depth of sensuality that made Nick's mind do flip flops. "I get all that pent-up sexual energy tonight? I'm down with that." Nick laughed as she lifted her eyebrows suggestively and reached around to unhook her bra and lifted it over her head agonizingly slow. Clearly, the woman knew each moment would add to his need for her, and she was right. She flung it to the floor and smiled as she slowly pressed her breasts against him.

Nick inhaled sharply and kissed her with ferocity. He felt that he would explode as he pulled his jeans off and flung them to the same unknown location on the floor where Noory's bra lay. Nick began to shake with need. He tried to put the brakes on and couldn't. He quickly took his underwear off and slid his hand into her panties as he felt her warmth and wetness against his palm. She sighed as he ground his mouth against hers in a need intense and sweet all at once.

He withdrew his hand and pushed her down onto the bed as he removed her underwear. His mouth found her breast.

"Please," she cried as she arched her hips.

He slid two fingers inside her as she pushed against his hand. He eased them in and out of her. "Please," she begged. He still didn't enter her but lowered his head between her legs and tasted her. "Nick, please."

She felt him smile against her. "You don't have to beg," he said with a husky voice. He lowered himself onto her and entered her slowly and moaned as he slid the rest of the way into her. Noory gasped and threw a hand out to grab the pillow beside her. He reached for the hand and grasped it with his own.

"Are you okay?" he asked as he stayed completely still.

She nodded.

His face was a mask of pure concentration. "Don't move, Light, or I'll come undone.

Knowing he wouldn't last long; he reached between them and stroked her. When he felt her contract around him, he began thrusting as she wrapped her legs around him and held on. He held her eyes captive, refusing to break contact as he thrust deep. He pressed himself against her one final time, savoring every inch of her as she breathlessly called out his name.

He didn't roll off her after they were both satisfied but leaned over and kissed her as if he were still just as hungry for her. He held his forehead against hers and spoke: "I want you to know I take what we've done here very seriously. I know we come from different places. In this time, what we're doing here doesn't always mean something, but to me it means I'm yours: heart, soul, body. You're it for me, Noory." He held her eyes, not wavering, making sure she knew his intentions.

"And you're it for me. I can't ever imagine anyone but you," she said.

He had a sly grin on his face. "If you're still here after all the shit I've put you through, then I couldn't doubt you. I just wanted you to know where I stand."

He held her that night, saying a prayer that he would be the man she deserved.

CHAPTER 60

The Templars had gathered in a clearing on John's land to witness a onetime event. They had come from all corners of the globe. Nick and Noory had been invited, too. It was time to destroy the relic. John sighed when he told them that even with the device gone; the people scheming behind the thing were still very much alive.

They all stood around the bonfire, waiting for everyone else to arrive. The sun was just beginning to set, and there was just enough light for them to greet each other before they began.

As Nick came into the clearing with Noory, John looked over at him from a distance. He studied him, and Nick shrank beneath the scrutiny. He knew with certainty that John had figured out that he and Noory had been intimate. Over the centuries, he'd watched as John correctly guessed that anyone from kings to congressmen was having relations with someone. He was never wrong. John held his gaze far longer than Nick was comfortable with. Oh, yeah, he knew. Nick also knew he'd rather get "the look" than have to discuss it with him. If that happened, he might have to jump into the bonfire with the damn relic.

Nick greeted his fellow Templars. Noory leaned over to John and whispered, "What's up with that weird handshake? Can I suggest that they do a little fist bump at the end?"

Nick cringed. Before John even spoke, he knew she had gone too far as he saw his posture change. "Careful, Noory. Any of these men here would give their life for you."

"Sorry, I guess it's a little strange for me because I actually do know that, and I'm just me, you know?"

John softened and said to her exactly what Nick was thinking, "I know you're the woman who jumped off a tower with that damn box,

290 ◆ *Kim Conrey*

knowing that your life could end right then and there. Hold your head a little higher. You've earned their loyalty and they know it, too."

William approached them. They hadn't seen him since Rosslyn Chapel. "Noory," he said with a smile in his thick Scottish accent. "You did well, scion."

"Thank you," she said. Nick noted that for the first time, she didn't look annoyed to hear someone call her that. They were both changing.

"You, John, and Nick should come visit me again when the fate of the world isn't at stake. I believe you would find Scotland much more lovely that way. I would be honored to be your personal guide," William said.

"I would like that," she said with sincerity.

William went to take his place among his brothers as Nick came to stand beside Noory. He took her hand and laced his fingers through hers as he watched the firelight dance in her eyes. As much as he loved seeing his Templar brothers again, he wanted to see Noory again later that night. He thought it possible that Noory might have been reading his mind as well. She winked at him at the precise moment he was going over what he wanted to do to her later.

Father Roy walked into the clearing holding the relic. The Templars were all up to date on exactly who he was. He was deemed the most trustworthy due to the fact that he had few ties in this world anymore.

John addressed the crowd. "Tonight, we have come together to witness the destruction of a device that threatens the free will of men everywhere. Our brothers have fought, died, and suffered torture to keep these rights safe and sacred. The fire itself represents our sacrifice." John paused and gazed into the flames.

Nick watched tears gather in Noory's eyes, no doubt over what he had told her in the cargo hold of the ship when they were held captive. It was hard to look into the flames. He saw it all again. He found himself squeezing Noory's hand tighter and forced himself to loosen his grip. "Sorry," he whispered.

She ran a soft thumb over the top of his hand.

"I don't know if this will work, but like all that we've faced through the years, we will figure this out together. Father Roy," he said motioning to him to throw the box into the flames.

He threw it in, and everyone held their breaths waiting to see if it would start to burn. It was wood but also metal. They knew it couldn't all burn, but the fire should have at least caused it to fall apart. "I hate that fucking thing," Noory whispered to Nick with venom.

"Pft! You and me both, Light," Nick replied.

"I was going to spit on the damn thing but when Father Roy walked out with it. I realized that was a no go."

Nick chuckled softly beside her. "Oh, I love you, Noory."

"Yeah, you need me." She laughed softly as she laid her head on his shoulder and continued looking into the fire.

After another twenty minutes, John called it. "It isn't working. It actually looks as if there is a thin shield around it where the fire isn't even quite touching it. It's protecting itself."

Nick was the first to speak after John drug it back out of the fire with a pitchfork. "I was hoping that I wouldn't have to bring this up, but I learned from Amaros that the device was forged in the in-between realms; therefore, it might only be subject to destruction by someone going in and destroying it there. I'll take it."

"No!" Noory said a little too loudly. Everyone jumped. "You've worked way too hard for your freedom to have to take that stupid thing in there with you. The second you show up with it, every dark creature here, there, and anywhere will feel it. It won't be but a few seconds before you will have dark entities clawing at your back."

Nick took a deep breath and spoke to her calmly. "Noory, I will do what must be done quickly and get back out of there. You know I travel there all the time. I'm the most qualified. If it looks like I'm having trouble with it, I will come right back, and we can figure something else out."

"No, I'll take it," Noory said with confidence.

"No," John and Nick both said simultaneously with looks of fear and stubborn determination on their faces.

While they were all discussing what to do, they barely noticed that one of the Templar brothers had stooped down and picked it up as he gazed at it like someone in love and possibly on drugs all at the same time.

"John!" Father Roy called as he pointed at John's fellow Templar.

"Barnabas! What in God's name are you doing?" John said.

"You're all confused about this thing from the start. Can't you see that it could—" Barnabas began.

John narrowed his eyes at the man. "I am not going through this shit again!" With that, he punched the man so hard, he fell unconscious and hit the dirt. None of the other Templars so much as blinked.

John leaned over and checked Barnabas' pulse. "He'll be all right," he said. "Now where did we land with this damn thing?"

"We landed with me dealing with it," Father Roy said.

"How?" Nick asked. "You've been sent back. As far as I know you can't get back in unless He brings you back."

"Yeah, I think you're right, but that wasn't what I was thinking. I *am* the in-between realm. What if it's just a matter of the thing not *detecting* the earthly realm? I can try shifting into spirit form and walking the thing into the fire with me," Roy explained.

"I don't know. Sounds risky. What if you can't hold your form or the thing somehow destroys you with it?" John said.

"I have peace about it, John. If it kills me, then it won't matter. I was already on my way home when I ended up here."

John swallowed hard before speaking. "If you can't hold your form, and you burn to death . . ."

"I've never had a problem holding one form or the other," Roy said.

Several moments of silence reigned.

"John, I'm respectfully asking you to let me do this. Please," Roy said.

John simply nodded and stepped back as Roy picked up the device, said a prayer, became translucent, and stepped right into the fire without another word.

The flames licked at Roy's body, but he appeared fine. They all began to hear roars as leathered hands reached for the box. With Roy being in his spirit form, he had inadvertently created a type of tear between the two realms. Just as Noory had predicted, the magic of the relic was strong enough that it rang like a bell in the other realm.

The other beings were simultaneously panicked that it was about to be destroyed and excited that they might be able to reach it and wield its power. Roy held the box fast with one arm and flung a concentrated flame in the direction of the leathery hands. Other arms reached, and soon, Roy appeared to simply concentrate, and he directed the flames. It was frustrating for a group of assembled warriors to not be able to help him, but the man was doing an admirable job of helping himself. Within a minute, the box itself began to burn and crumbled into the flames. When the thing was destroyed, Roy stepped out of the fire and became solid once more.

Noory sucked in a sharp breath.

"What's wrong, Light?" Nick asked.

"What if this is it? What if this is the last thing he had to do, and now he will be taken from us?" Tears rolled down her face. Nick understood. They had been through so much together. He was a true friend. John looked at them with a knowing look. Yet several minutes went by, and Roy was still there.

Roy came to them. "Apparently I'm not done yet," he said as he patted Noory on the shoulder.

John clicked on the camping lanterns he'd brought and poured water on the fire, then used a metal rake to sift through the ashes to see what remnants were left. There were none. He looked up at all his brothers, Noory, and Father Roy. "It's completely consumed. Oddly, metal too."

Nick felt his body relax. He hadn't realized he was still so tense about the relic until that moment. Beside him, Noory exhaled like air being released from a balloon. Clearly, she'd been worried too.

Everyone made their way back to John's house. They ate, drank, and talked well into the night. Nick watched Noory's fascination with the stories they told. He could tell she was surprised how being around these like-minded Templars freed John up to speak of things she had never heard before.

She leaned over to Nick. "This is good for both of you, huh? Your lives are so surreal that being able to talk about it with these guys, not having to hide . . . It's a freeing experience for people with such a heavy history."

Nick smiled. "Says the woman with the surreal life, but you can talk to me."

She leaned in closer to him. "Yeah. I can."

Eventually, one by one, they left. Before Nick and Noory left, Father Roy approached them.

"I've been thinking. I can't say for sure how long I will be here, but while I am, I might as well put myself to some good use," Roy said.

Nick looked both amused and a tad emotional as he answered. "Are you kidding me? You saved my life. You believed in me when I didn't dare believe in myself. To top it all off, you destroyed that evil ass box of doom. You've fulfilled your commission well."

"Yet I'm still here," he looked at them both as they all considered that. "Perhaps I could do more. While I was inside the flames fighting off the creatures, it felt right to me. Nick, I would appreciate it if you would consider bringing me with you now and then when you go out. Only if you're comfortable with it. Maybe you could use someone who can't be caught, and if I act quickly enough, I can't be punched, shot, or stabbed, either. Even if I were killed, I've been so close to the light that I have no grip on this life, anyway. Although I do love my new friends," he said with a gentle smile.

"I would be honored to go into battle with you, Father." Nick reached out and grasped his hand in solidarity.

"Good. You can reach me on my cell phone when you need me. John has decided that I must have one," he said as he pulled the device from his pocket.

Nick and Noory laughed.

John looked over at them and smiled.

CHAPTER 61

Noory jumped from one rooftop to the other with the stealth of a cat. They were tracking a teenage boy who was higher than a proverbial kite. Not only that, but he had also stolen from a drug dealer to get that way, and he was being hunted by the man. When he saw Nick, Noory, and Father Roy coming toward him, he had panicked and started running again. He couldn't tell friend from foe in his state of mind. She could hear Nick and Father Roy talking below. They all hoped to find him before the dealer did. Noory whipped her head around as she heard someone land on the rooftop behind her.

Claws sprang up in her face, and then quickly retracted. "Shit! Sorry, Noory. Didn't mean to do that; it's instinct." Damascus jumped back just before she drove a fist into his chest that would have likely sent him sailing through the air. "I've been following you guys for the last hour trying to talk to you when that berserker Santa Claus of yours wasn't around. I'm not looking for trouble. My teeth finally finished growing back in." He turned his mouth up in a wicked grin to show off his very off-putting, sharp, pearly whites.

"Damascus! To what do I owe the honor?"

"Wanted to see how you and your devilishly handsome boyfriend are doing these days," he said.

"Much better now, thank you," Noory replied. "I'm thinking this is unlikely to be a social call," she said, hoping he would get to it before Nick spotted him. It would likely get ugly.

"Can't it be a bit of both?" he asked.

"It could. I suppose."

Damascus sniffed the air, tilted his head to the side as if his nose told him something interesting, she wasn't privy to, and looked at her before speaking. "It seems you and I have a common enemy," he said.

"We do? The crazy box has been destroyed."

"Yeah. Word from my acquaintances is that they sensed the thing and tried to retrieve it moments before it was destroyed, and just a heads-up to your priest friend there: they recognize him now and are pissed that he destroyed the 'crazy box.' He also burned a couple of them pretty damn bad. If they run across him, they won't be gracious," Damascus warned.

Noory felt a chill that had nothing to do with the cold December air. "Noted. I appreciate you letting me know." She knew there was more.

"But our common enemy isn't any of them. If you hear of anything coming up with this Second Sight, 'yay for utopia' bullshit . . ." Noory laughed as his claws came out just long enough to make air quotes, then went back in again. She knew he'd done it for her benefit. He was a showman. "I want to know about it."

"Why do you care?" she asked.

Damascus looked off into the distance.

"Oh, Robert again," Noory said softly.

"He had to go answer to them. They beat him up pretty bad. It was actually a woman who did it, but Hades knows he wouldn't tell me that. I only knew because he had not taken a shower yet, and I could smell her battle adrenaline on him. Whoever she was, she had a temper. What a bitch!"

"So, you don't like powerful women?" Noory said feeling a little defensive.

"Oh, now, girl, you know that ain't true. I'm here talking to you, aren't I?" he said with a smile.

"True, but you want something from me."

"Yes, but who's to say that I wouldn't be here anyway. You've grown on me, scion," he said.

"I'll let you know if I hear anything." Noory listened closely, still feeling paranoid about the possibility of Nick catching them. "You're going to stay away from my kids, right?"

"I remember," he said grinning once more. "I have an alluring smile, and I'd like to keep it that way."

"Of course." Noory had more to say to him but felt awkward about it. He was still a killer. She couldn't keep her feelings to herself though. "I'm not quite sure Robert deserves you, Damascus."

"Of course, he doesn't. No one does. I mean, just look at me."

Noory laughed.

"You should laugh more. It looks good on you," he said. A moment later he turned to go without so much as a goodbye.

When Nick jumped up on the roof from the top of the opposite building, Damascus' sudden disappearance made sense.

"Were you up here talking to someone? I know I heard voices."

"Oh, no. Just looking around," she managed to stammer out.

"Noory, you're lying to me." The hurt in his voice was clear.

"You're right. I don't want us doing that. It was Damascus," she said. Anger swept across his face like a thundercloud.

"He's a murderer. You should be beating his ass, not having a conversation with him."

"I get that, but at the moment, he's sharing information with us."

The exasperation was clear in his voice. "Why in the hell would he even do that? You know these pieces of shit always have an angle."

"I know, Nick. I know his angle, and frankly, I understand it."

"How? Noory, come on!"

Noory hesitated to tell him the whole story. It felt like a betrayal. Then again, Damascus was a demon. It was strange to protect him. Yet she knew, though Nick might kill him for being a murderer, he wouldn't hold it against him for loving the wrong person.

"He's in love with Robert, and Robert got his ass kicked for failing Second Sight. He doesn't want Robert involved in it anymore and wants to stop them to keep Robert safe. That's why he's willing to share info. It could be mutually beneficial."

Nick's eyebrows shot up in surprise. "Oh. Well, Robert didn't appear to give two shits about him when I knocked his teeth out and slammed his face down on his desk."

"No, I think it's pretty much a one-way thing," Noory said.

"Yeah. Listen, I don't want you talking to him alone anymore. Tell him I promise not to kill him as long as he behaves, but I want to be around from now on when he comes to talk to you," Nick said.

Part of her wanted to give him hell and tell him he was being controlling and she could beat Damascus' ass all by herself if she needed to, but she knew he'd just seen way too much of the horrors in this world to let it go. "I understand," she replied. She couldn't help but feel that it was a little old-fashioned sweet that he wanted to protect her.

He put his arm around her. "There's just no accounting for love, is there?"

"Nope, not in our world." He leaned in and kissed her with a gentle passion. "All right then, Father Roy is waiting for us." They both jumped from the building with the cool night air blessing their descent.

Nick took a deep breath and focused once more as he tried to pick up the teenager's signal. "West," he said as he turned to Father Roy. "You ready for this?" he asked.

"Oh, yeah," he replied with a gleam in his eye as the three of them headed into the night.

CHAPTER 62

"Ready?" Nick asked.

Noory took a deep breath of the crisp December air. She looked around at the Atlanta skyline from where they stood on top of Nick's apartment building. The windows of the other apartments shone with festive twinkling lights of the season. She felt alive and secure all at once.

"Yeah, I'm ready," Noory replied.

The wind swept her hair up and swirled it about her. She reached up to contain it until she caught the look of fascination and wonder in Nick's eyes. Then he wrapped his arms around her as she laid her head on his shoulder.

Moments later, they stood in the darkness of the tiny Colombian village of Miguel Delgado, the man who had helped them escape from the ship that her father had captained. It had only been a few months ago, but after all they had been through, it seemed a very long time. Noory saw candles lit on the windowsill of a small house. It was Christmas Eve, and Miguel's family would leave for midnight mass soon.

"So, Saint Nicholas, what are you going to leave him?"

"He's been struggling since he left his job on *The Chalice*. I have a gift that will solve that."

To Noory's surprise, they didn't walk up to Miguel's door but followed him at a distance—all the way into the church. Noory knew if she was uncomfortable there, then Nick must have been barely able to breathe. They took their places at the back of the small church. Nick's hands shook as he made the sign of the cross. He didn't go down for communion like Miguel did, but Noory knew it was enough that Nick was here confronting his past, perhaps beginning to heal.

They walked out of mass and into the humid night air to the sound of Christmas Eve fireworks—a Colombian tradition that Noory hadn't expected. The church bells rang out across the village. Nick looked up at the exploding colors overhead, and she caught sight of his eyes shimmering with emotion. He said nothing but took her hand as they continued to follow Miguel.

After Miguel had accompanied his family inside, Nick knocked on the door. The sounds of laughter erupted within as the family became caught up in the mystery and magic of the night.

Miguel was smiling as he opened the door. Then a look of shock passed over his face before giving way to reverence and memory. "Bishop Nicholas," he said as he placed his hand over his heart. "You remembered me."

"Of course. I told you I would."

"Please come inside. You and your companion will be honored guests at our table." He looked at Noory. She gathered he was still struggling with what he'd heard or had come to another conclusion that wouldn't threaten his beliefs or scramble his brains.

She smiled at him.

"I won't keep you from your family for long, but there is something I must show you before we go."

"Of course, Bishop."

Nick led Miguel through the village in silence until they reached the docks.

"This is for you." Nick placed a set of keys in Miguel's hand and gestured toward a boat rocking softly in the water before them. "*Señor Miguel*," was painted on the back of the vessel. "The paperwork is inside. I was thinking you could start a business fishing or taking people out to the islands. The slip and maintenance are taken care of for the next ten years as well."

"Bishop, I can't."

"Sure, you can."

In the distance, Miguel's family began calling his name as they noticed his absence. Miguel walked a few feet from Nick and Noory and called out to them he was on his way. When he turned back, Nick and Noory were gone.

∞

"Where are we? Ugh! Never mind. I'm standing in sheep poop, aren't I?" Noory asked.

Nick laughed. "We're here for John's ritual. I haven't been in . . . a while."

Noory squeezed his hand and smiled up at him. "There he is with Father Roy. He's done this every Christmas Eve for as long as I can remember." The two said nothing more as they zipped up their coats. Nick gave Noory a quick kiss, and then the two joined John and Roy on the bench as they all gazed up at the night sky in quiet reverence.

Noory thought about the respect and devotion Miguel had on his face when he saw Nick. The way he said the word "Bishop" as if it were a holy thing, a thing of awe.

"May I ask you something, Nick?"

"Anything, Light," Nick said ever so softly. It wasn't lost on Noory that he said her name the way she'd heard Miguel say Nick's name.

"Do you miss being something . . . I don't know . . . holy?" Noory tried not to look at his face as he answered. Part of her feared he might miss being so esteemed by others.

John chuckled as he heard Noory's question.

Nick pulled her closer to him until she relaxed and laid her head on his shoulder. "What is holy, Noory? What we are called or what we do?" Nick asked.

"Amen," Roy whispered.

Noory thought for a moment. "Then anybody could be holy."

"Indeed, they could." John said.

The four of them sat bathed in the light of the brightest star in the sky on a quiet Christmas Eve.

Look for Book Two of the
Wayward Saviors Series
Noory and the Eternal Light
in 2024

About the Author

Kim Conrey is the author of The Wayward Saviors series and the sci-fi romance series Ares Ascending. She also writes about living with OCD. Her essays and short stories have been published in regional as well as local publications. You can find her marching in Atlanta's Dragon Con parade as a Box Hero Wonder Woman. In addition, she serves as VP of Operations for the Atlanta Writers Club. She also podcasts with the *Wild Women Who Write Take Flight* where they interview authors and industry professionals with a primary goal of supporting women writers.

Author's Note

The very best way to support a book or author you love is to leave an online review. It's a small thing that makes a huge difference!

Also, for more information about Book Two in this series or to sign up for my newsletter, keep up to date with book events, or to get occasional freebies, go to KimConrey.com.

With gratitude,
Kim Conrey

Learn More

Much of the inspiration for this story came from volunteer work that I've done over the years, especially with the Court Appointed Special Advocates (CASA) program. This is a program of advocacy for children who have experienced abuse and neglect. Volunteering there was truly a life-changing experience and might be in your life as well. Find out how you can become a CASA volunteer at nationalcasagal.org.

Also visit covenanthouse.org to learn how you might help homeless youth.

Additional Resources:

Alcoholics Anonymous: www.aa.org

Suicide Prevention: Call or SMS: "988" Suicide and Crisis Lifeline. Also: 988lifeline.org

CPSIA information can be obtained
at www.ICGtesting.com
Printed in the USA
JSHW080952300523
42346JS00003B/21